THE GLASS CENOTAPH

THE GLASS CENOTAPH

A CALL FOR TRUTH AND RECONCILIATION IN AUSTRALIA

PETER PURCHASE

DUNE

Perth Western Australia

First published in Australia 2019 by Dune Publishing
Copyright © Peter Purchase 2019
www.peterpurchasebooks.com

The Truth And Reconciliation Trilogy
Book I   The Glass Cenotaph
Book II   The Life And Times Of Gerrit de Waal
Book III Alicia

Cataloguing-in-Publication data is available from
The National Library of Australia

General acknowledgement is made to the following for permission to reprint previously published material: Mushroom Music Publishing, excerpts from Archie Roach song *Native Born;* Paraphrased excerpt from the song *The Dragon Song,* © Randy Farran of Tulsa, USA, permission courtesy of Randy Farran; Excerpts of *Trouble with a Capital T* © Horslips Group, permission courtesy of Barry Devlin; Excerpt from *Pale Fire* © Vladimir Nabokov Estate, permission confirmed by Stephanie Derbyshire, courtesy of The Wylie Agency (UK), Ltd. London WC1B 3JA; Use of the Australian Aboriginal *Malgana* language, permission courtesy of Ben Bellottie of Denham, Shark Bay; Photographs of the *Zuytdorp* wreck site, © Fremantle Shipwrecks Museum, permission granted by photographer Pat Baker, courtesy of Fremantle Shipwrecks Museum; Photographs of Jandamarra's Rock and the *Zuytdorp* Cliffs © Adam Monk Art Photography, courtesy of Adam Monk. Pendant on the cover designed by Kathleen Buzzacott, courtesy of Allegria Designs.

ISBN: 978-0-9756216-0-8 (paperback)
          978-0-9577364-3-6 (epub)

Other photos by Alexander Krivitskiy and Taylor Poe (from Unsplash)
Cover and interior designed by Julia Lefik

*Art itself may be defined as
a single-minded attempt to
render the highest kind of
justice to the visible universe,
by bringing to light the truth,
manifold and one, underlying
its every aspect. It is an
attempt to find in its forms,
in its colours, in its light, in
its shadows, in the aspects of
matter and in the facts of life
what of each is fundamental,
what is enduring and
essential—their one
illuminating and convincing
quality—the very
truth of their existence.*

Joseph Conrad 1897, novella
The Nigger of the 'Narcissus'— A Tale of the Sea.

*This book is dedicated to the estimated 20,000
or more known and unknown Aboriginal and
Torres Straits Islander people killed during the
Frontier Wars in Australia*

Acts	Pages

STEFAN

MELBOURNE, NEW YEAR'S DAY 1997, several minutes after midnight.

Stefan Novak was on the balcony of his third storey unit leaning against the rail in partial shadow, alone and still. He was peering up at rockets bursting into blazing spheres of red, green and blue beneath a cloud-streaked sky, before waning in a glitter of dust and smoke. More soared above the city's skyline, their detonations thumping among car horns blaring on Lygon Street beyond the courtyard below. Dazzling showers of sparks lit up his face, striking cheekbones and the shadow of a beard giving him a sombre, hawkish look.

It's time, he thought. *Time for a new beginning. Time to get my act together. Time to do something out of left field, to swim for it across the current to avoid going under.*

Then the telephone shrilled over the clang of pots and pans and voices yahooing on the balconies below. Desperate for a call from Tania, he scrambled through the sliding door.

'Steve Novak?' The caller was barely audible over the baying of the Dobermann next door, hysterical at the ruckus.

'Yes. This is Stefan.'

'Stefan. You're still up. Good. I haven't dragged you outta bed.'

'No, I'm watching the fireworks.'

'Good onya. Look, I know the timing's lousy and I won't keep you, but I've got a favour to ask. Something for you to mull over before you give me the answer I want.'

Stefan hesitated, frowning. 'What answer?'

He was disappointed and bewildered by an unexpected caller whose voice, though vaguely familiar, he failed to recognise.

'A simple yes will do me. That's all I'm after, bro. No argument.' And then, as the dog quietened, 'That noisy fella yours?'

No argument from you perhaps, and bro? Why bro?

On guard, he replied, 'No, the dog belongs next door.

What's the question? A simple yes sounds complicated to me.'

Who am I dealing with? Some crank who's hacked my name and number? About to slam down the receiver, he thought better of it and, as though sensing Stefan was about to ask who on earth he was and what he wanted at that time of night, the caller introduced himself.

'This is Lennard Currie, but you can call me Ace.'

Stefan was taken aback. While they'd never met, he knew Lennard's name and reputation. He had admired his work for years and now he recognised his voice—a resonant baritone with a characteristic outback intonation he'd heard for the first time last September when Lennard took part in the SBS television debate on Truth and Reconciliation. He'd spoken with passionate conviction that night, his argument laced with irony, his powerful frame standing out among the panellists. Some friends had considered his point of view convincing, but Stefan was sceptical of his line of reasoning that raised more questions than it answered.

There were voices in the background—laughter and the faint sound of a guitar with someone singing to it. Archie Roach? Surely not!

Where was he calling from? What was he after? If he was chasing a donation he was pushing his luck.

'I'm not expecting a snap decision,' Lennard continued. 'You've got three days to chew it over.'

'That's generous of you. So I do have a say.'

'Of course you do.'

'Glad we got that sorted. What am I agreeing to, then?'

'Just a minute, hold your horses.'

Lennard shouted and silence fell, broken by the muted song and the guitar. 'It's not so much a favour as a proposition; an offer too good to knock back. Hear me out. You'll get my drift.'

'Ask away.'

He heard Lennard speak to someone across the room and there was a burst of laughter. He stiffened. *Was the joke on me?*

Lennard Currie! He'd been at the cutting edge of Australian art since the early 1970s—Aboriginal Australian art. He was one of its leading lights; a maestro whose glass sculptures were acknowledged worldwide, fetching five and six-figure prices. Several of his pieces were on show in London's Victoria and Albert and New York's Metropolitan and Corning Glass Museums, and the Acquisitions Committee for the Quai Branly Museum of indigenous art proposed for Paris had recently approached him to prepare an installation as part of its landscaping.

A month ago, Stefan had visited his latest exhibition. He'd walked through the colonnades of the National Gallery into a breathtaking blaze of colour flashing through a forest of slender head-high glass sculptures radiating light. It seemed a liquid flame lit by the fiery desert sun glowed in the recesses of Lennard's imagination and by some magical sleight of hand and eye he'd brought the quartz outcrops and scorched red dunes and sweeping skies of the western desert indoors with him.

One sculpture, in particular, had caught Stefan's eye—the centrepiece, an exquisite, statuette of dichroic glass lit alternately from within and without, each flash lasting thirty seconds. It glowed in a magenta wash when light was transmitted from within, and reflected sensuous tones of aquamarine and turquoise when lit from without. The raw beauty of its colours and the patterns that materialised like fiery hieroglyphs through its core in waves of light on light enthralled him. How much colloidal silver and gold had Lennard used in the glass batch to create the effect? Or had he come up with an experimental chemical composition to achieve it?

Back on the street that afternoon, envy had speared through him as he'd compared the failure of his crystal ware business with

Lennard's success. He'd wondered bitterly how much of that success was attributable to Lennard's Aboriginality, singling him out for the approval and support of the art fraternity... then he acknowledged his thoughts were mean-spirited and regretted his prejudice. The sculptures were one of a kind; technical mastery and creative flair evident in their arresting brilliance. Lennard's streak of genius in combining glass and light the way he did deserved accolades.

About to tear up the exhibition catalogue, he'd changed his mind and folded it into his back pocket.

Now he looked down at the unopened letters scattered beside the telephone and rummaged through them to find it. On its cover, vermilion and scarlet patterns swirled through a glass figurine beneath the words *Earth and Fire*. On the back was a photograph of Lennard, masked and pouring a braid of red-hot light from a ladle brimming with molten glass. He had signed his Malgana name across it—*Malajarri*. Stefan read the translation and his smile was sardonic—*Thunder*.

'So what are you after?' He broke the silence.

'How old are you? In your late thirties, yes?'

'Give or take.' Stefan was mystified. 'I'm one year shy of the big four-o.' Then he added, with a touch of sarcasm, 'I can't bloody wait.'

'And I'm fifty-five as of yesterday. Fifty-five to the day if you count back twenty minutes. We're still celebrating here.'

He gave a caustic laugh. 'Congratulations! You're closing in on sixty and you're celebrating when you should be cursing?'

'Not when you're having fun, by crikey.'

'Having fun?'

'Sure am, bro. I'm packing it in before I pack it in. It's the only way to go.' And then, businesslike, 'Thirty-nine; what's that make the two of us? A hundred?'

'Close enough. Ninety-four.'

'Then we've got all the experience we need, all the know-how in the world.'

'What for?'

Stefan was unprepared for his reply.

'You and me, we're gonna cast a monument—a replica of Jandamarra's Rock.'

'Jandamarra's Rock?'

'The one in Windjana Gorge. You ever seen it?'

'No.'

'Then I'll take you there, to the Kimberley. You haven't lived until you've been. Like I say, we're gonna sculpt it in solid glass. It'll be the biggest thing since Palomar.'

'Big as Palomar?'

'Bigger. Half as big again.'

A brief silence was broken by Stefan's snort. 'Pull the other one, why don't you?'

'I've never been more dinkum in my life.'

Now he's really taking the mick, Stefan thought. He frowned, picturing Hale's gigantic Pyrex telescope disc, some twenty tons in weight, six metres across and two years in the cooling, it had taken eleven painstaking years to grind and polish into a flawless parabolic mirror reflecting the farthest reachable stars. He listened as Lennard suggested they put their combined experience in the technical intricacies of working with molten glass to good use. Then he was astonished to hear him mention the problems they might face firing a complicated mix including silicates of garnet sand.

'Did you say *garnet* sand?'

'You heard me right. Garnet *buthurru*. It's there by the truckload in the Hutt lagoon dunes, acres of it, in my Nhanda brothers' country, waiting for us to dig it up.'

He'd never worked with garnet silicates before, Lennard admitted, but he had a feeling in his bones that Stefan would revel in manipulating the extreme temperatures required to release the spectacular colours lying dormant in the garnet's carmine pink.

Stefan's thoughts raced. What a challenge! Garnet, with its unpredictable thermodynamic properties and precarious melting point! The chemical balance in the mixes, the subtle interaction with other metals for colour contrast, the complex process of bringing down the temperatures during the annealing, and always those unforeseen intractable problems to resolve with spotting or with air bubbles contaminating the final product.

He looked sceptically at Lennard's picture on the catalogue and slowly shook his head. Given garnet's hardness—it was seven on the Mohs' scale—he doubted the feasibility of using it in glass. It was useful in jewellery design or as a sandblasting abrasive or polishing agent, but surely nothing more.

Intrigued, he did not express his reservations. 'So fill me in.'

'We'll be playing with *garla*, bro, playing with fire, but it'll be a piece of piss for the hundred-year-old fella that's you and me rolled into one.' Lennard gave a throaty laugh. 'I can see us now, up in lights—the Freo Glassworks alchemists! I got a nose for these things. Trust me.'

He mentioned the staggering tonnage they'd need and pointed out how long the project might take—four years by his reckoning.

'I'm aiming to knock it over by December 2000.'

'To coincide with the millennium?'

'Partly.'

Four years! And garnet in the batch! Stefan found no words.

'Cat got your tongue, bro? What? Too big an ask? You chucked in the towel already? That's not what I hear around the traps. Word is you're still in the saddle, digging in your spurs.'

Digging in my spurs? Flogging a dead horse more like it, Stefan thought, baulking at Lennard's vision, at the overwhelming ambition of a glass pour of that magnitude requiring garnet sand by the truckload. *And a mould of that dimension; how does he propose building that? He's off the planet or having me on.*

'You still there, bro? *Nyinda jindithayinu?* You giving me the silent treatment? I haven't bored you shitless so you've done a runner, have I?'

'I'm still here. I'm gobsmacked is all, trying to get my head around it.'

Lennard said he was flying back to Perth that morning and asked Stefan to meet him at Tullamarine airport. He could think of no more appropriate a metaphor than the first day of a new year to begin exploring an idea as original as the one he had in mind. They could yarn about it while they sobered up over a coffee or two.

'Make sure you show, brudda,' he said when Stefan hesitantly agreed. 'You'll be doing us both a favour, so don't pike out and don't sleep in.'

He rang off, but Stefan failed to hear the disconnection. Unsure whether Lennard had more to say, he listened to the silence before asking, 'Are you still there?' Confused, he repeated the question and when there was still no response he laughed outright. *The story of my life! Listening for an enlightening reply from someone who isn't there.*

Now he was caught between Jandamarra's Rock and a mountain of garnet sand on one hand and his bankrupt business and recent split with Tania on the other. If he did take up Lennard's invitation things could hardly get worse but with his recent run of bad luck, why not?

Back on the balcony, he stretched across the railing to look up beyond the roof-line. The firework display was over. A classy celebration to commemorate the failure of his business and his finances going down the drain, he thought drily.

Scattered stars flickered through skeins of smoke drifting high across Melbourne's glow. For a moment he visualised their reflections in the polished mirror of the Mt Palomar telescope, waves of light transmitted into the eye of an observer, their illusory sparks transmuted by the trickster mind into particular images of aeons past.

Then, with a wry smile, he shook his head. *Lennard Currie, of all people! Who'd have guessed? It's perfect timing for such an unexpected offer though, now I'm skint and a month in arrears with the rent.*

So where should he go from there? He'd acted on impulse once before when he'd thrown the shackles off four years ago and pulled the pin on Pilkington Glass. What was there to stop him now?

For one lurching moment he was back in the factory, hanging his white coat for the last time on the hook behind the R&D laboratory door. They'd given him a boisterous roasting at his farewell, his manager wishing him well, toasting Australia's answer to Swarovski and Pandora, before predicting he'd last six months—six months at best—before he'd come crawling back to plead for his job. He'd promised to keep the revolving door open for him until then.

Stefan had thanked him for the gesture and then, 'Come back and work a conventional nine to five with the likes of you blokes? No chance! If it comes to that, I'll settle for a plot on the wrong side of the grass.'

'Careful what you wish for,' his manager had warned.

He'd walked out past white-hot furnaces roaring on the factory floor, flat ribbons of glass streaming across acrid baths of molten tin within the floats. A summer thunderstorm had loomed over the Dandenongs as he'd crossed the car park and strode down the avenue of purple jacarandas, his footsteps crushing fallen flowers along the road less travelled.

Before he'd reached his Ducati, heavy drops of rain had struck his shoulders in twos and threes. They had been warm and welcome and he lifted his face to them.

Then he recalled Lennard's warning. What was that word he used? *Garla.* It had been a baptism of rain that time, next time it would be fire!

By the time he'd accelerated onto Greens Road it had been lashing down, soaking him to the skin. He had been laughing fit to burst as he'd tasted the intoxicating freedom of following his dream, racing through this opening to the unexpected, never looking back and never mind the risks! He'd roared down the bitumen on a high, his severance pay in his wallet and a return flight to the Czech Republic to visit the Moser glassworks in his father's home town, booked for the following week. Each split-second moment had presented an exhilarating opening in the weave of his future, promising endless possibilities.

Had he been reckless? In hindsight maybe, but he'd known the risks. Did he regret the decision? In part, yes, but he'd given it his best shot. And he was young enough to start afresh. Besides, he'd met Tania as a consequence. That justified every move he'd made, even though she'd cut and run for whatever reason eight days ago. They were the best of years… and the most testing.

He sat at the balcony table and reached for the four-sided ivory *dreidel*, the spinning top dye lying next to a half-empty bottle of red wine. He spun it with a snap of thumb and fore-finger and watched it skitter across the tabletop until it slowed and keeled over to show the winning Hebrew letter g—*gimel*, the symbol indicating winner takes all. *Go for it*, his thoughts whispered. *Buy some time. I can't play for time when time runs out. So what if it's another dead end? Learn from it. Enjoy the adrenalin rush.*

There was enough fuel in the tank to get him to the airport and back, he calculated. He might come away from the meeting with an opportunity to escape the trap into which the financial downturn and bad luck had led him.

He imagined accelerating fast enough to reach escape velocity and break free of his disasters; the trunks of trees lining the Tullamarine Freeway a hypnotic blur.

THE AIRPORT CAFÉ was packed. Stefan saw Lennard through the plate glass door, seated at a table to the left. He was the picture of self-possessed relaxation. His legs were outstretched beneath the table, crossed at the ankles. He was absorbed in a book lying open on the tabletop. He appeared to be making notes, a silver pen in his left hand poised over its pages.

Lennard looked up and caught his eye. He closed the book, inserted the pen as a bookmark and stood. He was taller and broader than Stefan had imagined, with the first signs of middle-aged spread evident under a sky-blue shirt. The sleeves were rolled up, a narrow armband of raised scars visible in a diagonal pattern above his left elbow. His skin was light brown, sinews of sheathed muscle gliding beneath it as he extended his right hand, the palm was square and work-hardened, the calloused fingers powerful.

'Stefan Novak, I presume!' He flashed a radiant smile, all teeth.

'That's me.'

'G'day. I'm Ace.'

He waved Stefan to a chair and sat opposite, his elbows on the table, his chin balanced on the bridge formed by interlaced fingers. His face was broad and imperious, and although his eyes were shaded behind blue-tinted sunglasses, Stefan saw them dark and expressive. The wiry strands of his black beard were streaked with silver and his hair was unruly.

He stretched and leaned back in his chair. 'You have any trouble picking me out?'

'You're hard to miss.'

'I'm the only Yamaji here?'

'The biggest, anyway.'

'And getting bigger, so I'm told.' The brass eagle on the Harley buckle of his belt of polished snakeskin glinted as he patted his stomach. 'If my *wilygu warabadi* is anything to go by.'

'The TV doesn't do you justice.'

'It does if you've still got black and white.' He smiled. 'You know what they say—the bigger they are, the harder they are to fell.'

'That I can believe.'

Around his neck, Stefan saw a leather thong and, hanging from it, an oval of worn abalone shell patterned in a lucent swirl of sea-blues and greens. When he looked closer, he saw the outline of a bird carved in cameo in the nacre. It appeared to be an albatross, its wings spread in cruciform flight.

'It's good to meet you at last, brudda,' Lennard said. 'It's time we crossed paths. We've got things of importance to see to.'

At last? Am I the celebrity here, Stefan wondered, *the one with familiar features? Hardly!*

'Secret men's business?' he asked.

'You could say that, long as nobody's listening and you're not about to grass.' Lennard glanced at his watch. 'I'm catching the early flight. That gives us forty minutes, long enough to give you the heads up.' He stood to buy the coffees. 'You take yours white?'

'White and one.'

'I'm with Henry Ford—any colour, long as it's black.'

When he returned with the tray, he took a deep appreciative breath. 'Nothing beats that smell, that's for sure.'

Stefan was in unfamiliar territory, unused to the company

of a national celebrity, unnerved at the prospect of conversing for the first time with a charismatic icon of Australia's Aboriginal community. Ill at ease, he searched for something to say. Then he noticed the photograph of a high-winged, triple-engine monoplane skimming a line of dunes under a lowering sky imprinted on the side of his coffee cup. He held it up and examined it. Was it Kingsford-Smith in the *Southern Cross*? Or the *Kookaburra*, sent to search for the *Southern Cross* when it disappeared in the Kimberley in the late 1920s?

He tapped the picture. 'That's got to be the *Kookaburra.*'

'The what?'

Stefan turned the cup. 'The *Kookaburra*. The poor blokes on board crash-landed in the Tanami when they were searching for Kingsford-Smith. They died of thirst. They drank their own urine in the end, apparently, with a dash of ethyl alcohol and distilled water from the compass, would you believe, topped up with petrol mixed with oil.' He paused. 'Some cocktail that must have been.'

Lennard lifted his cup and studied the design. 'Sounds a likely thirst quencher, bro.' He took two spoons of sugar and stirred. 'Rather them than us. Let's hope this brew doesn't have the same ingredients, by crikey. At least we're not stuck way out there in the Tanami, but. It's hard *manangkarra* spinifex country, that Warlpiri land.'

'There was probably a waterhole within cooee.'

'Every chance.'

Lennard turned in his chair and, from an inside pocket of the worn leather jacket slung across its back, he withdrew a faded Kodak envelope. 'Never mind the *Kookaburra*,' he said. 'Let's kick-start this conversation and get down to business.'

He shook the envelope and spilled several photographs into his palm. He shuffled them, riffled them against the table like a card shark, squared them up and spread them face down across the table as though dealing a hand in blackjack. He waved a hand across them, inviting him to pick a card, any card.

Stefan flipped the first photograph to his left. A woman looked up at him. Waves of dark copper hair framed her fine-boned face. Her skin was pale and lightly freckled. He leaned closer, saw the hint of a smile. Beneath dark brows, her eyes were green and candid. He saw humour in them and, it seemed, a questioning; a fierce intelligence with a touch of… what? Mockery? *Who was she teasing*? He cast a quick glance at Lennard, who was observing his reaction with a half-smile. He turned back to examine the backdrop—a wall of weathered rock, white and marbled and immense, encircled by a dark reflective pool on which it seemed to float.

'Whoever she is, she's drop-dead gorgeous, Ace. And bloody hell! If that's Jandamarra's Rock you'll be working your ring off.'

'No doubts there, on both counts. That's my Rosie—Rosalie O'Sullivan. And that's Jandamarra's Rock. Top choice first up. The omens are good. Now check out the rest.'

Each photograph showed the rock from a different perspective as if the photographer had selected each new vantage point to show a different surface, an unexpected blend of sunburned colour, an unusual pattern of weathered angles and shadows. He noticed the photographer's footprints in the sand encircling the rock, as though he or she had walked around it many times deliberating over the composition or the light.

The rock stood solitary in the centre of the gorge, solid and angular and timeless. The sandbank leading to it was edged with an overhang of paperbarks. The jade-green water surrounding it mirrored the background of soaring cliffs, their cave-pocked limestone walls so still it seemed you could walk across the water on their rust and sepia reflections. In one shot, Stefan noticed a narrow-snouted crocodile basking on the sand as if carved to scale in polished rosewood.

He looked across at Lennard and held up the photograph. 'Is that what I think it is?'

'Yep, it's a freshwater croc. There's a few in the river. They won't bother you, long as you don't get too friendly.' He smiled, showed his teeth. 'Not like a saltie.'

In the last photograph, he saw Rosalie for the second time. The rock jutted sun-bleached from the river and she was seated on an upper ledge, smiling down at the camera, her beauty bathed in sunlight. Her hair flowed across her shoulders. Her arms were wrapped around her knees, her feet bare. Below were multiple tide-lines scoured by successive flooding of the river, which was shallow in the photograph, as though the wet season was recently over, or yet to begin.

Stefan peered at the rock. He visualised a two-storey monument, a pyramidal iceberg in glass and splintered sunlight.

Sculpt that? In solid glass? He looked up, shaking his head. '*No… bloody… way.*'

'*Yes way!*' Lennard cut him short, lifting his coffee cup in both hands as if warming them. '*No way*, no way. It's a memorial we'll be casting, remember? A memorial to my people.' He paused. 'A cenotaph.'

'A cenotaph!' Stefan exclaimed, and his heart sank.

'That's right! A cenotaph to commemorate our *wiyaband-inugu murla*, our known and unknown heroes.' After a tense silence he asked forcefully, 'Are you aware how many we're talking about here?'

'How many died?'

'Were massacred.'

'Since when?'

'Since the invasion.'

'You mean since settlement.'

'I mean since the invasion,' Lennard fired back. '*Nothing* was settled.'

'Oh, okay. If you say so. I'm not too sure, but I think I read somewhere it may have been around twenty thousand.'

'If not more.' Lennard leaned forward, adding tersely, 'Perhaps twice that. But we're not talking statistics here, bro, we're talking flesh and blood. We're talking *human beings*, by crikey. They lived. They died. And we're bringing them back to the place they belong.' He stared at Stefan. 'In this country's consciousness.'

Lennard's sudden assertiveness jolted Stefan. Riven by confusion, he looked away. How could he collaborate in commemorating Lennard's ancestors when he knew so little of their history and there were so many questions hanging over what he did know? And a *cenotaph*? A war memorial for massacred Aborigines? Was Australia prepared for that?

His face darkened as the disagreement that had erupted when he'd met Tania's brothers in Cairns for the first time two years ago flashed across his mind. 'So you're not sure where you stand or what to believe?' Richie, the older of the two, had growled sarcastically that dreadful afternoon, shaking an accusing finger as he paced the worn carpet in the lounge, his thickset frame bristling, his ponytail of dreadlocks flying. 'Is that why you're living in *our country* rent-free like you own the fuckin' place and never signed a lease?'

Stefan had reared back in his chair as though fending off a physical attack, looking towards the window to conceal how mortified he felt, gathering himself. Rain had been bucketing down the glass, wind gusts thrashing at the spears of sugar-cane across the road, their feathered seed heads ducking and weaving under the assault. In the uncertain light, he saw a patch of blue to seaward where the sun streamed through a break in the clouds and he thought, *If the sun can weather the storm, then so can I.*

He felt the same determination course through him now. Steeling himself, he looked directly at Lennard. 'Alright. Go on.'

Alert to Stefan's discomfort, Lennard relented. 'I'm not inviting you on a guilt trip, bro. Guilt gets you nowhere, especially if it's associated with events you're not personally accountable for. Justice, now that's a different story. Justice is at the heart of the matter, but we can save that discussion for another time. Let's say right now I'm looking for a cluey off-sider with his head screwed on to help me build the thing and let it go at that.' He looked shrewdly at Stefan for several moments before adding, 'But I want an off-sider who's onside.'

Stefan's thoughts raced. Guilt and justice? An off-sider who was onside and committed to his vision and all it implied? In a less charged political context at a more convenient time, perhaps yes. But right now? With his business in disarray and his finances on the line? And Tanya gone?

A long silence followed, during which Lennard coolly observed him. When he spoke at last, he left Stefan mystified. 'Let's split the difference and agree for now that twenty thousand were massacred. Twenty thousand—and *one*.'

He checked his watch and then glanced at the flight announcements. 'Time's almost up. Let's put this to bed, one way or the other.' He picked up the nearest photo and circled the rock with a thick forefinger. 'So how do you reckon we get this done?'

Relieved, Stefan took the photograph. He studied the rock's sweeping proportions. After several moments, 'It's a bloody big ask,' he said. 'Palomar wasn't solid glass. It was honeycombed, except for the lens surface. And they ladled the melt into the mould. They had the manpower and the time to achieve it, not to mention limitless resources.'

'If we need extra hands, I know people we can call on. All good blokes.'

'With glass experience?'

'Of course, what else? Even a couple of gaffers with lungs like Pavarotti. Mate, we'll have the full orchestra, right down to the little fella tapping on the triangle.'

Stefan scrutinised the photograph. 'My guess is you'd have to fire something that big in the mould itself.'

'We,' Lennard interrupted him.

'We?'

'You said you. Try we.'

'All right. *We.*'

'And *will*. Not would.'

Stefan responded with careful emphasis, '*We will* need a bespoke kiln with the proportions to cope. It's hard to imagine. There isn't one that size in the southern hemisphere. We'll have to knock one up ourselves.'

'That's more like it.'

'Not only that, the volume of batch to fill the mould will be humongous and we'll have trouble with the timing of the melt, let alone the cooling. With solid glass for something that size you're looking at eight years' annealing at a guess, or maybe nine.' He studied the photograph head down. 'You mentioned a four-year schedule. If that's the case, you've got to think a *hollow* structure, or a smaller one. Gut instinct tells me even then you'll be pushing shit uphill.'

'I understand the problems, bro,' Lennard broke in. 'Why else have I asked you along for the ride?'

Stefan did not look up. He scratched his temple. 'And garnet! Why garnet? Neither of us has experimented with it. If we miscalculate the proportion in the mix, I can imagine a furnace filled with black molasses turning into bitumen.' He gave a dry chuckle. 'Good for surfacing the Gunbarrel Highway and doing the outback tourists a favour. You'd be better off importing a chunk of obsidian from Yellowstone and carving that.'

Lennard listened, his head tilted like a bird of prey, before sweeping away Stefan's objections with an open palm as he reached for the photograph. 'Never say die, bro. It's not in my vocabulary. You think the project's bigger than Uluru? It is! It's bigger than *Ben Hur*. Did you hear me say it was gonna be a walk in the park? No! You're forgetting we're Aussies and we'll improvise. We've got the knack and that's where you come in, so don't get your budgie smugglers in a twist this early on the technicalities.'

Then he sat back and said it was good to see Stefan already setting his mind to it. 'Give the idea a chance to sink in. It'll be worth it.' He lifted his cup, took a swallow. 'One thing I know for sure and certain, bro—this is an opportunity too challenging for you to knock back.'

Stefan inclined his head. There indeed, Lennard had his number. He thrived on the technical intricacies of working with molten glass. He revelled in manipulating the fierce and unremitting power of the flame, in drawing living colour from opaque silicates and nursing temperatures down through the annealing process before opening up the mould to reveal, for that first ecstatic instant, glassy landscapes of the infinite reflected in grains of sand. He gambled his technique and creative intuition against the odds on generating colours and tones, shapes and movement in the viscous liquid, with white-hot flame his only ally and the cruellest of arbitrators, unremitting, taking no prisoners.

Lennard placed the photograph face-up on the table and veered in an unexpected direction. 'Tell me something, bro. It's none of my business, but aren't you on the bones of your *manda* right now? Aren't you in deep shit with your landlord?'

Stefan gasped. 'Who told you that?'

'I've got all the good oil. I know you're going down the tubes and you're about to hit rock bottom if you haven't already.'

Stefan braced himself. 'So I've fucked up big time.'

Lennard gave him a knowing grin. 'They also tell me you're rootless at the moment, except for our dancing girl, Tania Tibora.'

'You know Tania?'

'Small world. I know her brothers, Rex and Richie.'

Stefan froze. *So he knows about the bust-up, but he doesn't yet know about Tania.* 'You're behind the times. Tania's gone. She's back in Cairns. In Caravonica with the family, last I heard. Who knows? She may be heading overseas.'

'Sorry to hear that.' Lennard snapped his fingers. 'So you need cheering up and I've got the remedy.' He reached for the book he'd been reading—*Six Australian Battlefields*, Stefan noticed, by Al Grassby and Marji Hill, a book he'd never heard of. Lennard withdrew a Qantas ticket from between its pages. 'Maybe this'll do the trick. I'm a blackfella boy scout. I come prepared.'

Stefan read the destination and flight time—Perth, fourth of January, one way, requiring confirmation. He placed it back on the table. 'You may have come prepared, Ace, but we've only just met and this is very generous.'

'Not to mention presumptuous!' Lennard laughed aloud. 'Didn't think you'd take this long making up your mind. Crikey, bro, where I come from you make up your mind or you miss out. Being decisive is the name of the game, and I'm game if you are.' He gestured at the ticket. 'Use it anyway. Come over for a break. Check things out. Give it a burl and you never know, one of our good-looking Freo chicks might do the trick and keep you there. Forget Tania. Sounds to me she's bitten the hand that fed her. We'll find you someone with more chilli in her than a Fisherman's Friend, a bushfire blonde hot to trot to put the sting back in your tail.'

'I wish it was that simple.'

A speculative look passed between them and Lennard slowly nodded. 'Sometimes a change of scenery works wonders, bro. It'll take your mind off her, give you time to work out strategies for winning her back if that's what you want.'

Stefan looked down at the ticket. *If I accept his invitation, am I clutching at straws? Am I allowing my circumstances to force me into a decision I might regret? Do I have any alternative?*

He glanced up. 'What was that word you used last night? Alchemy? You're right. The technical challenges are undeniable. We'll be balancing on the razor's edge.'

'Nice analogy.' Lennard smiled. 'One slip and we're both talking with squeaky voices.'

Stefan felt a wave of irritation. *I'm not usually this backward in coming forward. Get over it! This offer is exactly what I need right now.* He reached for the ticket, folded it and slid it into his shirt pocket, brushing aside his reservations. 'Ah, what the hell, luck's a fortune and Freo's as far from Cairns as I can get.'

'Not to mention the landlord.'

'Yeah, her too.'

He looked at Lennard in silence, his mind churning. The unpredicted crossing of their paths, the disconcerting power of Lennard's presence, the certainty of his vision and his passion… tempered by what? His humour? There was all of that, but he also sensed uneasily the strangeness of things unrevealed, the uncanny mystery of things unknown.

'Okay, you can count me in,' he said at last. 'It's a yes. I'll give it a go.'

'*Gu'ugu! Nyinda wangganyina*! Now you're talking!' Lennard reached across the table to shake Stefan's hand in both of his, grinning broadly. 'You little ripper! So one door closes and another opens. Welcome to your next four years.' He scooped up the photographs and stacked them in front of Stefan. 'Study these and bring them with you.'

'You look like you've struck it rich.'

'Still panning bro, still panning, but I reckon I saw a flash of colour and I'm stoked.'

Stefan stifled a laugh. 'You sure it's not fool's gold, Ace?'

'I'll back my judgement.'

'Why me in particular?'

'Simple. You've got a handle on the technology I need for a project this challenging.' He tapped his forehead. '*Gambarra nyinda*—they reckon you're the real deal. Don't think I'm blowing smoke up your *manda*, but I've heard you've forgotten more technical tricks of the trade than I'll ever know. It's time we tapped in. And they tell me your *wurduru*—your heart—is in the right place for a *wajbala*. I've never known them to be wrong.'

'Them again! That's quite a network you've got out there.'

'That's the *gurdumutha* for you—the brothers.'

'You can't mean Tania's mob. I'd find that hard to believe.'

'Them too. The point is I can't do this on my own. It's too big and it's too important. It's gonna take the two of us.'

'To stuff it up?'

'To get it right. With my Yamaji vision and your *wajbala* technology we're on a winner.'

Stefan gave an explosive snort. 'Look where my whitefella technology's got *me*.'

'Deep in dog shit? Forget all that. When you've taken a fall, you pick yourself up and you don't step in the same *duthugura gunda* twice. It's on the nose if it sticks.'

Stefan raised both hands palms up and shrugged. 'I'm not exactly flush at the moment, as you know. I'll have to put the acid on you for a grubstake.'

Lennard pushed back his chair and stood. He looked briefly at Stefan over the top of his sunglasses, startling him with the intensity of his gaze and the colour of his eyes. 'We'll take care of you, bro. I'm not a short-armed tightarse with long pockets, you can rely on that. You're not gonna make a fortune, but we'll keep your head above water. This is about sharing in the spirit of what's mine's yours and what's yours is mine.' He glanced across at the departure times flashing in the frame to his right. 'And it's about knowing when it's time to shoot through.'

He hooked his thumb into his snakeskin belt, adjusted it and straightened his shirt. He noticed Stefan's curiosity. 'It's a rattlesnake skin from the Shenandoah Valley. The Powhatan who gave it to me said wearing it would preserve my magic. Let's find out, bro. It's time for us *gutharra thayadi*, us pair of snakes, to strike.'

Then he removed his sunglasses to polish them on his sleeve and Stefan saw his eyes once more—one was dark brown, almost black, with a hypnotic ring of amber around the pupil, the other a piercing arctic blue. Unexpected, startling, they were accentuated by the colour of his skin. He'd noticed this characteristic in Lennard's appearance on SBS but had no idea how remarkable it would be close up.

'Well, it looks like I'm bringing home the bacon,' Lennard said. 'I'll know for sure when you arrive. You got any questions before I do a runner?'

Stefan paused thoughtfully, and then, 'Why is December 2000 so important to you? You said it was partly to coincide with the new millennium.'

'It is bro, but the real reason?' His voice was intense, his words clipped. 'The 1991 Act has a clause bringing down the axe on the Council for Reconciliation by the first of January, 2001. We've been given ten years to negotiate for change across the country.' He raised his voice still further, turning heads at nearby tables and Stefan stiffened. '*Ten years*! The bastard pollies think turning around two hundred years of history is something with a decade's bloody deadline! It's not! It's gonna take more time.'

He broke off, replaced his sunglasses and put a reassuring hand on Stefan's shoulder. 'Scare you, did I, bro? Don't mind me. I get carried away sometimes thinking about it. The point is this—we need the cenotaph as a marker before the council is disbanded. It's the first step. To symbolise reconciliation as a process that's ongoing, not completed on a designated day.' He gave Stefan an engaging smile. 'There's that and the Sydney Olympics, of course. I thought you'd have that one sussed.'

Before heading for the door, he did something curious. He reached into his pocket and withdrew a polished silver coin, which he flicked into the air. It rang as it spun from his thumbnail. He watched its flashing arc, caught it in his right hand and slapped it onto the back of his left. 'Your call, bro. We'll let the coin decide.'

Stefan hesitated, and then, 'Heads.'

Lennard showed him the coin. 'Heads. You win. So you're coming, no ifs and no bloody buts. Now you're free because you no longer have to choose.'

'I'm free because I have no choice? That sounds contradictory.'

'There's nothing like a paradox to keep you on your toes.' Lennard leaned across and rapped the table with the coin. 'You're free because you're no longer at a loss on what direction to take. *Ngayiwu nyinda garlgunyina?* What's keeping you, bro? You're outta the cage. You can show us your fighting qualities.'

'So I'm out of one cage and into another?'

'That's up to you.' Lennard held the coin by its edge, twisting it this way and that. It glinted in the air between them. 'One thing's for sure—in my workshop, you'll be free to use your skills the way you want, instinctively. It's not my way or the highway. You'll be free to experiment, to use your imagination. You can invent and let things unfold, with the rock and garnet as your guidelines. You hear what I'm saying?'

The cenotaph would give them the artistic context, he said. How they got there was another matter. He contemplated the coin and suggested that Stefan might discover things about himself he'd never known, that he might learn to see both sides of the coin at the same time. 'It's the only cure for the one-eyed, bro. Not that you are, I'm not suggesting that.' He tapped his belt. 'You might learn to wear two skins like I have. Find out for yourself when you get to Freo.'

Stefan reached for the coin before Lennard pocketed it. It was Dutch; a Zeeland *schelling* minted in 1711. It was slightly bent and burred at the edges. On one face he saw a crouching lion holding what appeared to be a hat balanced on the point of a sword.

Lennard retrieved the coin. 'The lion was the symbol of the United Provinces, the Netherlands,' he said, 'and that's the hat of liberty on the end of the sword. Same as the hat you're wearing right this minute, only you don't know it yet.' He turned the coin over and showed him a lion rampant emerging from the sea embossed within a shield. 'And this is the Zeeland coat of arms. My mother gave it to me years ago when I was a *yamba*; a little tacker. It's a relic from the wreck of the *Zuytdorp*. She went down on the cliffs north of Kalbarri, in my country, Malgana country, up near Shark Bay. This is the memento I carry with me.'

'I thought you were Yamaji.'

'Same thing, bro. I'm Malgana, one of the tribal groups of the Yamaji nation.'

Stefan pointed at the coin as he pocketed it and suggested it must have quite a history.

'It's my lucky *bardalyi*; my lucky coin. It keeps away the *muwanuga wambu*; the bad spirits. It's a long story. I'll tell you about it when you arrive. It'll make the trip worthwhile.'

'You let the coin make all your decisions?'

'Only when I'm at the crossroads, bro. It reinforces my conviction I'm engineering the fate that's engineering me.'

'This is a crossroads?'

'For you it is.'

'You got that right.'

'And I'm the bloke handing you a map marking your escape route.'

'I'll need a compass to go with it.'

'No you won't. Travel due west. Follow the *wabarnu*; follow the sun.' He winked. 'Cattle class, down the back by the crapper like the rest of us. Only don't go down the gurgler on the way across.'

As he slung his leather jacket across his shoulder, Lennard asked Stefan if he had the feeling he'd been hijacked and before he had a chance to reply, he added, 'Consider yourself on the payroll as of now. I'll ring you from Freo.' Then he grinned. 'A friendly warning though—I'll have your nose to the grindstone. I'll be looking for blood along with the sweat and tears. I'll be extracting my full pound of flesh.'

'You're too late.'

'Why's that?'

'I've been circumcised already.'

Lennard roared, surprising a couple at the next table who looked up and laughed without knowing why. 'So you're the pride of the village! What do we call you? Horse? I'll warn that redhead to expect more than she's bargained for, by crikey!'

He picked up the book as his flight was announced and said he'd have to run or the plane would leave without him. Stefan struggled to his feet and Lennard shook his hand again. 'I'm not gonna twist your arm, but if you don't come over, bro, you'll live to regret it. Not for long, though, because I'll be back to break your bloody neck. I'll catch you later.

When you fly, travel light. I'll meet you at the airport on the Harley.'

He turned to leave, then hesitated at the door and looked back. 'Oh yeah, one thing I forgot. It won't all be plain sailing, but. We've been getting threats from some crackpot bastard aiming to put the stoppers on us.'

'Threats? What sort of threats?'

'Could be bomb threats.'

'Now you tell me!'

'I've had a few weird phone calls, but don't let that put you off. They've gone quiet on me lately.' He glanced back through the plate glass as it swung shut. 'So what's new?' he called out. 'No guts, no glory!'

Stefan watched him thread his way down the escalator through the crowd, and the thought struck him—bomb threats! A few crank phone calls! During the past few months as his fortunes had changed for the worst, he had developed tunnel vision and he needed a light at the end of it. Was Lennard showing him a light or driving a runaway locomotive in his direction?

He spread the photographs across the table. He looked down at the two pictures of Rosalie. When he examined the larger portrait, she seemed to challenge him once more. He sensed in her green and candid eyes a disconcerting, playful touch of will-you-won't-you irony and knowing humour.

'You're right,' he said to her, 'I must be going troppo. I don't have a clue what I'm getting myself into.' Then he smiled ruefully. *Here I am, talking to a stranger in a photograph. How desperate is that? She makes a good listener, though. No backchat, just that penetrating gaze as she reads my mind. What's her secret? Will she let me in on it when we meet?*

He slipped the photographs back into the envelope.

He walked out into the fresh wind beyond the airport

buildings and watched a Qantas Boeing 737 labour up into the empty sky, suspended impossibly between climb and fall. He imagined Lennard aboard, down the back next to the toilet, but in Lennard's case, definitely not going down the gurgler. As it climbed, he wondered if this was a crossroads or a parting of the ways. Was the spin of Lennard's coin another double-or-nothing moment in his life of uncertainty? Had he lost the call or won it?

ON SUNSET THAT evening, Stefan celebrated the improbable turn of events. He filled a glass from the bottle of wine he'd saved since Hanukkah—a Mount Mary Quintet he'd bought during a fire sale at the winery door. He conceded it wasn't exactly kosher, but the thought was there.

Then he took out one of the stylish crystal *menorot* candlesticks he'd salvaged from the stock in his workshop and did something he hadn't done since leaving home in Geelong as a seventeen-year-old—he loaded nine candles into its arms and lit the central *shamash*, the guard and the tallest of them, before lighting the remainder with its flame. Since Hanukkah was officially over, he lit them alternately from left to right, humming the first stanza of the *Ma'oz Tzur*, smiling when he recalled the opening reference to the Rock of Ages.

As he lit them, the sudden thought struck him. *Eight candles! Each marks one day since Tania walked out on me on Christmas Eve.* He felt a rush of anguish as he recalled her cutting him to the quick when she left, her tongue a scalpel as sharp as his for once.

She had been halfway through the door that afternoon when he'd returned with the last-minute shopping for the Christmas lunch he'd promised to cook for her. In his other hand, he'd held a bunch of her favourite carnations.

She'd stepped back to let him in. He saw that she'd been

weeping, but she was composed and, when confronted, she was unexpectedly self-possessed. She was so out of character she'd caught him off guard. Dancing on stage, she was a consummate professional; a graceful perfectionist absorbed in fine-tuning movements she'd been learning since she was six, but when she was at home and relaxing, even though she could arc up unpredictably at times, she usually displayed a mix of reserve and innocence he adored.

During the past week he'd felt gutted each time he'd pictured her standing in the open doorway, her green Adidas sports bag in one hand and her favourite bonsai plant—a Moreton Bay Fig tree her mother had planted in 1970 to celebrate the day she was born—balanced with great care in the crook of her other arm.

'I'm taking time out,' she'd said. 'I need some space.'

His mind in sudden turmoil, he'd stammered, 'You're leaving? Why?'

His question hung unanswered in the shocked silence between them. His thoughts had reeled. Was she bored with him? Was she going walkabout to recover between Yajarlu and Wirruwana Dance Theatre assignments? If that was the case, she would have said so, surely.

Was it the failure of his business that alarmed her? Or the age difference between them? Was she leaving him for another man, younger maybe, with better prospects? Or a woman? Was it the unexpected disagreement he'd had with her brothers? Or perhaps his point-blank refusal to have the child with her she craved?

Her last dismissive words before she'd disappeared had stunned him. She wasn't sure she'd be coming back, she said, and saw no point in explaining why. She'd send her sister Alexa round to pick up the rest of her belongings on Boxing Day.

'*Alexa* had a hand in this?' he'd snapped.

'No! This is my decision. Mine alone.'

'So you're leaving me for dead.'

'No. I'm leaving you for life.'

'What's that supposed to mean?'

'Never mind.'

'It's a simple question.'

'With a complicated answer.'

After a moment's charged silence, he'd asked, 'Does for life mean for good?'

'For my good, yes. You wouldn't understand.'

'Try me.'

'It's too personal.'

He'd lifted to shoulder height the bag of groceries and the carnations, which she hadn't acknowledged. His sudden gesture barely missed her face and she'd shuddered back with a sharp out-breath as though he'd slapped her, the rich whiff of Lion's Christmas fruitcake added to the cinnamon fragrance of the flowers. 'Nice timing, Tan. It's Christmas Eve, for Christ's sake. We can't waste these.'

'I'm sorry it doesn't suit you.'

'My oath it doesn't suit me.'

'I'm not under house arrest,' she'd said, her eyes alight, her voice unflinching.

She'd leaned forward and kissed him on the cheek before stepping back and waiting expectantly for him to move aside. He'd hesitated before doing so. She'd brushed past him. 'Look on the bright side,' she'd said, looking back, 'now you're free and so am I. It's not your fault. It's mine.'

He'd seen her eyes brimming. He'd dropped the flowers and groceries and moved towards her, off-balance, as if stumbling down an unseen step in pitch darkness, but she'd shied away and shaken her head. 'Not now!' she'd warned, and then she was gone, her sandals echoing down the stairwell.

Stung, he'd fought the urge to call her back. After several moments of resentful bewilderment, he'd checked the empty corridor before closing the door. He'd cursed himself for failing to read the signs. *What signs, for God's sake?*

Hurt, enraged and panicking, he'd looked down at her from the balcony as she'd walked across the courtyard, the eccentric combination of her bonsai and gym bag lending her the forlorn appearance of someone homeless carting all she valued to the next night's shelter under a forgotten bridge.

'At least tell me where I can contact you,' he'd called out. 'Don't leave things like this.'

She hadn't replied, but then, before she'd turned the corner, she'd slowed and glanced back, briefly. She'd nodded and he'd waved in return, a surge of hope racing through him.

In that frozen moment, he'd seen a Sikh couple walking arm in arm along Lygon Street. They'd hesitated at the courtyard entrance, alerted by his shout. Both had glanced at Tania, then up at him. They'd stopped, then the man had murmured something and they resumed their walk, the woman with her face framed in the cyan shimmer of her flower-patterned sari looking back at Tania. For one dizzying instant, he'd imagined Tania reflected in her gaze and the crazy hope arose that she might turn and bar her way, prevent her departure and convince her to return to him.

But no, they'd disappeared in different directions among the passers-by.

A weight had descended as she'd vanished, and it dawned on him how much he was going to miss her, how much he relied on her being around. Two years of happiness had been snuffed out and he hadn't seen the writing on the wall. Struggling to save his business over the past few months, he hadn't given her the attention she deserved. Had he taken her so much for granted that now she'd turned her back on him?

He'd filled a vase from the kitchen tap, set it on the balcony table and stood the carnations within in it, still bound by a twisted green rubber band. They'd be visible from the street.

That evening when he'd searched the flat, he found she'd sorted all her gear from his, down to their collection of CDs, to make it easy for Alexa. On her dressing table, he'd discovered the crystal bird of paradise pendant he'd made for her when they'd first moved in together. He'd spent days designing and sculpting it and she'd raved over it, rarely going out without wearing it. It lay with the silver chain coiled beside it, as though dropped there as a hasty afterthought. Or was it? Wasn't it a clear signal she was done with him? Another deliberate gesture, like the bonsai, to drive the point home.

He'd hunted desperately for the charm bracelet he'd fashioned for her birthday a year before. It was his business stock in trade and he'd added elements to it month by month, twelve abstract shapes in shimmering glass combined with fragments of a range of precious and semi-precious stones, each charm commemorating meaningful moments in the progress of their lives together. *They're my speaking stones*, she'd told him, a memory behind each. It seemed she'd taken that with her. At least she'd done that.

Nor did he find a farewell note of explanation. *Did she write one? If I hadn't turned up when I did, was she going to slip it beneath the door as she closed it behind her?*

He'd been distraught, confused and obsessed. For several days, he'd contacted her family and friends without success, until at last her brother Richie rang to confirm that she'd arrived in Cairns. She'd decided to break off all ties with him, he said. And then he dropped the bombshell. She'd been invited to Brazil to work with the *Sapatos Alados* Dance Theatre in Belo Horizonte.

'So *that's* the reason she walked out?' Stefan had snapped. They had offered her a contract to work on a production before she met him, and it had taken him an agonising week to change her mind and move in with him instead. 'When did they invite her back?'

'They called her yesterday. She's in two minds, but we're advising her to take the opportunity.'

'*Of course you are!*' Stefan had shouted after a stunned pause. 'Thank you very much, Richie, I appreciate your interference.'

'Hey! Try me, why don't you? I swear I'll take out a restraining order on her behalf if you make a move in her direction—'

Shaking with rage, Stefan had slammed down the phone.

Later, when he'd calmed down, he knew he must resign himself to her decision. Had she stayed it would have been against her will. Added to his financial troubles, her ill-timed desertion which, in his bitterness, he judged a betrayal, was unbearable, but he knew that worse was to come. When she'd moved to Brazil, she'd deliver the eighty-first blow, the most stinging of them all.

He snuffed out the eight lower candle flames, leaving the *shamash* burning. He deep-fried some hash brown *latkes* and heated three doughnut *bimuelos* he'd found in the fridge, washing them down with a last half glass of wine before the reek of mozzarella and pepperoni scorching in the ovens of the pizzeria across the courtyard drove him indoors.

When he cleared the debris from the balcony table the *shamash* waned, then flickered out. Had Tanya's love for him as well? She'd done a runner and wouldn't be back anytime soon. *If ever, for God's sake!* He reached for the wilting carnations, shook the water from their stems and flung them into the bin.

Later, on the verge of sleep, Stefan reconsidered Lennard's invitation. One nagging thought disconcerted him—the monument was intended as a memorial to twenty thousand massacred Aborigines about whom he knew next to nothing. While he acknowledged the number, he hadn't heard their stories and knew few of their names. *Would it make a difference if I did know? They're really no concern of mine. They're in the past, long gone and best forgotten. It's time to move on, isn't it? Time to keep pace with progress taking place across the country with frightening acceleration.*

When he and Tania had moved in together and his first meeting with her brothers had proved so disastrous, Stefan agreed to explore her Yirrganydji people's collective history to better understand their point of view. It was one way to repair the damage, she suggested.

So when they'd returned to Melbourne, he'd researched incidents arising from the clash of cultures during early settlement around Cairns. While there were some eye-opening moments, he was disturbed to discover conflicting narratives and records in some of the diaries and reports he referenced and he was disconcerted by contradictory interpretations and bias in passages from books Tania selected for him. Were the Aboriginal tribes made up of thinly scattered family groups or organised into sovereign nations? Were they primitive hunter-gatherers to be brushed aside or domesticated farmers in settled villages cultivating yams and native plants? Was the virtually empty continent there for the taking or was the Mabo decision a justified step in the right direction?

The more he read the more confused he'd become. Two hundred years loomed as an unbridgeable abyss so that in the end, nothing could shake his growing conviction that his research had no point. It was too late in the day for meaningful corrective action and any that was taken now would only widen the divide.

He didn't lie to Tania.

'It seems to me we'll never get a handle on the real truth, Tan,' he'd asserted one morning. 'It doesn't matter what steps we take to fix things now, it's far too late. Land rights granted because they were once usurped? A treaty negotiated two hundred years after the event? An apology to the stolen generations and compensation for past mistreatment? We both know whatever's conceded or denied, one mob or the other comes out of the process wanting more or feeling dudded.'

Tania was furious. 'We can't stop trying,' she'd exclaimed. 'The stakes are too high.'

'For your mob, maybe.'

'*For all of us*, Stefan! We have to set things right,'

'For all of us?'

'Are you blind? *For the nation!*'

'For the nation? Careful Tan, you're walking into quicksand.'

She hadn't replied. She'd stormed out to dance practice and given him the silent treatment on her return, relenting only when he'd picked up his research where he'd left off. But nothing changed his view. Though she hadn't pursued the disagreement, he was aware how deeply his admission had dismayed her.

And now, lying in the dark, he wondered how he could convince her to return. *How far do I have to bend?* he wondered. *To find the answer I need to work alongside someone like Lennard and hear him out.*

When he woke the next morning, he took the plunge before he had a change of heart. He confirmed his flight.

It took him the next three hectic days to wind up the paperwork for the liquidation, store the Ducati and clear the flat. He packed a selection of his crystal ware moulds and notebooks to work on during his spare time in Fremantle, including one of Tania's favourites—a delicate, sparkling mobile of blue crystals that had taken him weeks to fabricate.

The morning after his arrival in the west, he and Lennard were working for the first time in the vast and airy space of the glassworks on the foreshore of Bathers Beach.

LENNARD MET HIM at Perth Airport on Saturday evening, just after sundown. They roared into Fremantle aboard Lennard's Electra Glide, Stefan with his guitar case across his lap, bracing his pack against the backrest, leaning precariously with Lennard when they banked into the corners.

When they arrived at the house on Bellevue Terrace overlooking the city, Lennard parked in the carport alongside a vintage black scooter. He gestured with a thumb. 'This is my first Hog, would you believe? Bet you didn't know they built a scooter.'

'A Harley scooter? No way known.'

'Yep, it's a fact. She's a "Topper" I bought in 1963. Second hand. All I could afford when I was a student. She still goes like the clappers, even if she's farting more smoke rings than Groucho Marx these days. She took us everywhere, Rosie and me. As far as Kalbarri to meet the folks.'

'I'm a Duke man myself.'

'Not while you're working with me, you're not. Wash your mouth out!' Reaching into his back pocket, he extracted a set of keys, which he dropped into Stefan's hand. 'She used to have a rope pull-start like a lawnmower, but we converted her to electric to make it easy for Rosie. She's yours for as long as you need wheels, bro. Treat the old girl with respect and she'll return the favour in spades.'

He led Stefan to the entrance of the turn-of-the-century house, explaining that he and Rosalie had restored it in the mid-1970s; a long-term labour of love.

Four limestone steps climbed to the shadow of a bull-nosed veranda. When Lennard opened the red front door, Stefan groped his way down the passageway in the semi-darkness, his footfalls creaking on polished floorboards. He caught the pungent tang of... what? *Cointreau? Surely not! Are there oranges fermenting somewhere in the shadows?* Lennard switched on the passage light. Lemons and green apples were piled in a wooden bowl on the hallway table. Standing out among them was the scarlet globe of a pomegranate.

A life-sized gold-framed charcoal nude propped on an easel greeted them at the entrance to the lounge, her profile Grecian, her lines alive with movement in the energetic sweep of back and thigh, her fingers at the startling inward curve of hip and silhouette of breast. Stefan was astonished when he read the signature—Brett Whiteley!

In the lounge, a vast rectangular slab of glass two centimetres thick covered the rear wall. Stefan recognised an example of Lennard's early works. Lennard flicked a switch and it exploded into incandescent sparks, as though it was an aquarium swarming with luminous fish darting across a reef of electric coral. It lit up the room,

Packed bookshelves ran along the wall of clinker bricks to Stefan's left. On two shelves built into a recess was a collection of rocks of different colours, among them a pair of spherical stone flutes. A large olive green and brown turtle shell resembling a polished leather shield was mounted above them, a number of photographs lined beside it.

An enlarged portrait of Rosalie in a silver frame caught his eye. Serene, with a characteristic half-smile, it seemed she had a secret she was undecided about sharing with the photographer or was intrigued by a confidence just divulged to her.

In contrast, on the opposite wall, he noticed four framed black-and-white engravings of buildings and canals in a city he did not recognise. They appeared to be several centuries old. A windmill on one suggested they were Dutch.

Then his gaze fell on the glass model of a three-masted sailing ship in a bottle standing on a glass-topped coffee table in the centre of the lounge. He walked across to admire the delicate intricacy of its structure. 'This is quite something. Did you make it?'

'Yes. It's a model of the *Zuytdorp*.'

'Another labour of love?'

'Of course.'

'How long did it take you?'

'All of six months. The same time it took to build the real thing.'

'I can imagine.'

Lennard waved a hand around the room. '*Marugudu nyinda ngurrala nyinamanha*. Make yourself at home, bro. My young bloke Luke's away on tour in Canada and Europe until October, so you're welcome to his sleepout until then. And remember, when in Freo do as we do—live as laid back as nature meant you to.' He laughed. 'It beats living in a humpy. I've lived in a few of those, but. When you're out there in the desert you live like the Warlpiri people or you don't survive.' He thumped Stefan's shoulder. 'Ask your mates aboard the *Kookaburra*!'

He stepped back and studied Stefan for several thoughtful moments. 'There's something we need to get squared away right now,' he said at last. 'You've heard me talking language now and then. It's Malgana *wangga*. I'll be doing that a lot when you least expect it because I need the practice. Some people get uptight when they hear me speak it. They think I'm jerking them around, excluding them from the conversation, but I'm not. It's part of my culture. It's the cement that carries our history. If it gives you grief let me know.'

'No problem so far, Ace.' Stefan paused, in two minds, and then suggested, 'Maybe I could take lessons and learn it myself?'

Lennard gave a broad smile. 'Good thinking, bro. My *wajbala* offsider speaking Malgana! That'd be radical. Then you won't have to second guess me and we can work on it together.' He nodded up at Rosalie's photograph. 'Rosie's twin brother Max has been learning it as well. We'll get a three-way conversation going once you get the knack. I'll mention it to Alicia. She can knock you up a beginner's cheat sheet.'

'Alicia?'

'Been keeping her up my sleeve, bro.' He pointed at the far door to the back veranda. 'She'll be out the back. She's our resident linguist. She's been helping us resurrect the language and sort the syntax out… and she's my partner.'

'Your *partner?*' Stefan glanced fleetingly up at Rosalie's photograph.

Lennard noticed his double-take, but he didn't miss a beat. 'It's a dying language we're giving CPR to, so learning it's not a pushover. My mum thought it was extinct until she found these *marnkurru gambarra bugarra*; these three cluey old aunties from Denham who remember speaking it as kids. They're brilliant. They're friends of hers. She met them when she first moved to *Munimaya*, to Northampton, to teach, when she was in her early twenties. She was boarding with one of them and began learning it then. Now they're all working with Alicia, recording their vocabulary and sussing out the grammar. They're not fluent, but they're trawling through their memories like there's no tomorrow.

'I visited them last September before I came across to Melbourne. They gave me copies of their latest tapes. My pronunciation's not crash hot and I'm using words when I know zip about the fine distinctions in their meaning, but I'm getting there. I learned a few words from my mum when I was a young fella. I shoulda kept it up, but you know how it is when you're that age… too much time for everything else.'

He led Stefan towards the sliding door that opened onto the back veranda. He gestured through the glass. 'As I thought. There she is.'

Alicia was asleep in a hammock slung between carved jarrah pillars on the veranda. The lantern light washed over her. Her hair was drawn back, bound by a broad headband of white silk and the thick sable rope of her dangling plait gleamed as she breathed. An open book lay upturned across her breast. An empty wineglass and a plate with a paring knife and an apple core stood on a side table, an unbroken spiral of green skin discarded on the floor beside it.

'She's from the Shenandoah Valley in West Virginia, where they're all as good looking as her. What d'you reckon, there must be something in that water coming down them Appalachians?'

'Homebrewed Mountain Dew, perhaps?'

'That'd cover it, bro.'

Beneath the hammock lay a dog, a Malamute cross that scrambled to its feet. When it recognised Lennard, it yelped and bounded across to them. It leaned its paws on the door frame and looked from one to the other through the glass, its eyes a surprising sky blue, its coat the colour of sand with light brown flecking down its back. It contemplated Stefan, then turned back to Lennard and showed its teeth.

He tapped a finger on the glass. 'This is Skathi,' he said. He gave Stefan a sudden, wide smile. 'She's the other mixed-breed in the family.'

'Skathi? That's a new one on me.'

'The Norse goddess of winter or hunting or whatever. Rosie used to breed purebreds, but this one's mother, Freya, took a fancy to the Kelpie leader of the pack up on Wanamalu station run by my old folks and when he duffed her that was that. End of breeding project. She's a beauty, though. See the smile?'

'So it is. I thought she was snarling at me.'

'Nah, mate. She likes you.'

'She's a good judge of character, then.'

'If you say so yourself.'

He knocked on the door panel. Alicia stirred, opened her eyes and waved. As she did so, she dislodged the book. It fell to the floor and she reached for it languidly. She reached again, but it lay beyond her fingers. The hammock swung, and through its mesh, Stefan saw her broad face, angular cheekbones and eyes deep-set beneath the remarkable sweep of raven eyebrows. There was an eye-catching asymmetry in her accentuated bone structure, her wide mouth. She seemed at first glance ageless; a woman who took her striking looks for granted, carrying them unawares. He saw that she'd be as regal when her hair had turned to silver. In the half-light, she had a somewhat androgynous look, with skin the colour of caramel. He imagined she was Spanish, perhaps Mexican.

She leaned further from the hammock to retrieve her book and smiled up at them half-asleep, a dimple creviced in her left cheek.

'She's a dead ringer for Michelle Pfeiffer,' Stefan said, 'except for the hair.'

'Michelle Pfeiffer dunked in Grecian 1000, you reckon? You may be right, but let me warn you, bro, she's not big on compliments.'

'Tell me more,' Alicia said as she walked through the door that Lennard opened for her, Skathi following at her heels. She put a hand to her cheek in a gesture of self-mockery, her dark and forthright eyes sparkling. 'Michelle Pfeiffer, you think? No offence taken, kind sir, she'll do for now. Just don't mention Frida Kahlo. I'm bored to tears with being mistaken for her older sister.'

Stefan knelt to pat Skathi as she sniffed his hand and then offered him a paw with an approving tail wag. Then he glanced back up. 'No, I see you've got two eyebrows. But apart from that—'

'Second-hand joke,' Alicia interrupted him. 'Lead balloon, I'm afraid. I've heard them all before.'

Stefan stood and she took his hand in greeting. She was a head taller, broad-shouldered and athletic, her body faintly visible through the caftan. He took her to be in her mid-thirties.

'I'm glad to know you, Stefan Novak.' She stepped back with a look of appraisal. 'Or is it Joel Fleischman? You look like you've walked off the set of *Northern Exposure*, afro hair and Jewish nose… needing a shave is all. But it must have been the final episode, now I see the wrinkles. Welcome to Fremantle.'

Stefan noticed her Australianised accent, the occasional vowel revealing hints of a southern drawl, the word 'welcome' inheriting an extra syllable.

She gestured through the open door. 'The sleepout's to the right, at the end of the veranda. I've cleared away most of Luke's things but it's still a disaster.' She handed him a pair of keys. 'This one's for the sleepout and this one fits the back door to the house. We need the place secure when we're not around. Apart from that, the doors are always open. Grab your backpack. Follow me.'

In the sleepout, Stefan dropped his guitar and backpack on the bed as Alicia pulled open the door of an empty wardrobe, the coat hangers jangling. She closed it and walked across the room to the en suite entrance. 'You've got your own facilities in here.'

'I hope I won't be a nuisance,' he replied, 'imposing on you like this.'

'Don't let that worry you. We want you to treat this place like home. You'll be good company for Ace when I'm away, which is quite often these days. He may have mentioned I'm flat out researching the Nhanda and Malgana dialects right now, so I spend a lot of time working up in Geraldton with the Yamaji Language Centre.'

She pointed through the front window towards the top end of Bellevue Terrace, where a semicircle of double-storied townhouses stood around a cul-de-sac. 'Don't think we're trying to get rid of you already, but we've got you listed for one of those. They come up quite often and they're conveniently close. Meantime, you're welcome to Luke's pad till he gets back.'

She gestured at his guitar case. 'You'll find some boxes of Luke's music under the bed if you're interested. I'm sure he won't mind you looking through them.'

'I'm only a beginner. I'm concentrating on flamenco.'

She glanced at him in surprise. 'A beginner? And you're concentrating on *flamenco*? Then you're very welcome in this house, Stefan.' She paused. 'You'll be familiar with Paco Pena and Tomatito then, but tell me, have you ever heard of El Poeta?'

'I'm afraid not, no. Only Paco.'

'I mean José Cala Repeto. There are others with the nickname. He's brilliant. He's a master, truly authentic. I've got a couple of recordings Papá taped when he heard him in Andalusia in the sixties. They're very rare. On one of them, he's playing to El Chocolate's singing. Does El Chocolate ring a bell?'

'Sorry, no.'

'And I've got another of him with La Sallago. I'll get them out for you once you've settled in. If you like flamenco you're bound to like them.'

'I'm still in nappies, though.'

'With flamenco, you're always in nappies, aren't you? You never stop learning, Papá used to say.'

'He played?'

'He did, and my *abuelo*—my grandfather—before him.' She gave a smile as she pre-empted his question. 'No, not me. Not like them. I played, but never very well. I used to sing for Papá though, years ago, before I left home. And then I met young Luke and I picked up the guitar again.'

She pointed at a silver-framed photograph propped against the mirror on the dressing table and Stefan leaned closer to study four musicians lined up on stage.

'Luke was in his teens when I first moved in.' Alicia picked up the photograph and brushed her fingers over it. 'He didn't take to me at all at first. Lennard warned me he'd been very close to Rosie. It was very awkward. When we first met, I told him I wanted us to be friends if that was alright with him, and if it wasn't, I'd still be there for him if and when he needed me.

'Well, it wasn't. He avoided me like I was a Jezebel,' she gave a quiet chuckle, 'with leprosy. He'd lock himself in here and brood for hours on end, tinkering with his latest guitar. That's what broke the ice bit by bit—the music. It took me months to bring him round, but I worked on him. Eventually, he let me teach him how to fingerpick and improvise flamenco-style. I couldn't demonstrate it all that well, but I knew the finger movements and the chords. When I showed him the fingering for the tremolo, he was a natural and that was the breakthrough. He began warming to me. Sure, we still have our moments.' She gestured around the room. 'As you can see, I'm not his housemaid! But we are good mates and on the same wavelength now, much to Ace's relief.'

She offered Stefan the photograph.

'This is Luke's group?' he asked.

'It sure is. They call themselves *Ingga Thaaka*—loosely translated as the Cyber Sharks—and that's Luke.'

She placed her forefinger on a fresh-faced guitarist in

denims with a devil-may-care larrikin look of corruptible innocence about him. His long copper hair was held back in a headband woven in strands of red, black and yellow. His eyes were an indescribable luminous green.

'Those eyes, they're not that green, surely,' Stefan said. 'Is he wearing coloured contacts? Or is that some sort of photographic effect?'

'They're his, the way he was born. Hypnotic, aren't they? Inherited from his grandfather on Rosie's side.'

'He'd have no trouble reeling in the girls, I'd say.'

'God's gift.' She laughed. 'They're all over him, even when his eyes are shut.'

Stefan scrutinised the photograph more closely. 'You wouldn't pick him for an Aboriginal Australian.'

'Don't tell *him* that. Big mistake! Check out the headband. He's carrying the colours.'

Then she pointed out another member of the group, an Aboriginal with a rakish grin and a wild mane of hair gleaming silver against his coal-black skin. 'That's the Wildcat— Willie Deakin. He used to front the *Broome Wildcats* till they disbanded. Remember them?'

'Remember them? They were my all-time favourite way back when.'

'Lennard swears Luke and Willie are guitarred with the same brush.'

'Willie! He was a hero of mine.' Stefan nodded. 'Australia's answer to B.B. King. Jeez, he's aged some since then. Has he still got the voice?'

'He sure has, like he's got twelve testicles.'

Stefan laughed as he replaced the photograph on the dresser. 'I saw him once in Geelong, live, in his leathers. One of my mates was convinced it was a hernia.'

Smiling, Alicia looked back as she left the room. 'Come

and join us when you've unpacked. I've got dinner up and running. I hope you're not a vegan. It's roast chicken tonight.'

'No, I'm not. I've got no allergies. I'm not fussy. And right now, I'm starving.'

'Good. It won't be long.'

'I can help out in the kitchen, Alicia. Earn my keep.'

'There's really no need.'

'But I don't mind. I enjoy knocking up a meal when I get the chance. My mother's had me learning the ropes since I was an ankle-biter and I'm a dab hand with some of her recipes.'

'Well, you can take over when I'm working up in Geraldton. Lennard always balloons on his takeaways when I'm away. We can talk about it later.'

Stefan watched her walk away down the veranda. He shook his head. *Alicia, now there's a lookup for the books! How does she deal with Rosalie's presence in the house? She's every-where you look.*

And Rosalie? Where is she? When will we meet?

Before unpacking, he looked through the rear window and marvelled at the view through trellised grapevines and across rooftops angling down towards the city and the sea. The sun was setting, the last segment of its blazing disc edging below the horizon. He watched the colours on the ocean and across the sky fade to dark as though someone was drawing down a blind. Smiling at the thought, he reached for the sash and did the same.

THE NEXT MORNING, they were hard at it in the glassworks on the shore of Bathers Beach. Stefan heaved the rubber-tyred wheelbarrow filled with fine silica sand up a narrow plank across the threshold for what seemed the hundredth time. He hesitated there, standing half in sunlight, half in workshop shadow. He was not yet used to the rhythms of heavy work and the weight of the barrow wrung his shoulders. His eyes were blinded by sweat. His hands were blistered. He released the wheelbarrow and stood still, panting.

The sun streamed in through three tall windows illuminating diagonal columns of dust in particles of light drifting slantwise across the vaulted space towards the row of four kilns and the furnace against the far wall. Overhead, giant beams of century-old jarrah ran the length of the roof, a herringbone mosaic of timber panels between them. He found the cathedral-like effect stunning.

He wiped his face with a rag from his back pocket before reaching down to grip the handles. He balanced himself; and as he leaned into the load and took the first step a sudden blast of music struck him. He heard Lennard shout above it, 'This is Henryk Wieniawski, bro! His "Variations on an Original Theme", Opus fifteen for violin and piano in A major. Wait till you hear what's coming. That's me on the didge.'

Taken aback, Stefan listened for the rhythmic throb of the didgeridoo. He picked up its sonorous echoes in the background; an energetic pulse weaving through the melody, a bass voice calling up the country, the music of Australia's western desert echoing across the Russian steppes.

'That's loud enough to wake the dead!' he shouted.

'Exactly the point, bro. That way the ancestors can all tune in.'

'What about the pottery mob next door?'

'They don't mind. They know it's one of Rosie's favourites. The first time I heard it Igor—what's his name?—Oistrakh was playing it at a concert Rosie and I went to. Or rather, she went and I met her there by chance. In August 1963, would you believe, when I was still a young fella. When I heard him play that night, I told her all it needed was the didge to give it some Aussie zing. So later we recorded it in. And here,' he gestured around the glassworks resonating to the sound, 'you have it.'

I'm in a medieval abbey, Stefan thought, *and if this is heaven, it's close to hell*, as the wheelbarrow rolled towards the roaring mixer dragging him with it, his arms threatening to leave their sockets. He swung the barrow to tip the sand onto the pile beside the sieve, dropped the handles and rubbed his stiff-fingered hands together.

'My go,' Lennard said. 'You'll get used to it. Another month or two and this'll be piss-easy. Let me show you how it's done.'

He handed Stefan the shovel and removed his orange T-shirt. He rolled it into a sweatband, wrapped it around his head and knotted the sleeves. He adjusted it to hold back his hair, then crouched and stomped his way around the fallen barrow, head jerking, elbows out, lifting his knees and slamming his boots to the didgeridoo's rhythm, raising dust. He completed a complicated leg-shaking shuffle and froze stock-still with a wide grin as the dust settled.

'Rain dance, bro.' He shook himself like an overweight dog emerging from the sea, beads of perspiration sparkling around him. 'A rain dance for you *wajbalas* who still think we came down in the last shower.'

The gleaming pendant swung on the leather thong below his throat and when he was still, Stefan saw the wings of the albatross quiver to the pulse within the muscled curve of his ribs.

'How d'you like my *nyambi* shuffle? You reckon I got the right moves?'

'Tania could show you a step or two.'

'No doubt. And now you're gonna tell me I'd look the part in her tutu and leotards,' he looked down at his boots, 'not to mention her size sixteen ballet shoes.'

He broke the pose, spat on his palms and rubbed them vigorously together before reaching down to grasp the handles of the barrow. 'Let me show you us blackfellas don't turn to water at the thought of hard yakka. Watch this!'

His running shadow blocked the doorway as he went up a gear, sprinting out into the glaring sunlight, the barrow bouncing.

It struck Stefan then that he may have bitten off more than he could chew. He wondered if he had the tenacity and stamina to see it through, but there was no backing out now.

He listened to Oistrakh's exquisite violin as its lyrical upper register explored the gentlest of melodies before descending through a brilliant cadenza to a lower register. Then he heard the pizzicato sounds of falling water gathered in by the didgeridoo—brown sounds, sunburned sounds, the sounds of a rain dance, he imagined, rain falling from a darkening sky filled with clouds formed from smoking lines of blazing Spinifex sweeping in orange zigzags across the desert… rainfall pelting the scorched earth in the piano's muted thunder, splashing on the upturned faces of Warlpiri dancers whirling to the violin's energetic final passage, each drop raising a mini coronet as it struck red sand and doused the flames.

Lennard reappeared, struggled to unload the barrow, then released the handles. His body gleamed. 'It's a lousy rumour horses sweat and us Yamaji don't. Five more loads will do us. I'll toss you for the privilege.'

He dusted the sand from his hands and withdrew the silver *schelling* from his pocket. He balanced it on his thumbnail, inspected it, gave it a kiss and flicked it as he called out, 'Heads.'

'What's this, another crossroads?'

'You've always got a fifty-fifty chance of winning.'

'And losing, with my luck.'

They watched its glittering arc. When the coin fell, Lennard showed Stefan tails. 'You win again. It's all yours.'

'I win and I lose. I'm on a winning losing streak. That coin of yours must be loaded.'

'You make your choice and take your chances.'

'Story of my life.'

'Both our lives brudda, but one of these days it'll land on its edge and we both win.'

'That'll be the day.'

Lennard looked thoughtfully down at him. 'We're both winners already, but. We're members of the same tribes and we're on a mission, you and me. That's a win for starters.'

'What tribe is that?'

'*Tribes* Stefan, *tribes*. The same *brotherhoods*,' he said with sudden fervour. 'We're glassmakers, bro. We're artists. We're *Aussies*, even if there are times when we're not sure what that means. And one of these days, if I have my say, we'll be Malgana brothers too.'

'We're glassmakers without borders?'

'You got it in one, bro. You got it in one.'

He glanced at the clock on the wall. 'Another ten minutes and we're outta here.'

Stefan watched him make his way towards the CD player. *Wieniawski? That's one for the books! He's given me another insight into his unfamiliar world. Another random piece of the jigsaw with no clear reference yet from which to calculate its placement.*

With a wry grimace, he reached for the handles of the wheelbarrow.

LENNARD RESTARTED THE CD. He headed for the double doors open to the sea and leaned against the jamb. He looked across the sand to the water's edge where stick-legged gulls tottered seaward and back, some bickering with their necks arched, others lifting and gliding across the line of weed. A waft of iodine and saltwater reached him, fresh and tangy. He breathed it deeply in as sounds of the violin reached him. Another time another place, he recalled, as he sat on the bench beside the door and descended into reverie, the memory so vivid it seemed to be the present moment…

LATE EVENING, AUGUST 1963

HE WAS HEADING for the South Perth ferry on his way home and Rosalie was queuing for a concert in the foyer of the Capitol Theatre as he passed. He heard her shout and stopped abruptly. She emerged from the crowd and leaned against the curved balustrade three steps up from the pavement. Her wave reeled him in.

She was sheathed in white satin with a viridian silk scarf silver-toggled at her throat, her hair a shining fall of deep rich copper across her shoulders. She took his breath away.

'Hello stranger,' she said, her eyes alight. 'Don't I know you?' She snapped a finger. 'I remember now. You're the bloke who's been stalking me.'

'I've been looking out for you for weeks.'

'And now you've found me. What took you so long? Why don't you join me inside in case you lose me for a second time?'

'In these?'

His jeans were worn through at the knees. The collar of his polo T-shirt showed beneath a duffle coat that was his pride and joy, technicolour glass-spatter glittering down the front like paintball hits. The faint smell of furnace smoke drifted about him, overpowering as he got closer.

'Of course in those. You're a cannibal, remember? You're dressed to kill.'

Lennard smiled at her reference to their conversation in the operating theatre when they'd first met a month ago.

'Come and chew the fat with me inside. We may not get a better chance.'

He heard the five-minute curtain call.

Sweeping aside his apprehension and ignoring the

indignant looks that greeted him as he mounted the steps, he strode across to the box office. The crowd parted for him like the Red Sea.

The ticket cost him almost two quid. *Two quid! There goes my ferry ride*, he thought, as he passed the coins across. The booth attendant, taken by surprise and too slow to object, accepted the payment.

This better be worth it, Lennard thought, but knew he'd pay, whatever the cost. He was offered a choice of seats. Grinning, he stuck his dye-stained finger in the centre of the stalls—*row R for Rosalie*. 'I'll have that one, thank you.'

Alerted to the possibility of trouble, the theatre manager stepped up behind him and placed a hand on his shoulder.

'Excuse me… sir. May I ask what you're doing here?'

Looking him in the eye, Lennard waved the ticket. 'I've come down from Geraldton for this, so I'd better get value for money or I'll be asking for a refund.'

After a confused exchange of glances, the manager stepped aside.

He was the last one directed down the aisle. He followed the usherette's torchlight, scanning the audience for the gleam of Rosalie's hair as the lights dimmed and the roar of voices faded to the last anticipatory cough. He saw his empty seat in the middle of the row and clambered over the knees of hor-rified patrons *sorry-sorry-about-that-pardon-me-beg-yours* to get there, clumsy as Big Foot riding a tricycle, a Mexican wave preceding him as they bobbed up from their seats to avoid him.

And then, to his astonishment, he saw Rosalie two seats beyond his.

Her sister, or perhaps a girlfriend, was in the seat between them. She was eyeing him off as he progressed down the row, her lips pursed as though cut by tin snips. Rosalie glanced around as he hurdled the last set of knees and she impulsively changed seats, so that when he took his it seemed she'd reserved it for him.

'So who's jamming tonight?' he asked in a conspiratorial whisper as he leaned across to sit down and Rosalie's laughter rang out when he added, 'Let me guess. It's Willie Deakin and the Broome Wildcats and you're a fan, like me?'

She showed him the program. 'You wish. It's Igor Oistrakh.'

'Igor! The seventh member of the Rolling Stones! Is he gonna sing "Come On" with Mick and the orchestra for backup?'

'No, no orchestra and no Mick Jagger,' Rosalie giggled. 'His backup's Natalia Zertsalova on the piano. She's his wife.'

Smiling together, eyes locked, it seemed they'd been doing this for years.

The violinist walked out into the spotlight, tracking him straight-backed and aristocratic across the stage, the pianist following him out. The applause died and there was a moment of charged silence before the auditorium resonated to the sounds of the violin and piano launching into the energetic *allegro assai* that soared over them.

'This is Beethoven's "Violin Sonata in G Major",' Rosalie whispered, opening up the program in her lap. She pointed out the other pieces, running her index finger with its scarlet fingernail down the page. Then she pointed at the fifth and final item. 'They're all a build-up to Henryk Wieniawski. Wait till you hear that. He's my favourite.'

Like a gypsy organised to perform for them, there he was—Igor Oistrakh on his first visit to Australia. They were captivated by the passionate outpouring of the violin, its subtle switches in melody ascending and gliding gloriously through the registers to the piano's thunderous conclusion.

When the lights brightened at the end of the bracket, Lennard was captivated by a dazzling cut-glass chandelier suspended in a coved dome in the auditorium ceiling. It hung there brilliantly lit, the sparkle of its myriad crystals reflected in aquamarine patterns across the white plaster mouldings. He pointed it out.

'It's beautiful,' Rosalie said.

'It's what I do.'

'You make chandeliers?'

'I'm experimenting with glass and light, trying to sculpt something new. Something different.'

'Glass and light?'

'Multi-coloured light… and its effect on glass.'

'You mean stained glass, as in cathedral windows?'

'No. Three-dimensional glass sculptures with fluorescent light filtered through and round them. I'll have to show you.'

Then he gave her a wide grin and, pointing at the stage, said he hoped she didn't mind, but from among all his muso friends, Igor was the only one available for the night when he'd asked around and she'd have to put up with the occasional mistake in his bowing technique, since it was early in his career.

'I told him you'd be here and he promised not to let me down. I was gonna bring my didge along to join him up there in a duet just for you.'

'You think it needs the didge?'

'Of course it does, to spice things up.'

'Then why didn't you bring it?' Rosalie asked. 'You'd have stolen the show.'

'I tossed up with his missus. Her piano won.'

Rosalie laughed. 'Then let's wait for the Wieniawski piece and imagine you up there with him then.'

Her green eyes and his brown and blue were deep in silent communication for long moments after that, the improbable chain of coincidence in their earlier meetings and the synchronicity in Lennard's choice of seat not lost on them. It seemed some whimsical ghostwriter with a sense of the surreal was pulling the strings, including those on Igor Oistrakh's violin.

They were still whispering during the opening to the next item, a Prokofieff sonata, when Rosalie's father leaned across and glared at them from the end of the row. His arching forehead gleamed, the glint from his rimless lenses rendering his eyes reptilian.

'Would you two mind shutting up?' he hissed. 'We're here for the recital, or haven't you noticed?'

'Sorry!' Rosalie waited until the music rose and then she leaned across to murmur, 'My father, David. He has this thing about you lot. He probably thinks you're about to abduct me.'

'He's deadly right,' Lennard whispered in reply. 'I am. And I know exactly where to hide you.'

'Oh yes, and where's that?'

'Up in the hills where they'll never think of looking.'

'Sounds good to me.'

The huskiness in Rosalie's voice struck a deep responsive chord within him, opening up a curtain on what seemed the brilliance of day.

They were absorbed in the music till the bracket ended. When the piano stilled, applause erupted. They joined it, Rosalie stamping her feet joyously.

During the half-time interval, they remained in their seats as the audience shuffled out; and as they talked, they were surprised to discover they shared a love of the sea. When Lennard mentioned his interest in the *Zuytdorp* as a key to his Malgana family ancestry, Rosalie was astonished.

'The *Zuytdorp*!' she exclaimed. 'I don't believe it! You're stealing my thunder!'

She'd dived on the sunken remains of another shipwreck

the weekend before, she explained excitedly; the *Vergulde Draeck*—the *Gilt Dragon*—discovered in April, wedged into a reef south-west of Ledge Point.

'I'm preparing an article for the dive club magazine right now. I took underwater photos of the wreck site last weekend.'

'What about the *Zuytdorp*? Have you dived on her?'

'No one has yet. Some friends of mine from the club tried last March, but it was too rough. They're organising another dive next year. They found some relics on the cliffs up there and a pit of ash so thick it's lasted all this time. They think it's the remains of a beacon fire the survivors lit to signal passing ships.'

Lennard gave her a broad smile. 'That's my country and I've seen it too, that big ash pit!' He and his father had been visiting the site for years, he told her. 'And I've got some relics of my own.' He reached into his pocket and withdrew the coin.

She gasped as she inspected it. 'This is unreal! Where'd you find it?'

'My mother found it in an old tobacco tin up near Kalbarri.'

He described the crudely fashioned rock shelter in a cliff-top cave his mother had discovered on Wanamalu station, the pewter canister hidden beneath a pile of rocks in a recess at the back. 'That cave's a hundred and fifty kilometres south of the wreck. I played in it when I was a kid. I sat in it. I slept in it. The container had Table Mountain etched on its lid and there were other relics inside. That coin. An animal hair bracelet, plaited from lion's mane, we've been told. A silver spoon with a sailor's name inscribed on it—*Gerrit de Waal*. And this…'

He reached inside the neck of his T-shirt and withdrew the black leather thong. He ducked to lift it over his head, the abalone shell dangling. He laid it in her palm alongside the coin, turning it so that she could examine the albatross cameo. The theatre lights glimmered on its whorls of greens and blues, accentuating the outstretched wings and elongated head and beak. The carving was crude, but delicate and enigmatic.

'This must have taken ages to make with such a thin layer of mother of pearl,' she murmured, shaking her head. 'Someone's carved it with such care.' She looked up. 'Is it a storm petrel, one of Mother Carey's chooks?'

'I think it's an albatross, a *banduga*,' he replied.

'A *banduga*? What language is that?'

'My language. Malgana *wangga*.' He pointed at the carving. 'My totem is the osprey, the *wabagu*. I reckon this one here's a crossbreed. The *wabagu* for me and the *banduga* for Gerrit. It brings me closer to him. Puts us in touch. Same tribe, different bird totems. Same tribe, different centuries.'

'The *wabagu* and *banduga*. They're the gentlest sounds. I can hear the wind and the sea in them.' She returned the necklace. 'So tell me about him. Why do you feel a connection? Because you've seen the spoon?'

'He's my ancestor.'

'Your *ancestor*?'

Lennard described the tarnished tablespoon with the name etched along the handle in ornate script, a series of flourishes initiating the 'G' and a long curlicue extending the final 'L'; the sailing ship inscribed in the spoon's bowl, with the VOC insignia inlaid across it; and the 'Z' for the Zeeland charter stamped across the back.

'The VOC? You mean the Dutch East India Company?'

'Yep, that's it. The VOC.' He placed a clenched hand to his lips and cleared his throat as though preparing for a nervous recitation. 'How's this for double Dutch—the *Vereenigde Nederlandse Geoctroyeerde Oostindische Compagnie.*'

'My God, I'm impressed!' She gave a quick laugh, and then,

'If I tried that I'd spray you with spit. So you've been studying the *Zuytdorp*'s history?'

'I'm trying,' he shrugged, 'but there's not much information around.'

'It's early days, I guess. Do you still have the spoon?'

'No. It was stolen. My dad drove down to Geraldton to deliver it to the Maritime Display with some other artefacts and someone broke into his car. My mother wouldn't part with a handful of coins, but. And she gave me the necklace when I was eighteen. I've worn it ever since.'

'It's your dog tag,' she said as he put the necklace back around his neck. 'Your *sea-dog* tag.' She adjusted the pendant to the centre of his chest, looking up at him with concern. 'But an *albatross*? Around your neck? Aren't you tempting fate?'

'No. This one's alive. Very much so. And it's my link to Gerrit.' He smiled and added, 'But the spoon—seeing his name on it—that was a blast. It's given me a trail to follow and I'm gonna find out everything I can about him when I get the chance.' Then, sensing her scepticism, 'I'm not suggesting any of this proves that Gerrit *is* my ancestor, but it does prove he survived. I guess there were others who survived as well. I may be descended from one of them.'

The lights dimmed once again and they were absorbed in the Bach and Hindemith sonatas that followed until Oistrakh struck up at last the majestic *maestoso* passage that opened the Wieniawski piece. When the composition ended on a repeat version of the theme, lyrical and dance-like, a waltz that built into a brilliant crescendo, Lennard was entranced.

He looked at Rosalie, 'I'm hooked!' he said. 'The rhythm's perfect for the didge.'

She took his hand. 'Then we'll get together to arrange a recording.' She gave him a mock-serious look. 'About the kidnapping—you'll have to wait a while before dragging me off. We're organising a barbecue next weekend for the Georgian State Dancers. They're in town on tour at the moment.' She reached into her handbag for a pen and scribbled an address onto a page in the program. She handed it to him. 'There. You're invited. I want you to come.'

Lennard read it, frowned and rolled the program up. So she *did* live on Mount Street. In the dress circle overlooking the river. *Jesus*! *I'll be the one and only blackfella at a barbecue on Millionaire Row, with most of the other guests Russian ballerinas.*

Self-conscious confusion he hadn't displayed before coursed through him.

'Not a chance,' he muttered and looked away.

'What do you mean, not a chance?' She peered into his face, but he would not meet her eyes. 'Don't you dare give me the flick! Give me your address and I'll drag you there myself.'

'I'll stick out like a dog's.'

'Of course you will. But you'll be a celebrity, not a freak. Don't run for cover. You're gutsier than that. That's what I really like about you. I'm sure you'll enjoy it.'

'It's too far outta my league,' he said, then added defensively, '*You're* too far outta my league.'

She placed both hands on his forearm. 'No, I'm not. And besides, you don't decide that for me. Look around you, Ace. This is out of your comfort zone too, but here you are, with me, and we're having a good time, aren't we? It won't be so bad. I'll look after you, I promise. Let me prove you can trust me. Please.'

She grabbed the program, unrolled it and opened it at the page where she'd recorded her address. It carried a full-page advert for the Ansett-ANA airline. She read it, unclipped her pen and scored out 'Ansett-ANA'. Twice. She replaced each scoring with her name and telephone number.

'There you go,' she said. 'Now you *can't* refuse.'

A faint grin spread as he read her revisions, "You're in good hands all the way when you fly with *Rosalie O'Sullivan*," and, "For helpful and reliable service, ring *Rosalie O'Sullivan*."

'Now you've got *no* excuse. I've gone out on a limb. I've gone down on both knees. How can you resist?'

'Alright.' He paused. 'I'll be there… if I'm there.'

'Not good enough.' She gave him a coquettish flutter of her eyelashes as she rose. 'Just come.' She gripped his shoulder as she looked down. 'Don't disappoint me. I want you to meet my brother Max. He's the one you saw with me on the bus.'

'Your brother? I thought he was your fella.'

'My *fella*?' She gave a suppressed snort of laughter. 'That'll be the day! We'll set the record straight when you meet him. You'll have to take him with a grain of salt, though. He's studying law but thinks he's a QC already, with the IQ to match. Like he's some sort of smarty-pants cultured ocker.'

A confused look crossed his features, as though he was about to ask a question he'd rather not, but he did so anyway. 'So, what's your old man got against us lot?'

She turned, nodded and sat back down. She took his hand in both of hers. 'Apart from the fact that you're intending to kidnap his daughter and race her off into the hills?' She glanced at her departing family, now out of earshot, then carefully chose her words. 'Don't get me wrong, Ace, and don't let what I'm about to tell you spoil your evening.'

'That bad, is it?'

'No, I want you to understand. He really is a good man, deep down, but his prejudice—let's face it—goes back a long way. He's old-school and hard-nosed. He's a mining engineer, born and raised in Kalgoorlie, set in his ways and fixed in his opinions, no matter how blinkered or politically incorrect.' She was thoughtful for a moment. 'Ever since I was knee-high to a grasshopper, I've listened to him sounding off about problems with Aborigines in the mining game.'

Lennard interrupted her. 'Let me guess. It's the land. He's pissed off about the sacred sites and dreaming tracks he reckons we conveniently cook up to complicate things.' He gave her a knowing look. 'I'm right, aren't I?'

'That's partly it.' She squeezed his hand as though offering and seeking reassurance. 'But he points the finger at trade union activists for stirring things up. The Pilbara labour strikes on the cattle stations in the forties, for example. His latest gripe is last week's Yirrkala petition against the bauxite mine in Arnhem Land.'

'You're talking to someone who's heard this all his life, Rosie. From a different perspective. Next thing you're gonna tell me he reckons granting the vote to Aborigines last year was a step too far.'

She inclined her head. 'I'm afraid it gets personal, too. In the early fifties, he pegged a slate mine in the Chichester Ranges near Ngarrari, but when he began working the claim the local Yinjibarndi people objected. When they persisted, he had to shut the quarry down, but not before he'd made a small fortune. He set the family up on Mount Street, but he's never forgotten it and he's been dead set against you lot ever since.' She stood and held out both her hands to him, palms up. 'But listen to me. Neither Max nor I are chips off the old block.'

'That's a relief.'

'If anything, we're the opposite. We're always having a go at him about the issues. That's Mum's influence showing through, so please, please, please don't let Dad stop you coming. I really want you there. I'll be hurt if you aren't.'

She looked back as she walked away, sending him a smile of such tenderness it seems she'd handed him a winning lottery ticket. He gave himself over to its warmth as he responded to it.

THE CD ENDED and Lennard snapped from the flashback.

The onshore breeze was in, the sea wilder now with churning white tops. A cray boat thundered in from the Gage Roads channel, cutting the chop to shreds as it crossed the entrance to Bathers Beach. One deckhand was hosing down, another stacking pots. Diesels thumping, the portside bow unleashed a wave that curled towards the beach.

Lennard imagined the engine's throb vibrating through the aluminium deck beneath his feet and coursing through his body. He wondered how Gerrit would have felt if he'd experienced the juddering sensation and heard the twin diesels' growl instead of the creaking swing and sway of the *Zuytdorp*'s timbers and the whoosh of sheets and pennants as the ship surged down the backs of overtaking waves. He guessed that the wild expanse of ocean and the surrounding horizon's promise—and the promise of what lay beyond the horizon beyond that—would have mattered most to him.

The bow wave reached the shore, agitating the weed at the sea's edge and stirring up the gulls as he turned back into the shadows of the glassworks.

'Time to hit the road, bro! Let's shut her down and make tracks,' he called. 'We'll give Alicia Sunday night off. Whaddya say we load up with fish and chips from Cicerello's?'

Stefan parked the barrow and switched off the vibrating sieve. He joined Lennard in the open doorway. A sinuous track of foam marked the passage of the cray boat like a paper trail beyond which the mirage of Rottnest Island floated on the horizon.

Lennard pointed at the island's shadow. 'Wadjemup,' he said. 'The Alcatraz of Perth.'

'Why Alcatraz?'

'It was a prison for us blackfellas for close to a hundred years.'

'I didn't know that.'

'Neither do half the tourists who book rooms in the Lodge. That was once the Quod, the prison building holding seven, sometimes many more chained together in a cell.' He gave a disparaging snort and shook his head. 'These days you get a cell to yourself, with a king-sized bed and a spa bath with fluffy towels, not to mention a fully stocked bar fridge and tea and coffee making facilities.' He glanced grimly at Stefan. 'There were several public hangings in the quadrangle in those days and no one seems to remember or care. It's disrespectful, bro. Can you imagine the outrage if Auschwitz was converted to a five-star resort with the gas chambers spruced up into honeymoon suites?'

Stefan was stunned. 'Is that another of your reasons for the cenotaph? Deaths in custody?'

Lennard placed an arm across his shoulder. 'What do you reckon? But hey, listen, when I get too heavy bringing up our history and piss you off, feel free to tell me to back off and loosen up.'

'So my first lecture on Aboriginal Australian Traumascapes 101 is over?'

'Sure is, but it'll never be forgotten and it won't be the last.'

'So your history's like a stone in your shoe? One you can't remove?'

'A stone in my shoe? Nail on the head, bro! Nail on the head. Come on, let's go eat.'

Stefan was ravenous after the unfamiliar slog. He made short work of a thick slab of western dhufish fried in crisp batter and a mountain of chips over which Alicia had sprinkled sea salt and squeezed quarters of a lemon fresh from the garden.

Dinner over, he leaned back and gazed at Lennard across the table. For a man who had turned fifty-five, his looks had a vitality that put him about ten years younger.

'Hope I look as young as you at your age. What's your secret?' he asked.

'That's easy, bro. Slow down time. Shift gears from linear to circular time like us blackfellas, with six recurring seasons in the year.' He gave an infectious laugh. 'Then buy an Irish clock that runs backwards and have a good time with the time you save. Make every day count. Don't sweat the small stuff, as they say.'

'*Carpe diem*?'

'By the short and curlies, bro! Like my old man says, make the most of every moment. You want the secret to a happy life? Look for the eternal in the present, because the present's in the past before you know it and the future's already knocking at your door. That way you'll never fall between the cracks.'

Before Stefan could respond, Alicia came in from the kitchen with a tray of coffees and a plate of sliced lamingtons. She placed them on the table and took a seat beside Lennard. She stretched an arm across his shoulder. As she did so, the light turned her cheek and the corded tendons in her throat pale gold.

'Not to mention Alicia here, bro.' He looked at her with deep affection. 'She keeps me young.' He paused and smiled. 'And on the straight and narrow.'

'Never mind me,' Alicia broke in. 'Let's not forget the ties to the country you inherited and the hunter-gatherer in your genes.'

'Ah! Those.'

Both his parents were in their late seventies and still riding horses out on Wanamalu station, Lennard explained. 'The old girl used to ride like the wind. She loved breaking in the colts and going to the rodeos to watch the rough-riding. Not anymore, though. Now she's getting on a bit and lost a little finger.'

'Lost a little finger?'

'On her left hand. She was doing some woodwork one day and one of my *yamba* cousins switched on the bandsaw while she was clearing up the sawdust. *Ngubamutha*! Blood everywhere! But she never made a fuss, didn't wanna scare the little fella, who was shitting himself for his mistake. The finger was still in the glove when we found it. We packed it in ice and took it with us to Northampton Hospital, but there was nothing they could do. She doesn't break the colts in now, because the finger she lost was on her free arm when she was riding them and she swears her balance is cactus.'

Stefan reached for a slice of lamington. The plate lay beside Alicia's slender book. He studied the cover as he bit into the slice, flecks of shredded coconut falling into the hand he held beneath it. *The Jew-Jitsu Christ*, he read, *Poems by Max O'Sullivan*. He finished the slice, licked his fingers, pointed at the book.

'Interesting title. Is that the same O'Sullivan?'

'He surely is,' Alicia confirmed. 'He's Rosie's twin. You'll meet him when you least expect it. Be on your toes. He dances to a different drum.'

'Jungle rhythm, the smartarse,' Lennard added. 'He doesn't miss a trick. If you're not quick, you're dead, and he's real quick with that photographic memory and silver tongue of his.' Then he chuckled. 'He still has trouble with his women, but. He's got them queuing up, but his relationships don't last.' He tapped his temple. 'He's got some flash software up here cranking on all cylinders, but I reckon his hard-drive's in for repair.'

'He does all right,' Alicia interjected dryly. 'Perhaps it's the other way around.' She nodded at the book. 'He's well worth a read. And he loves his Shakespeare. He'll quote a line or two word-perfect from *As You Like It* or some other play to illustrate a point or catch you off guard when he's debating something with you.'

Lennard agreed. 'It's a courtroom tactic he uses to stir things up. There's nothing he likes better than tossing a feral cat among his fellow legal eagles to stir them up.'

'He's a lawyer?'

'A barrister actually,' Alicia replied. 'He does a lot of work pro bono for the Aboriginal Legal Service. He'll turn up one of these days out of the blue.'

'Like a bad smell, but I think you'll like him.'

Alicia shook a warning forefinger. 'We'd better warn you, though—he eats like a horse with hollow legs.'

'Bottomless pit.' Lennard grinned. 'When there's food around make sure you get in first.'

His face was etched by deep lines when he smiled, but his eyes were his surprising feature. Stefan found their different colours disconcerting and the piercing glint of ironic humour they often displayed unsettled him.

Lennard noticed his bewilderment. 'You're having trouble with my *gurunu;* with my eyes?'

'It's that obvious?'

'I recognise the signs, bro. Everyone's put out the first time we meet. It's heterochromia. I'm the only one in the family with it. My old man and a couple of his cousin-brothers have got blue eyes—both of them blue. The old man reckons he'd pass for a Scandinavian gigolo suntanned after a cruise in the Greek islands. I'm the only one whose *gurunu* don't match.'

'You're another David Bowie.'

'Not David Bowie,' Alicia interjected. 'Bad example. I used to think the same, but Bowie's eyes are both blue. He injured one, and the pupil's permanently dilated. Try Dan Aykroyd, or even Alexander the Great. I must admit they were confusing when we first met.'

'They are a bit.'

'Confusing? You hear that, Alicia? The brudda's picked me for a shifty fella.'

'Well, you are. You're an old shapeshifter from way back.' She turned back to Stefan. 'He's a chameleon living in two worlds. He changes his skin to suit the occasion and his eyes are his badges of belonging. You'll get used to them. The first time we met I thought they gave him an air of ambiguity like he was some kind of changeling. I kept asking myself where *does* this guy belong? Who is he today?'

'Who am I today?' Lennard ran his fingers through his salt-and-pepper beard thoughtfully scratching his chin, then gave a full-throated laugh Stefan was getting used to. 'I know you've been wondering bro, so what d'you reckon, it's time we got down to the *real* introductions?'

'The real introductions?' Unsettled by Lennard's bluntness, Stefan was unsure where the conversation was heading.

'I'm a full-blood half-caste, part Malgana from Shark Bay and part Dutch from way back,' Lennard went on, 'and that's on my old fella's side. The old girl's mob's Kurrama from further north, with some bog Paddy Irish thrown in for good luck!'

'That's quite a mix.'

'You're not wrong. They stirred up all the colours of the *Wagyl* when they dreamed me up.'

His mother's family was among the first to relocate from Yangkalinha Cattle Station to the Onslow Aboriginal Reserve at the start of the Great Depression, he explained, when her Irish stockman father was retrenched and abandoned them.

He pinched the skin on his forearm, lifting dark veins threaded across the muscle.

'My long-lost grandfather! Said he was going north to Darwin to earn a living for them and they never saw him again. She was two years old when he shot through. He left her and her mother and two brothers to fend for themselves.'

He lifted his cup, sniffed the coffee, sipped. 'I've tried tracking him down, but he disappeared off the face of the earth. Chances are he never got to Darwin. Who knows? His bones may be out there in the Great Sandy somewhere. I had less trouble tracing my Dutch ancestor on my father's side, and he took me back three hundred years.'

He crossed the lounge, picked up the crystal sailing ship and placed it on the table between them. Stefan inspected the three brittle masts, full-blown sails and delicately spun ropes, the lines of tiny cannon, the pair of dolphins set into waves at the prow. He read the name *Zuytdorp* etched cross the stern.

'Like I told you, she was wrecked up near Kalbarri in 1712. A fella called Gerrit de Waal was the senior carpenter on board.' He turned the bottle with a careful fingertip. 'If she hadn't gone down or he hadn't survived, I wouldn't be here.' He gave Stefan a bemused grin. 'In which case you'd be homeless, bro, sleeping on a bench in Fitzroy Gardens with one eye open for the gays and the other for the cops.'

'Rent-free?'

'Nah! Paying the fines every time you're caught.'

Stefan felt a spark of interest. 'So, Gerrit de Waal. How did you find out about him?'

Lennard told Stefan about the tobacco container, the spoon among the other relics and his lifelong research. 'I did a lot of sniffing around looking for Gerrit's roots because I like to think they're mine and I wanna know my ancestry. I was in the dark at first, going around in circles, by crikey. I found out the hard way historical research is like that, but it gets easier when you work out where to look and how to pick up on the clues.

'I found them in the archives in Middelburg and The Hague when I was working in the Netherlands in the eighties. When I found a connection between a sailor called Hendrick de Waal and an Italian merchant called Francesco

Carletti, I knew I was home free. It was like coming across a freshwater spring in Karijini when you're dying of thirst, the way the information came pouring out.'

The trail from Hendrick and Francesco had led him straight to Gerrit, who was born in Middelburg in 1686, he said. Once he had the goods on Gerrit the rest fell into place.

'There's been a lot of research done on the *Zuytdorp* here in Freo by the team at the Maritime Museum. They helped me out as well. Have you read Philip Playford's book *Carpet of Silver*?'

'No.'

'You should. It came out last year.' He jerked his thumb at the bookshelf. 'There's a copy in there somewhere. Give it the once over when you get a chance. It'll fill you in on the discovery of the wreck and signs of the survivors.'

Stefan ran his eye along the titles but failed to find it. 'I'll do that.'

'I've collected enough material to write Gerrit's biography myself,' he nudged Alicia, 'or bribe someone I know willing to write it for me.'

'Not without a six-figure advance!'

'You wouldn't do it as a favour? Out of the goodness of your heart?'

'Not a chance. Not with my workload.'

'Piker!' Lennard grinned, turning to Stefan. 'That's that, then. So what about your background, bro? With a name like Novak you must be another Aussie import.'

'I was born and bred in Geelong.'

'Geelong! So you're a Cats man, one of Polly Farmer's mob?'

'From way back, yes, I am.'

'Then you're in good company, bro. So, Novak. What's that? Polish?'

'Close. It's Czech. Actually, it was originally Novalecki.

The old man was going to anglicise it to Newman, but he decided to stick with Novak to keep the Czech connection. He came from Karlovy Vary—Carlsbad to the tourists. I visited the Moser glassworks there in '93 when I started the business. My mother was from Brno. She was taken to England on the Kindertransports in 1938. They migrated here after the war. They met in Melbourne. They were married there.' He paused, debating whether to go on, before reluctantly admitting, 'The old man was caught up in the Shoah.'

'The Shoah?'

'The Holocaust.'

'Is that right? Then he'd have a story to tell.'

Stefan frowned down at the ship, unwilling to continue. His father had died while working up at Tumut on the Snowy River scheme. Stefan had been ten years old and he remembered a reticent and secretive man who avoided speaking of his imprisonment in Terezin and Auschwitz. His only concession on rare occasions was to hint vaguely at a circumstance, before retreating into silence as though scalded.

At other times, when it seemed he was about to open the door on his experiences a fraction, he'd lapse into a triviality instead, then he'd clam up as if to seal away the unspeakable truth. Stefan had always respected his father's silence, his evasiveness suggesting incommunicable anguish. The wounds ran deep and he didn't want them exposed or to impose them on others.

Lennard raised an open hand, acknowledging Stefan's reluctance. 'So you're Jewish, bro. We share a similar history. That makes us two of a kind.'

'I'm Jewish, yes. But I'm not *too* Jewish, if you know what I mean. I'm secular. I'm an assimilated Aussie. My old man, he observed the traditions, after his fashion.' He hesitated.

'But look, don't get me wrong. I'm Jewish, and not only by inheritance. I wouldn't have it any other way.'

'So you're another Aussie wearing two hats.'

'Sure, but most times it's an Akubra.'

'Then we have a lot in common bro, and I'm not just talking glass or hats.'

A lot in common? Stefan recoiled and clamped his jaw. He'd heard this viewpoint before—Aboriginal massacres likened to legalised genocide and the murder of millions, prison cells and deaths in custody equated to the concentration camps and gas chambers, racism directed against the Aboriginal population and anti-Semitic persecution discussed in the same breath. He found the comparisons questionable and contemplating the monstrous injustice and oppression both peoples had suffered unhinged him. He did not respond. And in his silence, he thought, *I am my father's son.*

Lennard gazed intently at him, then broke the awkward silence. 'We both belong to a people who've *survived* is all I'm saying, bro.' He raised his voice and with his right fist gave Stefan thumbs up. 'We've *survived*, in spite of our bloody history.' He brought down his fist and pounded the table. 'Never mind smoothing the dying pillow for a dying race! We're still around to make our mark. Why else are we building the cenotaph, you and me? We're witnesses. We're witnesses to the *truth*! We're resurrecting the dead by remembering their names and stories. That way we'll celebrate their lives among the living.'

Alicia reached across and touched Lennard's cheek. 'Come on, sweetie. That's enough for tonight.'

'I'm getting some of the curly questions the brudda here wants answered put to bed. I'm breaking the ice.'

She placed a hand over his fist and held it there. 'No need to use a sledgehammer,' she murmured.

She stood and picked up the glass ship. She placed it back on the coffee table and then returned, removing her ribbon and unravelling her plait. She shook her head so that her hair glistened, dark and lustrous, around her face.

Looking up, Stefan was astonished to see, from his angle, her face beside Rosalie's photograph on the wall and it appeared both women were smiling down at Lennard. Then she leaned over him with a look of such tenderness it seemed a caress before she resumed her seat. She put her cheek next to his and her arm about his shoulders. With her extended hand, she passed the ribbon around the two of them and tied it so that they were bound by white silk. Her hair, or perhaps her skin, carried the heady scent of almonds.

She turned to Stefan, smiling. 'This brindle's learned to live with his Aboriginal and his European heritages and he makes it look easy.' She ran her fingers through Lennard's hair. 'Which is what swept me off my feet.'

She tilted her face to look up at Rosalie and, as she turned, he caught a hint of determined fearlessness in her dark eyes that had surprised him once or twice before. At that moment he sensed she'd come through fire, had known such terror that, in the knowing, she'd discovered her strength and her resolve.

There was a long silence before Stefan broke in, 'I brought the catalogue from your Melbourne exhibition with me to read on the plane, Ace. There's something I'd like to ask you. Let me get it.'

'Sales talk!' Lennard called out as Stefan crossed the lounge. 'A fella has a living to make. One way or another we have to finance the rock.'

ON THE VERANDA, Stefan looked up into the night sky. It was black as pitch beyond the aura of the city. He stood at the veranda rail and leaned out to search along the highway of stars for the tilt of the Southern Cross. He discovered it low on the horizon; so low, it seemed suspended beneath the ocean's edge. Then he looked southwards and saw reflected in the dark bowl of sky the scythe of an ashen moon on the rise.

There, in the south-east beyond the moon, he saw the glowing smear of the tail of the comet Halle-Bopp. He called Alicia and Lennard out to look. They admired the faint streak for some minutes before Stefan ducked into the sleepout to retrieve the catalogue.

Back in the lounge, they drew their chairs together. Alicia rested against Lennard's chest, the white ribbon hanging like an elegant scarf about his shoulders.

Stefan opened the catalogue, wondering once again at the display of tenderness between them despite Rosalie's pervasive presence. There were no photographs of Alicia on the walls, no shots of her and Lennard together, yet he sensed no tension between them, had witnessed so far only mutual devotion. *Is Rosalie in some way a consenting third party to their relationship? If so, how have they made that work? If not, is she perhaps estranged and overseas, as Tania is? Or dead? Surely not. Lennard would have mentioned it.*

He looked down and began to read aloud—

'He considers himself a painter sculpting in molten glass, whose pieces provide the eye of the imagination with a lens to the miraculous in this universe we inhabit, much as a prism operates on light. His intention is to offer his viewers an experience in which the simplicity of line and the interplay of colours in the glass structures fade as the ecstasy of vision overtakes seeing.'

'Seeing and vision,' Lennard interrupted. 'Vision and seeing. There's a difference, bro. You don't only see. You see with the eye of the imagination.' He tapped the centre of his forehead. 'With the eye of the spirit, as long as you learn how to open it and keep it open.'

'And you don't develop cataracts,' Alicia added. 'We colour the world by looking at it, don't we? What we see has qualities given to it by the way we see it. And the way we see it can inspire our wonder. Max would have quoted Hamlet on that. How does he put it? *There is nothing either good or bad, but thinking makes it so.*'

Stefan was struck by the catalogue's cryptic assertion—

'What he's after is the exhilarating freedom of a dreamlike dance of the mind swimming in light.'

He read the sentence aloud twice over and asked Alicia if that was what she meant.

'It's close to the mark.'

'They're Alicia's words, bro. More of her bulldust. Fair knocks you sideways, don't you reckon?'

'It does that.'

'I don't know what I'd do without her—my one-woman advertising agency.'

'You do all right when it comes to bulldust, Ace. I add a touch of… what? The light fantastic?'

'Swimming in light's one way of saying it, sister, but when the power goes off you gotta watch it or you'll drown.'

He was a Fellow of the Royal Society of Arts in the UK, the catalogue read. On the inside cover there was a comical picture of him as a younger man standing at a lectern, clutching an honorary degree. *'Awarded in Edinburgh'*, the caption read, *'Heriot Watt University, 1983'*. He was dressed incongruously in an academic gown, an embroidered cloak of scarlet brocade hanging to his knees. His mouth was open as if astonished.

Stefan told him he looked like a troubadour who had broken into song at the wrong moment and forgotten his lines.

'Sidney Poitier in drag at a fancy-dress ball, you reckon?' Lennard responded with a broad smile. 'Fancy-dress balls-up, more like!'

There was another shot of him working in a studio, his leather apron stained with metallic dyes, the furnace flame a blinding orange.

'In the early 1980s,' Stefan continued, *'he lectured on the techniques of working in glass at Heriot Watt University in Edinburgh and the prestigious Gerrit Rietveld Academie in Amsterdam. While he loved the pervasive sense of enthusiastic purpose and the opportunity for creative experiment at both, he hated the cold, the lack of ever-grey-green eucalyptus, the absence of leaf-shimmer in Australian sunlight. He missed the Pilbara pepper smell of dust after rain. He longed for the western desert edged by the sea and the myriad blues of the reefs of Ningaloo. He yearned for the colour and space of country, for its desert silences.'*

'I couldn't cut the umbilicus,' he grinned, 'but I stretched it to snapping point!'

'You must have found it interesting, meeting artists overseas and taking part in the global interaction?'

'Nah! I was out for a good time, but I couldn't stand the cold. I was having a ball until the brass monkeys got to mine. I couldn't wait to get home, to go walkabout in the sun, back in country.'

'Don't you believe him,' Alicia said. 'He's always swapping yarns with the world's best. They contact him all the time. He's a national international treasure.'

'You know what they say, brudda. No man's an island or he's in no man's land. That's another reason we invited you over here.' He stretched, yawned and pointed at the clock. '*Ngatha ngundamanha.* Time for a kip. Time to recharge the batteries.'

Alicia turned as she and Lennard left the room. 'Ace tells me you're keen to learn Malgana?'

'I'd like to.'

'Then here's your first word—*matharra*.'

'*Matharra?* What's that? Goodnight?'

'No, you'll find out in the morning when they turn up—our red-tailed black cockatoos. If you're not awake when they arrive you soon will be!'

'One question before you go. *Malajarri*. Why are you called Thunder, Ace?'

'You haven't heard me sound off yet? Thought you'd be deafened by now!' He laughed. 'All we need's the *lightning* to go with it, bro, and we're working on that, you and me.'

Stefan raised a hand as they disappeared into the bedroom.

STEFAN CLOSED THE brochure. He stretched out in the chair and raised his arms above his head to ease the bruised sensation in his shoulders. Then he relaxed and with an elbow on the table propped his chin against his fist and exhaled a long sigh through his fingers.

His first day's hard labour was over. How long would it take him to adjust? The quicker the better. Or would he? If not, how could he back out if push came to shove? With a resigned sigh, he acknowledged it may be too late for that.

He stood and headed for the sleepout, pausing when Skathi bounded up, showing her teeth. He bent to pat her, caught the faint smell of citrus on the night air and his mind lurched as he recalled how he'd flinched at talking about his father.

As he scratched Skathi behind the ear, he vividly remembered his mother telling him about his father's death when he was ten years old. She was unpacking his belongings returned to her from Tumut.

He'd been working on the final grade of a rain-soaked embankment for the Jounama Dam, she was told, when his off-side grader wheel bit into the verge and the earthworks failed to hold. An avalanche of mud and rock buried him and his young survey hand, the grader on its side, one slowly spinning wheel protruding. The rescue crews reached them too late.

He'd watched as she'd withdrawn from among his things the yellow star his father had saved, one he'd been forced to sew onto his jacket during his incarceration in Terezin and Auschwitz. He'd mounted it in cellophane along with the red triangle marked with the black 'T' he'd worn indicating his Czech nationality.

It was the last thing she'd expected. She'd squatted, grief-stricken, on the edge of the bed, her body doubled over and shaking as she'd ducked her head to sob. She'd held the packet at arm's length on her upturned palm, staring at the star and the letter 'T', her fingers rigid, before she'd turned her hand over to drop it back into the battered leather suitcase as if her skin was scorched.

She'd pinned the badges to his suit at the cremation. They may have been intended to symbolise the fact that he had been among the less-than-human when imprisoned, but to Stefan's young mind, he'd worn them with defiant and dignified pride on that last day, as though the victory was his.

His father's will had been specific and his mother observed his wishes—he insisted on cremation despite the Halachic prohibition, followed by the scattering of his ashes at Barwon Heads.

A gusting wind had snatched at the smoke from the crematorium chimney after the funeral, driving ash across the handful of mourners outside the chapel as his mother thanked them for attending. She'd handed out roses and lilies to them, detached from the wreaths and sprays she'd unravelled. Faint traces had settled across her shoulders and Stefan remembered the grainy feel of it as he'd brushed it away. He'd looked down at the residue of white dust on his ten-year-old hands and was aghast at the sudden thought— *So he ended up in the ovens after all.*

The world had fallen away beneath his feet. Drained and emotionless, he could not drive away the emptiness he'd taken for indifference and he felt the guiltier for that. He'd buried the moment deep within him. It had taken him years to forgive himself for what he'd experienced that afternoon when he'd found himself standing paralysed and seemingly unfeeling on the edge of an abyss.

He took Skathi's head between his hands, gently shaking it as he looked into her pale blue eyes. Then he straightened and strode to the sleepout, closing the door firmly behind him.

LATER THAT NIGHT he woke to a piercing cry. For a moment his blood froze. He listened intently. Was it the high-pitched cry of a seabird? Was it Skathi? Or the wail of a distant scavenging dog?

He held his breath. The house leaned into the night wind. Then he heard the prolonged, orgasmic call of a woman's ecstasy, agonising and unmistakable, the wordless inflection of uncontrolled joy torn from the back of the throat, the cry of the body carried away into the deepest recesses of sensation. In the stillness, he heard the sound again. We were two, the cry announced, and now I am one.

The house whispered as a tree branch swished across the corrugated iron and he heard the stone wind-chimes clinking on the veranda. In the broken silence he recalled Tania returning from the secret place to which her sighs had once carried her and he read the eloquent language of her eyes—I was one and now we're two. Stay.

He felt a pang of longing and stretched out across the

empty bed. Behind closed eyes and half-asleep, he saw her standing in the doorway looking back at him on Christmas Eve. He was torn by desire for the cool smoothness of her skin, curving from flank to rib, for the swell of her breast, for the erotic glide of sinew in her thigh and the exquisite pool of skin where thigh met pubis, and when he called out to her she did not leave but crossed the floor. As she approached and he moved to embrace her he saw the vaguest contours of her face beneath the sweep of dark hair. The crystal bird of paradise she once wore for him no longer glistened at her throat.

She faded, and he drifted back into fitful sleep disturbed by part-remembered dreams of unfulfilled desire, as though estranged and abandoned in an alien place.

He woke in the half-light surprisingly refreshed. He rose and flicked up the blind on the sleep-out window. The image of Tania came to him as he did so and he was pierced by regret. A wave of unbearable emptiness welled through him.

Reaching for the windowsill, he steadied himself and looked out at the view. A calm day's empty sky curved towards the Antarctic, sunlight flickering across the ocean towards the streak of Rottnest Island. Within the breakwaters he saw masts, pennants, sails, yachts and gulls massing in the wake of cray boats churning about their early morning business.

He crossed the veranda and sat on the lower step, his body waking to its aches. Skathi greeted him there in a gentle mood.

Tania would love it here, he thought, as though she was sitting beside him as he looked around. Above him, a Norfolk Island pine creaked with the lightest breeze. In the middle of the lawn, a pond of tropical water lilies displayed violet and yellow blooms on slender stalks as they opened.

A juvenile white heron swept down from the roof and settled, unbalanced, on the fence. It saw Skathi bounding towards it and abandoned its hunt for the elusive goldfish, spreading delicate wings and launching itself with a honk of alarm towards the rooftops below.

To the right, a garden shed was hidden beneath a lemon tree, its branches glowing with fruit. Beyond it was an area of exposed soil pitted by a number of Skathi's excavated dens among the roots of two pomegranate trees. Passion vines covered the bottom fence, fruit like green grenades and flowers hanging in white starbursts among the leaves.

Through it all, the sea smell drifted like a welcome to a different world, and he was captivated. With a faint smile, he imagined Tania comparing it to their favourite retreat—the converted boathouse on the Lake Macquarie foreshore they'd visited last October; the orchids in hanging baskets around the eaves, the heavily scented Brunfelsia bushes beside the jetty. Kiss Me Quick, she used to call them, or sometimes Yesterday, Today and Tomorrow. His smile turned rueful. *Not much chance of that now!*

Then Lennard emerged from the shadows of the house, a faded scarlet towel around his waist.

'Good to see you up this bright and early, brudda,' he called as he came down the steps. He squatted next to Stefan and pointed at the ocean. 'Great time to check out the *wirriya* to make sure no one's pulled the plug out during the night and let it drain away.'

He carried one of the stone flutes in his left hand. He held it out. 'Ever seen one of these? There's a hippie fella makes them up in Darwin. He comes down to Freo every few months and flogs them off on Market Street. You should hear him. He's a belter. He attracts the crowds like you wouldn't believe.'

He lifted the flute to his lips and blew a succession of notes from the four holes, their pitch light and airy. To Stefan's astonishment, he recognised a simple derivation of the song *Africa*.

Lennard played it for several minutes, then handed it to him. 'Something else for you to learn while you're here,' he said.

'Toto. Great song.'

'Another one of Rosie's favourites. She used to play for hours on end. Go for it. Let's see how long it takes you to give us your version of *Hava Nagila*.'

Before Stefan could experiment with it, Lennard waved a hand at the horizon. 'Imagine Dutch sails appearing from the west three centuries ago, changing course northwards to tack towards Batavia.'

He described the appearance of de Vlamingh's three Dutch ships anchoring off Rottnest in 1696. The sailors had dragged their dories over the silted river mouth to explore the river's upper reaches, he explained, shooting black swans and then tasting the bitter poison of zamia nuts as they investigated the footprints of phantom tribesmen who'd vanished among the trees to observe the freakish strangers from concealment.

'Think about it, bro,' he raised his voice, 'think about the Nyungar asking over and over, "Who are these wajbala? Are they our dead back from the spirit-world?"'

He glanced at his watch, stood and stretched before turning back up the steps. 'It's back to the land of *ngundhanyina* for me, bro. Time to catch a few more zeds before breakfast.'

Distracted by persistent thoughts of Tania, Stefan pocketed the flute. She'd left him without warning for reasons of her own, she'd told him. That couldn't be entirely true. Had she been softening the blow? What had he done to drive her away?

For a moment his self-reproach generated a burst of frustration. *It's time to stop brooding about her. Time to suck it up and get on with it!*

He scratched Skathi's ribs as she asked for more, a rear leg twitching. The growing light spread a wash of colour across the buildings below, where pigeons scattered as if thrown skyward, wheeling and turning and gliding in unison across the warehouses beside the docks where they briefly caught the sun, then, like a single flame immediately doused, descended in scattered ash towards the river's entrance.

Moments later, he was deafened by the demented screech of red-tailed black cockatoos attacking pinecones overhead, pine nuts clattering on the corrugated iron, torn branchlets spiralling to the lawn.

'*Matharra*,' he whispered, and a series of questions came to mind. What was the first word Gerrit had learned when he survived among the Malgana? How had he communicated with them at their first meeting? Had there been a stand-off after an unintelligible exchange, with the Malgana melting back into the saltbush and wattle thickets to survey the unlikely visitors from a safer distance? Or had both parties been struck dumb, overcome with mutual suspicion, unable to recognise in the gaze of the other a common humanity? Had that moment of misunderstanding translated into impulsive acts of murder and self-preservation as they'd reached for spear and infantry musket?

The cockatoos took off as suddenly as they'd arrived, their raucous discord fading. He picked up a pair of red and black tail feathers from the grass and climbed back up the steps with Skathi at his heels. He smelled bacon cooking, saw Alicia moving behind the kitchen window and heard the sound of running water as she topped up four jars lining the windowsill in which sprouting avocado pits were balanced on toothpicks driven into their sides.

She waved and opened the window wider. 'Hi there.' She sent him a broad smile. 'So much for Joel Fleischman! In this light, I see you're Dustin Hoffman made up for your part in *Little Big Man*—Jack Crabb on his hundredth birthday. Lennard's slave-driving has aged you overnight!'

'And a good morning to you too, Mrs Robinson. You're looking younger by the day.'

'I wish! Come on up and have some breakfast. The coffee's on. The eggs are done.' Then she noticed the feathers. 'I see you have Yagan's headdress there.'

'Yagan?'

'A Nyungar warrior of high degree—a *Whadjuk Ballaroke boordier*. I'll leave it to Lennard to explain.'

Stefan looked down at the feathers. 'I'll look forward to it.'

He turned on the top step and gazed back at the horizon where the ocean was a sheet of pale blue ice. A quiet smile. A new day. A fresh start, and he was in it for the long haul.

ROSALIE

Moments later, Lennard joined them on the back veranda. He made short work of the scrambled eggs and bacon and was spreading plum jam across a slice of toast when he pointed his knife at the sky, a tracery of runaway clouds unfurling across it.

'Looks like another good one,' he said. 'Reckon you're up for a stroll to work before it gets too hot? I often walk it.'

Stefan peered doubtfully at the distant glassworks, its grey rooftop and tall windows barely visible. *How far is it? Five clicks?*

'Sure.' Then he grimaced. 'I could do with a push start.'

Lennard stood, picked up his toast, took a bite and looked thoughtfully down at him. 'You and me both, bro, and it's downhill most of the way.' He took another bite and nodded. 'Big day for us today. Now the fun really starts. They're delivering the garnet sand. I'm not sure how early. We'd better get moving.'

As they crossed the lounge Lennard stopped and gestured at Rosalie's photograph with the half-eaten toast.

'Rosie. Why don't I tell you about her on the way? How we met. How she died. I know you've been too polite to ask.'

'How she died?'

'I should have told you earlier.'

'I've been wondering. I wasn't sure. I'm sorry.'

'It happened ten years ago, now. In the Kimberley.' He looked up at the photograph. 'Not a day goes by. But thank you, bro.'

'I'd like to get to know her...'

'No, you *need* to get to know her. She's the reason we're modelling the cenotaph on Jandamarra's Rock.'

They walked out into sunlight glimmering through coral gums lining Bellevue Terrace, the pavement strewn with tiny gumnuts crackling underfoot. Stefan struggled to match Lennard's strides, wincing at stiffness in muscles he wasn't aware he had. When a gumnut flicked up and lodged behind his heel, he stooped to remove it. Unable to do so with his forefinger, he limped on for several strides before kneeling to remove his shoe.

Lennard looked back and slowed as he retied the lace. 'Looks like you're feeling it,' he said. 'Another week or two of hard yakka will put that right.'

They turned in silence down the hill towards the city, and then, as though talking to himself, 'I met Rosie in late July 1963 in the Repat Hospital in Shenton Park. In the operating theatre, of all places.'

He had been in his third year at UWA studying Fine Arts and strapped for cash, he explained. He had been working through the semester break as a casual orderly. He'd worked there over the previous summer vacation and was filling in again, allocated to the cardiac ward at first and then one morning, the matron offered him a secondment to the operating theatre.

He'd jumped at the chance, he said, and copped blood, shit and gore—and rushes of adrenalin—for the rest of the break.

'That choice was a turning point, bro. It changed my life for good. I met Rosie on my first day there.'

Stefan smiled. 'I'm all ears,' he said. 'Fire away.'

'I went into the theatre part way through a kidney oper-ation,' Lennard went on. 'I was wheeling a reserve oxygen cylinder the anaesthetist had called for.' He tapped his nose. 'It took me a moment to get used to the stink of cauterised flesh and antiseptic agent in there.'

A gloved, five-foot-four surgeon wearing a green mask and matching cap and gown, a Scot with a fearsome reputation Lennard had been warned about, was manipulating a slender silver instrument, excavating for a pair of staghorn stones grinding in the kidney he'd opened up. He was delicately pris-ing them out with a casualness that suggested it was second nature to him.

'As soon as I walked in he pointed at the bank of overhead lights, and I had to realign the focus on the gap in the green sheet.'

It was stained with saline ice slush, with glinting instruments fanned around the incision, holding it open.

'A bit further... thank you.' The surgeon glanced up at Lennard and then back at the kidney, feigning shock. 'Good God! What the devil has she sent us this time? A cannibal?'

Disconcerted, Lennard searched for a response. None came. He stifled his surprise and held his composure.

'A joke son. It's a joke,' the surgeon grunted in his broad Glaswegian accent, teasing at the kidney. 'No need to take offence. Although I understand the fat around the kidneys was particularly prized by your ancestors, so keep your hands to yourself. It may have been a delicacy once, but I expect you'd be too young to have had it on the menu.' He gave a caustic laugh. 'We can only hope.'

He began to hum and the theatre sisters listened to *Bolero* while he probed and his assistant cauterised. The faster the rhythm, it seemed, the better he liked it. He paused, peered into the cavity, and one sister rolled her eyes while another laughed obligingly at the punchline of an outdated joke he'd clearly told them before, 'And after the appendectomy the poor old sod, still half-under, thought we'd said a *penis*-sectomy. When we showed him his appendix floating in a jar of formaldehyde he reached down to check his crown jewels and screamed, "If there's any damage, I'll sue you butchering bastards!" Swab please, sister, and how many swabs is that?'

When the surgeon asked her for the count, Ace was electrified. There she was, holding the dish and counting the swabs. *He knew.* He knew in that mind-blowing moment as she looked at him, her mesmeric green eyes widening in surprise and her face on red alert, that his life was forever altered.

How had he missed her up till then?

Flushed with sudden adrenalin, his pulse hammered at his throat. The floor plummeted away below him and his mind raced as he heard her hesitant response. 'Eight, I think.'

'Eight *you think*?' The surgeon glared at her. 'What do you need? An abacus?'

'I'll check.'

'You do that.'

The low-pitched breathiness of her voice, the warmth of it, set Lennard on fire. She disappeared into the autoclave room with the kidney dish, so he followed her there. She was counting out the swabs into the waste.

'Eight,' she said. 'Thank God for that. I don't know what you did to me in there, but you put me off my count. Don't do that again. I have to concentrate.' She stared at him, hostility turning to surprise. 'It's got to be the eyes! My God, what's with the eyes?'

'Transplants,' he retorted, a comeback line he'd used for years. 'Different donors.'

It struck him clear as day—*this is the woman of my dreams. This is she!*

'I've been having this recurring dream,' the words came to him unbidden, 'and you're in it.'

'In your dreams!' Her eyes flashed. 'Dream on!' But then, mischievous, 'No bloody wonder I woke up tired this morning.'

'We were *flying*,' he assured her as she walked away.

She looked back as she was about to exit. 'You sure it wasn't a nightmare? Hey, I'm Rosalie.'

'I'm Ace.'

'Nice meeting you, Ace. Don't allow pea-brain in there get to you with his insults, even if he is the best microsurgeon in the world between these four walls.'

'Micro's right,' Lennard responded. 'How tall is he?'

'Tall enough to be long on smarts and longer on sarcasm, so tread carefully.'

'I noticed.'

Then she glanced at his groin and her eyes lit up. She gave a flirtatious chuckle. 'Oh! My *goodness*! Looks like things are on the up and up. It pays to advertise, does it?'

She spun around, walked back into the theatre and the spell was broken.

They reached the crossing on Hampton Road, where the lights were red.

As they waited, Lennard told Stefan that the swaying floor had settled as the hormonal rush from his overworked adrenals eased, making *his* kidneys ache, let alone the patient's.

'*Jesus!*' Stefan broke in. 'He was *digging* out the stones? What, with a *spoon?*'

Lennard laughed. 'No shockwave treatment way back then. No lasers either.'

The lights changed and, as they crossed, he admitted that in that strange, electric moment he had been head over heels. Turned inside out. Taken apart. Rewired in every convolution of the *Kama Sutra*.

'It was love at first sight, if there is such a thing. Max suggested *lust* at first sight, and it was, for sure and certain. But love? Well, it had never happened to me before, and now it had. Don't forget I was twenty-two at the time, green as grass, straight from the bush, without a cynical bone in my body.' He grinned. 'And the testosterone was *pumping*, bro! Was it ever! It was quite a moment, something I'd never experienced before. I was grateful for that gown! I had to bend forward for the rest of the operation… and bend over backwards for Rosie for the rest of her life!'

There'd been a quake at the centre of his being, he said. Off the Richter scale, and Rosalie had felt the same, she'd told him later. They had tuned in on recognition so overpowering it had blown them away.

'Recognition? Re-*ignition* more like it. We were struck by lightning, like we'd never been struck before.'

They turned into Alma Street and walked on in silence, Lennard deep in thought as he recalled what Max had said about their meeting, 'Shakes-no-peer has Juliet say something about that—*My bounty is as boundless as the sea, my love as deep: the more I give to thee the more I have, for both are infinite.*' And Rosalie loved it. The metaphor suited them both—*the sea.*

'She was away the next day attending a training course,' he continued. 'I saw her again a week later. Unexpectedly.'

His scooter was under repair and he was travelling home by bus. It was raining and he was soaked as he sprinted for the bus shelter, blinded by the glittering lights of an oncoming bus. As it drew up, he read the number and destination in time to know it wasn't his.

'I saw her in the front seat. She was miming hello through the window. Some young bloke was seated beside her.' He looked across at Stefan and smiled. 'It was Max, bro, but I didn't know that at the time.'

He saw the shadows of other passengers blurred behind the glass as the bus began to move. On an impulse, he leapt for the step as the doors hissed shut.

He had no idea where he was going, except that it was with her and away from his destination. He did not care. The only seat available was at the rear next to a sleeping drunk whose face he turned away to avoid the heady stench of rum and hint of vomit on his breath.

Rosalie removed her raincoat hood. She slid her fingers through her hair, drawing it in a burnished fall across her shoulders. She talked quietly to the young man, who seemed absorbed in what she had to say. It may have been the reflection of the dashboard lights, but it seemed to Lennard that her skin glowed and and her hair was a headdress of feathered light.

The impression persisted as they rode up King's Park Road towards the city. He was on a trip to who knows where in the rain accompanied by a spirit being, it seemed. How far was he going? To the end of the line, he'd told the bus-driver. *All the way*, his mind whispered, *as far as it takes*.

Once, when she looked back at him, he was aware of an intimate connection across the separating distance, deeply personal and intriguing. They shared a moment of profound familiarity, as though they were in some euphoric elsewhere, as they had in the operating theatre.

Was he aware of the future in that moment? Was it wishful thinking? Either way, he sensed she was aware of his will to surround her in his wonder at seeing her again. She knew and she was pleased.

Telepathy? He thought sceptically. *On an ancient MTT bus? Rattling along King's Park Road over potholed bitumen under the peppermint trees, with the rain leaking through the window and the overpowering stink of diesel? Who's kidding who?*

The bus slowed at the top of Malcolm Street and Rosalie reached up to ring the bell. She and the young man stepped down into the rain.

She looked up as Lennard reached across the sleeping drunk to wipe the fogged window clear. Under the hood of her raincoat, he caught the flash of her face, her lips forming goodbye. Then she was gone.

Hello. Goodbye. Now you see me, now you don't! Her exit brought him back to earth and it was only then, since she had someone with her—her boyfriend, surely—that he wondered if he'd been led astray by an overactive imagination driven by a surfeit of testosterone. Home was now miles away and he was in for a long, wet walk to the ferry.

He jumped off at the next stop.

'We're not there yet, mate,' the driver reminded him. 'You paid full fare. You gonna get your money's worth, or what?'

'I will. Trust me, mate. I will.'

He trudged down the hill past the dilapidated wood-and-brick buildings of the PWD workshops beside the barracks archway. He peered with rain-stung eyes at the labyrinth of mansions terraced down the slope of Mount Street overlooking the Swan River, wondering where she'd disappeared to with her friend and half his luck.

It was a long, empty month before he saw her again; an eternity, and it seemed she was gone for good. He began thinking maybe that was for the best. She clearly belonged to a world beyond his reach.

'So there I was,' Lennard told Stefan. 'Way down the back.'

'So near and yet so far?'

'Too right.'

He did meet Rosalie again, he went on. At a concert, when he heard the Wieniawski piece for the first time and she invited him to a barbecue the following weekend. Her parents were hosting the Georgian State Dancers and she wanted him to meet Max, her twin.

'I'd mistaken him for her boyfriend and she had to put that right.' He laughed. 'She said it was an insult to her taste in men she'd never live down.'

'Did you go?'

'I did, but it took some doing, bro. I caused a stir when I first walked in, but not for long. All those ballerinas Max had the hooks out for were copping the limelight.'

'Did he score?'

'Not a chance. That was the story of his life at the time,' he shook his head, 'and nothing's changed. It has to be his line in charm. He uses the wrong lure. You know the story—tag and release. He gets them to the boat but rarely sinks the gaff. He told me once he was staying single to avoid becoming single again after he was hitched.'

'That makes good sense. What about you and Rosalie?'

'Ah bro, now *that*, that was different. Let's just say we burned the rubber on the bitumen.' He laughed aloud. 'But don't expect a blow by blow description. I was still inexperienced in those days, remember, so we'll leave the details to my memory and the rest to your imagination.'

They walked on in silence, until Stefan asked, 'So, the barbecue?'

'That was some night. It was deadly.'

HE CLIMBED JACOB'S LADDER, winding up the cliff to Mount Street, his nerves on edge. He paused halfway up the stairway to inspect the house set into the hillside above. The lawns ran down to a wall of moss rock at the cliff edge, and there were people sitting on the parapet. Below them, beds of nasturtium blazed orange and yellow across the cliff face in the last of the evening sunlight.

He sat on the step, looking across the spread of city lights emerging in the dusk, their fractured patterns quivering on the slick dark river, blurring and dissolving and reappearing in fresh graffiti scribbled by the wind. The evening traffic streamed towards the river narrows and the bridge below and, on the opposite point at South Perth, he saw the sail-blades of the old flour mill, stilled and silent.

At that moment it seemed the mill sails stirred and the axle ground and creaked as its story unfolded frame by frame—the story his father had often told him when he was a boy, a story that illustrated who the ancestors of the Aboriginal Nyungar people were and how strong he as a

Malgana tribesman should become.

Once again, he heard the wild war cries of the ochre-painted spirits of Marniong and Yadong and thirty warriors of the Pindjarup tribe as their leader, Calyute, pinned the miller George Shenton at spear point to the ground, spread-eagled and terrified among the flour bags they'd come to raid a century and a half ago… then a wind shift brought him the sounds of a piano and he gazed back up at the house.

An overpowering surge of pleasure at the prospect of seeing Rosalie in a few moments ran through him as he resumed the climb, pausing again when he reached the top. Animated voices drifted, the sound of the piano louder now. After several minutes, once more gathering confidence, he walked on up towards the ivy-covered entrance to the mansion garden.

He stood at the arched gate looking at the house. It was two-storied, Tudor-gabled and imposing. He tore a variegated leaf from the creeper and twirled it between thumb and forefinger, wondering what league he was getting into. *Ivy, nothing surer*, and he was once more swamped with doubt. *Who am I to venture into a world so different from my own?*

'Ah, the hell with it!' he growled, forcing himself to lift the latch and open the jarrah-timbered gate, and then in a barely audible whisper, 'Bring it on.'

He stepped beneath the archway, one foot following the other across the paving to the front door. He caught the smell of barbecuing steak and onions and heard the roar of conversation and laughter as he rang the bell.

There was a bicycle propped against the wall and he tested the pressure of the front tyre as he waited. The thought of escaping on it if anyone but Rosalie opened the door crossed his mind, but it was too late. The door opened a crack, then widened as Rosalie's father peered around it, his raptor's green eyes narrowing behind his rimless glasses.

'Ah, Rosie's painter and decorator,' he said, giving Lennard's extended hand an abrupt shake and ushering him in. 'David. And it's Lennard, isn't it? Come along in. We weren't sure you were coming.'

He led Lennard across the white-marbled tiles in the hallway, past the stairs, as Lennard cleared his throat and muttered, 'I promised Rosie I'd come if I could.'

'So you did, so you did, and Rosie will be pleased. She's been looking out for you all evening. Come through to the garden. She was out there last time I saw her.'

Groups of people were gathered in the lounge, vivacious women among them uniformly dressed in strapless gowns of gleaming apricot and green and crimson, all strikingly lithe and slim. Some surveyed the room from an upper balcony, others clustered in a vibrant blur around a white grand piano on which a balding pianist was tinkering.

Others armed with fistfuls of multi-coloured gambling chips surrounded a circular coffee table draped with green baize on which a French roulette wheel spun, the intermittent clatter of the ball echoing in the silences between cheers and groans of disappointment.

Lennard sensed people turning to peer in his direction as he crossed the floor, the invisibility he usually relied on deserting him.

A waiter in a blue tuxedo was serving white wine poured from a crystal decanter on a silver tray. He accepted a glass as he passed.

He hesitated before a pair of landscapes by Sidney Nolan on one whitewashed wall—storm-grey Kimberley skies lowering over rust and ochre cliffs. On the opposite wall, he recognised a large exuberant water surface painted by George Haynes.

As he slowed to examine it, David interrupted him, 'As I expected, there she is.'

Rosalie looked up at him through the glass of the double doors, her eyes shining. Caught in the garden floodlight, she was breathtaking. Folds of hair were clipped at her temples, a thick chignon coiled behind them. A pearl gleamed on a band of black satin at her throat. She wore a white pencil skirt, her green silk blouse glinting with sequins.

He raised the wine-glass to her and their eyes locked as they stepped towards each other.

'Hello, handsome,' she welcomed him, and then with one voice, 'It's great to see you,' they said.

She took his hand as he stepped down to the lawn and, with her free hand, waved dismissive fingers over her shoulder at her father, who watched them as the doors swung shut. Lennard saw him raise his eyebrows in annoyance or disapproval or both as he turned away.

'See? You made it into the lion's den unscathed!' Rosalie gave his hand a reassuring squeeze as she led him to the wall at the end of the garden, where people were seated holding plates of frankfurters and eye-fillet and salad, wine and beer glasses balanced precariously between them.

She waved a hand across the crowd. 'Max is on barbecue duty for the moment. He's got the steaks and snags going. He's in his element, feeding all these gorgeous ballerinas watching their calories. He thinks he's going to pot them off like a row of ducks.'

'Crack shot, is he?'

'Thinks he is. Thinks he's the drake the ducks are after—the one with the curly tail,' she laughed, 'but with his luck, he'll be out *for* a duck and his tail's staying curly. Score zero.'

'Or score one of the older ducks?' Lennard nodded at a stately silver-haired matron crossing the lawn towards them before he recognised Rosalie's mother from the recital.

'Hey!' Rosalie responded in an Australian accent you could cut with a knife. 'Take it easy, mate! That's me mum, that old duck you're referring to!'

Her mother joined them and he discovered that his reputation had preceded him.

'Ah, Lennard, I've been so looking forward to this. Rosie's told us all about you. I understand you work with coloured glass.' She waved an empty wineglass towards the house. 'You saw the latest additions to our art collection, no doubt? What did you think?'

'I couldn't miss the Haynes. I like it.'

'I like it too,' she said. 'I picked it, actually. What about the Nolans?'

'Did you pick them as well?'

'No, no. They're David's. He bought them last month at the Skinner exhibition. He thinks they're a shrewd investment. I chose the Haynes, with some help from George himself at his studio.'

'Then you've got a good eye, Mrs O'Sullivan. Why did you pick that one in particular?'

'It matches the rug,' Rosalie interrupted with a teasing smile.

'Nonsense, dear. We bought the rug to go with the painting.' She turned back to Lennard. 'And never mind the Mrs. It makes me feel old. You must call me Phyllis.'

'Well, there you go!' Rosalie exclaimed in mock triumph. 'Meet Phyllis... my Philistine mum.'

Lennard saw an older version of Rosalie's elegant beauty in her mother's fine-boned face—the delicate structure of the cheekbones, the same sublime shape to the eyes—though hers were hazel with a captivating blend of severity and humour in them—the curve of her forehead, accentuated by the upward sweep of silver hair pinned at the temples by two tortoiseshell combs, beneath which three-tiered pendulum earrings glittered with emeralds.

'Rosie would have been so disappointed if you hadn't come, Lennard.'

'Thank you for the invitation.'

'We're pleased to have you here. I want you to feel at home.'

'I do. Now.'

'Fair go, Mum! Stop fussing over him. He's fine. I'll take good care of him.'

'You can rest easy.' Lennard shared her smile. 'It was deadly coming up Mount Street, but.'

'No doubt it was.'

'I'll make sure he's well looked after, Mum.' Rosalie paused, and then, 'If your roles were reversed and you'd been invited by the Nyungar to attend a dance at their Coolbaroo Club you might have felt the same as Lennard did just now, and then you'd have been pleasantly surprised once you got inside. We share the same sky, don't we? And none of us is out of place under that.' She gave a wicked chuckle. 'You'd have attended solo, of course. I can't imagine you dragging Dad along. He'd have faked a seizure or suffered a real one to avoid it.'

'I'd have left him behind in any case, him with his two left feet.' Phyllis turned to Lennard and handed him her empty glass. 'If you'll do us the honours Lennard, the drinks are on the terrace. I'll have another white wine, thank you.'

'A stubbie for me, please,' Rosalie said. 'Any kind'll do.'

'I do love his *eyes,* Rosie,' he heard as he made his way back up towards the house. 'Did you say one of them was glass?'

When he went back with the drinks, he met Phyllis on her way to the terrace.

'Don't think me rude, Lennard, but hostess duty calls,' she explained as he handed her the wine. 'Max is down there with Rosie. We'll catch up later.'

'I'll look forward to it.'

'We'll make it soon. I'll ask Rosie to arrange a dinner.'

As she walked away, he wondered how she'd react to meeting his feisty mother Mary, how they'd get along. One the down-to-earth, no-nonsense matriarch to their extended family—what you saw... and heard—you got. The other smart and socially privileged, the sort of woman Mary, as a member of the stolen generation, had been trained to serve as a house-maid when she was in her teens. He shook his head. *I know who I'd back if they disliked each other and fought like alley cats.*

Max sat alongside Rosalie on the parapet. He wore a navy blue and white striped butcher's apron and a crumpled chef's skull cap, spikes of red hair protruding beneath it. His narrow face and striking green eyes hinted at a sharp intelligence. He held a pair of silver tongs carrying a steak wrapped in a salad leaf in one hand and a brandy balloon of red wine in the other. His mouth was full. Rosalie removed a fragment of lettuce stuck to the corner of his lip with her fingernail.

'Ace, meet Max,' she said.

Max placed his glass on the parapet. He scrutinised Lennard and gave him a nod of recognition as they shook hands. 'So it *is* you. I've seen you on campus.'

'Am I that obvious?'

'Well, you are the one and only in Fine Arts, aren't you?'

'I can't say I've ever noticed you.'

'Us whites, we all look alike?'

'Can't tell you apart.'

'And I thought I was one of a kind.'

'You are,' Rosalie broke in, 'the dickhead kind.'

'You hear that, Ace? And you still want to get to know vinegar tits here? Your agates must be big as watermelons, or they'd better be. You're going to need them. Either way, it's good to meet you.'

'Likewise. Actually, I have seen you. On the bus, last month.'

'Rosie told me.' Max pointed a thumb at her. 'Seriously, mate, you must have a roo loose in the top paddock to get mixed up with this one. Take my advice, don't. She should've been born a bloke. Ever since she followed me down the birth canal, she's been at me for snaffling her share of the family jewels.'

'*Your* family jewels? Give me a break, Max! When I saw how small they were I knew I'd won the lottery.'

Max laughed, choking on a fragment of steak as Rosalie pounded his back.

'Wrong hole,' he said, his eyes watering. 'God knows who put them so close together. I'll have to sue the bastard for the lousy plumbing.' When the coughing eased, he peered up at Lennard. 'The *Zuytdorp*, Ace. Tell me about the *Zuytdorp*. Rosie says you're descended from Dutch sailors. What's that make you? A high-bred hybrid?'

'I'm not sure about high. I believe my Dutch ancestor was on board. He survived the shipwreck.'

'Careful,' Rosalie interrupted. 'The silk's about to subject you to the third degree. Don't tell him anything he doesn't already know.'

Lennard heard Rosalie's directness reflected in Max's sharp retorts. He imagined the two of them trading insults, alert and on guard, before sparring like a pair of fencers, sparks flying. Rosalie had warned him at the concert about Max's sometimes scathing humour.

'I've been thinking about the *Zuytdorp* ever since Rosie mentioned you,' Max said, as she reached across and put a hand over his mouth.

'Max, don't you dare!'

'She hasn't stopped talking about you since...' his voice came muffled through her fingers, 'the concert. It seems you believe Australia's answer is blowing in the wind.'

'Blowing in the wind?'

Max lifted her hand away and held it. 'Wind-blown ships and Dutch sailors. It's an interesting idea. Dutch seamen in a race to mix the races, starting with your mob up north.' He waved a hand across the myriad of city lights, their reflections blending on the darkly sinuous river. '*Multiracial miscegenation*! I like it! Miscegenation on an industrial scale, with the emphasis on *nation*! All our genes whisked together in this continental Petri dish incubated by our southern skies.' He gave Lennard an ironic grin. 'Look at you, for starters, Ace! You're right on the money.'

'Right about what? You've lost me and I haven't said a word.'

'Because you can't get a word in,' Rosalie murmured.

'He doesn't have to. Look at those eyes! You're showing us the future!' Max raised his glass to toast Lennard and drained it. 'I might go down to the sperm bank myself on Monday. Make my donation to the gene pool. Short-sighted donors barred, visionaries welcome. No wankers.'

'*That'd* make it difficult, but save us the gory details.' Rosalie laughed.

Max vaulted onto the parapet. He spun to face them, legs dramatically apart. He waved his tongs like a wand at the sky, his face edged by streaming stars. Lennard thought for a moment the wine had unsettled him and he was about to fall back over the edge, but he steadied himself.

'Dutch semen!' he intoned. 'Shipwrecked sailors, they're the answer to a Malgana maiden's prayers!' Then he took a breath, as if hyperventilating and in a frenetic rush, with no pauses till he ran out of breath, '*O Lord methought what pain it was to drown what dreadful noise of waters in my ears what sights of ugly death within my eyes methought I saw a thousand fearful wrecks a thousand men that fishes gnawed upon wedges of gold great anchors heaps of pearl inestimable stones unvalued jewels all scattered in the bottom of the sea…*'

'Oh, God save us!' Rosalie groaned. 'Don't let him get his second wind! What can we stuff into that ginormous mouth of his?'

She shoved Max at the knees so that he fell from the wall into the darkness beyond. They heard his voice continue as a hand reappeared. He leaned an elbow on the parapet, ruefully inspecting the steak covered in grass clippings. Then he reached down to retrieve his chef's hat and set it back on his head.

'You'd make a great didge player,' Lennard commented drily. 'Your breathing doesn't interfere with your talking.'

'So now you've met my twin sister,' Max responded. 'Don't trust her good looks, mate. Man may have evolved from the shrew, but let me warn you, this woman's evolving back into one. See the teeth?' He shook his head. 'And she's cunning with it. You know how it is, *make the doors on a woman's wit, and it will out at the casement; shut that, and 'twill out at the keyhole.'*

He climbed back over the wall and dusted himself down. 'Talking of Dutch castaways, did she tell you about the *Gilt Dragon*? Show him the article you wrote, Rosie. It's a skilful bit of journalism. And your underwater photographs aren't bad either, even if it pains me to say so.' He turned to Lennard. 'She couldn't have done it without my editing, though.'

Rosalie clipped him lightly over the ear. 'I got you to check the punctuation, that's all, which, by the way, you forgot in your speech back there.'

She stuck out her tongue and the tongs clicked as Max snapped at it, dropping the steak.

'I know when and where I'm wanted,' he said, looking up towards the house, 'and right now it's at the hot plate. Let's get this party sizzling—Anna, Elena, Marina, Kristina, Katya and the rest of you Georgians I haven't met yet! Even husky Russki Olga! Dear God, help me to convince at least *one* of these irresistible women not to resist me tonight. I'll turn on the charm like never before.' He groaned aloud, turning faces in his direction. '*Come, woo me, woo me; for now I am in a holiday humour and like enough to consent!*'

Rosalie nudged Lennard. 'He's got the hots for a Catholic student in one of his tutorials at the moment, but he hasn't scored. He blames the verbs in the Eucharist Latin—all she does is decline.'

'Can you knock me for trying?' Max grinned. 'So much for RCs. I'm into Russian Unorthodox tonight and the more unorthodox the better.' He placed a hand on Lennard's shoulder. 'You've been warned, my friend. Don't chance it! Don't rely on Rosie here for support. Rely on your legs—and keep running.'

'We've chanced everything so far, with great results,' Rosalie said.

'In that case, if you're going out later, don't leave without me. Unless I score me a cygnet or two from Swan Lake and I'm otherwise occupied.'

'*Two?*' Rosalie laughed. '*One* is wishful thinking, kiddo. You may as well join us as soon as it's over.'

'See how sharp her tongue is, Ace? And I see it's still forked.'

He ducked away through the guests before Rosalie could respond.

Lennard watched him walk away. He was unsettled. He found the unfamiliar free-for-all in his conversation disconcerting and his theatrical mannerisms and unexpected quotations bizarre and pretentious. While he knew he'd encountered someone exceptional, he was troubled, unsure how he'd respond next time they met. Rosalie had referred to his 'urbane ockerism' at the concert. Now he'd experienced it… and it put him on edge.

'His bark sounds worse than his bite,' he suggested warily.

'It is. It is, and he is my twin brother, so let's forgive him.' She placed a hand on Lennard's forearm. 'We can forgive him the Shakespeare too. He's been learning passages by heart ever since he played the first witch in *Macbeth* in primary school and never put a foot wrong—*a sailor's wife had chestnuts in her lap, and munched and munched and munched!*' She tapped her temple with a forefinger. 'He has this photographic memory. Part of his brain was wired by Kodak, so learning the part was cinchy for him, even then. He loved it when he was that young and he's been hard at it ever since.'

Lennard recognised the strength of her affection for Max. He sensed in their co-dependency an unconditional relationship. Their bond was non-negotiable and he wondered where that would leave him down the track. Would Max come between himself and Rosalie as their relationship developed? He corrected the thought—*if* their relationship developed.

And he'd witnessed Rosalie holding her own, heard the flash of her wit so that, for the first time since they'd met, he felt uneasily alert. She was outgoing and self-assured. She displayed a confidence and strength of will he wasn't yet used to and he wondered what the future held.

'He's been really keen to meet you, though,' she said. 'You can expect the third degree next time he sees you on campus. You'd better prepare yourself. I'm surprised he didn't quiz you tonight.'

'About what?'

'Oh, things to do with Aboriginal issues and Australian law, of course. Things he's been driving me bonkers about since I mentioned you.'

'I'm flat out with my degree. I don't have time for politics.'

'But you're Aboriginal. Doesn't that make you an activist by default? Max is interested. He knows things are hotting up over east to give Canberra a shake-up. He's been arguing endlessly with Dad about it.' She ran through the names as though ticking boxes, 'Chicka Dixon and Aboriginal Advancement, Charlie Perkins and student action, Lake Tyers, the Yirrkala petitions—'

'Thanks for the warning,' Lennard interrupted her. 'I'll give Max and the law faculty a wide berth in future.'

'No, you won't. I know Max and I'm getting to know you. He'll have you up to your neck the minute my back's turned.'

At that moment, David appeared on the terrace, the glass doors flung wide. He tapped on an empty wine glass to bring the night to a close, announcing a pair of black-shirted, baggy-trousered Cossack dancers who began an energetic display, leaping in unison in their silks and leather boots across swords laid in parallel on the slate paving on the terrace, the piano resonating.

THEY REACHED THE corner of Essex Street.

'So you made it,' Stefan commented. 'Sounds like that took some doing.'

'Tell me about it, bro. I surprised myself, but I wasn't gonna prove myself a gutless wonder. Not after coming that far.' He flashed Stefan a quick smile. 'Took a mighty risk, though. All my money on the black! And not only on the black, *on the black twenty-two*! With no plan B.'

Stefan laughed. 'Stuck your neck out. I know the feeling.'

'It was worth it, but. Rosie was waiting for me and I couldn't let her down.'

The smell of fresh bread in the ovens of a Vietnamese bakery pervaded the street corner.

'Smell that!' Lennard said. 'Bloody beautiful. Fancy a croissant with your coffee?' He reached into his pocket and sorted through the change.

'Sounds good.'

The baker was washing down the pavement and she kinked the hose to stop the flow as they walked around her.

They bought a croissant each and walked on towards Marine Terrace as Lennard took up the story.

'YOUR LEDGE POINT dive, Rosie. Are you gonna show me the article you've written?' he asked as the sword dance ended.

She slipped her arm through his, interlocking their fingers. 'Of course I will.'

'And the pictures?'

'They're embedded in the text.'

'You and me, we should dive on the *Zuytdorp*. You could teach me how to use aqualungs,' he suggested.

He was planning a trip to Wanamalu Station for the long weekend early in September. Would she like to come?

'We could go on to Kalbarri and cross the Murchison River there. It's hard country, but I know it like the back of my hand. I can't wait to explore it again.'

He was convinced that most of the *Zuytdorp* survivors had trekked north, he said. He and his father had driven southwards down their path the year before, from Denham and along the cliffs to the wreck site.

'How can you be sure they travelled north?'

'Some clues they've found around Shark Bay confirm it.'

He described a swivel cannon they'd carried, perhaps to signal passing ships. Rusting water barrel hoops. Brass buttons. The lid of a pewter tobacco canister found at Wale Well, a long way north of the wreck site. And three crude rock shelters erected on Freycinet beach that whalers had subsequently used.

'There has to be a lot more lying around up there,' he suggested. 'It looks like they were making a run for Batavia. I guess they died trying. Who knows? Except for Gerrit. They must have left him at the wreck site. Perhaps he was injured.'

'You really think he survived long enough to live among the Malgana?'

'Definitely.'

'How can you be sure?'

'I think his spoon confirms it. My mum found that a long way south at Wanamalu, so he must have travelled in that direction. How could he have done that unless he was with a group of Malgana, living off country? They would have been moving down to the Murchison River for the blue manna crabs right then. They're in season in the estuary from June to August and the mulloway follow them in.'

'Couldn't *they* have found the canister at the wreck site and taken it with them?'

Lennard pointed at his blue eye. 'So where'd I get this?'

'Transplant!' Rosalie laughed, squeezing his fingers. 'Gerrit's got you hypnotised, Ace.'

'He's got my attention, that's for sure.'

'I'll say.' She went quiet for a moment and then looked up enquiringly. 'Who's imagining who, I wonder? Are you conjuring up Gerrit or are you a blip on his radar?'

He inclined his head. 'I'd have to say both.'

They crossed the lawn. With each step, the silk-sinew of her waist shifted against his forearm. Before they reached the steps to the terrace, she guided him towards the garden wall where they stood looking back at the cityscape, breathing the cool night wind coming off the river.

'It's the funniest thing. When I mention your experiments in glass and light to Mum, she thinks you're into lead lighting. She wants to commission you to make her a porthole for the front door. Something chic. Something stylish.'

'A cockatoo among the gum leaves?'

She screwed up her face. 'I'm sure she'd love that! And

yes—Kalbarri,' she went on. 'Of course I'll come. I liked Mum's remark about your eyes tonight, by the way. Brown land, she said, blue sea.'

'And neither of them glass?' He closed the brown and gazed at her with the blue. 'See any wrecks in there?'

'Full fathom five?' She stepped closer and gazed deeply into him, a hand to his cheek. 'No, Ace. Fathoming *you* is what I want. And your pupil's dilating! Any wider and I'll be reading your thoughts. Not that I can't already, they're that transparent.'

She tilted her face and they kissed, light and fleeting, a brushing of lips, the faint taste of beer and wine. Lennard looked down at her in expectant surprise.

'That was nice,' she said. 'Still waters run deep, that's what I saw.'

She withdrew her hand from his cheek and ran her fingers through his hair, pulling him down to her.

'Now that we've started,' she murmured.

They kissed again, and he quivered as she moved her hands to the small of his back and folded into him, on her toes, unbalanced in his grip, her slender body's length against his. He began to shake, so that she relaxed and withdrew, settling back on her heels, her hands on his hips.

He reached out and drew her back to him, his cheek to her hair, breathing her scent. *'Ngathangura warlu, wurlathayi,'* he whispered—*my lover, come closer*.

'What was that?' Rosalie asked, alert to his inexperience. 'It sounds like you're purring.'

'I am.'

The pearl trembled on his chest alongside the albatross. Then she took a step back, holding his hands at arm's length. She was silhouetted against the lights of the house, shadowed people moving behind her, their voices muted. She tried to move but he held her there.

'Stay,' he said.

'What are you doing?'

'Drinking you in, taking photographs I'm saving for tomorrow.'

'Ah, so that was the blinding flash!' Her sidelong glance touched with impish humour delighted him. 'Beauty for the two of us is in the beholder of the eyes. I'll show you mine if you'll show me yours; your glass sculptures for my dive article. Deal?'

'Deal! Which one first? My glass sculptures? Why not tonight?'

'There's no time like right now,' she said, as Max joined them.

He was alone, as predicted. His clothes and hair reeked of cooking oil and jarrah wood smoke. He didn't say a word until they were descending Jacob's ladder, and then, 'Missed out again. Wrong bloody pheromones.'

'Never mind, Maxie,' Rosalie commented, verging on laughter, 'ballerinas need their sleep. There's always next time, or the time after that, or even more likely, the time after the time after—'

'*Because I will not do them the wrong,*' he interjected, '*to mistrust any, I will do myself the right to trust none; and the fine is, for the which I may go the finer, I will live a bachelor...* and there's a fucking end to it!'

'You never know. The night's still young,' Rosalie reassured him.

They made it onto the last ferry to South Perth, sprinting hand in hand towards the jetty, Rosalie laughing, her hair loose and wild, and Lennard yelling at the deckhand casting off not to leave them behind. All three leaped aboard as the gangplank was withdrawn.

Max made his way to the bows; a melancholy figurehead peering across the scorched earth of a Georgian retreat as the ferry thrust through the wind and spray, the city lights swarming on the river smashed to smithereens against the hull.

Short on fuel, Lennard had parked his repaired scooter at the Mill Point jetty. An electric milk cart was the only other vehicle on the street as they puttered past the lion-grunting zoo and over the switchback into Victoria Park, Max perched on the handlebars with his feet propped on the mudguard and Rosalie on the pillion.

A grizzled, sway-backed Alsatian guard dog snarled at them from behind the glass factory gates, until he recognised Lennard's voice. He sniffed around Rosalie with interest, and then followed them to the studio door at the end of the building, where Lennard rattled the key into the lock, dew dripping into his hair and across his shoulders from rust-encrusted eaves.

'Stay here while I prepare the display,' he said as he swung the door open.

He weaved his way between three suspended glass sculptures chained to the crossbeam. Rectangular panels of coarse-cored glass a metre across, two metres tall and two centimetres thick, with concealed fluorescents inserted into the top and the base, they hung at an angle across the room. A control switch lay on the table beside the camp bed at the far wall, where a jammed electric clock flashed the wrong time—eleven past eleven. There'd been a power cut weeks ago and it needed resetting.

Lennard reached for the switch. 'Okay,' he shouted. 'Come on in.'

They stumbled through the door, guided by the flash of the clock. When they were halfway across the room, Lennard turned on the switch.

Lit from within, the three glass panels burst into colour, intense and blinding.

'Bloody *hell!*' shouted Max, caught off-guard. 'Lennard said let there be light, *and there was light!*'

Rosalie was dazzled in the crossfire, her hair a cascade of bronze and scarlet, till Lennard turned off the switch and left them in darkness, their eyes flaring with after-images.

'And then kept us in the dark for the rest of eternity,' Max observed.

Then he switched on one sculpture and coloured light poured across the room as though refracted through a prism, crimson and vermilion auroras swirling about them, the walls and pitched ceiling ablaze.

They stood enthralled.

'It's like standing in a *holy*gram,' Max suggested as he walked around the sculpture, his shadow merging with it. 'Do you have any music to match this? It needs something Ptolemaic. Something cosmographic. Majestic. No, *Almagestic.*' His face in flames, his cheekbones stood out in eerie purple shadow. 'Something, I don't know, Saharan. Primordial. Berber music inspired by the sands of time or, better still, *timelessness.*'

Rosalie walked across and sat beside Lennard on the bed. She hadn't said a word. She reached out with both hands cupped to catch elusive colours that slipped through her fingers and then extended both arms as if reaching for the light's essence.

Lennard saw her eyes glisten. He stiffened. 'What is it? Is it too bright?'

'It's the beauty. I've never seen anything like it.'

'It's just glass. It's just light.'

'No. It's more. It's much, much more than that.'

She stood and drew him up with her. She put her arms around him, her face to his chest, before turning to Max, who was leaning against the panel, peering in, his arms outstretched.

'Crucifried, Ace. That's how I feel. Crucifried. In your

sun-painted desert.' Then over his shoulder, 'How's the time? Do I smell a coffee coming on?'

'You can sleep here,' Rosalie pointed at the camp bed. 'We're going into the hills.' She looked back at Lennard. 'Is that okay with you? We'll be back in the morning. Do you have some coffee he can brew?'

Lennard pointed at mugs and a canister of instant coffee lined on the sideboard. He took a box of matches from a drawer and lobbed it onto the gas rings in the corner. 'You'll find bacon and sausages in the fridge and bread in the freezer, so you won't starve.' He turned back to Rosalie, 'We can refuel at the airport turnoff on the way.'

They left Max silhouetted in the doorway. 'Abandoned,' he complained. 'First the Georgians and now you guys. A bloke could get paranoid.'

The door closed; Max's shadow caught behind the whitewash of its panes.

THEY TURNED INTO Marine Terrace, the morning breeze stronger now, blowing directly into their faces.

Stefan was distracted by a stocky, dark-tanned shopkeeper in a tawny apron opening up a delicatessen. Boxes of fruit were on display behind the window, highly polished green apples among them He was hefting two plastic buckets filled with bunches of carnations, moving them to a display table on the pavement. The wind brought Stefan their unmistakeable scent and with it a confusing burst of longing and regret that stopped him in his tracks. He clenched his jaw and rubbed his cheek.

Get over it, for God's sake! he thought, before raising his open hand to the shopkeeper, who nodded back. He turned away and walked on, picking up the pace to catch up with Lennard.

They reached the end of the Terrace and crossed the railway line, climbing between two stationary goods wagons.

A flattop truck had reversed up to the front door of the glassworks with the consignment of superfine waterjet garnet sand. Lennard unlocked the door and they helped the truckie offload twelve bulging sacks, propping them against the wall in the alcove. They were labelled GMA—Garnet Mines Australia—and originated from the Hutt Lagoon at Port Gregory, in Nhanda country.

He and Stefan gripped a sack each and dragged them to the sieve.

'One more'll do us for starters, bro,' Lennard said as he inspected the sacks. 'This is where things get interesting. We'll see if your predictions are on the money.'

Stefan gave him a sceptical nod. 'No bets this time, but you know what I think. I hope I'm wrong.'

'We've got our work cut out for us for the rest of the week, bro.'

'Sure have,' Stefan grunted, as he hauled the third sack across. *What surprises does the furnace have in store?*

Lennard prepared coffees while Stefan set about checking the equipment, flicking switches and monitoring temperature gauges, logging the results.

Lennard opened the double doors to the beach and walked with his croissant and steaming mug to the water's edge, as he always did before work began.

The tide was receding, the breeze raising whitecaps.

He squatted on the sand and stared for several minutes with a faraway look at a line of figures standing on the boulders of the South Mole breakwater. He recalled the warmth of Rosalie leaning into him on the pillion that night, the feel of her breasts… and then he noticed the fishermen cast and occasionally retrieve the writhing flash of small fish.

Herring on the run, no doubt. He looked more intently. *Or garfish.*

He breathed the rich aroma of the coffee before sipping, and then gazed at the horizon, turning his mind back to the clearest of memories—when he and Rosalie rode up into the hills.

The cold wind whipped past them as he revved up the Kalamunda zigzag. It wound up to the summit, where he turned onto the viewing platform and switched off the engine.

Below them, the city lights spread westward to the edge of the ocean, flickering beacons lined across it. Beyond them, the intermittent flash of the Rottnest lighthouse pierced the darkness. The wingtip lights of a descending plane strobed the air over the city, its landing lights spearing down towards the runway.

'Happy landings,' Rosalie whispered, her breath gentle on his neck. Her hair strayed over his shoulders. Her arms were around him, her body cradling his. She slipped her right hand beneath his shirt to feel for the abalone shell and with her fingertips, she read the contours of the albatross, like braille.

'The wandering albatross,' she murmured, and then, 'Zeeland and the *Zuytdorp*, they're your keys, Ace. They'll help me unlock you.'

He leaned round to look at her.

'Don't wind me up, sister,' he warned. 'You know there's no stopping me once I'm up and running on *that* topic.'

'Winding you up? I like the sound of that. And once you're up and running who wants to stop you?'

He smiled. 'The spoon's one key. I've held it. Weighed it. I've even *eaten* from it. And I've thought about other keys. Especially the ship.'

She leaned her cheek into the back of his shoulder. 'Don't start searching for them now. Let's save that for later.' She drew him closer, her ear to the muscular drum of his chest as she listened to his heart thumping deep within it.

'What's the Malgana word for heart, Ace?'

'*Wurduru.*'

'*Wurduru.* That's *exactly* what I can hear. *Wurduru. Wurduru. Wurduru.*'

Then she placed her hands on his shoulders and ran her fingers through the hair curling over his collar.

'When was the *Zuytdorp* built?'

'Her keel was on the Middelburg slipway in January 1701. That much I know for sure. Her hull was launched in July.'

'Well, this is now,' she said. 'And this is us.'

She pointed towards the inland hills where the lights of Kalamunda vanished into darkness. 'Let's find somewhere we can overlook everything. Somewhere we can see the land and the ocean and the stars. Somewhere we can watch our first sunrise. I want to see the light in *our* sky.'

'I know the very place.'

'Show me.'

They coasted through the Kalamunda streets, skidding round a cat on one corner, the eerie green of its eyes flaring before its ginger shape, caught in the headlight, raced behind a whitewashed wall. They turned to glide down the hill towards the Bickley Valley, sweeping through a swath of mist and the sudden scent of wild Boronia as they crossed Piesse Brook Bridge, before climbing towards Mundaring Weir.

The silhouetted avenue of eucalypts and jarrah trees cut the sky above them to a channel of stars they followed to the dam. They heard the rush of water across the weir as Lennard slowed and turned into a firebreak, the glimmer of the lake beside the rocky embankment to their left.

A lookout tower straddled the track a mile from the road. When its pillars loomed out of the darkness, Lennard pulled the scooter to a stop and switched out the light.

The platform sailed above them and they began the climb, feeling for the wooden ladder rungs.

'It's breathtaking,' Rosalie said when they reached the open side-panel and climbed in, 'and I'm breathless.'

The wind had died and the night was still, the canopy of leaves around them glimmering.

She looked around the cabin. 'However did you find this place?'

'We were scavenging for rock samples for a uni project last year.'

'And you've been bringing all your girls here ever since? The ones you kidnap.'

He shook his head.

'So I'm your first?'

A faint grin as he showed his hands palms up. 'You could well be.'

She put her arms around him. 'Then I'm honoured.'

Then she stepped back, her hair falling around her face as she took off her jacket and laid it on the bench that ran along one wall. She put her finger to her lips as a night bird called; three notes dovelike in the dark. Another answered further down the valley with the plaintive sound of an underwater bell and called again, and they saw a momentary flare of soundless white curve in among the trees beneath them.

She leaned into Lennard, asking if the bird was an owl, and he replied that yes, he supposed it was, an *inngabalayi wangganyina*; an owl calling.

She reached over her shoulder to undo the first of her blouse buttons and when the next button caught in its thread she guided his hand to help her untangle it. He undid the rest. She slid the elastic of her skirt belt down over the curve of her hips, thumb-hooked her pants to her knees and stepped out of them, lifting her blouse over her head and bending to remove it, her breasts hanging beautiful in the moonlight.

She stood pale and naked and smiling as he undressed, then opened her arms to him.

'I know,' she whispered. 'I know. We have all the time we need.'

She held him in a moment of touch and caress, his hands moving tentatively across her hips to the curve of her lower back, her fingertips running down the ridge of his spine. Anticipation coursed through them as they kissed. Then she led him to the bench. She stretched out, her right knee raised, her left slanted to receive. She pulled him down to her and when they'd settled, she leaned her face away to expose her throat and he kissed her beneath her ear.

'You can touch me anywhere you like,' she sighed.

He tensed and arched as she guided him, and then looked down at her in amazement as he entered her. It was over in moments, but his erection remained.

'Keep still now,' she said. 'Don't move.'

Still joined, he felt the lightest of muscular contractions that held him there. And then, with a groaning sigh, she began to move, subtle and slow. He responded to the pressure of her rhythm until she shifted sideways and turned him on his back.

'Give him to me,' she demanded, gazing intently into him, panting as she bore down. 'Deeper!' Then she gave a wild, ecstatic cry torn from deep within her, a hot gush of fluid bursting between them, before shuddering as a burst of sobbing laughter swept through her.

At last, she lowered herself and rested her body across his chest, her face nuzzling his shoulder.

'Now *that*,' she said at last, 'was really something. That, I needed.'

Lennard was enraptured. He turned and propped himself on his forearms, looked down at her in disbelief and shook his head in silence before kissing her with renewed force.

Languid, Rosalie stretched her thigh over his. 'Are you all right now?'

He shook his head again yes, and she moved with a delicious lasciviousness beside him as he whispered, '*Ngathangura warlu, wurlagura.*'

'You're purring again and I feel ravished. Beautifully,' she said. And then, smiling, 'You found my sweet spot.'

A wash of light was spreading across the eastern sky when she stood and walked to the rail.

'Come and look,' she said, pointing through the window at the ocean, the city outstretched beyond the shortening shadow of the hills. 'This is all ours, forever.'

He held her from behind, cradling her breasts and breathing her rich musk as she leaned into his shoulder, her hair coming to coppery life. They watched the sun edge over the inland treetops as the canopy brightened, the fading moon floating like a pale ceramic high above the roofline.

'That's our *bira* up there,' Lennard told her. 'She's smiling especially for us.'

'Yes, she approves.'

Then a movement below caught Rosalie's eye. She pointed at the long olive sash of a dugite gliding along the track into pools of sunlight. She shivered as it coiled into a cluster of kangaroo paw in red-green flower, half its body exposed, before resuming its slow glide into the undergrowth.

Lennard held her flank, stroking her back and hip, warming her. 'This wouldn't be paradise without one,' he said, moving his hand to caress her breast.

'Not to mention the forbidden fruit,' she replied, 'which is forbidden no longer.'

When the snake reappeared, it stretched out in the sunlight for a moment, raising its head and quivering, as if searching for a sensed presence, before accelerating with sinuous speed into the chequered umber shadows of the trees.

As Lennard watched, a recollection sprang to mind. 'It's like a bullwhip,' he reflected. 'The sort they used on us in the old days.'

Rosalie gazed intently up at him before placing her fingers to his lips. 'No, no, don't go there. Don't spoil things, my darling,' she said, sensing once again how deeply each would rely on the other for reassurance when venturing into their separate worlds.

A flock of emerald ring-neck parrots whirred past. They settled in a white-flowered eucalypt directly in front of them, screeching as they attacked the pendulous nuts and scattered torn leaves.

'Time's on the wing,' she suggested, brightly. 'We should go before the forestry people have us up for trespassing,'

'That was no trespass, sister. That was you and me becoming us.'

'You want to know the best part? I can't wait for you and me to become us again.'

And they did.

When Stefan had completed his rounds and checked the equipment, he downed the rest of his coffee and joined Lennard on the beach.

'Take the weight off, bro.' Lennard patted the sand beside him. He glanced at his watch. 'There's no rush, now we've got the garnet. Park your *manda* and I'll finish off Rosie's story.' He glanced up at Stefan. 'Unless I'm boring you shitless?'

'You're not.'

'So where were we?'

'Max was back in the Vic Park Glassworks. You and Rosalie were heading into the hills.'

Lennard gave a burst of laughter. 'Nice try, brudda! That chapter's strictly censored. Let's just say my cherry went walkabout.'

'So I miss out on the juicy bits?'

'You do. You do, by crikey.' He paused, stretched out both arms and then, turning on his side, made himself comfortable on one elbow.

'When we got back to the studio, Max was stretched out on the camp bed, wrapped in a sheet and reading a newspaper.'

THE UNLIT SCULPTURES hung like flags in a mediaeval hall-way, their honeycombs of colour shimmering when they burst in, arms around each other, joyous.

'A*haaa*!' Max sat up and grinned. 'I don't have to be Sherlock to see you two have set the wheels in motion.' He placed an imaginary meerschaum in the corner of his mouth, took several puffs before removing it and stood on the bed to serenade them with an air violin. 'You look *wheelie* emotional!'

Rosalie grinned up at Lennard. 'Let's break the Stradivarius over his head. He thinks he's a dead ringer for Igor.'

They tangled him in the bedclothes and dragged him out through the door, where the dog joined the fray. They tore away the sheet and locked him outside in his underpants, pleading to come in, as two women cleaners on the Sunday morning shift came in through the gate. They looked across laughing, and one shouted, 'Come here handsome… if you're game enough for a threesome!' And the other in a shrill voice, 'You proud of what you've got there, sonny? Looks to me you've been to see your shrink!'

Rosalie called out that it was his chance of a lifetime, while Lennard lit the gas to boil water for coffees. Then he picked her up and carried her back to the camp bed where they stretched out together, Max hammering at the door, pleading to come in.

Rosalie looked over at the sculptures. 'I love the colours you've used, especially the blues and aquamarines in the middle one,' she said. 'It's like you're diving under a breaking wave, looking up at the undersurface of the sea through all the foam.'

Lennard got up to unlock the door. Max came in, picked up the sheet and threw it over his shoulder, knotting there it like a toga. He pointed across the room with a flourish, his unruly ranga hair spiked into a victor's laurels.

'*I come not, friends, to steal away your hearts, I am no orator…*' he paused, '*but as you know me all, a plain blunt man, that love my friends. For I have neither wit—*'

'Right on!' shrieked Rosalie, 'you witless twit! Look out, Ace. He's winding up.'

'*…nor words, nor worth, nor action,*' he looked down at his front, 'least of all action—*nor utterance, nor the power of speech—*'

'We wish,' Rosalie interjected again.

'*…to stir men's blood; I only speak right on. I tell you that which you yourselves do know… there is a tide in the affairs of men which, taken at the flood, leads on to fortune; omitted, all the voyage of their life is bound in shallows and in miseries.*'

He jumped several times on both feet, moving slowly across the room towards them, before ducking behind the amber sculpture closest to them, where he stood one-legged, his left knee raised, his foot resting against his right knee. He raised a hand to shade his eyes as though searching the horizon as the patterns in the glass turned his toga deep rust and lined his face with streaks of ochre.

'*…On such a full sea are we now afloat*—like your Zeeland

sailors, Ace—*and we must take the current when it serves*—like they did—*or lose our ventures.*'

'Ventures, Max?' Lennard broke in. 'What ventures? What are you rattling on about?'

Max picked up the *West Australian* from the floor. It was a week old, folded inside out. He showed them a recruitment advert for vacancies in the Pilbara. Its bannered headlines read *Railway Survey Hands.*

'Check this out. AAM Surveys are calling for labourers. They've completed the aerial mapping for a railway from Dampier to Mount Tom Price. CRA is opening up an iron ore mine there and they've let the contract to AAM to do the groundwork through the sticks. They're looking for survey hands, starting in November. The timing couldn't be better. Exams will be over. The money should be good. We need the cash. We'll have three months off for the long vacation. What do you say we get our names in early?'

He looked expectantly at Lennard, who was stirring the coffees.

'The extra brass would be a bonus,' he agreed. 'What about you, Rosie? Could you make it?'

'Would there be any work up there for nurses, do you think? In a first-aid post, maybe? I've got a stack of leave overdue. I could ask for time off.'

'We'll have to find out,' Lennard said, handing out the coffees, 'because I'm not going anywhere without you.'

'If you're both happy with the idea I'll register our names during the week,' Max said. 'I'll let you know how it goes.'

He settled into a chair beside the camp bed and waved a hand around the room. 'You struck lucky, Ace. How'd you score a joint like this? Right next to a glass factory of all places?'

'It's a long, long story, bro.'

Rosalie snuggled into him. 'Does it have a happy ending?'

'I don't know yet.' He lifted her hand and kissed it. 'This is just the beginning.'

'I'm hooked already.'

'Then I'll tell you the rest, as long as you come up to Wanamalu with me.'

She adjusted the pillows against the wall and placed an arm around his shoulder, making them both comfortable.

'Fair exchange?' he asked.

'Fair exchange. I said I would.'

Max laughed aloud. 'And you're going to ask Dad for his approval? I can't wait to watch his reaction.'

'No way. I'll just go.'

'Then prepare to cop an earful when he finds out where you've been.'

'Never mind Dad. Go ahead, Ace.'

'Alright then. I'll start with the auction. I was about six. Imagine big mobs of farm machinery lined up at a fire sale on a farm outside Northampton. Some of it rusted out, the rest in working order, and my old mum—well, my much younger mum then—she spots this sit-down potter's wheel screaming for her to buy it. She couldn't resist it.

'So when it came up, she bid… and she was that keen she upped the bid because she thought someone else had raised her but no one had. She'd bid against herself and ended up paying more than she had to.' He grinned. 'She laughs about it now. She didn't then, but. Money was that short. She blew a dozen fuses because no one let her know about her mistake till after she'd paid.'

She'd bought it for the school, he explained, for the art and craft classroom. It was a broken-down potter's kick wheel and she had to learn to use it herself first. It had a wrecked electric motor his father dismantled and fixed. It took him two months to get the parts, so she had to learn how to sit at the wheel and kick-start it herself. Once she got the knack she was in her element, and her secondary career as a hand-crafted potter took off. One thing led to another.

Within a year, she had a wood-fired kiln and a pottery shed on the farm and she was selling the work she produced at the end of the driveway.

'She was a natural,' he said. 'She had a great eye and a wicked sense of colour with her glazes.'

She became so proficient people used to drive out to buy her work. She held her first exhibition in a gallery in Geraldton and won a number of blue ribbons with her bowls and vases at successive Perth Royal Shows.

'Quite the local celebrity, she became! She still takes on commissions now and then.'

'Where were you while this was going on?' Rosalie interrupted.

'In the thick of it, Rosie! She had me mixing the clay for her from day dot. Wet clay and dry clay—powdered, that was—brought in from Queensland. I can still feel it in my fingers—wedging it, kneading it like dough, getting the lumps and bubbles out, punching the shit out of it, by crikey.'

As he'd progressed, she'd showed him how to mix and apply the glazes, firing the ceramics in the kiln and nursing them down through the cooling process. She'd turned him into an expert by the time he'd reached his teens; worth his weight in gold.

'Throwing that clay onto a spinning wheel. You ever tried that? It's addictive, Rosie. There's a magic to it, centring the clay and working it up. You shoulda seen my first try when I was seven. What a mess! I was watching the old girl get better and better and developing the skills myself.

'Talk about hard work. Beats going to the gym. I had muscles like Hercules by the time I hit my teens. You couldn't tear me away from the wheel once I was on a roll, developing something from nothing but a lump of wet clay. Sunup to frigging sundown some days. The oldies, they always knew where to find me.

'By the time I got to high school the old girl was displaying some of my pieces in with hers... and selling them, too. We used to compete over who sold the most each month and there were times she had to admit I'd beaten her to the punch.'

Then he was introduced to Picasso and that was the making of him. His art teacher had looked over his work and thought he saw some potential. He gave him an American magazine one day—*Craft Horizons*, with illustrations of finely crafted and glazed Japanese and Korean raku vases and an article on Picasso, with photos of his off-centre chunky work and painted plates and pots. They struck an immediate chord.

'When I saw *them*, I was up and running. *Full bore*, let me tell you! That Swede Stig Lindberg was in there too with some of his work, and he clinched it for me. I've been a fan ever since.' He smiled thoughtfully.

'Next thing that teacher—Mr Argus his name was; John Argus—he arranged an interview for me with the Abschol committee. They were visiting the school from over east, wanting to promote Aborigines into uni. They picked me for one of the first-ever scholarships. Threw me in the deep end, chasing an art degree at Perth Tech, with units in Fine Arts at UWA for good measure.' He paused, gave them a wide grin. 'And here I am! Me! Close to qualifying!'

'So you are,' Max said, then nodded at the glass sculptures. 'That's interesting, but the glass?'

'Natural progression, bro. Two years ago, the Vic Park glassworks next door advertised among us Tech students for part-time helpers to join the team, working at the furnaces and off-siding the gaffers, blowing glass at the glory holes. How could I resist? Once I saw the raw melt being worked on, I was hooked. I knew I'd found my medium. It was countdown to blast-off, bro! I was up there with Yuri Gagarin!'

The Italian brothers who owned the glassworks had treated him like royalty, he said. He wasn't sure why.

'Maybe it's the skin. They're Sicilians—blacker than me, by crikey.'

Before migrating to Australia in the 1950s they'd trained in Venice in one of the famed Murano glassworks, he explained.

'The best experience you can get.' He gestured around the room. 'This used to be a storeroom full of junk. We cleared it out and they let me stay here free of charge, long as I help out in the glassworks and keep an eye on the place.'

'You've fallen on your feet,' said Max.

Lennard looked at Rosalie and squeezed her hand. 'You can say that again. Nothing's surer.'

In mid-November, the AAM recruiters contacted Max to advise him that all three had been selected to work for three months on a limited contract. Lennard, experienced on farm machinery, signed on with the scraper crew. Max was appointed grade checker to the surveyors and Rosalie, who took all her accumulated leave and was granted a further sabbatical, accepted a position in the first-aid post, assisting a charge nurse.

Early in December, they flew from Roebourne to the camp at the townsite planned for Mount Tom Price. The Cessna followed the fresh scars of gravel pits and bush tracks snaking between spinifex-covered coastal hills from the port construction works in Dampier towards the plains and mountain ranges beyond. To Lennard's eye, the pools along the creeks between the trees were heliographing an eye-catching welcome for him, like scattered mirror fragments as they caught the sun.

Then the plane's shadow winged across the creviced, ancient ironstone walls of the Karijini ranges. It banked over a crest, skimming the summit to glide into the neck of a valley beyond, an amphitheatre shadowed by surrounding peaks. The wheels bounced on the gravel airstrip raising dust, its peppery smell filling the still air as they climbed out into the late afternoon chill.

They clambered with their gear into the back of a slat-seated Acco truck with three other recruits and drove down the graded road to the tent encampment at the townsite. Flocks of pink and grey galahs feeding on the seeds of purple-flowered *Mulla Mulla* along the verge squawked in last-minute alarm at the spinning wheels.

Lennard's mind resonated with the choreography of the journey. This was the eastern edge of his mother's country and he felt himself opening up to the landscape. *I'm coming home*, he thought, *this time bringing with me the woman of my dreaming*.

Formalities over, Lennard and Rosalie walked along the track towards Mt Jarndunmunha in the last blaze of sunset, the facets of its rock bastion splashed in reds and golds. They sat beneath a ghost gum on its lower slopes, Rosalie wedged between his knees, her back to his chest, his arms around her. They did not speak as the olive greens and ochres of twilight deepened into darkness and stars swirled into view in astonishing profusion.

Rosalie was fascinated by the unfamiliar beauty of the landscape but intimidated by its vastness. She'd experienced the sensation once before when she visited Wanamalu, and now she leaned into Lennard, uncanny dread spreading through her. He felt her shiver and tightened his arms around her.

'I told you this is Mary's country,' he said. 'Remember the Nhanda song she sang when she introduced you to the ancestors at the Hutt lagoon? They'll keep you safe.' He gently rocked her. 'We'll have to find a pool for you to swim in like you did that day with her. That'll settle you down. You'll love it once you get used to it.'

They did not speak for several minutes. Then Rosalie broke the silence. 'Remember the fire tower? Remember what we saw that morning?'

'The dugite?'

'Yes, but how did you describe it?'

'A snake in paradise?'

'That's right, but for you, it metamorphosed into a whip, remember?'

'It did, and then you shut me up.'

'Can you blame me? We'd made love for the first time, and B&D's not my scene.' She gave a sudden throaty chuckle, 'But did you bring the handcuffs just in case?'

Lennard squeezed her shoulder. 'The snake appeared at the wrong moment.'

'It did.' She peered around at him. 'Snakes! Will I *ever* get used to them? Do you know what Max said when I told him about it?'

'Another quotation?'

'No.' She laughed. 'He said "Snakes, Rosie? Are you *afreud* of them?" Yes! I am. I can't stand them. What are they like up here?'

'There's plenty, but they'll leave you alone if you respect them. The king brown, she's the aggro one. Don't get her cornered or she'll go you. She's big and quick. She'll flatten out her head when she's on the charge, a bit like a cobra. The copperhead, she's shy, comes out at night. The green tree snake's harmless. She'll dance for you.

'As for the black-headed banded python, the *yididibarndi*, she's a beauty. She lives along the creeks. You pick her up by the tip of her tail and walk with her and she'll take you to water for a swim or when you're dying for a drink. The one you have to watch out for is the death adder.'

'Why?'

'She's small. She fits in the palm of your hand. She's quiet. She's fearless. She's got perfect camouflage and she strikes like lightning at anything within range. Her fangs are longer than most snakes and she'll rarely miss.'

'The death adder,' Rosalie shivered. 'I'll keep an eye out for her.'

'She's deadly.'

The next morning Lennard was drafted to the twelve-man earthworks crew working on the haul road to a gravel pit close to camp. He was assigned the role of spotter, directing a pair of scrapers spreading their loads on the newly graded surface. They'd give him time out, they told him, to learn how to operate one.

During the first smoko break, he met the team, surprised and pleased to find Tommy Mills among them, their leading hand. A part-Aboriginal from Wittenoom, he was nuggety and broad-shouldered, with canny smoke-grey eyes. His square face was cleanly shaven, his broad forehead topped by a crew cut. Light-skinned and laconic, the few words he spoke were directly to the point. He exuded self-contained toughness. He took no nonsense and people respected him.

At the end of the break, he took Lennard aside.

'Good to have you on my crew, brother,' he said. 'What's your mob? Nhanda or Malgana?'

'Malgana. How'd you pick that?'

'The blue eyes, even though you only got the one. Sure sign of your mob. I'm Yingardda from down Wooramel

River way, but I married a Banyjima sister from Wittenoom.' He looked shrewdly at Lennard. 'No special favours here, bro, except for one. That white sister I see in the first-aid post, she with you?'

'We're together, yes. That's Rosie.'

'Good. Just one thing. Any of these whitefellas here get the idea she's easy meat because she's chosen a blackfella and figures that gives them God's own permission to make a move on her, I'm right behind you. Anything you can't handle on your own, you let me know.' He gave a sardonic laugh. 'They don't call me the "Windmill" for nothing.'

'Thanks for the warning. And the support.'

'When they find out you're on my crew, I reckon they'll leave you both alone, but you put Rosie in the picture all the same.'

'I will.'

As the day wore on, waves of pleasure ran through him. He felt a deep sense of reassurance and connection to the red earth, to the spinifex and ghost gums, to the rock faces, to the kestrel hovering overhead and the shadow of the Square-tailed Kite he saw late in the afternoon, gliding against the blue before falling like a stone below the tree line and sweeping up again. Several times between scraper loads, he opened up his hands, palms up, and moved them slowly to his chest, inviting the country in.

He had come home.

THE SUN WAS higher now, so they moved to the bench shaded by the Norfolk Island pine on the lawn beside the glassworks. Lennard was deeply thoughtful, gathering himself. When he continued, his voice was charged.

'She died twenty-four years later,' he began, 'in Windjana Gorge, in the late afternoon. She was swimming in the pool beside the rock. I was reading on the sand. It was deadly quiet.'

A vehicle travelling at high speed on the main road revved down and swung into the campsite beside the entrance to the gorge. It was hidden from view. The engine shut down. The dust settled and there was silence.

He listened for the slamming of doors. Heard nothing. Alert, he stood and walked into the shallows.

'Someone's coming,' he told her. 'Maybe we should make a move.'

'Chicken,' she replied, floating on her back, her blue bikini exposed. 'Is it too cold for you?' She sprayed water at him through pursed lips, challenging him.

He looked around, uneasy, searching the trees a hundred metres away. There was no movement. No sound of approaching voices. No dogs. No excited children running towards them across the sand. No calls in greeting.

He rose to her challenge, as he always did, and dived in.

She was in his arms and they were both laughing when the first sharp crack of the shot that missed whipped overhead, twinned by an explosive thump that stunned Lennard, leaving him paralysed in shocked surprise.

And then he heard the deliberate four-beat click of a rifle reloading. His mind contracted in horror. How close was he? Which side of the river?

'Dive!' he shouted. 'Dive! Dive! Dive!'

His feet were in deep water. He had no leverage. He splashed clumsily, gripped her upper forearm vicelike to submerge her, shielding her body as she looked wildly around at him, her mouth wide and swallowing water, screaming an unheard question.

He went down with her.

The second shot thumped into the water, targeting the chaos of their churning bodies.

Unprepared and panicking, she tensed and arched her body, fighting for air as he dragged her farther down. Thrashing wildly, they broke the surface. He heard a third shot as he wrestled her beneath him, felt her shudder, saw a faint brown stain spread around them and she went limp.

He came up for air and dived at once, taking her with him, struggling to gain the shelter of the rock. Behind it, he took another breath and ducked, holding her beneath the surface, the water reddening around his open eyes. Then he surfaced, straining in the silence to hear the slightest sound, bringing her up with him.

He supported her beside him, where she floated motion-less, spread-eagled, groaning.

Seconds passed, an eternity, and then he heard the high-powered whine of a vehicle out on the main road approaching from the east. Before it reached them, a door slammed close by and the roar of an accelerating motor echoed down the gorge. He saw a trail of dust beyond the trees as the unseen vehicle tore down the driveway towards the entrance. It turned left and accelerated towards Fitzroy Crossing, tyres squealing.

Rosalie was alive but dazed and shuddering when he dragged her from the water. He laid her on the gravel at the far edge of the pool and screamed at her to stay with him, a purple hole below her clavicle pulsing blood he couldn't staunch, the shattered shoulder blade grinding beneath his fingers.

The bike was three hundred metres away downstream at the campsite. He picked her up and ran, stumbling across rocks and exposed tree roots in the riverbank. She looked blindly up at him, and he heard her whisper something that he didn't catch.

'Don't talk,' he panted. 'Don't talk.'

He struggled knee-deep across the river and up the other embankment bordering the campsite.

At the bike, he stretched her out and bound a towel around her upper torso. 'You'll be all right. Stay with me!' He forced the words between gritted teeth, each outcry a demented prayer. 'Stay with me!'

He threw on a pair of jeans, withdrew the belt and lifted her across the pillion, binding her to the backrest. Her body buckled forwards, then held, slanted sideways. He mounted the bike, started it and rolled forward, her bare feet juddering against the gravel as he steered towards the main road. There he stopped and lifted her legs across his thighs. They slid away. He tried again, again they slipped away. He reached back, tore a shirt from the pannier and used that to tie her ankles across his waist.

Then he opened up the throttle, engaged the cruise control and veered towards the Gibb River Road junction, forcing her against the backrest to hold her steady, drawing from her groans that echoed his.

The race towards the turnoff was a horrifying blur as he slid through rutted sand traps, accelerated across corrugations and fought the steering to hold the camber in the road. Cold panic rushed through him as her blood seeped down his back, spreading across his shoulders and his ribs. Now and then he rode one-handed as he adjusted her position on the pillion and the placement of her feet.

Then, careening round the bend at the turnoff, he swerved to avoid a Troop Carrier parked beside the road. A uniformed tour operator was lowering the jack after a tyre change, while two passengers were hoisting the flat tyre onto the roof rack. Another passenger with his back to them was urinating into the scrub.

'I need help!' Lennard shouted, gravel blasting across the vehicle as he braked and skidded to a stop.

They milled around him as he untied Rosalie and staggered with her to the vehicle. With terse efficiency, the tour operator swung open the split rear doors, assisted Lennard in lifting her inside, and parked the bike deep in the scrub off the verge.

He directed his passengers to climb aboard.

Lennard sat between the seats, Rosalie's head cradled in his lap, both hands pressing a rolled-up towel to the wound, listening to her faint, intermittent gasps as responses from Derby Hospital and the police crackled over the two-way. One of the tourists tended to her grazed feet.

An hour later they reached the hospital in the last light. Lennard carried her through the doors into Emergency, into waiting arms and onto a gurney. He followed them to the cubicle where they lifted her onto the bed.

Minutes later, an Aboriginal nurse looked back at him, her eyes wide with alarm, before she looked away.

He stood paralysed for a moment, then rushed forward. He brushed aside the team around her, took her face in both his hands and kissed her. And then, consumed with overpowering rage, he stumbled back out into the dusk shaking his fists and roaring at the sky, a prolonged involuntary howl drawn from deep within him.

Dazed, he staggered around the bitumen, thrusting aside the policeman who stepped forward to console him, before leaning against a parked ambulance, arms outstretched against the bonnet, head down and weeping as another thump of the defibrillator reached him.

Exhausted, he turned towards the hospital entrance and sat on the step, his head between his knees, heartbroken. A policeman detached himself from the watching group and settled next to him in silence. He placed a tentative arm across his shoulder. After several minutes he removed his arm but remained alongside Lennard in the gathering darkness.

It was pitch dark before he climbed to his feet and re-entered the hospital. He was directed to the mortuary, where they had washed her and laid her on a trestle. He leaned across to kiss her and then sat holding her hand until the cold of the morgue drove him out.

Showered and in borrowed overalls, ignoring a bed he was offered, he spent the night in the hospital canteen sleeping fitfully at one of the tables. At one point during the night, he called Phyllis and then Max, who was attending a conference in Sydney at the time. At daybreak, he barely recalled the conversations.

The next afternoon, after a long interrogation, the policeman drove him back down the Leopold Downs Road to retrieve his bike. They were silent for most of the journey, Lennard breaking down now and then, staring through the open window, his elbow on its sill, his thumb and forefinger squeezing shut his eyes.

'You sure you'll be all right?' the policeman asked when they reached the bike.

'I'll be okay.'

'We picked up your camping gear last night. It's back at the station.'

'Thanks. I'll follow you back.'

'We've heard the TRG boys nailed the gunman this morning, so you're safe. He was a German tourist, I understand. He shot two victims up at Timber Creek and another three on the Pentecost River. That's all we know so far.' He paused. 'I have to ask you this. What were you two doing out here when we put out warnings he was on the loose ten days ago and possibly heading this way?'

'We hadn't heard,' Lennard replied as they hauled the bike out to the road. 'When we're in the bush the outside world is the last thing on our minds.'

'You were lucky to find Barnesy and his group out here.'

'He saved my life, driving past when he did. Pity he wasn't ten minutes earlier.'

'He was running for cover from Fitzroy Crossing to be on the safe side. He took them over there from Broome for the weekend rodeo, but with all the hysteria he thought better of it. It was his duty of care.'

His duty of care! The words ran through him like fiery ice. Where had his duty of care left Rosalie?

He started the bike. He turned towards Derby to follow the police vehicle, but swung round on impulse and accelerated towards the ruins of the Lillimooloora homestead and the entrance to the gorge. Uncertain what had prompted him to ride back, he parked at the campsite.

He stepped over tape erected by the police and walked out to the rock.

He climbed to the shelf as the dusk descended and sat there through the night, bereft. At times, he felt he was the only man alive in a silent and indifferent world, denied the opportunity to farewell her; at others, crushed by guilt that he hadn't died in her place.

The persistent thought assailed him that he'd led her to her death; that he hadn't saved her, despite his desperate attempts. Consumed with anguish, he fought to keep his grief at bay before submitting to it now and then and breaking down.

Sunlight seeped into the gorge at last, taking the edge off the chill and brightening the cliffs. He climbed stiffly down from the rock. He washed in the pool, staring bleakly down at his reflection as each cupped handful of water fractured its surface, then turned and walked away.

Before crossing the tape, he gazed back and he was mesmerised. The cliffs were alight, the rock between them a glittering monument of glass between walls of fire. It was a setting she loved. One that summoned up her presence. A sacred place that held her now, making her eternal. And the thought pierced him—*I must pick up the pieces.*

His vigil through the night had been a cry for courage. He would not shroud in silence a martyrdom not of her choosing.

LENNARD LEANED FORWARD, staring at the ocean. Stefan broke the silence, 'The shooter, Ace? Did they confirm it was the German tourist?'

He shook his head. 'Not for certain. The cops believed it was, but without proof, the coroner signed off with an open verdict. They never found the cartridges and I didn't see the vehicle. Neither did Barnesy. So who knows?' He hesitated, then said, 'There were some half-wits who suspected it was an accident and I was involved, for God's sake!' He straightened up and looked at Stefan. 'Max thought it was political. Still does. Someone with a personal grudge. There was talk of it in his legal circles, he told me.'

'I'm sorry.'

Lennard shook his forefinger. 'No, no. None of that.'

Stefan bit his tongue as he recalled Lennard mentioning twenty thousand at Tullamarine… twenty thousand and one.

'When I told people I was going back to the gorge with Rosie's ashes soon after her cremation, people thought I'd lost it,' Lennard went on.

'Is that what you did?'

'Yes.'

WHEN LENNARD ANNOUNCED his decision to spread Rosalie's ashes across the pool beside the rock, he received a mixed reception. He was prepared for it. He'd thought it through and ignored friends who suggested it was too soon, that he should wait for the coroner's verdict, that another 2,500 kilometre journey to the Kimberley aboard the Harley was risky in his present frame of mind.

When Max surprised him with the warning the assassin

might still be out there, Lennard said he had to stare down his demons. 'When you're down you don't roll over. You get back up and you look your enemy in the eye.'

Max placed a hand on his shoulder and held it there. 'Nothing changes, Ace. She's still putting words in your mouth.'

'No, she's not,' and then he conceded, 'but if she does, I'll be listening.'

'You're still attentive to a fault. Now she's gone you really think you'll call the shots?'

'Bro, we were a team. Now the buck stops with me.'

Lennard had Phyllis's blessing though. Aware that Rosalie would have approved, she'd silenced David's objection that the gorge was inappropriate.

'We have to give this idea more thought,' he'd protested as they prepared for bed the night Phyllis told him. 'It's hardly rational under the circumstances.' He had slowly unknotted his tie, his eyes flashing as he'd tested her resolve. 'It's a so-called sacred site, is it not? We won't be welcome. And Jandabloodymarra! We both know his murderous history. I won't go near the place, so I'll have nowhere to mourn her. She's our daughter! Have you thought of that?' He'd whipped the tie from around his neck. 'Why in God's name return her ashes to the place she died? It makes no sense.'

Phyllis was having none of it. 'Because Rosie loved it there. That's where she went to recharge her batteries. It was her spiritual home. She told me so herself, with prophetic irony, now I come to think about it. "When I'm there I come alive like there's no tomorrow." They were her exact words.'

She'd removed her emerald earrings and loosened her silver hair with an irritable shake of her head. 'And another thing, you can't continue censuring Rosalie's relationship with Lennard now she's dead. Let it go! You can't blame him for what's occurred.' The explosive *clack* as she'd snapped shut the lid of the mother-of-pearl shell case into which she'd dropped her earrings echoed like a gunshot. 'Besides, she always said Luke was conceived there.'

SHOCKED BY THE news of his mother's death, though spared the details, eleven-year-old Luke was unnerved and disbelieving. Confused by Lennard's despair and occasional bursts of outrage, the boy longed for reassurance, distrustful of the sympathy shown by unfamiliar people among the gathering of friends and relatives in the house.

Dazed and withdrawn, his feelings swerved between paralysing numbness and surges of grief he fought with teeth clenched until he was alone when his tears fell hot and uncontrolled, an unbearable admission against his will that Rosalie had been torn from his life for good.

At the funeral service, he was disturbed by the touching eulogies and the scattered laughter that greeted stories of her humour and her sense of irony, then he was transfixed by the remorseless glide of the coffin towards the red velvet curtains that opened and then closed to the melancholy thrum of Lennard's didgeridoo.

When Lennard invited him to ride pillion on the Harley for the journey north, he latched onto the prospect with unrestrained excitement. He unfolded the well-worn road map dusted with red fingerprints that Lennard handed him and explored their route, running a finger along the highway and sidetracks, examining the stopovers that Rosalie had marked on it over the years, reading the barely legible notes she'd pencilled in—*Look out for feral foxes*; *Fresh water in the gnamma hole on Grey's Road*; *Threadfin salmon in season*, among them.

Luke's twelfth birthday fell on the day following the cremation and he agreed to postpone its celebration until after their return. For days, he suppressed the image of roaring furnace jets torching his mother, picturing her ghostlike instead, as she lit twelve candles for him a month late.

'YOU WILL TAKE good care of her,' Phyllis said on the morning of their departure, before adding, 'I know you will.'

She held the front door open, allowing Lennard to cross the veranda carrying the rectangular jarrah urn with great care in both hands. She reached out to touch him as he passed. 'I wish I was coming with you.'

Lennard descended the limestone steps and strode to the carport, his riding boots crunching wet gravel. When he reached the Harley, he retrieved a beach towel draped across the seat. He wrapped it around the urn, then paused to feel its weight and his heart was wrenched as he recalled Phyllis's whisper the day they'd collected the ashes from the funeral parlour.

'Sweet Jesus,' she'd murmured, dry-eyed, her face drained, 'she weighs the same as she did the day she was born.'

He glanced up at Phyllis in the doorway, intertwined gold dragons breathing fire across her satin dressing gown. Her face was filled with concern, her eyes locked on his as though reading his thoughts.

Suppressing a surge of anguish, he secured the package upright within the pannier. His hand rested there a moment. *So it's come to this*, he thought, then shut the lid.

'Time to go, my beauty,' he said. 'Time to go.'

Overnight showers had fallen across the garden. Lennard glanced up at the line of clouds lifting. 'Like a row of can-can dancers showing off their blue knickers,' he imagined Rosalie saying, and the thought of her continuing, 'stonewashed denim, no doubt, with everyone hoping for see-through lace,' brought a wry smile.

A breath of wind rustled through the leaves of two olive trees lining the driveway, airbrushing sunlight across them. He'd raised a sweat twelve years ago, digging the holes, and Rosalie had planted the saplings into the reeking mulch he'd brought back from his father's stables. She'd ceremonially watered them in. 'Now you won't have to pee on them,' she'd joked.

'Why not? My magic formula's never failed. Ask the lemon tree.'

'So that's your secret?' Rosalie had opened up the tap and turned the hose on him in a swirling figure of eight. 'And here's me thinking it was your green thumb.'

Lennard straddled the bike and settled into the seat. He reached for his helmet propped on the fuel tank and adjusted the intercom built into it, before cramming his hair under its rim. He lifted the visor and looked round at Luke clattering down the steps, unrecognisable in his brand-new black leathers and top-heavy in his helmet. Lennard shifted his broad frame forward, allowing Luke to clamber aboard, then switched on the intercom.

'There's a stack of room for both of us,' he said. 'Lean into the backrest. Make yourself comfortable. Now try talking.'

'I can't see around you, Dad.' Luke's complaint crackled.

'Come on, Superman, power up your x-ray vision.'

Luke clicked his tongue twice, turning imaginary switches at each temple. 'That's better. Now I can see around corners.'

'No need for a periscope, then. You all set? Make sure you hang on tight.'

PHYLLIS RAISED A hand as the bike roared into life. It whined into gear and slid forward off its stand as Leonard manoeuvred it up the driveway. Beneath the olives, a stronger gust showered droplets on both riders in epaulettes of sunlit sparks.

Out on Bellevue Terrace Lennard turned right and slowed to a stop. He looked back and raised both hands, all ten digits extended. Then he pulled on his gloves and lowered the helmet visor before accelerating out of view.

She listened to the characteristic thump of the motor as they roared up onto Swanbourne Street beyond the crest above the house until it blended into the early morning rumble of distant traffic.

She gathered herself, locked the door behind her and made her way back through the silent house she'd agreed to look after while they were away. She took an apple from the bowl on the table in the passageway, polishing it against her hip as she crossed the lounge. She looked up at the photograph of Rosalie and stood on tiptoe to transfer a kiss to its glass frame with her fingertips.

'They're their way at last my darling,' she murmured.

On the back veranda, she wrapped her dressing gown tightly about her before sitting on the top step. She called for Freya, and the dog, confused by the disappearance of her mistress, warily climbed the steps before settling beside her and allowed her to stroke a shoulder. They sat on the top step sharing an uneasy silence, as awkward as newly acquainted strangers.

She took a bite from the apple as she contemplated the coming day. She considered waking David, then changed her mind. Another half-hour wouldn't hurt. Give the ocean and the city outspread below her time to come to sun-warmed life.

IT WAS A painful journey. Lennard imagined Rosalie with him, reliving shared moments as they visited her favourite places along the way—the empty sands of Sandalwood Bay; the reefs of Ningaloo; the pools beyond the railway bridge on the Fortescue River where flotillas of red-beaked black swans cruised effortlessly midstream until alarmed by pebbles Luke skipped across the surface; the gorges of Karijini, shaded streams deep within them icy; the night sea sweeping in towards the windswept dunes at Cape Keraudren.

It took some time for Lennard to get used to Luke's movements behind him, the weight of his body at his back when he slept, his waking now and then with a start, as Rosalie used to.

The sound of Luke's voice over the intercom disturbed him. He expected her voice, her lively commentary, her throaty laughter that set him alight.

At one point he caught the sound of Luke humming and the uncanny echo was reminiscent of Rosalie's favourite song, 'Warm Sweet Breath of Love'. Lennard loved to hear her sing it and he was overcome. He pulled over to the verge and parked for a minute to distract Luke, their arrival disturbing a mob of scrawny sheep that clattered across the gravel and vanished into the scrub.

They reached Windjana Gorge in five days. It was late afternoon and the place was deserted. They set up camp, then waded barefoot across the river and climbed to the shelf on the rock, where they sat in the quiet till dusk, when the light took on the clarity Rosalie admired, turning the rock into polished marble and the pool a deep silver-green as the shadows lengthened on the cliffs.

Lennard unscrewed the wooden urn and found the sealed plastic capsule inside. He had no idea how to open it. Screwdriver in one hand, container in the other, momentarily at a loss, he imagined Rosalie's gentle mockery. 'Same old story, Ace—it takes a woman. Here, it's a no brainer.' He turned the urn over and, as though she'd pointed it out, he spotted the concealed line of the seal that he prised open.

He spilled a handful of her ashes into his palm, closed his fingers, kissed her farewell and stood. Luke followed his lead. They scattered her ashes across the pool and the finer particles drifted before settling in a circle that widened over the water, spreading around her, it seemed, as her hair used to, in a shawl of silk around her face. He imagined her laugh as she'd invited him into the pool that last time, her slender sunburned body treading water green as glass beneath her.

He reached into his shirt pocket for a letter he had written to her while she'd been swimming the first time he'd brought her here, twenty-four years before. He'd watched her wade into the pool, easing into the deeper gulley at its centre. As the water had closed around her, he'd felt his hands on her, his fingers the water's caress, his palms the pool's liquid touch. He'd handed her the letter when she climbed out. She'd stood as she read it, pearls of water rolling down her skin, onto the paper and onto him.

Then she'd looked down at him, cross-legged on the sand. 'I'm flattered,' she'd said, nudging his lower ribs with her toe. 'This reads like a commitment, all the bells and whistles. And I have it in writing! Now you're really in the deep end. Sure you can handle it?'

He didn't know that she had kept it. She was no magpie, but when he'd sorted through her belongings, he'd found it in a drawer. The ink had blurred where the droplets had struck.

He unfolded the page and swam out to the circle of ashes, where he released it. The paper gathered globes of water and slipped beneath the surface, washing away his words as though erasing her epitaph.

When he climbed out, his body was streaked with ash.

Later, with Luke asleep and snoring gently beyond the firelight, Lennard felt for the first time reconciled to the fearful emptiness that had swept over him the night she'd died. He sat on his haunches before the embers, stirring them with a green stick, releasing a torrent of sparks. Magical sparks, he mused, stirred with a green wand, its smouldering end wisping like a stick of incense that smelled of citronella and kept the sandflies at bay. Beside him the rock, now black as obsidian, was glazed by the dying fire.

He remembered her with the letter in her hand, looking down at him that day, her eyes mischievous as she'd reached round to release the clasp on her bikini top. She'd removed it and held it out between thumb and forefinger as she'd patted the rock with her free hand. 'I think we should set this in stone, right here, right now,' she'd said. 'Don't you?'

Now, for the first time, he felt the cold. He stood and walked barefoot across the sand towards the overhang of trees to find more firewood. Partway there, the glint on the jagged stripes of a still, coiled shape caught his eye. Alert, he hesitated—a death adder.

He slowly backtracked and retrieved the folding shovel beside his sleeping bag. He locked the blade into place and, with both hands on the shaft, cautiously retraced his steps.

The snake was motionless and then, as though sensing his return, it raked back its head like a wound spring to strike across the thick coil of its body. He leaned forward, lifted the shovel, then changed his mind. He took another step forward, inserted the shovel into the sand, lifted the snake. As it uncoiled to escape across the blade, he manoeuvred the shovel to hold it there and carried it to the tree line, where he flicked it into the undergrowth.

'Live, you little *thayadi*,' he said. 'Like I have to.'

He dragged a dry branch back to the fire, snapped it in two and laid both pieces on the embers. When the fire crackled into life, he reached for the empty urn and placed it among the flames that flared green and blue as they darted around its base, the lacquer smoking.

As he watched, the moon sailed free of cloud and bathed the gorge in uncanny light, turning the rock into a monument once again—the monument in glass he'd visualised once before. He crossed the shallows and leaned against it, both arms outstretched for balance, the quartz still warm, the water freezing. He remained there for several minutes, spellbound.

At one point he imagined Rosalie calling out, 'Hey! Sisyphus! You may never shift it, but don't stop trying. And don't do your back in. I need you in good nick.'

He climbed to the shelf, where he sat and waited for the breaking dawn. It was not over. It would never be over. But it was done.

LENNARD

ONE AFTERNOON IN LATE March, Max O'Sullivan appeared unexpectedly at the glassworks. He'd been negotiating with the Minister for Lands for a lease on the grassed half-acre on the banks of the Swan River beside the Narrows Bridge, on which Lennard was determined to place the cenotaph.

Lennard had explained to Stefan why he considered it the perfect location. 'It's a sacred site next to the Old Swan Brewery, in full view of King's Park. The Whadjuk Nyungar call the place Goonininup. They've given us the green light as long as we tread lightly and don't disturb the *Wagyl*—the sacred rainbow serpent. That's the spot where the Poms first landed upriver in 1829. They saw chief Yellagonga's campsite by the freshwater spring there and stepped ashore to meet him.'

He took a long breath, expelled it through his teeth. 'And so the invasion began. I want our dead to stand witness to that first *wajbala* bootprint.' He scrutinised Stefan for several uncomfortable moments. 'Hey! That's a lookup for the books.' He raised a triumphant fist. 'You've been here for two months and you didn't flinch at the word invasion! We're making progress, brudda.'

'Must be something in the air.' Stefan grinned. 'You think you'll get permission?'

'Trouble is it's a heritage site. That means the Minister for Works *and* the Minister for Heritage are both involved. The red tape's a nightmare. That's not all. It's directly below the Anzac memorial. That makes it political dynamite.' Then he growled, 'All the more reason.'

Stefan was flat out, pouring a measure of cornflower blue glass pellets into the vat, absorbed in the glittering fall of the beads. When he looked around he was startled to see Max squatting on his haunches behind him. He was fending off Skathi excitedly licking his face.

Stefan saw the still, sharp face of a fox—small, sunburned brown, quick, his cropped hair dark copper, his scalp tanned beneath it. His eyes were yellow-green in the workshop light, ironic humour lurking. In contrast, two deep vertical lines between his eyebrows gave him a relentless air; he was not to be messed with. His lips seemed sun-freckled and his long neck sinewy and wind-burned. He appeared half-starved and somehow battle-hardened, straight from the desert, at home among dry creeks and scorched rocks, used to travelling rapidly across the treacherous no man's land between evaporating waterholes.

Then Max grinned and laughter lines curved from the corners of his eyes, his sudden smile like water welling into sand. An eye tooth missing on the right lent him a comical, roguish look.

'Max O'Sullivan.' His voice rang deep and clear. 'You need a hand?'

Lennard appeared alongside him, exotic as Bluebeard. He'd been using the sander; his cheeks and shoulders powdered in fine blue dust. A facemask hung around his neck, safety goggles balanced on his forehead. He had a plate of Alicia's lamingtons in one hand, two coffee mugs in the other.

'Well, bless the Pope, Ace—*nyinda ngugurnu*? How are you, you old bastard?'

'Good to see you, Max. I see you two've met.'

Max gave an explosive laugh. 'You look like a black and blue minstrel about to break into the blues—Al Jolson jamming with Johnny Lee Hooker.'

Still on one knee as though genuflecting and waving an imaginary straw hat, he sang in a hoarse but tuneful baritone with a captivating resonance—

'Oh! So-ho-nny boy!

Well Mama chopped the snake up and she put it in the stew,

Told you it was ox-tail when she served it up to you

You got to drink the home brew down and go… my sonny boy, uh-huh!

You got to drink the home brew down and go,

Before she tells you that she pissed in there as well, my sonny boy!

Oh! So-ho-nny boy!'

Lennard looked good-humouredly down at him. 'You got your timing right as usual bro, to the minute. There's lamingtons for smoko and you turn up, skinny as a roo-dog like you still got worms. *Nyinda thalbadi? Nyinda ngarniya* coffee?'

'*Yungganangana wigimutha manga.* You can give me a cold beer if you like. But if you're out, a coffee'll do the trick. You like the song?'

'Don't give up your day job till you get the land deal signed for us.'

Lennard offered him a lamington and turned to Stefan. 'We warned you about this bloke, but you haven't seen his jaw in action yet. Better get your share, bro, before he eats the lot.'

Stefan shook loose the last of the beads stuck to the base of the measuring urn. He wiped his fingers across his T-shirt and shook Max's hand.

Max looked down at the cobalt dye smeared across his palm. 'What's this? Woad?' He gestured at the circle of head-high multi-coloured glass statuettes standing like misshapen obelisks in the middle of the floor. 'You look like a couple of druids about to sacrifice a virgin or two in Glasshenge. Whose heart are you ripping out this time? The ugly one who's still intact? The sexy second-hand one who's had a skin graft? Or the ninety-five-year-old wearing pantyhose?'

'That was the Aztecs, dickhead.'

'Alicia will appreciate it, then. She'll be happy to know you're spilling blood for Quetzal-what's-his-name and the sun'll rise tomorrow on another day in Chihuahua.' He bit voraciously into the lamington and continued through a mouthful. 'I'm afraid I've got news that won't please you, Ace. *Ngatha ngangguyanu yuganga…* I heard our application was chucked out at last night's meeting. I went to see the minister this morning and found out we've been shafted.'

He took another bite. Carefully breaking off a piece of sponge cake from its centre, he offered it to Skathi, which she delicately took, and then he crammed the rest into his mouth, licked his fingers and reached for another.

'We were rejected without so much as a by your leave, apparently. The site we want is reserved for a car park, according to the committee. They've allocated us a plot on Heirisson Island instead, next to Yagan's statue.'

'*Heirisson Island?*' Lennard roared. 'That's a bloody insult! No one will see it there.'

'Yeah. I figured that was coming.'

'Out of sight out of bloody mind, as usual.' Lennard fumed. 'They make my blood boil, those bastards in denial.'

'Chill, Ace, chill. Don't go ballistic. You'll have a coronary. We'll have to go higher. Talk to the premier. We'll soar with the vulture and leave the dodos where they belong—so far out of tune with the times they deserve their extinction.'

Lennard held himself in check. 'If they won't give us the time of day, we'll stick the boot in where their mothers never kissed them, when it'll have some effect—Stadium Australia, before the opening of the Olympics. With the world watching. It'll be the perfect place for a showdown.' He scratched his chin through his beard, dislodging a faint shower of blue flakes. 'We'll set up another tent embassy with an open invite to the foreign journos to have a yack with us. That'll euchre the committee, for sure. They'll pack the shits.'

Max turned to Stefan. 'Sounds like the black brother's

contemplating blackmail and that may be appropriate,' he said, 'but there's a lot we can do before that. We can do some lobbying. Make noises in high places. Squeaky wheels get the good oil, the higher up you go.'

'Or fall off,' Lennard suggested.

'Yeah, that too.'

With one hand he offered himself the last of the lamingtons and with the other, he accepted it.

'*Ngatha bulyarru.* I'm starving and you blokes are too slow. Besides Alicia'll take this as a compliment to her baking.'

'That'll be the day,' Lennard replied as Max handed him the empty plate. 'She'll probably hope you choke on it. *Nyinda bulanu nganiyanu?* Sure you've had enough?'

Max walked around the circle of glass statuettes, inspecting them. For weeks now they'd been firing experimental mixes using traditional components and different metals, casting sculptures in moulds of wet olivine sand, exulting over unexpected colours and patterns emerging as they cooled. When they stood them upright, concentric circles and ellipses and half-moons swirled within them like oil spreading across water in a peacock sheen.

Earlier, they'd abandoned the idea of using garnet in the batch. To Lennard's dismay, each successive experimental melt had reverted to a viscous black mess they'd had to cart away and dump. Stefan's pessimistic predictions had proved correct. They'd saved the surplus garnet for use with the waterjet for cutting and polishing and they'd cancelled further orders.

'Looks like you blokes've been putting in the hard yards with the stone that flows,' Max commented.

'Flat out,' Lennard replied.

'Lizards drinking,' Stefan added.

'That hard? No bullshit.' He turned and gestured at the largest of the statuettes. 'Is this for sale?'

Lennard laughed. 'Don't tell me you're developing an eye for a good investment in your old age?'

'I couldn't afford your prices, Ace.'

Lennard pointed out a sledgehammer among the tools beneath the bench. 'They're experiments, bro. We'll be breaking them into chunks of cullet and refiring them later.'

Max ran a hand down its surface. He tracked the shadow of his fingers gliding among the colours. 'That's interesting. The shapes and colours change as you move. They dissolve and reappear like you've trapped chaos in there, caught in a state of flux. They're like those paintings that eyeball you as you walk around the room and you wonder what you've done to deserve the attention.'

He circled the sculpture, his silhouette whirling as he peered into it. And then, against the far wall, he spotted the clay replica of the rock that Lennard had modelled. Scaled at five to one, it was baked brown, nondescript; an anthill a metre high. The full-sized mould for the monument would be based on its proportions.

'What's this?' he asked, walking over to it.

'The rock. A model,' Lennard explained.

Max looked back at Lennard, incredulous. 'Well fuck me sideways! Is *this* what all the fuss is about? This piece of dinosaur shit? Where'd you find it? Next to the Stegosaurus tracks on Gantheaume Point?'

'I knew you'd recognise it, Max. You're always up to your neck in it.'

'That's a turn-up for the books. You're always telling me I don't know shit from clay.' Max glanced at Stefan. 'The Trickster Ace strikes again. The sorcerer Prospero and his apprentice Ariel turn cretaceous dinosaur-do into glass and a pile of shit becomes a masterpiece. Ingenious! Or ingenuous! *Such stuff as dreams are made on*!'

He zipped his mouth shut with thumb and forefinger. 'If this is the secret of your success, my lips are sealed. It's safe with me. *Your rough magic is a potent art* and no one will ever know your inspiration came from the back end of Tyrannosaurus Rex.' He grinned broadly. 'The dark matter of the unconscious; you focus on faeces and create order from ancient ordure. I won't ask what sort of music you've arranged for the opening ceremony. Thunderous, no doubt. Who's composing it for you, Ace? Awesome Wells? A symphony for his back-passage didgeridoo?'

He walked back to them, brushing flecks of coconut from his mouth.

Lennard turned to Stefan. 'How can I top that? Awesome was a friend we worked with in the Pilbara in the sixties. He had trouble with flatulence.'

'To put it politely mate,' Max added. 'He had a supreme gift for the timely fart, a God-given talent for blowing an argument away. And he never hesitated to use it. What was it he used to say, Ace? "I think your idea stinks! Let me far-ticulate one of mine! You want to hear me turn fart into art? Eff off!" And we did. He'd clear the room in no time flat.' He rubbed his temple with a forefinger. 'What's Prospero's take on it? *I have required some heavenly music, which even now I do, to work mine end upon their senses, that this airy charm is for.*'

Glancing at his watch, he passed between them. 'Talking of which, *ngatha yaninyina*. It's time to rock 'n roll.'

He strode to the door with Skathi loping alongside, looking up as though begging him to stay. He gave a brief wave. 'I'll keep in touch.'

He was a frilled dragon, Stefan thought as he disappeared—small and fearless and quick to take on the world with controlled and comical fury.

'I see you're on the run as usual,' Lennard shouted, 'and

thanks for leaving us some lamingtons. At least you spared us more of your Shakespeare, for once.'

Max's shadow reappeared in the doorway and he strode jauntily back to them. 'You want some more Will Shakescene? Don't tempt me, Ace. But I forgot. I've got some good news from Tassie you'll be pleased to hear, and it's reminded me of this Tassie joke that's doing the rounds. Stop me if you've already heard it. It goes like this.

'There's this forty-five-year-old Sydney accountant who's been working his arse off in the city and he has a nervous breakdown. Mid-life crisis, bi-polar manic depression, suicidal tendencies, the works. He decides it's time to quit the world. So he sells up the Pittwater house, divorces his wife and kids, packs his bag and heads for Hobart. Then he makes a beeline for the backwoods. Backwoods? I'm talking *wilderness* here. He buys a property south of Wynyard and west of nowhere, a few goats, fruit trees and scrawny chickens, all thirty kilometres from the nearest neighbour he avoids like the plague. Somewhere he can drink with the flies.

'Six months pass. Nine. A year.

'He slowly regains his sanity. He discovers what it means to survive. He learns to live with his solitude, to tolerate his own company and the goats. Then one afternoon, there's an unexpected knock on the door. A horse is tethered to the veranda rail and a big, red-bearded hillbilly in torn jeans and a red check shirt's looking through the flyscreen door. A mirror image of *him* by then!

'"I've come to invite you to the party we're having," says the stranger, "to welcome you to Tassie. You're the guest of honour."

'*Well!* The guest of honour! It's been over a year, he thinks. He's been in solitary long enough. What the hell, it's time to get out and socialise, meet the neighbours.

"'Sounds good," he replies.

"'Has been known for there to be plenty of drinkin' at these parties," says the hillbilly.

"'I'm an ex-accountant. I used to go to conferences and drink everyone under the table. I can hold my own with the booze."

"'Has been known for there to be fightin' sometimes."

"'I'm a trained negotiator. I can talk my way out of trouble."

"'Has been known to end up with an orgy of wild, wild sex."

"'Now that I'll *really* look forward to. It's been a year between drinks. What's the dress code?"

"'Come as you are."

"'Come as I am?"

"'Yup. There'll only be the two of us.'"

They burst into laughter as Max raised a hand to silence them. 'That news from Tassie, Ace—there's been progress this week in the talks with the trustees of the British Museum to repatriate Truganini's skin and hair and those two bundles of Tasmanian cremation ashes. Once the legislation's in place they'll all be coming home.' He paused as the news sank in. 'How d'you like *them* green apples? The Palawa *pukana* have had a field day.'

'About time!' Lennard burst out. 'I hadn't heard. The Palawa will be rapt to get them back.'

'They're over the moon. Then there's Yagan's skull, of course. You know the delegation's bringing him back to Perth in August. At least, that's the plan.' Max gave a sardonic laugh. 'With all that blackfella magic around it's no wonder the pommy curators are concerned about losing their marbles.'

He turned towards the door. 'Nice meeting you, Stefan. Watch out for the big fella. Don't let him put one over on you. *Marugudu ngatha nyinda gutharra nangiyanmanha.* I'll catch you both later.'

He disappeared for the second time into the afternoon glare. Skathi sat in the doorway looking across the lawn as he walked towards his Toyota Troop Carrier, in two minds whether or not to join him, but she trotted obediently back to Lennard when he whistled, her tail a metronome signalling she knew on which side her bread was buttered.

'So that's Max.'

'None other,' Lennard replied as he pulled on his goggles and fired up the sander. 'Don't tell me we didn't warn you. They made him and then they broke the mould. I reckon they did us all a favour. Rosie used to swear they should have broken it with him still in it.'

THAT EVENING, WHILE Lennard was shutting down the workshop, Stefan took out his notebook to write up the formulae used in the morning's glass pour, as he had since his arrival. He looked down at previous entries on the page, rubbing the pencil on the benchtop to sharpen its edge. Then he turned impulsively to the back page and jotted down Max's anecdote.

He completed the passage before recording the day's formulae and observations in the front. Then he flicked through all the pages. The diffusion coefficients measuring the reactions of elements in the liquid glass in the furnace and the temperatures at which unexpected hues materialised during the cooling were scribbled on the opening pages. He was familiar with the formulae, had used them all his working life. And now, in the back, was Max's joke.

As Lennard turned out the lights, Stefan recalled Max's reference to Yagan's skull. During his first week in the glass-works, Lennard had explained that Yagan was a Nyungar Whadjuk Ballaroke warrior of high degree, a murderer according to the British settlers, with a substantial reward

on his head. He had been shot in 1833 by a teenager he'd
befriended, and his severed head was sent to England to be
measured and probed and sketched and weighed in the name
of scientific enlightenment. Now the question struck Stefan
like a blow—*Who was it spent three patient months smoking
Yagan's skull for that investigation?*

He reopened the back of the notebook and began writing
in the half-dark. Who was it crouched at the smouldering
eucalyptus trunk in which he'd wedged Yagan's head, his
clothes reeking of red gum wood-smoke and charred flesh,
breathing the nauseous stench of scorched skin as the eyes
burst, the face shrivelled and the hair singed? Had his hands
been blackened as he'd removed the trophy at last? Had he
held it at arm's length on the stick he'd poked through an eye
socket, turning it this way and that as he'd judged the result of
his skill and estimated the price it would fetch?

Had his own skin tanned as he'd watched and waited, his
eyes blinded by the smoke? And did he later learn that the
skull, thanks to his handiwork, served antiquarian Thomas
Pettigrew in his London residence as a dinner table ornament,
a fascinating conversation piece adorned with two feathers of
a red-tailed black cockatoo? And later, according to rumour,
as a paperweight for an Oxford craniologist who prepared an
article on the skull's phrenology to determine its evolutionary
classification as savage or barbarian for the coming edition of
London's *Literary Review* before it ended up in the archival
cellars of Liverpool museum and eventual burial in Everton
Cemetery in a plywood box, packed in there with a Maori
skull and a mummified Peruvian child?

And the trapezoid slice of skin bearing intricate tribal
scars of seniority that ran across his back and shoulder, flayed
from his corpse and tanned as a memento, where was that? In
the dusty recesses of an antique shop in Chelsea or Tottenham

Court Road, stitched into a unique shade for a Regency lamp-stand or fashioned into a stylish handbag?

Stefan looked up at the window. *Even a murderer with several killings under his belt deserved better than that*, he thought. *But those were the times. The settlers were here to stay and meant business. The Nyungar had to learn the hard way that British common law now governed their lives and protected settler land tenure and property ownership.*

Lennard had previously mentioned that it may have been a servant assigned to settler Henry Bull who'd carried out the smoking. Or had it been Ensign Robert Dale, who'd transported the skull to England?

He felt a surge of revulsion.

He stifled it.

It began to rain, a light drumming at first, deepening to a summer thunderstorm that swept across the channel. The solid grey sheet roared in from the sea, turning Bathers Beach to foam and bringing down the night, pulses of sheet lightning flaring at its core. The roof thundered.

He was deafened by the workshop's percussive detonation. Then he heard Lennard call out and saw the flash of his torch. For a moment he could not move. *How does Lennard deal with despair when it comes upon him? By what chemistry did he turn his powerlessness to outrage when he was young?*

He watched Lennard pace the workshop, his shadow swooping across the walls like some avenging archangel. He was shielded by his purpose, by the actions through which he declared himself. And by his humour. He was single-minded even as his torch shimmered over the circle of statuettes and swept across the sand moulds and the kilns and the windows as he checked the locks.

He recalled part of Lennard's impassioned argument during the reconciliation debate on SBS the previous September—'You wonder how my people survived for sixty thousand years across this continent?' his voice had rung out. 'They were stoics! They were resilient! They were raised in an ancient culture red in tooth and claw, with close kinship and self-reliance at its core! They knew that independence and selflessness weren't contradictory characteristics. They had the brothers to draw on, and the sisters. They were tough. They laughed at life.

'How could they not survive? They were bound to country and lived uncompromisingly by the law. Those characteristics are in our DNA, so we've survived the last two hundred years as well. Even though most of us were displaced and exiled to missions and reserves after resistance had been beaten out of us. We learned to adapt and bide our time.' He paused. 'Well, let me tell you now, our time has come!'

Lennard called out to him once more. Stefan put the notebook into his rear pocket and tracked the flashlight to the door. He looked back as lightning flared. Wall to wall, the workshop was momentarily ablaze and he was blinded. The burst of thunder was directly overhead and, when sight returned, the glassworks was enveloped in a smoky darkness.

He worked his way towards the exit and Lennard opened an umbrella they shared as they walked into rain that beat into their faces. The wind snapped at its blue and white panels. Behind them, waves thumped on the sand and slewed up the face of the seawall, spindrift spraying across the lawns. Along the Esplanade, the pavements gleamed in successive pools of streetlight and they stepped across water gliding down the gutters in quicksilver rivulets, the wet trees glinting.

'What kept you back there?' Lennard asked.

'I was writing up the notebook,' Stefan replied, then added, 'I took down Max's joke and made some notes on Yagan. From now on, I'm recording the things we talk about. It'll help me come to terms with how I think.'

'How you think? You're not sure?'

'It'll focus the questions I need answers to. It'll help me understand the things I need to know,' he gestured into the darkness, 'in the context of the rock.'

Lennard's teeth flashed. 'Whatever it takes, bro.' He placed an arm across Stefan's shoulder. 'Let's get back to Bellevue and see what Alicia's knocked up for dinner. She'll be interested to hear her flamenco player's become a budding author.'

'Stranger things have happened.'

'They sure have.' Lennard wrestled with the umbrella. 'But remember, get your priorities right—*first* the monument, *then* the best seller.' Then he stopped abruptly and Stefan, who had taken several onward strides with Skathi, turned back. 'I've had a brilliant idea—*Gerrit's story!*' he exclaimed. 'You know I've broken all the ground. Now I need his story written and you're a writer-to-be, looking for something to sink your teeth into!'

Bewildered, Stefan took several moments. 'Me? Write Gerrit's story?' He gave an embarrassed gasp. 'I don't think so.'

'Why not? I've read the articles you've published. You've got a way with words.'

'For a factual report, maybe. But a full-length novel? There's a big difference. Writing up the findings in a glass experiment and ghost-writing a biography are poles apart.'

'Writing the biography of a ghost, you mean.' Lennard glanced at him thoughtfully. 'I reckon you could bring him back to life if you put your mind to it.' He gave a dry laugh. 'But there you go again, bro—undervaluing yourself. What is it with you? You're putting up hurdles before you've given the idea the once-over. Bad, bad habit of yours! We all have our limitations, but we shouldn't let them cripple us. Before you put those hurdles up you gotta check if you can jump them. Take risks.'

'I'm here, aren't I?'

'That's different. That's your outside circumstances making your decision. I'm talking about your inner demons. Face up to *them* and you'll change your view of the world.' He raised his eyebrows with a nod. 'Do that, and we'll make a new man of you yet, Mr Novalecki!'

Stefan smiled, then asked, 'What about Alicia? She'd be far more skilled than me. I'd be a hack compared to her.'

'She doesn't have the time. Tell you what, though, I'm sure she'll do the editing. Give you some tips. Maybe even coach you, if you ask her. She wants to see it written as badly as I do.' He chuckled meaningfully. 'I reckon she'll jump at the chance to crack the whip.'

'Oh, terrific! I can feel the sting of Madam Lash already!'

They resumed their walk in the dwindling rain as Stefan considered Lennard's suggestion. True, the commitment with which Lennard had researched his Zeeland ancestry impressed him. Gerrit's elusive ghost, peering across three centuries, haunted him. The boy's shadow was emerging from his research as he added colour to him layer by layer, as he flushed him out, as he *fleshed* him out, adding the appropriate touches of black to white.

Then Stefan recalled the ship in the bottle. As he'd made it, had Lennard relived Gerrit's voyage aboard the *Zuytdorp* through his own artistic journey?

'So when am I going to hear the full story?' he asked at last. 'You promised to tell me if I came over. So far, you've only skirted around it.'

'Of course I'll fill you in. You'll have all the facts, right down to Napoleon Blownapart.'

'Napoleon Blownapart?'

'All in good time.' Lennard's voice became intense. 'I know it's a big ask, but hey, it is a great idea. Think about it. Gerrit was the first *wajbala* to reach a compromise with the Malgana. He had to, to survive. He depended on them. They had things of value to teach him and he had skills to offer in return. I like to think Gerrit integrated with the Malgana and together they're showing us the way forward for future generations in this country. I put that badly, bro, but you get my drift.'

'He had no other option.'

'You both have that in common.'

He closed the umbrella as the shower eased to a fine mist, and with a thoughtful glance, 'He must have been the first *wajbala* to come to terms with Aboriginal Law and custom. The first European to set foot on this continent who didn't assume the land was there for the taking and it was his way or the highway.' Then he surprised Stefan. 'Gerrit would understand exactly why we're working on the cenotaph, bro. If he was around, he'd be the first to acknowledge the need to commemorate our dead. He'd be our prime *wajbala* witness to the heroes of our resistance movements.'

He broke into a wide, challenging smile Stefan had come to recognise. *Here we go*, he thought. *What's coming next*?

'Not only that, bro, I reckon he'd be the first to support the Tent Embassy call for recognition of the First Nations People in the Aussie constitution. He'd wonder why we're dragging our feet on something so critical to the nation's vision of itself.'

'He's that important to you?'

'My oath he is. He's my first white ancestor, but he's not around to confirm it, so we'll use your book instead. We'll have signed copies at the entrance to the cenotaph. We can flog them off; recoup some costs.'

'Whoa, one step at a time Ace!' Stefan laughed and then, 'It sounds like Gerrit's been whispering in your ear since the day you were born.'

'Since before I was born, bro. The young fella gave me tinnitus when I was in the womb.'

They walked on in silence and then Stefan said quietly, 'In that case, maybe it *is* time to give him a hearing. But there are conditions.'

'*Now* you're talking! So what are you proposing?'

'Well, I know I can write a decent report. I enjoy gathering data, sorting it out. Making sense of it. Your research notes present that kind of challenge. *That* I can handle. But turning them into a readable novel? Like I said, I'd be in the deep end. I couldn't do it justice.'

Lennard clapped Stefan on the shoulder. 'Brudda! Relax. That's where Alicia comes in. You write the long version as best you can with Alicia's editing and coaching, but with you in the driver's seat. Then you hand over to the sister and she uses her know-how to cut it back to the version we publish. Make sense?'

Stefan nodded as he listened intently.

'That leaves you free to select the scenes you reckon are important for the story. Get a handle on the characters. Develop the story and the plot—the conflicts—and whatever other bollocks you pen-pushers get up to. It saves Alicia the back-breaking hackwork of going through my notes. How's that suit you?'

'If she agrees, I guess I could deliver on it.' Stefan hesitated. 'But time might be a factor, with the cenotaph and all.'

'We'll *make* time, by crikey.'

'In that case—'

Lennard did not allow him to finish. 'Good! Done! I'll talk her into it. And I tell you what, soon as we get a chance we'll go round to the Shipwrecks Museum. It's time we went. There's a certain little lady there I want you to meet. She'll tell you more about Gerrit than anyone can. We'll go and have a yack with her.'

'Is she that young redhead you promised me?'

'No, but she's got the wood on any redhead you'll ever

meet. She's made of solid Estonian white oak and she's three hundred years old.'

By writing Gerrit's story, he'd repay Lennard for the generosity he'd shown, Stefan thought. True, he was helping with the building of the cenotaph, but Lennard was paying him a retainer for that. *The book will be something more, something of real value, a gift in return for Lennard's open-handed hospitality and friendship.*

At the same time, Alicia would be mentoring him, editing his progress, guiding him through the complexities he'd no doubt find in Lennard's notes before she trimmed it back. That would give him an opportunity to get to know her better, to feel less intrusive while living under her roof. Then the thought crossed his mind—if he started walking on eggshells around her, he'd know it was time to leave.

When he'd completed the first draft, he realised, he would not only have brought Gerrit back to life, he would also have a deeper understanding of Lennard himself. That thought raised a question that stopped him in his tracks.

'What about the Malgana, Ace?'

'What about them?'

'You may be a full bottle on your culture today, but what about three hundred years ago? Unless you've got a psychic channel to your ancestors, we know bugger all.'

Lennard nodded. 'That's crossed my mind too, bro. We ask around. We shoot up to Shark Bay and I introduce you to the extended family. We find out how they reckon our ancestors would have reacted to the *wajbala*. We get a consensus. We do some sniffing around, check out country. We make some educated guesses.' Then he broke into a wide smile and clapped Stefan on the shoulder. 'And we go walkabout. We take the long walk.'

'The long walk?'

'From the wreck site to the Murchison, bro. We follow the

songline south the way they used to in the old days, stopping off at the inland soaks and waterholes. That way you'll get to know country first-hand.'

'Jesus! How far's that?'

'Depends how fast the crow flies.'

'Seriously.'

'Seventy clicks in a straight line along the cliffs. Eighty if you count climbing Womerangee Hill and both sides of all the gullies we have to cross.'

'Along the cliffs? You're making me nervous, Ace.'

Lennard gave a dismissive shake of his head. 'See? You're getting cold feet again before you've begun. You won't have them out there, but. Not when you're walking on hot sand and ankle-breaking Tumblagooda limestone in forty-five degrees! Trust me, brudda, you'll get to know exactly what Gerrit went through trekking south.'

'Oh, that's great.' Stefan laughed. 'Forty-five degrees and blistered feet. That clinches it for me. I'm in.'

They continued their walk.

'I think Gerrit would have been ready to make the trip in August, two months after the ship sank,' Lennard conjectured. 'By then it was either walk south or die of thirst. If he had any sense he'd have waited for a three-quarter moon, or a full one, to travel at night. Even if that slowed him down.'

'How long would that have taken him?'

'Four full nights at least, maybe five. Possibly six if he was recovering from an injury.'

'Bloody hell! That's what you're suggesting we do?'

'Why not? But not this year. Too much to do, and we have to get you fit. Coupla years, I'd say. Plenty of time for you to deal with Gerrit's life in Middelburg building the ship.' He gave Stefan a reassuring smile, 'Now we've planted the seed we let it germinate.'

It was Alicia's idea to split the model of the cenotaph in two. When she suggested it one afternoon, Lennard was non-plussed.

'Cut it in two, sister? Why?'

'So people can walk through it, not just around it.'

'This is not Hanging Rock we're sculpting.'

'No, it's not, but you said it yourself—they need to *experience* it, not only see it.' She paused. 'Let's invite them in. Unlike Hanging Rock, they won't be smothered by a rockslide. They'll reappear. They'll walk through and come out the other side…' she searched for the word, couldn't find it, 'not *transformed* exactly, not that, but with a raised awareness. It'll deepen what they've come looking for in paying their respects.'

'Ha! Born again, you reckon? Now you're stretching it.'

'I didn't say that. But they will be touched. It'll be a touchstone.'

The idea took hold. 'It would grab their attention. Give the rock a different dimension.'

'Exactly. The reproduction of a rock is a rock. But a rock with a channel through the centre? That changes its character. They'll be passing through a gateway. A gateway to understanding.'

'A gateway to the heavy-duty hallelujah! Now *that* I do like, sister!'

She gazed at him thoughtfully. 'They'll find a rock within a gorge, then walk through a gorge within a rock.'

Lennard peered down at the model on the veranda. He'd paced around it all morning, measuring the angles, selecting the surfaces he intended squaring for the inscriptions.

He called out to Stefan, who was feeding the heron-shy goldfish, coaxing them from the shadow of the water lilies. Skathi was beside him, alert to their splashing, head down as she circled the pond, giving them the eye.

Stefan retrieved the chainsaw from the shed and they heaved the model down into the blazing sunlight on the lawn.

Lennard picked up the saw, inspected it, slotted the wooden rope-toggle between his fingers and, in one move, swung it as he pulled the cord.

He roared as it whined into the clay he'd spent weeks meticulously shaping. 'Dinosaur *gunda* Max called it. What are we gonna find when we open it up?'

The halves separated. He nudged them apart with his foot, the saw clattering as he doused it. 'Now we're in business. We'll need a corridor wide enough for people to reach out and touch both sides.'

'That's brilliant!' Stefan exclaimed, stretching out both arms, fingers extended. 'People reaching out, making contact with the separate halves… lighting them up like fuses. The rock will be a beacon; a boundary marker with a passage through the centre. A bridge between different worlds.' He nodded. 'People passing through it will be crossing borders.'

He looked up, shielding his eyes with an open palm. 'If we locate the halves north-south, the sun will penetrate the passage once a day. They'll be walking through fire. We can have floodlights on at night to achieve the same effect.'

Lennard waved the saw. 'They'll be firewalking inside the *Wagyl's* skin! Through all the colours of the rainbow serpent!' He tipped one half on its side and stared down at the flattened surface scored by the saw's teeth. 'This is where we'll etch the names of the warriors.' He ran his hand over it, sweeping away the dust. 'Along here. On a wall of glass, like the names etched on the black granite memorial to Vietnam in Washington.' He pointed at the other half. 'And the message of reconciliation will go there. A line from the Nyungar *Karni Wangkiny* song.'

'What song's that?' Stefan asked.

'Their *Truth Telling* anthem.'

He squatted on the grass, squinted up at the sun and placed the halves in parallel with the passage in shadow. It was perfect. The names on the left; acknowledgment of the past. The quotation on the right; reconciliation for the future.

'The past will connect with the present as you walk through it,' Alicia suggested. 'The ancient dead will speak to the living. They'll invite them to commit to a future they *can* change by coming to terms with a past they can't.'

Lennard looked up at her with a sudden broad smile, 'We'll be giving them a voice, sister.' He beat his fist into his palm. 'We'll give them a *voice*! We'll give *all* us blackfellas a voice, by crikey!'

He spent what was left of the afternoon with a scroll of drafting paper unrolled across the veranda, chunks of rose quartz pegging down the corners, photographs scattered across it. He sat comfortably cross-legged, sketching between his outstretched knees with a stick of charcoal he'd sharpened on a shard of sandstone. Skathi lay beside him, following his movements, her muzzle on her paws, occasionally rolling her eyes up at him approvingly. Now and then he blew across the drawings, clearing the charcoal dust, breathing life into the lines, deepening the shadows with his thumb.

He showed in his bent back the relaxed concentration of a desert artisan as a series of drawings emerged. In each successive sketch, the halves of the model were rotated on their axes as if he was walking around them. He had an uncanny eye for detail. Each crevice and outcrop, each plane, each jutting angle abutted to the next appeared.

As he created the designs, he traced in the background— the Swan River stirring wavelets at the embankment; the Narrows Bridge straddling its reflection in the river; the coppice of flame trees at the base of Mooro Katta Hill standing among fallen leaves; the fountain of chief Yellagonga's spring concealed in an overhang of ivy; the empty windows in the Old Swan Brewery walls shadowed in the brickwork with two Aboriginal flags draped full-length across the fence, speared to the barbed wire.

In one space he sketched the first momentous meeting between a startled Chief Yellagonga and Captain Irwin as he disembarked from his boat with a bodyguard of redcoat foot soldiers, rifles at the ready.

He worked late into the evening. As night fell, he continued beneath the veranda lamp. His last sketches were of the passage walls. He worked in the names and the quotation, but he found it difficult as he varied the shape and slant of the script, altering its placement and adjusting its size. He sketched furiously, growing more and more frustrated.

When Alicia stepped carefully across the drawings carrying a tray of salads and glasses of wine out to the wrought iron table, he flicked the charcoal stick away and removed the rose quartz paperweights.

'These bloody inscriptions!' he growled. 'We can't afford to get them wrong.'

'Sleep on it, Ace,' Alicia said, as she retrieved the charcoal. 'You've been at it long enough. Have some wine. Listen to some music. How about *Charcoal Lane* to calm you down?'

She switched on the CD player and Archie Roach's voice echoed from speakers angled across the veranda as she knelt behind him, reaching over his shoulder to place a hand beneath his shirt and over his heart. She looked up at Stefan in mock surprise. 'It *is* still beating. Four beats to the bar, ideal for the alpha waves!' She chuckled wickedly, 'And the pecs aren't half bad either,' she gave them a squeeze, 'even if they are heading south.'

'You can play with my *bibi* if I can play with yours.'

'That's my man!'

She linked her arm through his and led him across to the table.

Lennard looked back at the sheet of drawing paper as it scrolled back on itself, taking the photographs with it. 'Now there's a critic who knows his shit, giving my blueprint the big up yours,' he said. 'It's not within a bull's roar yet.'

Leaning back in his chair, he sipped the wine and looked thoughtfully at Stefan as they listened to the lines of 'Native Born', Archie's voice evocative and smooth, the occasional unexpected vibrato—

'Albert Namatjira painted
Not so much the things he saw
But what he felt inside.'

'We need the words to describe the rock standing at the water's edge, bro,' Lennard suggested at last. 'We need to have a written record of it. We need to hear it talked about. I wanna listen to someone who's just walked through it. A *yamba* talking. One of the stolen generation. An old Digger.' He snorted sardonically, raising his glass. 'Even little Johnny Howard with an apology to us blackfellas on behalf of the nation, s-s-stuttering over the word s-s-sorry that's giving him s-s-so much grief.'

'Without choking on it or finding it's cost him an arm and a leg,' Alicia murmured.

'That'll be the day,' Stefan interjected.

'Yeah, I know. He's blind Freddy where that's concerned, blind as a welder's dog. But it's gonna happen, bro, even if it takes the next prime minister. I can hear him now, whoever he—or she—is. On the big screen. Saying sorry three times over to make sure the message gets across. Restoring dignity where it belongs. Under the flag of the Aussie Republic...' he paused and smiled, 'with the Union Jack replaced by the red, black and yellow.'

'Ha! The apology maybe,' Stefan grinned, 'but the flag? There'll be pork sausages grilling on Jewish barbecues way before *that* happens.'

'Where there's a *will*, bro. Tooth and nail, that's us, down to the last frigging tooth and the last frigging nail. We're here for the duration, so what's another decade or two? We think in centuries. In *millennia*, across sixty thousand years. Never mind the fat lady singing! Nothing's over until you give up the ghost, and we're not doing that any time soon.' He lifted his glass and saluted Stefan. 'You're the up-and-coming pen pusher. I'll do the sketching, you do the scribbling. Let's hear what you come up with.'

STEFAN BEGAN WRITING that night.

Outstretched on the bed, staring at the ceiling, he imagined the rock in its white expanse. He tore a page from a pad and took up a pencil, but he had no idea where to start.

Suddenly he was back in Geelong, listening to the rasping voice of his high school English teacher as he raised the board ruler and gave his desk an explosive crack, 'Begin at the beginning, boy, and when you reach the end, *stop*! Let the middle take care of itself.'

But the only words Stefan saw then were those crudely carved into the wooden desktop at which he sat, distracted by the bitter flavour of wood and graphite in the end of a chewed pencil.

He imagined the feel of Lennard's heartbeat through Alicia's fingers. *There are secrets there*, he thought, *encoded in the pulsing tempo of his spirit evident in the flickering wings of the albatross.* If he was to decipher them he needed to understand how Lennard felt, immersed in his history and bound to his traditions.

He unfolded the art show catalogue on the table beside the bed.

He considers himself a painter sculpting in molten glass, he read. *He missed the Pilbara pepper smell of dust after rain. He longed for the western desert edged by the sea… he yearned for the colour and the space of his country, for its desert silences.*

He recalled the wistful lines of *Native Born* and wrote—

> *And mother land still sheds her tears*
> *For lives that never stood a chance*
> *And Albert Namatjira cried as we all cry*
> *The Native Born*
> *We cry the Native Born.*

Lennard's creative impulse. His technical skill. His love of country. His feeling for his people. He must start somewhere— in the Kimberley perhaps, at the gorge. Touch the rock. Climb it. In the photographs, Rosalie was seated on a ledge facing the pool. Write as if he was sitting there alongside her.

Then he visualised the cenotaph completed, a glass monument standing beside its reflection in the river.

He began to write again.

> *In its dimensions and volume, the cenotaph*
> *is the largest structure sculpted in solid glass*
> *the world has seen.*

He stared at the words. What was he composing? An entry on a facts sheet? Then he recalled an earlier conversation with Lennard and continued.

> *The rock has always been deeply significant*
> *to the Bunuba people of the Kimberley.*
> *Windjana Gorge is the place where the*
> *uprising of the Bunuba warriors began*
> *late in 1894, under the leadership of*
> *Jandamarra.*

> *For the first time in Australian history,*
> *the encroaching settlers faced a group of*
> *Aboriginal warriors who had levelled the*
> *playing field. Armed with stolen rifles,*
> *they resisted the incursion of the first wave*
> *of pastoralists and their cattle herds into*
> *Bunuba territory, holding them at bay for*
> *the next three years. The rock marks the place*
> *where the first battle was fought.*

> *The monument is a memorial to that heroic*
> *campaign. More than that, it commemorates*
> *twenty thousand other unknown Aborigines*
> *massacred as the bloodied line of invading*
> *colonists advanced across the continent.*

He reviewed the page, pausing at the word 'heroic'. He considered deleting it, changed his mind and tossed it to the floor.

He tore off another.

> *People have access through it. On one wall*
> *of the passage through the rock are inscribed*
> *the names of Jandamarra's warriors and*
> *others who died in the name of Aboriginal*
> *resistance—Yagan, Midgegooroo, Calyute,*
> *Pemulwuy, Windradyne, Dundalli,*
> *Mosquito, Walyer, Multeggerah.*

> *Into the other wall is incised a Nyungar*
> *quotation commemorating Aboriginal*
> *survival across the continent; a line from an*
> *anthem of reconciliation.*

He heard the chainsaw whine through the clay, saw Lennard nudge the halves apart, imagined sunlight flashing through refractive glass.

Sunlight radiates across the passage in waves of colour. People traversing it find themselves walking through a natural hologram, through the veiled mysteries of the rainbow serpent patterned in light. Their outstretched hands touch the sides. They bridge the gap and close the circuit.

From concept to completion, the sculpture has taken the four years that Lennard allowed himself, although he has lived with the idea since further back than he can remember. It was conceived long before he was—it dreamed him into being before he dreamed of it.

The memorial reflects the dark side of Australia's history. Its paired halves present his vision of complementary ideals—truth-telling and acknowledgment on the one hand, apology and practical reconciliation on the other. In doing so, it celebrates

what's possible by way of understanding in Australia's future.

When he reviewed the words, they fell short of the mark. To his mind, they read like an entry in an encyclopaedia written by a novice. How could he give credible expression to the complexity of a man he'd just met and a project that, in all conscience, he considered politically controversial and technically unachievable? *How can I write about that?*

He placed the paper to one side, turning instead to the back of his working notebook. He thumbed forward to the technical records of their daily progress. The pages in the centre were still blank, and a thought struck him—as he filled the book from both ends, what he learned of Lennard's story recorded in the back would one day meet the chemical formulae, the graphs, the diagrams and the results of their experiments in the front. He'd have his impressions of Lennard's worldview and his art in the back and a metaphor for them in the opening pages.

When the pages meet and the notebook is complete, will I then have a window into Lennard's soul?

He'd already discovered the obvious. Lennard was tough, passionate, at ease with himself. He laughed at life's challenges. What you saw you got.

But there was more. He was an explorer, another Ernest Giles, travelling through the heart of the desert and the deserts of the heart. He'd been searching all his life for a meaning to his existence in this bewildering, bewitching universe.

He was awake to his Malgana culture, awake to his culture's reawakening, and that drove him—restoring and reshaping the Malgana belief systems, giving them a fresh vitality. He had broadened the restrictive interpretations of his traditions through his art, moving freely in the modern world without losing touch with his cultural roots. At the same time, he was seeking out his European heritage, and Stefan wondered how he had maintained that balance. *How often has he spun the coin?*

Stefan had asked Lennard one night about the turtle shell in the lounge and Lennard's response had intrigued him. 'That's my *buyungurra*; my special turtle shell. I speared it in Shark Bay when I was a *birrduwangu* during my initiation. The Big Men sent me out to hunt it for the *ngabu*; for the fat. They needed it for the ceremonies. I keep it up there as a reminder of the chase.'

He'd contemplated the shell for several moments before looking back at Stefan. 'Whenever I look at it, I'm reminded of Hermes and the story of the birth of music. You'd understand that, you with your guitar.'

As he'd continued, Stefan had imagined him in the dinghy with the outboard going full bore, bouncing over the choppy sea, leaning forward in the bows with his hair flying and his spear poised, the turtle skating the sand and weed below in a desperate zigzag to escape the chasing shadow, the thrust of the spear and the cord dragging him at the wrist into the water and below the surface.

And then the animal hauled aboard, on its back and helpless on the floorboards, the throat slit and the red plume of blood, the eyes glazing over, the rich dark meat. And later, the shell scraped clean, experimental strings of twisted gut tautened across it and the sound of the first musical note plucked by the craftsman's fingers from a magical nowhere.

'It's the liar's lyre, according to Max,' Lennard had explained. 'He sees it as a metaphor for the inventiveness of art, for the creation of something out of nothingness.'

'I wondered about the source of your inspiration when I visited your Melbourne exhibition,' Stefan had commented.

For a thoughtful moment, Lennard had not responded, and then, 'Try love of country, bro. Start there. You'll find country's part of me and I'm a part of it.'

Stefan closed the book and stretched out, his thoughts drifting once again to the problem of the monument's construction.

When he closed his eyes, the image of Redegalli's sculpture, *Cascade*, in Adelaide's Botanic Gardens came to him—five hundred horizontal panels of clear glass glued together in the towering shape of a wave breaking in a pool. He'd given the manner of its construction some thought when he first arrived in Fremantle but had not pursued it when Lennard insisted on using solid glass.

Now his memory of the sculpture re-emerged and with it, a flash of insight—splitting the monument into halves of similar dimensions offered new perspectives. There were two models now, with the inner walls flat surfaces. Forget the huge inverted mould, gigantic kiln and a furnace with the capacity for a pour of molten glass of implausible tonnages. Think *laminate* instead! *Illuminated* laminate, stacked panels of cold-worked float glass cut to size.

Pilkington to the rescue! They could construct the rock in two halves, he thought, stacking horizontal float glass panels one above the other, cold and cut to shape, pinned to uprights of stainless steel set into a concrete base. That way there'd be no annealing time. It was simple and elegant and easily achievable within the four-year time frame.

He sat bolt upright, reached for the pencil and tore off several fresh sheets of paper. As the concept raced through his mind, he quickly sketched one segment of the rock, simulating a three-sixty-degree 3D laser scan and marking out its contours.

Then he drew the edges of the glass panels in ascending layers up the flat inner surface.

He visualised one panel extracted midway up the structure. He drew its shape seen from above and imagined cutting its outline with the garnet waterjet. Then he pictured all the panels cut to shape and installed until the rock was complete.

He spent the next hour deep in concentration as he refined the designs and drafted a flowchart and timeline to discuss with Lennard the next day. When satisfied, he lay back on the bed holding the pages out in front of him. His hands were trembling. It *was* possible.

And it was time to put the foot to the floor!

He was unable to sleep as random thoughts surfaced. They'd contract for float glass panels that were optically pure and they'd intersperse other panels comprised of iridescent mixes of dichroic glass through both structures. These would react to natural and artificial light, generating dynamic colours deep within each sculpture with luminosity, depth and vibrancy to kill for.

At last, he visualised the best part, the part he couldn't wait to watch—Lennard working on the completed monument, grinding and polishing the two halves to their final shapes and etching the warriors' names and the songline into the passage, realising the vision he'd nursed for so long.

I wouldn't miss it for quids!

AT BREAKFAST THE next morning, blissed to the gills, he slapped the pages triumphantly on the table. 'Here you go, Ace, here's half that pound of flesh you were going to extract from me. The other half's my help in getting the job done.'

As Stefan ran through the process, Lennard studied each page, moving the dishes and cutlery aside to spread them across the table, his frown deepening.

'You're coming at me from left field, bro. Cast glass is my scene. You know that. Glass with muscle. Glass that really puts your skills to the test. You're showing me a Clayton's technique. It's a short cut. The easy way out.'

'Yeah, it is outside the box, but it's the easy way *in* Ace because it'll do the job brilliantly well in half the time.'

'What about the inscriptions? I want them in the passage. There's no way I can etch them into the edges of laminated sheets.'

'I've got that one sussed. We embed a panel in each passage wall to carry the names and the songline. At shoulder height. A panel that's any dimension you want. And we use some garnet in the mix to darken it. I'm sure we can experiment with minimal proportions to create the right effect without it turning into tar. That way at least you get *some* garnet into the sculpture.'

'*Now* you're cranking, brudda.'

'Think about it. It's simple. It's solid once it's stacked. It'll weather well outdoors. Look at Redegalli's *Cascade*—that's lasted and it's eye-catching. The reflective and refractive qualities will look as brilliant. And I can use my connections with Pilkington to get our panels prepared exactly the way we want. What more could you ask for?' He paused. 'It'll come at a price, of course.'

Lennard roared with laughter. 'Here we go, big spender! Break the bank, why don't you?'

'I'm not talking cash cost, Ace, although it won't come cheap. I'm talking site. I'm talking placement. It'll be impossible to shift it on a concrete base from Freo to Yellagonga's spring or Heirisson Island without risk once it's assembled.'

'So we build it where we want it—on-site, by the Old Brewery.'

Stefan shook his head. 'I'm thinking Bathers Beach.'

'*Bathers Beach*?' Lennard exploded. '*You outta your frigging mind?*'

'Next to the glassworks. It's got all the advantages.'

'Except for the symbolism, bro. I want it right where Irwin first landed.'

'Exactly! You told me yourself Governor Stirling established his headquarters on Bathers Beach after moving across from Garden Island. *That's* the place the settlers first camped on the continent. That's where the British left their first boot print. That's where they first raised the flag. Irwin's trip upriver was some time later.'

Lennard put two fingers to his lips, exhaled a lengthy breath. 'Good point, I'll grant you that. I'm listening. So convince me.'

'Where did Stirling have Irwin read his proclamation

claiming the western half of the continent? Right there, on Bathers Beach, beside Arthur Head. The place he landed upriver is dead and buried. We'll never get permission. Let's save Max a shitload of trouble and throw the application at the Freo Council instead. The thought of a Currie sculpture in their own backyard'll have them bending over backwards, especially for one that size and that significant. It'll be the first thing you see when you approach the city from the sea, even at night. An Aboriginal cenotaph that's a monument to reconciliation giving you a welcome to Australia! You want symbolism? How symbolic's that?'

'I'm still listening.'

'And the best part is we'll have it ready with time to spare.'

'You telling me we can take the weekends off?'

'Too right we can.'

'So I can start working on another exhibition on the side?'

'Not to mention the Quai Branly installation you've been thinking about, and I'm here to lend a hand.'

'Then okay, brudda! If we can meet the deadline and open it before the end of December 2000, then I'm in like Flynn!'

Stefan grinned with relief. 'I didn't think you'd be such a pushover.'

Lennard beamed. 'Quick on the uptake, bro, that's us black-fellas! Why else are we so good at Aussie Rules? When we see the chance to score six points, we don't miss it, by crikey!' He pounded Stefan's back. 'And here's me wondering when you'd come up with a workable plan. But I knew it—you're the right man! Hey, Alicia, give the genius here another steak and egg sandwich. We're up and running' He gathered the designs together and looked down at them. 'Max'll be interested in seeing this. The sceptical bastard still doubts we can deliver.'

'I'm with you, Lennardo da Vinci. Let's bust a gut and take no prisoners.'

Lennard scrutinised each page once again, then looked up and nodded. 'Now we can estimate the cost in dollars, bro. But we both know the cost of *not* building it would be greater.'

MAX VISITED THEM the following month. He called in late, arriving in the Troop Carrier from which he worked when he was in the northwest. He carried everything he needed in it—a generator, his files, a laptop and reference library of legal texts, his outback survival kit. He worked beside it in the open when he visited remote communities, his consulting room the shade beneath a blue tarpaulin lashed to trees beside the parked vehicle.

When his clients joined him, he gestured at tin mugs and a fire-blackened billy perched in glowing coals, a spiral of smoke rising in still air. He patted the red earth beside him, 'Come in. Come in. Don't bother to knock. Tea's on the boil. Make yourselves comfortable, my friends.'

He sounded his lairy two-tone horn before bounding across the veranda. He burst in and withdrew a bottle of Henschke's Hill of Grace Shiraz from a brown paper bag, as if conjuring a black and silver rabbit from a hat. '*Nhurra ngugurnunugu*? You mob all right?' he asked. 'You like that trick?'

They were at dinner. Ace was about to carve a leg of roast lamb he'd skewered from a baking dish filled with steaming sweet potato slices and carrots swimming in the meat's juices, the room filled with the mouth-watering smell of rosemary spiced with mint.

He placed the meat on a cutting board before looking up. 'I should have known,' he grunted, 'the hyena's arrived. We should have roasted this downwind.'

He was on his way to Geraldton the next day, Max explained, and needed a bed. 'The hammock will do me and breakfast won't go astray.' He licked his lips. 'Not to mention dinner. I reckon you'll need a hand to polish that lot off. Looks like you've done us proud as always, Alicia. Let's drink to it.'

'Not me this time. It's Stefan's shout. He's the chef.'

'Better still. We'll toast you both.'

The cork squealed and he sniffed at the bottle's neck, then took four wine glasses from the cabinet, sliding their stems two at a time between the outstretched fingers of his left hand. The wine swirled into the globes he held at eye level. He placed them on the table with great care.

'Years of practice,' he observed.

'Just as well,' Alicia replied, reaching for a glass. 'Spill any and I'd have to leave the stain as a memento to the hundred dollars' worth we didn't get to drink.'

He settled into a vacant chair. 'Any progress with the omphalos since we last met?'

'So it's a stone belly button now?' Alicia asked. 'The centre of the world?'

'The centre of Australia, more like. A mini Ayers Rock.'

'That's progress,' Lennard said as he carved, 'one step up from dinosaur *gunda*.' He passed Max the plate he'd filled to overflowing. 'Sit down and eat, scumbag.'

'Takes one to know one.'

'Yeah, but I was paying you a compliment.'

'Settle, boys,' Alicia broke in with a long-suffering shake of her head. 'Let's talk about the sculpture. Stefan's got it all worked out, down to the last nut and bolt. It's a neat solution, Max. I think you'll be impressed.'

Lennard turned to Stefan. 'Show numbnuts here what we're planning.'

'A *plan*? You've been at it for God knows how long and *now* you have a plan? My money still says your stone of splendour's never going to see the light of day.'

'So put your money where your mouth is.'

Max examined the first of the diagrams that Stefan showed him, his concentration growing as Stefan turned the pages, pointing out the principles. He glanced up at Lennard after peering at the last page.

'At least young Heckle here's checking which way the wind's blowing before he takes a piss. So it's been a dress rehearsal up till now and I turn my attention to the town planners on the *Freo* Council, do I? That should be a walkover.'

'You think so?'

'She'll be apples, mate. Trust me.' He loaded his fork and lifted it, but before taking a bite he gestured at Lennard. 'So how long's it going to take to get your hands on the glass panels? They're all bespoke, aren't they? That'll take time. You're already six months in.'

'Another six and we should have them,' Stefan said. 'I should be able to accelerate the process in Melbourne. Pull a few strings.'

'That gives us three years,' Lennard pointed out. 'Time enough, I reckon. We got hold of a panel this morning, similar size and thickness. It'll do to test the cutting equipment and the glues.'

'Better get to it, then.'

'We're kicking in tomorrow morning, brudda.'

WHEN ALICIA AND Lennard left them after midnight, Max and Stefan moved to the back steps, sitting with their backs to opposite pillars. The city lights spread before them, channel beacons sparkling on the black sheet of the sea and the distant Rottnest light flickering eight flashes to the minute; night's pulse.

'Mind if I ask you something about Rosalie?' Stefan asked. Max looked sidelong at him, an eyebrow raised. Stefan suspected he was sizing him up, wondering what he was about to ask, how much he needed to know, how much to hold back.

He took a Drum tobacco pouch and a cigarette paper from his back pocket. He tapped the pouch. 'Do you mind? I'm not a smoker, but I don't mind one now an again after a decent meal. I keep this on me for my clients out in the scrub.' Stefan nodded and Max took his time with the roll, licking the paper before he looked up. 'Ace hasn't told you about her?'

'He did when I first arrived. I know how they met... and how she died. But I'm confused. He clammed up when I mentioned it. I don't like to pry.'

'She's out of bounds.'

'I don't want to put my foot in it.'

'So you're prying now? What's bothering you?'

'Lennard told me about her murder, but he didn't confirm who pulled the trigger. I gather some people thought it may have been an accident, but he said you have different ideas.'

'An accident?' Max looked out into the darkness as he lit the cigarette. 'You don't get murdered by accident. You remember the tourist who went berserk in the Kimberley in the late eighties?'

'I looked him up. He went on a killing spree.'

'He did. According to most reports, Rosie was his last victim.'

'That's why I'm asking. Lennard wasn't clear.'

'Well, she died the same time as the other victims. Ten days of terror. No one knew where he was going to turn up next. He was sighted heading south from Kununurra one day and that put the wind up everyone down here. We had no idea how to contact Ace or Rosie. They'd gone bush when the killer was on the rampage. Then he ran out of fuel. He was holed up on a station near Fitzroy Crossing and there was a shootout. The tactical response guys brought him out in a body bag.'

'That's right. They did.'

'They never found the shells or bullets that killed Rosie, so it wasn't proved he shot her, but who else was out there? Ace heard a bolt-action rifle reload during the shooting and they found a bolt-action Ruger in his vehicle. For some investigators that decided it, even though the coroner found it controversial enough to record an open verdict.' He paused, then added, 'You're right, I've always had my doubts. Windjana Gorge is a long hike from Fitzroy Crossing and for him to make a detour there and back for no apparent reason makes no sense. Mind you, his vehicle *was* parked up with an empty tank, so it's possible that's exactly what he did. It was sighted by a chopper pilot mustering cattle. Ace hasn't told you about that either?'

'No. Not the details.'

'Well, you want my spin on it?'

'Sure.'

'Ace has always been a target for his politics. He still is.' His cigarette glowed brighter in the dark as he drew on it. 'He's been getting threatening phone calls about the cenotaph, as you know.'

'They've gone quiet since I've been here.'

'Have they?' For a fraction of a second Max faltered. 'Have there been any threats through the post?'

'Not that I know of.' Max's hesitation prompted Stefan to ask, 'Is there something he hasn't told me?'

Max shrugged. 'Sleeping dogs, Stefan, but watch your back. Ace is in the public eye and he speaks his mind. You've probably noticed. He's uncompromising on some issues. He doesn't hold back. He's not concerned with risks to himself. Do you remember the neo-Nazi firebombing of Chinese Restaurants in Perth, also in the late eighties? I think Lennard was targeted then as well. The bicentennial was due in '88. He was active in the push for land rights and he was on the working committee for the treaty campaign. You remember how divisive those issues were, especially when the Silver Bodgie ran hot and cold on the promise of a Makarrata by 1990?'

'They're still waiting.'

'They sure are.' Max gathered his thoughts. 'Anyway, for what it's worth, I believe the Kimberley killings were a timely diversion. They provided the opportunity and the cover for Lennard's assassination. I know it sounds far-fetched—we're living in *Australia*, after all—but it's possible someone followed him and Rosie up to Windjana and she was in the line of fire at the wrong moment.'

'You really think that?'

'It's a strong feeling I have, with no evidence to go on. I simply can't believe the German tourist fired the shots.'

'You must have been devastated.'

'We all were. We went through hell.' He paused, then gestured at Skathi asleep beside him. 'There was another incident sometime after that, when Lennard was in Brisbane setting up for the World Expo. I was living here, keeping company with Luke. One night we were woken by a God-awful howl in the garden. When I got out there Rosie's favourite dog Freya—this one's mother—had been shot with a crossbow. The arrow was buried in her chest, right up to the fletching. She died while I was holding her on the way to the vet.'

'Jesus!'

'Yeah, it wasn't easy. She was a brilliant dog. Purebred. According to the police report, she must have bailed up an intruder breaking in. *Carrying a crossbow*, for God's sake?'

He flicked ash from his cigarette, then blew a spiral of smoke towards the veranda lantern, enveloping the moths gyrating around it.

'Either way, Ace has always lived with the knowledge that Rosie died not only in his arms, but in his place.' He gazed out over the city. 'Imagine the guilt. It's taken him years to come to terms with it, if he ever has.' A moment's thought, before he murmured, *'Where joy most revels, grief doth most lament, grief joys, joy grieves, on slender accident. The world is not for aye, nor 'tis not strange that even our loves should with our fortunes change.'*

Stefan leaned back into the pillar. 'It must have been heart-rending for you as well.'

'That's an understatement. Part of me died. And it's the strangest thing—before I heard about it, I knew for certain something shocking had happened to her. I was in Sydney at the time, at a conference. The sickening feeling was so overwhelming I had to leave and make a phone call home to check. My mother hadn't heard from them and she couldn't contact Ace. As it turned out, he was carrying Rosie's body out of the gorge while we were on the phone. He rang us that night, from Derby Hospital.'

'I'm really sorry.'

'It's strange, though. I often look in the mirror and it's like she's in there with me looking out, as if I'm living for the two of us. I still talk to her, even though she's not around to listen.' He smiled. 'That may be a blessing, I sometimes think, with her gift for putting one over on me. You'd have liked her. She was a fiery one.'

About to mention his conversation with her photograph at Tullamarine, Stefan changed his mind. 'Something else has been bugging me.'

'Still to do with Rosie?'

'To do with Alicia actually… and Rosalie. How can I put this? Wouldn't most women in Alicia's position resent being constantly reminded of their partner's previous relationship, particularly one that deep? Rosalie's photos are on the wall.

I see her touches everywhere—in the house, in the garden, even in *Luke*, for heaven's sake. How can she stand it? Wouldn't she be permanently upset by the thought that she's a substitute? Never able to take her place? Or match her?'

'Ah,' Max murmured, 'you're touching on sensitive issues there, with a very private answer. Best left alone. Except for Luke. He was a tough assignment for her at first. He was fifteen when she first arrived and he was very close to Rosie, very. You can imagine how negative he was at first. She had a lot to put up with. But she's a force to be reckoned with and she battled on until they found some common ground. She won him over when she taught him some flamenco finger-picking on the guitar. It took her almost eighteen months.'

'She mentioned that the day I arrived.'

'I'll never forget the first time Luke first played for us using her technique. The two of them prepared a concert for Lennard and me, out here on the veranda. We'd never seen the young buck as pleased with his performance as he was that evening. He was even togged out in some Mexican gear she'd sent for, snappy black hat and long-sleeved scarlet silk shirt to match. When he struck up the Malaguena and went through it note-perfect, he was grinning like a shot fox. He brought the house down.' He smiled. 'He became something of a cult hero at school. He and Alicia haven't looked back since. When they do take each other on, as a stepmother and stepson always will, it's usually in good spirits and there's not that much blood spilled.'

'I'm looking forward to meeting him. But how she deals with Rosalie's presence, that's off-limits?'

'Better that way. You need to hear it from Alicia herself. That calls for trust and you haven't been here that long.' He breathed out, not quite a sigh, 'Let's just say she and Ace both share a similar loss and leave it at that. They each lost someone so close to them both their lives were changed. They both know how the person they've lost lives on inside them.' He drew on his cigarette. 'More than a collection of memories. Much more. She understands the guilt Lennard felt, and still feels. That gives them a mutual understanding you and I can only dream about.'

Stefan slowly nodded. 'I get the picture.'

There was a prolonged silence. They watched the lift and fall of lights on a mulie boat moving across the channel searching for sardine shoals, its reflection shifting on the rising swell.

'Has he told you why he chose garnet for the glass, by the way?' Max broke the silence.

'Only what we both know—the chemical content and the range of colours he thought it would deliver. It didn't pan out the way he hoped.'

'He told me, and that's a pity. You know the garnet comes from the dunes at the seaward end of Wanamalu? Rosie loved it there. She used to swim in freshwater pools not twenty metres from the pink lake, which is saltier than the Dead Sea. Those pools are a miracle of nature, fresh water alongside salt and pure enough to drink. They're a sanctuary for wild birds.' He shifted for a moment, rubbing his back to and fro against the pillar. 'According to his log, that's where Pelsaert marooned two mutineers from the *Batavia*, beside the Hutt Lagoon. On its eastern bank at the foot of a limestone bluff where there are some freshwater springs. You know the story?'

'Vaguely. Lennard's hinted at it.'

'Wouter Loos and Jan Pelgrom de Bly. They were the first recorded Europeans to settle, if you can call it that, on the continent. The first whitefellas to walk those dunes.'

'Lennard told me he took Rosalie up there after they met.'

'When she was in the pools, she used to imagine she was swimming with them. Her friendly ghosts she called them, in spite of their murderous history. It was one of her favourite places.' Max looked out into the darkness. 'Want to know another reason why the place was so special?'

'Sure, if you've got time before hitting the sack.'

'That first time Lennard took her up to Wanamalu his mother Mary welcomed her to country. It was a very private ceremony. It spoke to Rosie, and there was no looking back.'

She raved about the open spaces, he explained—the Hutt river gullies, the driving winds blowing trees parallel to the ground so they permanently grew that way, the creak of spinning windmills at the dams and drinking stations, the horses running wild.

He gave a sudden laugh. 'Except for the snakes. She *hated* them! The dugites sleeping on the window ledges in the house or in crevices among rocks beside the pools she was swimming in. She had a deadly bayamalu join her in the toilet once while she was peeing! She had to squat on the seat until it worked its way out under the door. Good practice for a trip to India or China, she told me later... with forced bravado, mind you. It was all so different from her life on Mount Street.'

He nudged Skathi with a toe as she whimpered in her dreams, her forelegs twitching, then he looked up with a knowing grin. 'When she got back to Perth she was radiant, but our old man, bless his suspicious soul, he couldn't handle it. He lost it. Went right off the deep end. He thought she'd been living on a reserve out in the sticks, washing in the creek, if she washed at all. He probably thought she'd brought back scabies or nits or a dose of the crabs, or worse—that she'd fallen pregnant and he'd have a bastard grandson to deal with, one with a touch of the frigging tar at that. They *were* the sixties, remember. White Australia was alive and kicking, well and truly.'

As Max brought the episode to life, Stefan recalled details

that Lennard had described to him during a coffee break on Bathers Beach.

EARLY SEPTEMBER 1963

SHE'D NEVER BEEN further north than Gin Gin before, an hour's drive from Perth. She was amazed as the country first opened up and they swept through it on the scooter, but when they reached the red sandplains of Eneabba and beyond, she found herself fighting to suppress her growing alarm at the emptiness, at the sweep of a cloudless sky in which the sun blazed. The landscape seemed somehow malevolent and hostile, and she was uncharacteristically dispirited when they arrived at Wanamalu six hours later.

But not for long. Lennard's mother, Mary, buxom, silver-haired and smiling, welcomed them both in a matriarchal embrace, before submitting them to a barrage of questions interspersed with good-hearted laughter that went on well into the night.

Lennard's father, Andy was the quiet one, contributing a terse comment to the conversation every now and then. Rosalie observed him watching her with appreciative shrewdness through the evening as he turned kangaroo steaks sizzling on the smoky barbecue, giving her a knowing wink each time Mary embarked on yet another anecdote that was news to Lennard.

The next day, at Mary's invitation, she and Rosalie rode horses down to the largest of the freshwater pools beside the Hutt lagoon.

'I wanna welcome you to country, Rose,' she'd said the night before, sensing Rosalie's apprehension.

They stood on a rock platform at the water's edge, the wind gusting, Mary's unruly hair a whirling silver mane. 'This is my special place. It changed my life when I was very young. Let's you and me share my story.'

She sank to the rock, her legs crossed and her elbows on her knees. With a gesture, she invited Rosalie to sit. 'But first,' she said, 'I'll introduce you to this place and let the ancestors know we're here.'

She looked up at the limestone bluff and then quietly sang for several minutes. Her voice was high-pitched and rhythmic, the melody shifting across two simple notes as though climbing and descending across an imaginary landscape. Rosalie found her chanting strangely soothing and the intonation other-worldly.

The song ended and, in the silence, Rosalie asked, 'Was that Malgana?'

'No, this is Nhanda country, girl, so that's the language here.' She pointed northwards. 'We sing the same song in Malgana over there, when we're crossin' Andy's country. Country gives you your language and with it, your voice.'

'You mean the naming of ten thousand things?'

She smiled brightly, her eyes sparkling. 'That's it, girl. Our Dreamtime creator singin' the world into existence. We all need a voice to keep the land alive and talk to the ancestors in languages they understand. Even you.'

Then she held her right hand out, fingers clenched, before opening up each finger in turn as though revealing something hidden in her fist. She held it out, palm up, and with the forefinger of her left, she traced the line of a pale scar curving across it from the webbing to the wrist. She showed her other palm. It was diagonally scarred as well, a ridge that ran across the web of palm lines as though cancelling them out. Rosalie noticed the stump of the missing little finger.

'Onslow Hospital,' she said simply. 'I was hidin' under there.' She rubbed her palms, flexed her fingers and then placed her hands on her knees. 'You shoulda seen me! I was hangin' on to them floorboards like a goanna up a tree! I wasn't givin' up without a fight. When they dragged me out, kickin' and screamin', I didn't know them nails were stickin' through. All these other lines here tell my fortune, but these two scars? Well, girl, they tell my *story*.'

In 1934, after a devastating cyclone that all but flattened Onslow, she went on, she'd scuttled under the timber floors of the hospital to escape patrol officers who'd arrived to take her and her half-caste brothers away. She sprinted to the hospital from the Masonic Hall, where she'd sheltered with her mother and her brothers for three days until the winds blew themselves out.

'Our tents on the reserve, they were blown away, halfway to Africa,' she said. 'The jetty, it was gone, with half the buildings in the town. When it was all calmed down, the officers came for me and my two brothers. Out of nowhere, they came. We got no warnin' so we didn't expect them. When we saw the truck arrive, my mum and me, we knew what they were after. She sent me out the back way and I gave them the slip, but they tracked me down. They grabbed me by the ankles and dragged me out from under there. So I was taken away as well.' Then she giggled. 'You should have seen that one officer though—that officer Amos. He was the one I'd always liked up till then—his clothes, his face, even his glasses so he couldn't hardly see, they were covered with my blood. You shoulda seen me slappin' him around!'

She'd heard the screams of her mother mingle with her own as she was dragged into the blinding sunlight, her last jolting image of her mother glimpsed through the slats of the *Reo* cattle truck carrying her to the tender that would take them to the *MV Koolinda*, anchored beyond the remains of the jetty.

'When we got to Perth, I was one of the first put into St Lelia's home. That was the year it opened.'

She said that she and Lennard had recently found her

name recorded in one of the archival ledgers there. 'They got my name right… Mary McDonnell. And they guessed my age right, too. I was twelve. They put me in Kiara Cottage and gave me a registered number—zero, zero, one, one; number *eleven*. That was me, from then on. And I spoke Yamaji, accordin' to them.'

'You speak Yamaji? I thought it was Malgana?' Rosalie asked.

'Hey, you're a smart one! No, they got my language wrong. I spoke Yarnarri. That's a dialect of Kurrama, but they wouldn't have had a clue 'bout that, so we can forgive them.'

She looked across the lagoon towards the Shoal Point dunes, their curved peaks marking the place the Hutt River estuary once broke through to the sea.

'They took me away so I wouldn't be brought up Aboriginal, but little did they know I already *was* one. I was older than the others, so they were too late.'

'How long were you in St Lelia's?' Rosalie asked.

'Until I was fifteen… three years, but less if you count the times I ran away and was brought back. My brothers, they were sent to San Benito. Things were different for them there. Things were harder. More discipline, more religion pumped into them poor little tackers by those Spanish monks with the cane in their hands.

'For all of us, speakin' language was forbidden, you know? After a while, I got real rusty, but my English was all right. What I did remember all that time was my memories of bein' happy in Onslow. Livin' on the reserve, sure, that had been hard, livin' in a tent and sometimes sleepin' down the beach in summer with the sandflies. It hadn't bothered me, but. They were good days, fishin' and crabbin' and all that. Maybe I didn't know any better, so who cared? Not me!'

'So what happened?' Rosalie reached out impulsively for Mary's hand and held it in both of hers.

'It all worked out. It always does when you've got patience, and me, I can be patient, girl. I'll hang in there till doomsday when I'm after something, doesn't matter what. Just watch me!' She gave an exuberant laugh, each exhalation succeeded by an asthmatic indrawn wheeze. 'What's that word describes it?'

'Tenacious?'

'Stubborn. I'm stubborn. Tenacious too, especially when I'm playin' cards. Never take me on, Rosie, let me tell you. With my talent, I'll whip you every time, you'll end up broke.'

'I'm broke already, but I'll keep that in mind.'

'Anyhow, the way it all turned out, I came back to St Lelia's three years later, to live there for the second time. A glutton for punishment, I was. I looked after those kids while I was trainin' to become a teacher's aide at Claremont College. Those *yamba*, those ankle-biters, we used to scrub them in the bath with bars of Mitchell's wool fat soap. You ever hear of that?'

'No, it's new to me.'

'Well, it didn't sting like carbolic, so we used it on them. I can still smell the lanolin. And taste it! Oh yes, and I can taste the carbolic too! I remember that. There was this one house matron used to lather out my mouth with it every time I swore at her in Yarnarri. I never forgot the swear words! And you know what?' Her glance was mock-serious. 'That carbolic taste got me through my teacher training. I only had to think of it and my English was word perfect.'

'So your memories of St Lelia's, were they positive?'

She raised her eyebrows. 'You take the good with the bad, Rosie. They weren't as bad as some people make out. But you know the worst? Apart from losin' my family, the worst was the shame I'd never felt before and couldn't understand. Why was I there? Had I done somethin' wrong? Had I broken some *wajbala* law? I felt like I was to blame, but I had no idea what for.'

Her voice rose. 'Look, don't get me wrong. I wasn't stupid. I knew 'bout the colour of my skin. I was old enough to know that. It wasn't anything I'd *done* that was wrong, it's what I *was*! I was white and I was black at the same time. My mother'd told me 'bout my father runnin' off from Yangkalinha, and he was white. I knew that. So the idea sank in I wasn't white enough.'

She nudged Rosalie, her eyes twinkling, the lids almost closed, her face a riot of wrinkles cobwebbed every which way. 'You know somethin'? One time when they told me to scrub myself in the bath I asked if they wanted me to scrub out the black. I asked them that. I did! I was riled. "*Then I will*" I screamed at them and I started scrubbin' and scrubbin' until almost bled. And *that* upset them, I can tell you. They had to stop me.

'They expected a tame one, but I was wild. I was hangin' on to my dignity, showin' them the black was there for keeps.' She rocked back and forth, and then, 'I took them on because I wouldn't let them break me, Rose. They thought they'd turn me into a housemaid tame enough to clean their houses in Nedlands and Peppermint Grove. Me? Wait on *them* hand and foot? *Never*!' She paused. 'They did help me get through the teacher training, but. And I'm grateful for that.'

'Did you see your mother again?' Rosalie asked.

'Oh, that was easy. I saw her every day.' She gave a secretive smile, tapped her forehead. 'In my mind, see. We never had nothin' in Onslow, but we did have this old car. It was a Buick, parked up in the Onslow dump. I can still remember it like it was yesterday. Paint peelin' off it. Dark red it was, but eaten through with rust, with nothin' but the engine block sittin' under the bonnet.'

'Did it go fast?' Rosalie asked, smiling.

Mary squeezed Rosalie's hand and bellowed with laughter. 'Eight straight, that engine, and let me tell you, girl, she was

red so she went like the wind! On an empty tank and nothin'
but three rims and one flat old worn-out white-walled tyre!

'My mum used to take us kids down there and we'd squat
on those mouldy purple leather seats with the redback spiders
and the springs showin' through, my mother hangin' on the
steerin' wheel and my brothers makin' engine noises in the
dickey seat whenever we went ridin' down the highway to
Perth or paid a visit to our family in the desert.'

Her laughter subsided and she caught her breath. 'So, yes, girl,
I saw my mother every day. Her and me and the boys, in that old
wreck. And I talked to her, too… lookin' out through that cracked
windscreen I told her everything. And every day I used to hear
her promise me she'd start that car and come and fetch me.'

She was suddenly serious. 'That kept me goin' in St Leila's,
knowin' I could tell her how I was, tell her what was happenin',
share my secrets. That's one reason I survived. But don't get me
wrong, girl. Those Irish nuns and their volunteers, they weren't
bad people. I came to like some of them, once I got over bein'
stuck in there. They did their best for me, for all the *yamba*, but
they couldn't get rid of the insecurity we felt. How could they?
We were the ones feelin' it, not *them*. It turned out a different
story for my brothers, though.'

'So did you see your mother?' Rosalie asked again.

'No. She was passed away. I found that out after I left St
Leila's when I was qualified. I went back to Onslow first. I
found her grave there. Then I came down to Northampton to
start teachin'. That's where I met Andy. He was workin' out on
Wanamalu,' she said, with a spark of mischief, 'and here I am.'

'Yes, here you are.'

'Here *we* are, girl.' She pointed at the pools. 'Now then,
this place. This place turned my life around. I came down here
one day when I was twenty-one. I was livin' with Andy at the
time and I was pregnant with Lennard, a few weeks to go and

I was huge! He was no bun in the oven that boy, let me tell you—he was a damper cake bigger than a basketball. It was blindin' hot and we came down here for a swim.'

She looked into Rosalie's eyes and described how she'd stripped and walked naked out into the water and, when she'd looked down, she saw her reflection mirrored full length in its surface. She was transfixed. She was looking at herself from the inside out and from the outside in, and she saw no shame there. She saw only her dark beauty, the swell of her belly and her body's intimacy.

She'd leaned forward and gradually immersed herself in the reflection beneath her. When she'd emerged, it was with a deep sense of joy, as if the spirit in her that had gone to ground was back in the light. She'd flung her hair about to wring the water from it and danced on the rocks like some wild, ecstatic water nymph in the hot sun in a fresh new world with Andy cavorting around her.

'I'd already decided to teach,' she said. 'No way wasn't I goin' to teach. I've spent the rest of my workin' life giving the *yamba* in Northampton some pride in being black and Aboriginal. I've taught the kids to wear their skin like a flag of defiance,' she chuckled, 'and do they wave it, hey? Do they *what*!'

'I guess we all have those moments,' Rosalie said.

'Well, you're right, and this is one for you.' Still holding Rosalie's hand, she stood, reached out for her other hand and held them both. 'Come on, girl. Don't be afraid. There's no crocs in here, 'cept this old crock when I get in. It's time for you to get baptised.'

She pulled Rosalie to her feet and led her to the edge of the rock.

'You ready, girl?'

Rosalie nodded. They stepped in unison over the edge into breast-deep water, their blouses floating up around them, their feet raising a cloud of fine white sand that drifted to their knees. And again, in unison, they ducked beneath the surface and came up laughing.

'Welcome to Andy's country and mine,' Mary said. 'Welcome to our people's country and the country of our ancestors.'

WHEN MAX PAUSED and looked out into the dark, Stefan knew he'd added another piece to Lennard's jigsaw. He understood the deeper implications of his relationship with Rosalie, but there were still some unanswered questions.

Was country truly the bedrock to his inspiration and his thinking, as Lennard had suggested? Had he seamlessly dove-tailed his Malgana roots into his Australian and international persona by some mysterious shift in consciousness? Like the fractal patterns permeating his sculptures, was the whole in the least part and the least part in the whole?

The mulie boat was floodlit as a circle of nets was set; a luminous disk in the dark ocean, the sky black as jet glowing pearl above it.

'Lennard tells me you're learning Malgana,' Max said.

'I'm giving it a go, but I get tongue-tied. You speak it well, though.'

'Nowhere near as well as the Black Messiah, but I'm doing my best.' Max noticed Stefan's raised eyebrows and responded with a quick laugh. 'Rosie's private nickname for him. She used it like a piece of four by two if he ever big-noted himself. He let me in on it once. The first time she christened him they were making love. "Well," she told him. "I'm done. So what're you waiting for, my Black Messiah? The second coming?"'

They heard the distant sound of music at the waterfront and the voices of people passing in Hampton Street below, their conversation quietening as a woman among them began to sing.

'Sounds like someone appreciates Crowded House,' Stefan observed. 'That sounds like "Better Be Home Soon", but she's off-key. Neil Finn'd have a fit.'

At that moment a meteor flashed a blistering trail of light across the sky. Max pointed upwards. 'She must be that mermaid King Oberon overheard. You ready for another quote?'

'Be my guest.'

'Once I sat upon a promontory and heard a mermaid on a dolphin's back uttering such dulcet and harmonious breath that the rude sea grew civil at her song, and certain stars shot madly from their spheres to hear the sea-maid's music…'

The song faded into silence, overtaken by the hiss and squeal of trucks braking at the traffic lights.

Max looked across at Stefan. 'Tell me something. What do you see when you look at Ace's sculptures?'

'Apart from the hard work that's gone into them?'

'Of course.'

'Well, the interaction between glass and light is there for all to see,' Stefan suggested. 'The sheer illusory beauty of it.'

'And?'

'He manipulates light through the medium of glass in such a way that you experience the workings of nature, maybe?' He hesitated, searching for the words. 'No, I mean the workings of *your* nature. Doesn't the experience enable you to focus on the processes of your *perception* somehow? Don't the sculptures have perspectives that affect the way you see them so that you sense the difference between vision and seeing, as Lennard puts it?'

Max gave him an ironic look. 'Yeah, I've heard him say that. The Black Messiah miraculously restores sight and insight to the blind!' Then he grinned. 'It's interesting, though. You're another one. I've asked a lot of people and my question is always answered with a question.' He paused thoughtfully. 'The effect of light. Can you ever put a finger on it?'

'So what's your answer?'

'I'm no different, Stefan. I'm still working on it too, but I may have found a clue to the sources of his inspiration. Has he told you that when we were students, we worked on the first survey crews brought in to construct the railway line from Mount Tom Price to Dampier?'

'Yes, he has.'

'Well, the rock walls blasted through the hills fascinated him; hurt him deeply too, ripping up the landscape the way we did, tearing country apart. He used to photograph the rock faces in the cuts and quarries after the blasting.' He leaned forward and removed a leather-bound notebook from his back pocket. He withdrew a battered photograph from a plastic holder within it and handed it to Stefan. 'Here's a shot of him with the scraper crew in those days. He's sitting up front. What d'you reckon? He's stacked on the blubber since then?'

Lennard was squatting on the mudguard, thin-ribbed and thoughtful. He was wearing shorts, resting his chin on one raised knee with his hands clasped around it, his other leg dangling. He had the beginnings of a sparse beard. A length of red plastic survey ribbon tied back an Afro shock of black hair. In the ribbon's trailing end was a pair of white-and-brown-streaked feathers.

'*Gutharra walgabuda bardudap*,' Max explained when Stefan pointed them out. 'They were his trophy from a bush turkey's wings. He trapped it on New Year's Day in the Canyon, I remember. It was delicious on the open spit,' he chuckled, 'but took some chewing.'

'He looked like an Apache then.'

'He's changed, and then some. Same bloke inside, though.'

'I don't see you in here.'

'No, I took the photo.'

Stefan looked down at several other men in the photo-graph before seeing a woman sitting behind Lennard, her face barely visible beneath the rim of a blue baseball cap. 'Isn't that Rosalie in the driver's seat?'

'That's her, at the controls as usual.'

'I thought she worked in the first aid post?'

'She did. That was taken back in camp at the end of a shift. Look, you can keep it. It'll give you an idea what Ace looked like in those days. I'll get a reprint.'

'You sure?'

'It's yours.'

Max explained that Lennard saw works of art where others saw formless rubble in the texture of the rock walls after the dynamite had blown. The diversity of colours and patterns fas-cinated him—the streaks of red and yellow jasperite, the rare tan and gold of tiger eye, the chunks of rose quartz embedded in the shale like crystalline flowers.

'He told us he was gathering evidence for what he called the sacred discord from which the universe emerges. He was seeing country from the inside, as it were.' Then he gave a quiet chuckle. 'One day he took a spectacular shot of a row of live charges that hadn't fired, the dynamite still in the drill holes and the lines of red wire linking them. They began a delayed detonation in sequence from the far end of the cut as he snapped the picture.

'He came out of there like a frigging Bondi tram, quicker than Ben Johnson on a bucket load of steroids. I've never seen him move so fast. He was lucky to get out alive. Just as well he was skinnier then. I'd hate to see it happen to him now. It cost him two days' suspension after the Safety Committee gave him a bollocking, but it was worth it for the photograph, he reckons.'

'I've seen his rock collection in the lounge.'

'He collected most of the pieces in the Pilbara, except for the two fragments of trinitite he's got. He was given those when he visited the States with Alicia.'

'Trinitite?'

'Chunks of glass fused from the desert sand at ground zero after the first atomic blast at Alamogordo in 1945, when they tested the Nagasaki bomb.'

'Which rocks are they?'

'They're not on display. He keeps them secure. One of them is green; that's the bigger piece, the size of your hand. It's shaped like Australia, with Tassie hanging off it, joined by an isthmus, which is why he chose it. The other's red, the size of your thumb. That's the rarer piece, contaminated by the copper in the bomb device. They're both opaque and covered in blisters.'

'Are they still radioactive?'

'Mildly, but they're safe. Get him to show them to you when you get the chance. They're interesting, especially the story about how they got the name. You know that "trinity" was the code word for the bomb test?'

'No.'

'Rumour has it, Robert Oppenheimer was inspired to call it that by the poetry of John Donne.' He gave a brief, ironic out-breath. 'How do you like *them* green apples, Stefan? A poem by the Dean of St Paul's and seventy thousand die in Hiroshima in a single blast, followed up by many thousands more in Nagasaki. An interesting conjunction, don't you think?'

He stretched, nudged Skathi and went down the steps. He walked across to the pond and stared down at the water lilies with the dog at his heels. The flowers were closed within their calyces, stirring like a field of blue-green tulips as he spoke from the shadows, '*What shall my west hurt me?*' He was silent for several moments, as though running through the verses in his mind, and then as he turned back, '*Therefore that he may raise, the Lord throws down.*'

He looked up as he reached the steps. 'Maybe you'll find his secret in those rocks, Stefan. There's no more blinding light than an atomic explosion and all it leaves behind is shards of glass.' He slowly shook his head. 'Remember Maralinga and the British bomb tests? I once had a Tjarutja client who was a kid when they went off. He was going blind as he got older. They thought at first it was the delayed after-effect of flash blindness. Turns out, he'd suffered a retinal burn and it was gradually detaching. He was chasing compensation for the trauma.'

Then Lennard appeared, scratching his tousled hair, fending off Skathi as she raced up the stairs to greet him.

'Talk of the devil,' said Max, before turning back to Stefan. 'That client. He won it in the end.'

'You blokes woke me, and I thought I heard my name taken in vain. What're you doing still up?'

'Stefan wanted to hear about you and Rosie so I've spilled the beans.'

'How far did you get?'

Max pointed at the photograph in Stefan's hand. 'We've been taking a gander at the survey crew.'

'That's taken you most of the night?'

'And then some.' Max somersaulted into the hammock and turned his back on them. 'Don't mind me, I'm dog-tired,' he said as he settled. 'I'll have a kip before I hit the road.'

Lennard looked down at Stefan. 'Max'll sleep through anything.'

He squatted on his heels and leaned back into the pillar. 'So what's he been yakking to you about?'

Stefan handed him the photograph. 'It must have been quite an experience for Rosalie, getting to know you and your world, Gerrit and all.'

'She didn't know what she was letting herself in for, bro. And neither did I, come to that, getting mixed up in hers. But whenever I got the chance to talk about Gerrit, she copped an ear-bashing. It took her by surprise the first time, but we soon found out we shared an interest in that history, so we checked out Gerrit's story together.' He paused. 'Tell you what. Let's get some sleep while we can and knock over today's work early. Then we'll go around to the Shipwrecks Museum. Give you a chance to get a fix on all my notes you're ploughing through.'

'Promises, promises. I've been looking forward to that since I arrived.'

'Yeah, we should've made time.'

He stood and turned to leave.

A breeze agitated the pond, stirring the veranda lantern's reflection across its surface in an illusory string of gold coins, the lemon tree brushing laden branches across the shed, fruit thumping on the corrugated iron. Stefan heard the phantom swish of seabirds heading for the ocean and saw them flare in the streetlights below, which were suddenly extinguished, leaving him in darkness paling into day.

He reached up to switch off the lantern.

Now that was a night to remember, he thought, *a conversation I'll be coming back to again and again.*

THEY SPENT THE next morning cutting the sheet of plate glass, working in turn to test and adjust the waterjet. The glass panel was supported underwater, the cutting carried out there for their protection. The high-pitched screech of the garnet mix exiting the cutting head nozzle at high pressure reached them faintly through their earmuffs.

By midday, Lennard was satisfied with their progress and called it a day. Manipulating the cutting head along the line from piercing to piercing required a high degree of concentration, and Stefan was quick to remove his safety gear after shutting down the servo pump and closing the valves.

He relished the prospect of a break and his first browse among the Shipwrecks Museum relics. He untied his leather apron, strode to the doorway and stretched his arms towards the sun, peering appreciatively across the lawn, his eyes aching after squinting at the precise line of the cut. He breathed the still salt air deeply in as he held the door ajar for Lennard.

On the Esplanade they disturbed a trio of cantankerous crows attacking a dustbin for leftovers. They retreated to the branches of a Norfolk Island pine, leaving a gang of gulls to wrangle over a torn brown paper bag spilling fish batter and chips across the grass. *I'm like those noisy buggers*, Stefan thought wryly, *scavenging through Lennard's research notes and foraging through his observations.*

He looked over at the museum, his anticipation growing. Would the visit give him some new direction?

They crossed the forecourt to visit volunteers building a replica of the *Duyfken* in a work shed. She was modelled on the first Dutch *jacht* to visit the Australian coast in 1606, when her *schipper*, Willem Jansz, explored the western shores of Cape York in the Gulf of Carpentaria, charting the coastline south of the Pennefather River before turning north for Batavia at Cape Turnaround.

Shouting over Pink Floyd blasting from a sawdust-covered CD player, Lennard introduced himself and Stefan to one of the four shipwrights working that day. The shipwright turned down the music before showing them over the recently laid stem and sternpost.

Stefan was fascinated by the original handcrafted shipbuilding tools and techniques he showed them, and he was struck by the range of unfamiliar sights, sounds and smells—the variously patterned grains of timbers the shipwright pointed out, the resin yellow of Latvian oak imported for the outer planking and the lighter tan in the composite keel, the rasp of saw and file and the hammering of mallets, and the pungent, spicy scent of wintergreen given off by shavings spread across the floor. His mind locked onto the images, aware he'd be transcribing and reshaping them later in descriptions of the Middelburg shipyard, the *dokhavn*.

'Would you credit all this, bro?' Lennard asked as they walked the seventeen-metre length of her keel. 'Check out the workmanship. The muscle power that's gone into it. How did they do it centuries ago, building their ships by hand? And so bloody quickly?'

'You said the *Zuytdorp* took six months from the laying of the keel to the launch?'

'That's right. They beat us at it hands down, that's for sure. This one's gonna take two years, they reckon, and we've got modern tools and measuring devices if we need them.'

Stefan was astonished as the shipwright described the traditional Dutch technique of building the ship without plans and by eye, preparing the outer hull planks first, bending them into shape over an open fire before fitting the inner frames and strakes from tree branches sawn and carved in their natural shapes.

He ran his hand over the thick right-angular wedge of a hanging knee joint on a workbench that would be used to tie the decking to a vertical framing piece, visualising Gerrit doing the same during his apprenticeship. As he did so, a splinter lodged deep in the base of his thumb and he spent several moments extracting it between his teeth, then gazing at it in the palm of his hand and wiping away the beads of blood with an ironic smile as Lennard's warning about blood, sweat and tears ran through his mind.

Then they crossed the paving to enter the museum and he was blown away by the dimensions of one of the *Zuytdorp*'s bower anchors standing in the gallery entrance. He gazed at it in disbelief. The rusted shaft towered sheer to the second storey, the flukes sweeping sideways to eye level.

'Think of the effort on the capstan to get *that* back up to the ship,' he muttered at last. 'Imagine the size of the chain and hawsers to hold it in place.'

'Gives you a good idea of the ship's dimensions,' Lennard agreed, 'it does that, bro. Now let's go upstairs and check out the sexy lady we've both come to admire.'

'The one you tell me needs a facelift?'

'That's the one, but don't you get too horny, now. I know you're gonna get the hots for her.' He chuckled as he repeated, 'You and me both, bro. You and me both.'

She was a wooden statuette the survivors had salvaged from her position between the gallery windows at the *Zuytdorp*'s stern and propped up on the cliffs above the wreck. Lennard was convinced that Gerrit's grandfather Laurens had chiselled her from white oak in the *dokhavn* carving shed. At first, he'd thought she'd been modelled on Nehalennia, the Roman Goddess of sailors and fertility, to protect the ship from storms, promising safe return with a full cargo.

'They found some granite carvings of her buried in the sand dunes at Domburg,' he said, 'on the coast near Middelburg. Religious altars, I guess you'd call them. I've got some photos Rosie took in the Abbey Museum when she and I were there in 1983. I'll show you later.'

He'd assumed she was Laurens's model, he explained. But he was wrong. He'd found out later she was inspired by images of the Grecian sphinx.

She stood four feet tall in her glass case. She wore a victor's laurels over hair that swirled around her upturned face. Her mouth was pursed and her cheeks filled to blow wind at the sails. She was lion-breasted for Zeeland and pregnant for the ship's cargo. Her wings were furled, a scaly serpent's tail extended beneath her. Sun-cracked and worn by three centuries of neglect, she stood in the corner of the glass case surrounded by other relics from the wreck—coins, broken bottles, barrel hoops, breech blocks for the bronze swivel guns, rolls of lead and a fractured section of yardarm.

The survivors had left her on the cliffs as a memorial to mark their arrival, Lennard explained. He believed she may have alarmed the superstitious Malgana, who subsequently kept their distance, so that many other relics were still intact when stockman Tom Pepper discovered the wreck in 1927, including a treasure trove of broken glass which the Malgana would have prized for spear tips and cutting instruments.

Lennard leaned forward, peering intently into the cabinet. 'She's a dead ringer for the bronze statue they're designing for the HMAS *Sydney* memorial in Geraldton,' he murmured. 'We'll soon have a second woman on that stretch of coast looking out to sea. But in *her* case, she'll be searching the horizon for 645 drowned Aussie sailors.'

Stefan raised his eyebrows. 'That has an interesting symmetry to it,' he said. 'Another stricken woman staring out to sea.'

Lennard stepped back with a cynical shake of his head. 'It sure does, but what d'you know,' his voice rose, 'us blackfellas, we miss out once again! We ask for a plot on Yellagonga's campsite and get knocked back in favour of a patch of ground on Heirisson Island. The *Sydney* memorial needs half an acre on Mt Scott in the middle of the CBD and they hand it to them on a frigging plate.'

'There's nothing wrong with Bathers Beach, Ace. Provided the Freo Council comes to the party.'

'Yeah, you're right. Max'll wrap them around his little finger with his sweet-talking.' He broke into a hollow laugh. 'He'd better, or we'll sack him!'

AFTER THAT FIRST visit, Stefan took time out whenever possible to view the *Zuytdorp* relics and other VOC exhibits on display. In the evenings, he pored over Lennard's research documents, uncovering pointers to Gerrit's family background and upbringing. The boy locked onto his mind like a burr as he materialised from the shadows of the *Zuytdorp*'s sunken timbers.

One evening, Lennard took down two of the engravings of Middelburg from the wall in the lounge. He and Stefan examined them using a magnifying glass. They were based on sketches by Mattheus Smallegange, dated 1699. The first showed a view across the inner harbour towards the *dokhavn*. In the foreground, an old man and teenage boy were pictured beneath the archway entrance to the VOC headquarters.

'I like to think that's Gerrit and his grandfather on their way home,' Lennard said. 'I found out Gerrit attended the Latijn School where he coped okay, without excelling, and his granddad Laurens worked for years in the carving shed.' He tapped his forefinger on the two figures. 'I like to think he's called into the carving shed after school to join the old fella for the walk home.'

Surprised by Lennard's suggestion, Stefan closely examined details in the picture. The boy was not elaborately dressed. He was wearing a buttonless shirt and long trousers beneath a knee-length coat, an open leather satchel displaying several books slung across his shoulder. Examining the tilt of the boy's head and jut of chin under the magnifying lens as he spoke to his grandfather, Stefan saw a sturdy, square-shouldered boy whose animated expression suggested someone learning to stand his ground, perhaps downright obstinately on this occasion.

'If it is them,' he glanced up at Lennard, 'the young bloke may respect his grandfather enough to walk him home but he looks like he's got a serious streak of the larrikin in him.'

'Could be. Take a look at the old bloke's face. Whaddya see? A patient frown? Someone who knows the young fella takes shrewd handling?'

Stefan shook his head. 'He looks one tough old bugger. I wouldn't like to cross him. I reckon he'd rip the kid gloves off to put the young bloke back in his place when he's crossed the line.'

'What about those books in the satchel? Do you see a kid interested in the busy world opening up around him?'

Stefan scanned the crowds milling on the quayside, the dogs running wild. 'Busy's the word for it, Ace. Half the city's out on the streets, by the looks.'

In the other engraving Lennard pointed out a group of four ratcatchers in a corner of the picture—two men and two women—with a pack of dogs hunting excitedly among three wheat silos on the east bank of the Haven Canal, the waterway leading ships from the *dokhavn* and the quays in the city centre to the sea.

While Stefan was peering at on the engraving, Lennard said that he imagined it was Gerrit—he leaned across to point him out—and a cousin or friend assisting a pair of kennel maids handling yapping terriers rooting out rats infesting the wheat. The boys were armed with slingshots. Gerrit had several dead rats suspended by the tail from his belt. He was adding another to his tally before unhitching his catch and throwing them onto the growing pile of vermin.

'So what's he shouting at the others, bro? Any idea?'

Stefan leaned back and glanced at him. 'They've reached their quota?'

'Bit more than that, you can put money on it. I reckon he's letting them know how much they'll earn from the Wheat Merchants' Guild—enough for a second round of Polar Bear beer, the latest brand from Haarlem that's all the rage and putting the local Three Barrels brew out of business!'

Stefan chuckled. 'Jeez, you've got an active imagination going there, Ace.'

'Showing you the ropes, bro. Come on, tune in. Fire up those creative brain cells. "Another ten," I can hear him yelling, "and we'll be washing down hot buttered bread and roast beef with our second refills!"' He pointed down at the other boy swinging a rat by the tail and suggested, 'Can't you hear that young fella? "Hey! You girls hungry? We can always put one of these little beestjes on the spit! Give me the word, by crikey!"'

Stefan laughed. 'I'm not so sure about the "by crikey".'

Lennard had discovered that the De Waal family were once engaged in the timber trade. 'They were timber merchants,' he said, 'not short of a bob. I also found out they were Republicans, and I found that *real* interesting. Gerrit must have listened to them chatting around the dining table favouring the idea of a republic from the time he was an ankle-biter.'

'Yeah, I've come across that suggestion in your notes.'

'You've got that far already?'

'Mate, I'm only partway through. Give me a break.'

Lennard's research had revealed that bitter political rivalries between Republicans and their opponents, the Orangists, supporters of William III, the Prince of Orange, had simmered beneath the surface in Zeeland society during Gerrit's boyhood and teenage years.

He retrieved a sheet of paper and a pencil from the writing desk. He drew a line down the centre of the page, headed each column 'Republican' and 'Orangist', and for the next few minutes, he listed Dutch surnames into the separate columns.

'The Orangist families,' he said as he wrote, more to himself than to Stefan, 'the Duvelaers, van Citters and Thibauts among others, they held the upper hand for over thirty years, up until 1702, when William died. The Republicans kept a low profile all that time.'

'Why?'

Lennard looked up from the list. 'They had to. They depended on William for protection. They were at war with Spain. Zeeland was on the front line in the south, with every chance of coming under fire.' Then he grinned. 'Different story when he died. Then the Republicans went berserk.'

He added the name Daniel Fannius into the Republican column, underlining it with two heavy strokes.

'This wild young fella was a Republican firebrand. He organised a group of rebs and staged a coup. I reckon Gerrit was caught up in the thick of it—a sixteen-year-old who figured he was bullet-proof.'

Stefan gave a quiet chuckle. 'Sounds like someone after your own heart?'

'Gerrit, you mean? For sure, no worries! But Daniel Fannius? Nah! Too rebellious for my liking. Nutcase, bro. If you're gonna start a revolution you've got to be *smart* about it.' Then he added with a snort, 'His coup didn't last. You'll find that in my notes as well.'

Stefan watched as he stood to replace the engravings on the wall. 'Those photos of the Nehalennia carvings you mentioned. Have you got them handy?'

Lennard retrieved a photograph album from the bookshelf

and flicked through several pages. He laid it on the table opened at a double-page spread with several pictures of a votive altar carved in granite. A Roman goddess in a flowing toga was seated in a grotto, a dog crouching beside her on the right, a basket overflowing with apples on her left.

He looked down thoughtfully. 'Rosie was fascinated,' he said. 'She did some research of her own while I was tracking Gerrit down.'

It turned out she was a Germanic goddess adopted by the Romans, he explained, with ties to Rosie's favourite Norse goddess, Freya.

'Freya's father was the sea god, Njord, so one link was the sea,' he said. 'Another was fertility. See the apples?'

Stefan pointed at one of the photographs as the thought dawned on him. 'And the dog?'

Lennard smiled. 'Yeah, Rosie named all her dogs after the Norse gods. Freya. Frigg. And Loki before that, granddaddy to them all. Mischievous old dog, he was. Shapeshifter from way back. My favourite. Went everywhere with me.'

'And Skathi?'

'That was Phyllis's idea, after Rosie died. She was in Freya's last litter, born before she copped the arrow.'

He closed the album and gazed at Stefan as he raised a separate finger with each word—'Fertility. Love. Wisdom. They were Freya's bag. Knowledge of life and death. Rosie uncovered the lot when she was researching her connection to Nehalennia.'

'Your notes,' Stefan said, as Lennard closed the album, 'they're something else. I have to compliment you on the way you've sorted them out. And the detail! I've already drafted a couple of passages almost word for word.'

Lennard laughed. 'I've made it easy for you?'

'Easier than I expected.' Then he grinned. 'Apart from the illegible handwriting, of course.'

'What did you expect? Copperplate, bro? I wasn't taking it slow. I had a lot to get through.'

'You must have been stoked diving into the archives.'

'I was. Over the frigging moon. It was the opportunity I'd anticipated all my life.'

Stefan looked thoughtfully up at the engravings. He was breathing life into the first European known to have survived among the Malgana and he wondered if Gerrit would guide him through the minefield between their differing cultures. He glanced across at Lennard, who had urged him moments ago to use his imagination as he fleshed Gerrit out, and the sudden thought struck him—*Gerrit's first child! Is that where the answer lies? In Lennard's first mixed-blood ancestor?*

In The Hague, he and Rosalie had visited the *Algemeen Rijksarchief*, the National Archives of the Netherlands, Lennard went on, looking for the names of the crew that sailed aboard the *Zuytdorp* on her final journey.

'I knew the boarding registers and the ship's log were missing,' he said. 'They went down with the ship. But with the help of the boss cocky there we did find the VOC recruiting roll. It gave us the names of a hundred soldiers and four tradesmen who signed on. That gave me a head start.'

Then he was shown something startling—an invoice prepared in Cape Town referring to repairs carried out by the ship's *oppertimmerman*, the senior carpenter, on the wooden Triton fountain in the outdoor swimming pool in the gardens of the Groot Constantia vineyard. The payment of seven guilders was credited to the ship's accounts on 21 April 1712.

'I got in touch with a contact I was given at the Cape Town archives right away,' he said, 'and they found his name, by crikey! On a page of the senior surgeon's journal—the one who ran the hospital, the *Gasthuis* they called it then. Gerrit de Waal! He was a patient there for five days in March 1712. I couldn't believe my luck.'

In Middelburg, he'd examined records documented from the late 1600s in the city's *Zeeuws* Archives. He had been working blind, running through microfiche films and turning the pages of fragile three-hundred-year-old ledgers with meticulous care, his hands in white gloves, the archive custodian hovering over him like a protective vulture.

He had the name de Waal and a series of dates to guide him—January 1701 for the laying of the keel and June of that year for the launch; August 1711 for the departure from Wielingen; March/April 1712 for the stopover in Cape Town.

On the first morning, he had been astounded when he'd unearthed Gerrit's name on the page of a *dokhavn* payroll ledger. Gerrit was listed for the first time as an apprentice *timmerman,* a ship's carpenter, on 3 January 1701. There were several subsequent references to him, barely legible, the last recorded on 14 June 1711. The records included another de Waal—Laurens, described as a *beeldsnijder*, a woodcarver, with records dating back a decade.

'I'd uncovered the name I was after. *Two* names,' Lennard said, 'and that was a mighty step forward. But Laurens? Who was he? Was there a relationship? I had my work cut out,' he paused before adding emphatically, '*and then some!*'

There was something else about the *dokhavn* records that struck him—the number of names that did not appear to be Dutch. 'There were big mobs of them working there, bro, names that sounded Spanish or Portuguese, Belgian and German, Scandinavian and one or two that looked Asian. That gave me a blast. Middelburg must have been a melting pot in Gerrit's day, one of the earliest multi-cultural societies. A lot like us today, I reckon.'

He'd beavered away without further success, he said. Then, on the advice of the archive custodian, he changed tack and examined the land tenure transactions and censuses for the 17th century. His persistence paid off. Late on the third afternoon, he'd found a transfer deed transacted on 25 October 1602 that led him to a Hendrick de Waal. On that date, he'd acquired an acre of land close to the west bank of the Haven canal, half a mile beyond the city gates.

'I couldn't believe it! I read the lot number and asked the custodian to translate for me.'

The land, she'd told him, had been bought in exchange for timber salvaged from the demolition of a Portuguese *carrack*, the *Santiago*, captured off St Helena that year. The record indicated that an unspecified number of diamonds and several pearls had changed hands in the transaction, along with the timber. Some of the jewels were catalogued as belonging to Francesco Carletti, an Italian merchant recorded as Hendrick's silent partner.

'The *Santiago*, bro! And a *third* de Waal; Hendrick this time… and *Francesco Carletti*!' Lennard exclaimed. 'And I had an address. I was certain there was a connection to Gerrit. I was that fired up I went off my rocker, dancing the *nyambi* round the archives like I was taking the lead at my one-man corroboree!'

He'd asked the custodian to cross-reference the lot number for its location.

'She was confused by my Aussie accent and euchred by my blackfella phrasebook Dutch, but she got the message. After a phone call, she suggested it might be one of the old houses behind the Middelburg cemetery.'

The land was located on Kruitmolen Lane, to the south of the city, she'd told him.

'What more could I ask for? I was up and running, by crikey!'

MIDDELBURG, JULY 1983

HE ARRANGED FOR Rosalie to look after his notebooks and papers and he took the library stairs three at a time, unfolding the street map as he sprinted across the town square, past the *Stadhuis* Town Hall and packed open-air cafes and over the canal bridges. He turned left past the railway station, not stopping until he reached the point opposite the Buitenhaven where the entrance to the Haven canal was once located.

The Haven canal, which used to carry ships southwards to the Westerschelde estuary at Fort Rammekens and the open sea beyond, had been filled in. It was buried beneath the bitumen road south to Nieuw-en Sint Joosland, but its raised embankment was still there, carpeted in thistles and grasses and ragtag patches of orange and scarlet poppies pulsing in the wind as he ran through them. He angled down past the cemetery gardens lined with overarching beeches to a cul-de-sac running off Kruitmolen Lane.

And there he found the row of houses he was looking for. They were part of the city's historic heritage trail.

Standing beside a shallow canal bordered by reeds and willows, they had a quaint and cheerful look. Lennard ran across the wooden bridge that led to the laneway. It shook under his footfalls. The tranquil brown water was swarming with dragonflies, some zipping through their lively callisthenics across its surface, others piggybacked in the mating ritual, riding the air in tandem, their linked abdomens curved like pinwheels on transparent wings. *They're as high as I feel right now*, he thought as he jogged past, barely able to suppress his anticipation.

Smoke from the chimney in the first house led him to the caretaker. A hostile border collie bailed him up, hackles raised, teeth showing as it backed him into peonies that lined the driveway, until the caretaker appeared at the door to silence the dog and confirm that the houses were open for viewing.

He was supposed to accompany Lennard, he said, but he was halfway through a meal and would join him later.

Lennard could barely believe it. The de Waal house—and he assumed it was Gerrit's—was the fifth one along, at the end of the row. Fixed into the brickwork beside the door he found a ship's bell. He read the name etched on it—the *Sao Jago, Lisboa, 1591.*

He struck it with his knuckles, listened to its echo and rang it another three times, a series of images springing to mind—bleary-eyed crews relieved after a watch change, a call to battle stations before the deafening crump of cannons and the crackle of small arms fire, funeral rites as corpses wrapped in sheets and weighted with cannonballs slid down the chute into raging black seas.

Alongside the bell, he saw a small heraldic shield painted with the Zeeland banner, its red lion rampant on a yellow ground emerging from blue and white waves. The Zeeland motto was inscribed beneath it—*Luctor et emergo—I struggle and I emerge*, he'd been told. *I battle to win.*

He opened the door and stood on the top step, his heart thumping. He gripped the thick post and ducked beneath the lintel. His eyes took a moment to adjust before he stepped inside.

In the dim light of oil lamps, he saw the gleam of a full-length mirror facing him across the floor, framed in ebony, and within it, he saw his own uncanny reflection step forward to greet him. He waved and his shadow waved back, more cautionary than welcoming, it seemed. In his elevated mood, he had to be attentive to every step, not get too carried away, not allow his heightened expectations to misread the story about to open up to him.

The afternoon sunlight streamed in behind him, illuminating the room. Alternate lines of red and yellow tulips hand-painted on enamel tiles ran along the walls. To his left, stood a glass-fronted display cabinet of oak and polished walnut. On one shelf, a row of blue and white china plates glimmered and, on a lower shelf, as he peered closer, stood a display of ornaments, among them four grey-green pottery mugs with austere faces set in relief and a pair of foot-high porphyry statuettes of what appeared to be a shepherd and a shepherdess.

To his right an oak bench with red leather cushions was set along the wall, and, for the second time since his arrival, he read the Zeeland slogan carved along its backrest. He sat down on the bench and, with his fingers, explored the gouge marks of the letters.

Luctor et Emergo. That has to be my motto from here on in! he thought.

Diagonally across the floor stood a small rectangular clavichord with an open sheaf of music set in its lectern. He crossed the room and struck middle C. Its tinny note rang true. When he walked across the room with the note still sounding, he felt he was stepping back in time, crossing a threshold into his history, as though a part of him was coming home. It seemed he could have found his way around in the dark, as if he'd lived there all his life.

He walked across the front room, through the wood-panelled archway and into the main hallway. There the floor was tiled in small black and white squares. *If walls and floors could speak*, he thought, *they'd tell me things there are no words for*. He stepped forward, as though making his first move in a game of chess. *I've chosen black*, he smiled exultantly, *and I'm playing to restore part of my Malgana people's collective memory*.

Each step he took seemed charged, each square a soundscape of polyphonic impressions hinting at complementary stories—the shuffled footfalls of felt and velvet slippers, the leather thump of polished boots, murmured conversations, the tinkling sounds of the clavichord, the dry screech of a boy's stick dragged across the tiles or the clink of his green glass marbles rolling across them, the sputter of peat fires and the crackle of poultry roasting in the kitchen ovens beyond. Bursts of explosive laughter. Family arguments. The sigh of an old man half-asleep or deep in contemplation, puffing at his pipe, even the daily slurry of a mop of boiling water dragged over them... and now the echo of *his* footsteps!

He turned right, to the narrow flight of stairs that wound up to the mezzanine. In the stairway banisters he found four polished uprights of carved ash—the lucky timber, he discovered later—stained butterscotch brown. He ran his hands over them. They were the chiselled figures of mermaids salvaged from who knows where aboard the *Santiago*. He felt the shape of the first of them—the breasts and the belly. The wood was warm where he expected it to be cold. The carving was meticulous, the grain running with the figure's lines worn smooth by the hands of people passing up and down the stairway over the last four centuries.

Part-way up the stairs he paused to admire the reproduction of a large half-length portrait of a naval officer suspended on the wall. The sitter was middle-aged, his square face austere beneath the black leather peak of a rakish sun-bleached red cap pulled low across his forehead. He was surprisingly unlined for a man of the sea, the finest tracery of lines fanning from the corners of his eyes. He wore a salt-and-pepper goatee and his lips were compressed into a thin line with no hint of a smile, giving him an authoritative take-no-prisoners look. He was wearing a simple pale blue uniform jacket silver-buttoned to his lace-collared neck. His hands, with fingers linked, rested across it, lurid tattoos of tiger salamanders breathing scarlet and orange flames on the backs of each.

Lennard read the label on the gilded frame as he passed—Hendrick de Waal, 1610, by Salomon Mesdach. The artist had captured a pair of arresting grey eyes so piercing they seemed to look through Lennard as he examined them. And when he glanced back, they followed him up the stairs.

It looked to Lennard as though Hendrick was in two minds, undecided between approval and displeasure at his intrusion. *On guard!* Lennard thought as he climbed further. *He'd be one hard bastard to get to know, with his frown a front to keep the world in its place.* But he suspected there was a gentler Hendrick behind the mask, reserved for those he chose to reveal himself to, those closest to him.

He took another upward step and looked back. *Am I right?* he wondered. *Have I got you sussed? Have I gone up in your estimation? Don't you realise I'm a long lost relative, a descendant come to pay my respects?*

He resumed climbing the stairs to the second storey landing, where he found a bookshelf. He ran his finger and his eye along the leather spines, reading the embossed titles—Jacob Cats, he remembered from his research, Roemer Visscher and Vondel, the diaries of Baldaeus and van Spilbergen, and a history of the Batavian Republic by Hugo Grotius, alongside a copy of his pamphlet—the *Mare Liberum*. They were twentieth-century reprints of the originals. Then one book in particular caught his eye—the *Reis om de Wereld, 1594–1606* by Francesco Carletti, the chronicles of the Italian merchant's voyage round the world.

He lifted it out and opened it.

He knew Carletti was a silent partner in Hendrick's land transaction, but he didn't know about his book. It was a reproduction of the 1701 Dutch translation from the Italian, printed in Amsterdam. When he flicked through it, he found several references in the last fifty pages to the *Santiago* and to Middelburg and the *opperstuurman* Hendrick de Waal aboard the *Zeelandia*.

He sat on the top step and skimmed through the pages, but the Dutch was beyond him. He replaced it on the shelf, determined to look for an English version later.

Across the landing, he found a ladder to the attic roped with plaited leather to a pulley. He swung it down. The smell of polished leather and dust spread as the ladder creaked down towards him. It was the well-worn smell of a page of history, he thought, in which he was about to read his past and, in some uncanny sense, discover part of his destiny.

'Aspire to become who you were,' he murmured—an obscure quotation of Max's he recalled as he placed his foot on the first rung.

He scrambled up into a small rectangular room with black beams running the length of its ceiling. A print was hanging beside the window and he saw the seductive eyes of Jan Steen's *Girl with Oysters* follow him across the room, a rosette attached to the ribbon in her hair, offering him, with feigned innocence, a plate of shucked oysters.

On another wall, he discovered a series of engravings of Middelburg, signed by M Smallegange. Several of these took Lennard's breath away. In one, the artist had captured the *dokhavn*, a view across the waterway with shipbuilding in progress. In another was a panorama of the Haven canal, with Middelburg in the background and the De Waal house alongside what appeared to be a line of ramshackle greenhouses. In another was a view across the Buitenhaven canal towards the VOC headquarters, with the arched gateway to the *dokhavn* alongside it. To Lennard's astonishment, he saw a man and a boy standing in the gateway. Could they, by coincidence, be Laurens and Gerrit? He inspected the engravings closely, determined to procure copies back in Middelburg.

On a shelf beneath the engravings was a row of wooden toys, some crudely carved, and others with remarkable accuracy.

A bed was set against the wall. At the foot of the bed,

propped in the corner, was a battered kite. Its silk panels were faded scarlet and green. The crosspieces appeared to be made of pliable whalebone baleen. A large rusted key was attached at its centre, where the crosspieces met.

'So here I am, Gerrit,' Lennard murmured, 'this has to be your bedroom! I'm three hundred years late, maybe, but I'm here to lead you back into the living world. So where are you, bro?'

On the bed lay a polar bearskin rug. It was a synthetic copy of the original, Lennard assumed. He pictured Gerrit lying back on it, his feet raised against the wall, eating roasted almonds coated in rose-watered marzipan prepared by his mother, reading his books of exploration, listening to the wind in the rigging of his ghostly ships and the cries of gulls wheeling above sailors marooned on the windswept coasts of his imagination.

The day was overcast. Pale light filtered through the latticed window. The panes were opaque and dusty. It was difficult to open and for a moment he thought it might be nailed shut, but it gave and he latched it as wide as it allowed. He looked down at the garden, where a pair of wrens splashing in a birdbath were disturbed and fled up into the silver branches of a birch tree pendulous with catkins, where they chattered at him in alarm.

Then, in a display cabinet with a sliding glass lid, he saw an ancient brass telescope and, next to it, what appeared to be a spyglass wrapped in snakeskin. They were lying beside two bleached conch shells washed up from who knows where, each with a small aperture perforated at one end. Alongside them lay a walrus-tusk sheath-knife, its handle a carved dolphin, and beside that, a palm-sized silver medallion minted in 1603 to celebrate the *Santiago*'s capture.

The glass lid was locked, but the key was in it. He ignored the prohibition notice on the glass and unlocked it. He took out the spyglass, unrolling it delicately from the crackling snakeskin. It was feather-light, the tube covered with a membrane of tanned leather, fine as parchment.

He sat on the window ledge and was surprised to hear the spyglass rattle as he lifted it slowly to his eye and looked in. To his amazement, he was looking through a myriad of patterned colours to the beech trees in the graveyard. He saw the crematorium, and beyond it, the traffic moving on the roadway. They were mirrored in the spyglass as he swept it across his field of view. They were coloured by it, forming part of its intricate patterns, like a trembling glass mobile. It presented him with a visionary shift in colour and dimension, so he bent to examine it more closely.

It was a primitive kaleidoscope. The inner barrel was highly polished, the lens at the end part-closed with an inward-facing mirror. Fragments of coloured glass inside were reflected along its inner surface. It was a cunning instrument and he looked into it again for a second or two, enough to brand it on his mind for good.

He rewrapped it and put it back in the display case, deep in thought. He imagined Gerrit peering through it at the *Santiago* in his mind the day it arrived at St Helena when it was captured by his great-grandfather Hendrick's ship.

And then he visualised the boy reaching for a conch shell and blowing at the sounding hole to signal the attack, as Lennard then did to warn of his arrival. He was astonished at its tone and tested it again. It sounded like a didjeridoo with a single low A note.

He sat looking over the beech trees in the graveyard. Everything he'd wondered about, everything he'd researched, made perfect sense in those moments.

Lennard explained that the Middelburg Archives library was closed when he arrived back after visiting the house. 'It was pitch dark and Rosie had gone back to the hotel. I'd lost all sense of time.'

The next morning, they discovered that the archive custodian had located several other records she thought might be of interest. She had translated and photocopied them. They included a complete list of buyers and the prices transacted at the auction of the *Santiago*'s timbers, Hendrick de Waal's name among them.

She'd also uncovered some cryptic details of the Admiralty court case featuring Francesco Carletti suing to retrieve his goods, seized when the *Santiago* was taken as a prize of war. In the final judgement, his cargo was declared forfeit. The Italian received a laughable amount in compensation. He'd been obliged to spend most of it on a traditional dinner he hosted for the judges who had passed sentence and the advocates who had unsuccessfully represented him.

'She saved the best for last,' he said. 'She opened up a genealogical census ledger and showed us several single-line references. Yep, Laurens *was* Gerrit's grandfather… and Hendrick his great-grandfather.'

And then, out of the blue, she presented Lennard with photocopies of two documents that astounded him. She'd discovered references to Gerrit's father, Maarten. The first was an ancestral record of Gerrit's christening, when he was six months old, on October 17, 1686, in the church at Aagtekerke. Maarten de Waal and Anneka, née Tuineman were recorded as his parents.

The second was a page from the *Daghregister*, the daily register of bookings into the VOC crew lodgings in Vlissingen. Along with a group of six other officers, Maarten de Waal had spent two nights there on 8 and 9 July 1693. The entry against his name confirmed that he was the *onderstuurman*, the second mate aboard the *Ridderschap van Holland*. She had sailed from the Wielingen channel on 11 July 1693.

'I was so shocked I couldn't speak,' Lennard said quietly, looking at Stefan. 'The *Ridderschap van Holland*... I knew about her. She reached Cape Town on time and in one piece. She left on 5 February 1694, but she was never seen again. She disappeared clean off the face of the earth. She didn't make it to Batavia. A total mystery.' He hesitated before shaking his head and adding, 'Gerrit lost his father when he was eight, the poor little fella.'

He was silent for several minutes. Studying him closely, Stefan thought he was wondering what it must have been like for the boy at that age, whether it had played a part in his determination to become a ship's carpenter, to work his way halfway around the world on a quest to find his father, only to end up on those godforsaken cliffs. But Lennard took a deep breath instead and gave him a knowing look as though he was aware of Stefan's thinking and wasn't about to elaborate.

'I couldn't believe my luck in uncovering so many connections to Gerrit in so short a time,' he went on. 'I thought we'd had Buckley's.' His smile developed into a chuckle. 'I turned to the lady who'd given us the goods and gave her a hug she'll never forget! Left her gobsmacked. Especially when I told her, "Dinner's on us tonight at the restaurant of your choice. It's our shout." Rosie had to translate my accent for her.'

It had cost them two dinners, two nights in a row. And on both occasions, they were lucky to get seats in the Spanish restaurant the librarian selected. They had been there during the tourist season, he explained. 'That's when Middelburg is buzzing. People visiting from everywhere. Bloody beautiful city, though. *Speaks* to you, by crikey. Like you're back in the Middle Ages. If you ever get the chance, go.'

He paused thoughtfully. 'Hey, I might have to send you there, come to think of it. Give you some insights for the book. Some atmosphere.' He looked shrewdly at Stefan, who hadn't responded. 'Let me think about it.'

THE CUSTODIAN UNDERTOOK a book search for Lennard before they left for Amsterdam. She found Carletti's book on the market in an English translation and he bought the second-hand copy she scored for him through a contact. He devoured it in an afternoon and read it again the next day. It was among the notebooks and papers in the box he'd given to Stefan who hadn't got around to reading it yet.

Before he left Middelburg, he also bought copies of the Mattheus Smallegange engravings he'd seen in the attic. He had them framed on his return to Fremantle and hung them in the lounge, with Rosalie checking their alignment.

He stepped back and, with his arm around Rosalie's waist, admired the effect with deep satisfaction. There he was—Gerrit de Waal, a boy from Middelburg, determined to set out in search of a father he barely remembered... a century after Galileo had confirmed the earth was not the centre of the galaxy and reduced man to a bit player in the universe, now hanging on the wall of his house in Fremantle.

CALYUTE

IN AUGUST, STEFAN MOVED into one of the vacated town-houses. It was a short walk to Alicia and Lennard and he often spent his evenings there, enjoying a meal and then playing cards or scrabble or occasionally chess, contests in which he found himself more often than not outfoxed by Lennard, despite making what he considered canny moves.

Ignoring Lennard's warnings, he accepted Alicia's challenge to a game one evening and she checkmated him in no time flat.

'Where'd you learn to play like that?' he asked. 'I'm humbled.'

She broke into a captivating smile. 'Alejandra's Great-Aunt Alfonsa taught me. Have you read *All the Pretty Horses*?'

'No, not yet.'

'Or *The Crossing*?'

'No.'

She gestured at the bookcase. 'Cormac McCarthy. His descriptions of Mexico are second to none. You can borrow my copies if you like. That old Dueña Alfonsa spent most of her evenings studying the game.'

Then, her eyes alight as she reset the pieces, she added, 'Seriously, Papá taught me. When I was four years old, he had me setting up the pieces and moving them around the board for him when he was playing against himself. I was bound to get the idea. Eventually, he let me take him on.' She gestured with a forefinger from one ear to the other. 'He grinned from here to here, the first time he conceded and I held him to a draw. I was ten. I can still feel his arms around me.' She laughed. 'He was so pleased he wouldn't let me go.'

Impressed by her expertise, Stefan asked her for some coaching and she introduced him to a range of opening moves, following through to mid and endgame variations that took some memorising. Practising at home, as time passed, he took on Lennard with growing confidence. His new-found skill won him an increasing number of games, advice from Alicia often his guide. 'Try the King's Indian defence,' she'd whisper. 'He's weak against the Sicilian,' and after weeks of instruction—'It's time for the Latvian gambit! That's it, Stefan! *Go for the jugular tonight!*'

He participated in tutorials with her as he learned Malgana. He found it complicated and tongue-twisting at first, but she set him achievable goals and he slowly picked up a basic vocabulary of everyday words.

One evening, when the lesson ended, Alicia asked him what language Tania and her brothers spoke.

'I'm not sure,' he replied quietly. 'She's a Yirrganydji woman, but I've got no idea what dialect she speaks, if any. She didn't mention it and as far as I can remember, I never heard her speaking anything but English. Or her family, for that matter.'

'Where are they from?'

'Caravonica. In Cairns, just north of the Barron River. Next to the cane fields there.'

Alicia frowned, then nodded almost imperceptibly. 'Then it may have been one of the Djabugay dialects. Yidiny, perhaps. Or Yirrgay, but that's unlikely. It's almost extinct.'

'I've no idea, but the name Djabuguy rings a bell. There's a Tjapukai Dance Theatre down the road from her place. She worked with them when she was in her teens, long before she met me.'

Gazing steadily at him, Alicia asked, 'So where *did* you two meet, if you don't mind me asking?'

'In Kyoto, of all places. In the foyer of the Granvia Hotel. I was stocking a glass cabinet there with samples of my jewellery and miniatures.'

Sales in Japan had taken off, he explained, and he'd had contracts in several different cities.

'Including Nagasaki, which was interesting. I didn't know

it, but the Wirruwana dancers were in Tokyo presenting *Oceans* at the time. When I turned around after locking the cabinet, there she was, standing behind me with another dancer.'

They had been admiring the collection of crystal marsupials he'd made—koalas, bandicoots, numbats, bilbies.

'She told me they'd snuck in a trip to Kyoto between performances and she'd admired them when she'd arrived the day before. She was surprised to find big mobs of Aussie fauna there to welcome her.'

They had been on their way to the station that morning and had seen him arranging the display.

'She was particularly taken with the cassowary. She said it had a particular significance for her. I wasn't sure what she meant and was about to ask when she picked up her bags to leave.' He paused thoughtfully. 'It was her clan totem, she told me later.'

On an impulse, he'd unlocked the cabinet, selected a cassowary from the three on display and given it to her.

'It was the wrong move. She didn't have the money on her to pay for it and she refused to accept a gift from a stranger, fellow Aussie or not.'

She'd taken his card, said she'd get in touch back in Melbourne, and disappeared through the revolving doors.

'I didn't believe her,' he went on, 'so I did the next best thing. I posted it to her via the Tokyo theatre with the message that payment wasn't necessary and returning it to me would be a disappointment. To cut a long story short, she turned up at my glass studio in Brunswick one morning to return it and one thing led to another.'

Alicia watched in silence as he shook his head. 'We were together for over two years. I look back on them as the best of my life, even though my business was failing towards the end. I was hopelessly undercapitalised. Customer interest was there, especially in the jewellery, but I couldn't produce enough to meet demand. It was the biggest mistake I could have made.'

And then Tania had walked out on him.

'There was no orange light, none I could see. No warnings. She went,' he snapped a finger, 'like *that*, and my world fell apart.' He was unable to go on for a moment, then gave a long sigh. 'The day she left I felt as if she'd driven a dagger through me. I think she felt the same. I had no idea what the problem was. I've been wondering ever since.'

Alicia clicked her tongue. 'Poor you, Stefan, let down by the woman who stole your heart. And you still don't have a clue?'

'Not for sure. She may have met someone else, I guess.'

'If she had, it would have been written all over her. You'd have picked up on changes in her behaviour she couldn't hide—those tell-tale hints that surface once the lying begins. You'd have sensed it the first day she met him.'

'Or her.'

'Or her.' Then she frowned thoughtfully. 'Was it the money, perhaps? She must have been concerned about your prospects… and hers.'

'She was, but she was helping me deal with it.'

'Perhaps she made herself scarce to give you one less thing to worry about?'

'I can't believe that. She'd been very loyal up till then. If we were going down, we were going down together.'

'So what else was there?'

'I figured it may have been her brothers, the Aboriginal thing. The resentment. The misunderstanding. The first time I met them early in the piece it was a disaster. We spoke at cross-purposes and I was totalled. I was completely unprepared for the outburst they delivered at my expense—at my ignorance of their circumstances and my apparent lack of concern for their history. Tania came to my rescue that afternoon.

Just as well, but the damage was done. Maybe she thought the bridges were beyond repair.'

'I doubt that, but it's possible, I suppose. Irreconcilable differences.'

'I've wondered. She had me reading up on her people's history before she left. She believed it would give me some insights and help me patch things up. But my heart wasn't in it. I know she was upset.'

He glanced beyond her through the glass doors for a moment. 'That was before I met Lennard and I'm learning to see things in a very different light.' Several moments of silence followed, and then, 'I really don't know what else could have upset her. She wanted us to have a child, but that was out of the question. We were in the red and she agreed to wait.'

'That must have concerned her. How old was she?'

'In her mid-twenties.'

'And you were what, in your late thirties? A twelve-year difference is neither here nor there.' She leaned back in her chair and broke into a peal of laughter. 'Until you hit the slide in the sixties and she's in her sexy mid-forties and having her midlife crisis!'

She resumed her original position and carefully chose her words, 'Maybe she wanted her *freedom*, Stefan. For the time being. She's a dancer. She's used to expressing herself freely through her body as she follows the choreography she's learned. She's disciplined, but she gets carried away in the flow of the moment. The freedom of it must be intoxicating.

'Perhaps that's how she was feeling. She needed space. Time out to reassess things. And she couldn't talk to you about it because she didn't want to hurt you. In the end, she couldn't help it.' She raised her eyebrows. 'If that is the case, my friend, I think your luck is in. I think she'll come back to you as freely as she left. I really do.' She smiled brightly and put her hand on his forearm. 'Wait for her to make the first move, but make sure she knows you'll welcome it.'

WHENEVER HE SENSED that Lennard was receptive, he bombarded him with questions about Gerrit. He especially looked forward to finding him in an expansive mood, needing no prompting, when he riveted Stefan with conjectures concerning Gerrit's survival on the cliff top and later among the Malgana.

The situations he described stretched Stefan's imagination—their first meetings after the shipwreck, when momentary fear and self-protective aggression were succeeded by curiosity and mutual interrogation, erupting into shared laughter. Their conflicted languages and abortive attempts to communicate. The early bouts of gift-giving and reciprocal exchange that descended into acts of communal sharing that the Dutch considered theft, leading to outrage, fiery recriminations and vicious fighting.

The bush medicine healing of Gerrit's wounds and his growing dependency on them. His painful trek south across the semi-desert clifftops to the Murchison River and the long period of tolerant indifference with which they regarded him when he caught up with them, his dependency a disposable nuisance before they eventually accepted him the stronger and more useful he became.

And there were weeks when the house was overrun with relatives and friends visiting from Denham or Geraldton or Mullewa and other inland towns in the Murchison. Stefan enjoyed meeting them and sharing in the chaotic interaction— the rowdy camaraderie, the teasing and contagious laughter among the adults. Then there were the antics of the younger shy yet extroverted children showing off their handstands and cartwheels and airborne somersaults, kicking a football across the lawn or pedalling furiously up and down Bellevue Terrace on two rusty bicycles Lennard stored for them. They did spec-tacular wheelies back into the gravel driveway, their ecstatic show-off smiles all flashing teeth, while older girls danced in an inner bedroom to deafening music on a ghetto-blaster Alicia regularly turned down before her patience wore out and she confiscated it.

On one occasion he spent time sitting on the back steps with a solitary teenage boy less well-adjusted than the rest, who astonished him by taking from his trouser pocket a Rubik's cube he solved with blinding speed, presenting it to Stefan with a lopsided smile, more in acknowledgement of his interest than satisfaction at his achievement, as Stefan reset it for another demonstration of his proficiency, his hands moving so fast he could barely make them out.

At night, with the children half-awake and whispering together in sleeping bags spread along the veranda, he joined the circle of adults reminiscing around the barbecue fire, their laughter carrying, stars in their millions sweeping across the sky.

On one such evening, he broached the question of Gerrit's arrival with the other survivors and the likely reaction of the Malgana to their uninvited appearance on country.

Opinions were divided. One, more forthright than the others, suggested outright slaughter. 'I reckon they massacred the lot,' he growled, 'which is how we shoulda reacted here in Perth in 1829. No questions asked. No quarter given!' Sticking out his tongue and with a blood-curdling gurgle he drew his forefinger across his throat and then, adopting a stage whisper, he hissed, 'Can't you hear them shoutin', "*Bloody boat people*! We have the right to protect our borders! We will decide who comes to this country?"'

He stared across the fire at Stefan with an ironic glint in his eye, so that Stefan wasn't sure whether his comments were tongue-in-cheek or not until he broke into a wide grin and gave him a gotcha wink.

Others believed there'd been a more humane reaction, with Gerrit accepted into the family once doubts about his white skin and incarnated return from the dead were put to rest.

Stefan listened keenly and gathered images he wrote up the moment he returned to the unit. He dragged his work desk onto the upstairs balcony where he had a clear view across a line of coral gums to Rottnest and the ocean beyond. Their grey-green foliage and russet flowers framed a glimpse of the city below and the glassworks on the foreshore.

He liked the solitude. He enjoyed the silence of the empty unit, filling it with music when he chose to.

It was conducive to the writing process, but he faced a dilemma at first. Given the depth and extent of the archival material Lennard had unearthed, he had to determine whether he was writing a factually accurate biography or a historical novel—part-fiction, part-speculation.

He asked Alicia. Her answer was straight to the point. 'Both,' she asserted. 'You don't have all the facts, so there'll be times when you'll have to be creative. You have a wealth of information, so you'll have to be selective. Decide how much to include, how much to ignore. When you do, *keep the reader in mind*. Always. Golden rule! So what's the answer? Write an entertaining *story*, Stefan. Don't digress. Keep her interested. Keep her on her toes.'

'Her? So my reader's a woman?'

'Of course! It's me! I'll be looking over your shoulder every word of the way.'

'That's good to know. So what do I do with facts that may be a diversion but, to my mind, should be included?'

Alicia answered at once, 'Use footnotes! That way your reader has an option to read or not to read. But make certain the inclusions are absolutely necessary. And keep one principle in mind—cut the crap! Because if you don't, as we agreed, I'll be doing it for you.'

'Footnotes? In a novel?'

'Sure. It's been done before. *Moby Dick*, I remember from High School.'

'And Douglas Adams!' Stefan exclaimed. 'In *The Hitchhiker's Guide*.'

She smiled. 'Even masters like Jorge Borges have used them. The Argentinian. We had to study some of his short stories in Linguistics, I remember. For the Spanish.'

'I'll be in good company, then.'

'You will.'

The balcony was the perfect place for him to read and record his ideas, but the writing did not come easily. His skills and experience in the composition of scientific reports and analyses for Pilkington gave him a command of the basics, but he underestimated the complexity of storytelling, of developing credible characters in authentic scenes, launching them into the maritime narrative emerging from the smoke and mirrors of Lennard's research and his own flights of fancy.

The writing was painstaking and progress slow and often disheartening. But he persevered. Lennard had set him the target of completing the book at the same time as the unveiling of the cenotaph. Writing in longhand, he maintained his schedule by force of habit, scattering completed pages onto the bedroom floor behind him where they were sheltered from the wind. Later, he leafed through and sorted them, before transcribing corrected versions onto a laptop he borrowed from Alicia.

Often discouraged when he examined what he'd written and tempted to tear it up, he worked on revisions instead as he strove to make the writing captivating, as Alicia had instructed.

He wrote when he was home from the glassworks in the late afternoons, now and then leaning back in his creaky swivel chair, occasionally listening to Leonard Cohen or Paul Kelly or his favourite Creedence Clearwater Revival tracks, the afternoon sea breeze rattling at the windowpanes.

At other times, needing a break, he reached for his guitar and tinkered to the flamenco tapes Alicia had lent him as he looked out at the sweeping sky down which the sun's blinding disc inched towards the horizon until it sank into the ocean, swathes of red and orange fading to a burgundy veneer soon overshadowed by the dark.

By MID-DECEMBER 1998, the two master sculptures were taking shape. They stood on a concrete base in the annealing room, which they'd converted into a secondary workshop alongside the glassworks. They'd re-laid its roof with transparent corrugated sheets, to monitor the effects of sunlight.

They were making steady progress. Stefan had tapped into his network at Pilkington to negotiate a contract for optically pure float glass sheets to the size and thickness they'd decided on and he'd approached a friend operating a glassworks in Caulfield to apply a dichroic patina of selected colours to two dozen sheets which they were laying at intervals through the sculptures. The sunlight was already refracting and reflecting colours of startling intensity and brightness from the first of these, four layers up, the lustrous effects arresting.

Both sculptures were several layers deep. Each sheet, cut to shape, was glued in place, pinned by three central stainless steel uprights painted to resemble authentic memorial poles, embedded in the concrete base. A mobile gantry was suspended above them, its cables ready to swing the next sheet from the glassworks into place.

The Fremantle Council had surprised Max by signing off on the project without objection. The vote was unanimous. The annealing room would house the sculpture during construction, and the town planners had arranged to dismantle the walls and landscape the area around the concrete foundations when it was complete.

It would stand in a floodlit pool, facing the ocean and accessible to the public via walkways at either end. The first designs were on display in an advertisement on the front wall of the glassworks. The aesthetic effects were remarkable. Whenever Stefan inspected the draft presentation, he felt a deep satisfaction, gratified that he was involved in the project.

At their present rate of progress, barring the unforeseen, they expected to meet the completion target with months to spare.

In May 2000, they spent a morning hoisting the final panel onto the right-hand sculpture and fixing it in place, completing both halves of the rock.

Lennard was euphoric. '*Yes!*' he shouted, stepping back to admire the effect, his arms crossed, before he caught Stefan by the wrist. 'We've done it, bro!' Arms upraised and carried away, they danced like a pair of drunken Greeks in a triumphant figure of eight around each sculpture, Lennard's yells echoing in rhythm with his footfalls as though responding to a balalaika, '*Yes! Yes! Yes! Yes! Yes! Yes!* And one more *yes* for kicks and luck, by crikey!'

To Stefan, cavorting breathless through the filtered light, the sculpture was inexpressibly beautiful, a stunning metaphor for aspects of Lennard's mastery he'd come to admire—his creative insight in capturing form, his perceptive instinct in working with the medium, his aesthetic sensibility, his technique.

The sculpture's proportions were exactly as designed and the effects striking. Aqua tints radiated from the dichroic sheets, lending it a cool translucence. When he and Lennard calmed down moments later and set to work removing the transparent roofing, the monument glowed in direct sunlight with a radiance more remarkable than they'd anticipated, ambient light and colour shimmering across the room.

After a phone call, Alicia and a reporter from the *West Australian* newspaper arrived, followed by Max and Luke, who assisted Stefan in wrestling a jubilant Lennard across the sand and into the sea. It took some doing. The commotion and laughter as he resisted raised consternation among the bathers at the beach, the sand sent flying, until Lennard dragged them all fully clothed into the water in bursts of spray. They emerged soaked, jogging back up to the glassworks to share a bottle of champagne.

The reporter recorded the celebrations on a video camera. Lennard raised a glass to toast a successful job well done, and then, looking directly into the lens with a triumphant glare, he challenged the faceless few who'd opposed the project, 'And here's to you, you gutless wonders, who threatened to derail us,' he growled bluntly. 'Thanks for doing a runner and taking your racism and bigotry with you!'

'Risky move, brother,' Max murmured. 'Risky move. That might make the headlines.'

'Risk? Never mind the risk—the job is done!' Lennard countered. He raised his glass and thumped Stefan's shoulder as he took a swallow. 'Here's to you, my brother. You've done us proud!'

THEY EXPERIMENTED WITH a mix of silicates including a reduced proportion of garnet to create two panels of an opaque blue-grey glass similar in colour and texture to opalite.

Lennard etched the songline message into the first panel, which they'd embedded into the right-hand wall the week after completing the sculpture.

He prepared stencils for etching the names, dates and family groups of those he'd decided to commemorate on the second panel.

'They've all got their stories,' he said when he selected the first stencil and began the etching process. 'They need to be heard. Doesn't matter how confronting.' He was warming the panel with a butane flame before applying the stencil. 'You gotta know their stories backwards, bro, to give you a handle on what went on during settlement. All the violent confrontations.' He shook the flaring torch at arm's length to emphasise his point before redirecting it at the panel. 'No more whitewash! You need to hear the truth about their lives to get the big picture. So you can acknowledge it... and get rid of any bias you may still have, my *wajbala* brother!'

'*Me? Bias?* Give me a break, Ace.' Stefan gave strained laugh, concerned his expression may be showing the lingering scepticism that occasionally surfaced despite his efforts to ignore it. 'I may have had my doubts when I first arrived, but after four years working with you, whose story *haven't* I heard? I know all the names and most of the history, thanks to you.'

But he had to acknowledge there were questions still haunting him. *When people visit the cenotaph in the future, will the commemoration of the names and narratives move them? Will they arouse curiosity and interest? Inspire empathy and understanding? Will the experience of reading the names and examining their stories from a new perspective dispel cynicism, disbelief and prejudice?*

It pained him to admit that even he was having difficulty at the deepest levels reconciling the two diametrically opposed narratives, the white and the black, still coming to terms with

Lennard's determination to expose the trauma in the history of his people.

Lennard reduced the flame and scratched his chin. 'So you know them all, you reckon? There's no one I've missed?' He switched off the torch, looked down at the stencil he was about to apply and grunted, 'Calyute! What about him?'

Stefan looked over his shoulder. He read *Calyute* of the *Nyungar Pindjarup*. 'No, you've got me there,' he agreed, as Lennard leaned forward to attach the stencil to the panel, smoothing it in place before laying strips of sanding tape to protect the rest of the exposed glass.

'Okay,' he said at last. 'That's done. Time to give it a go.'

They lifted the panel into the sandblasting cabinet. Lennard inserted his arms into the gloved apertures, checked the dials and then peered through the screen as he squeezed the trigger of the sandblasting gun, testing the air pressure.

As he watched, Stefan asked, 'Why are no Malgana names represented, Ace? You have several Nyungar warriors. And the Bunuba of course, with Jandamarra and his mob, as well as others from the eastern states. Why's that?'

Lennard didn't reply for several moments as he reengaged the sandblaster, and then he began talking over its hiss, weighing his words as he directed the blast.

'Us blackfellas, we're all brothers. We share our ancestors who died for the cause.' He broke off as he redirected the jet, and then went on, 'The Nyungar took the brunt of the invasion down here in Perth by the bucket load from day dot. And they died fighting back.

'It was different for us up north. The settlers took a while to reach that far. Never mind the handful of ships that called in along the coast—a pearling lugger here, a whaling crew there. Until the sheep stations opened up. All that took the next hundred years. It was gradual and less confronting. That's not to say we didn't resist the land grab. We did.'

He released the trigger, checked the etching and then looked out through the doors across the water. He inclined his head towards the haze of Rottnest Island. 'Many of my mob ended up in chains and lie buried over there—in unmarked graves.'

He went back to the etching for several minutes, then switched off the sandblaster and withdrew his arms from the cabinet. 'That's one etching down,' he said, wiping his hands across his apron. He suggested a coffee would go down well.

They took steaming mugs out to the bench on the lawn where Lennard leaned back, stretched out his legs. 'You want another answer to your question?' he asked. 'Try this for size—you'll find our Malgana heroes emerging *today* bro.' He looked keenly at Stefan. '*Taking responsibility*! Taking responsibility to make something of their lives in spite of their disadvantage. No, *because* of it.' He took a deep breath and, with his mug partway to his mouth, he added quietly, 'Proud to be black. And some of us not ashamed to be white as well.'

Stefan nodded thoughtfully and then asked, 'So, Calyute?'

'Another long story, bro.' He looked at his watch. 'Long enough to give us both a decent break.'

'Sounds good to me. You've been doing all the work today and I've been flat out watching.'

Lennard grinned as he leaned into the backrest. 'So what's new?'

Then he took a deep breath, 'Calyute,' he began. 'It happened in April 1834, if I remember right. I forget the actual date. At the South Perth flour mill on the Gareenup foreshore of the Swan River. Young George Shenton was the boss cocky there. Twenty-three years old, and he'd only been out in the colony for a year. Still wet behind the ears.

'He was alone when Calyute arrived with thirty or so of his Pindjarup tribesmen. Calyute asked him to come down to the river to signal to Captain Ellis on the far side to come over with the punt and carry him and his warriors across to Goonininup. There was a supply depot there and Ellis was the superintendent. Anyway, Shenton saw them coming. He hit the panic button and barricaded himself in.'

Captain Ellis had reduced the flour rations for settlers and Aborigines alike, Lennard explained. Supplies were running low and he had to conserve them. It was a sore point across the settlement and Calyute had come to pick up supplies for his tribe before they ran out.

Suspicious of Calyute's intentions and alarmed that he was out of ammunition for his Brown Bess musket after a duck shoot the week before, Shenton had blockaded himself in behind the wooden door and shuttered windows.

'I can imagine the young fella watching shit-scared through the cracks as the group camped in the scrub around the building. All they wanted was a lift across the river, they told him, and a midday meal would be the go. So he agreed to give them some flour for damper if they left him alone.'

They did disperse, a couple of them waiting for the handout. He'd served them through a window. When one of the two went down to the river for some water to bake damper, he'd ventured outside to talk to the other.

'While chatting with him,' Lennard went on, 'he caught sight of others moving in to ambush him. So he bolted, chased by the tribesman he was talking to, slamming the warrior's fingers in the door.'

The other tribesman had returned with the water. He'd started a fire and began cooking damper in the embers, inviting Shenton to open up and join them for a bite. But the miller stayed put. A short while later, with the damper baking on the coals, the whole mob had stormed the door and windows, fighting to rip away the boards and break in. Shenton had held them at bay for several minutes. And then, desperate, he'd offered each of them a further issue if they stopped.

Lennard gave a grim chuckle. 'Way I see it, bro, they were pushing all his buttons, bashing at the door to get him to dish out further helpings. He was terrified and agreed in the end, and while he was handing it out through the window slats, they charged the door again, smashing the latch apart and tearing away the rope ties.'

They'd burst in, snatched up his unloaded musket, dragged him outside and pinned him to the ground, a spearpoint at his throat.

Then they'd helped themselves.

'Imagine it, bro! A rampaging free-for-all. Flour everywhere. Blackfellas turning white until they up and outta there with every pot, pan, basket and dilly bag they could lay their hands on. All filled to overflowing.' He laughed. 'Half a ton they got away with, according to the records.

'In the end, Calyute let Shenton go, but not before he'd sliced the quartz spear tip across his throat and left him bleeding like a stuck pig. Gave him a scar to remember him by.

'Now I find that an interesting move. He had him at his mercy. Why didn't he do him in? You'd expect him to, wouldn't you?' He looked up, but Stefan shrugged. 'I reckon he was adjudicating in a public trial, bro, the Pindjarup way. Shenton was in the dock representing all the settlers. His tribesmen were the jury, each having his say. He heard them out, each one in turn, and when he passed judgement, he made a fair exchange—Shenton's life for nine hundred and eighty pounds of flour.'

'He knew there'd be serious consequences if he'd murdered him,' Stefan suggested. 'Surely?'

'He knew there'd be consequences anyway, and there were. But by letting Shenton live, I think he was showing the settlers he had the upper hand. He had the power to enforce the law *his* way, to deliver justice on *his* terms. He granted Shenton a favour.' He looked thoughtfully across the channel. 'In return, the settlers took his gesture as an insult... and a challenge. His crime was one too many and their revenge wasn't long in coming.'

He broke off with a warning look as Stefan interrupted him. 'Ah, come on Ace, what do you expect? He'd broken the law. He stole a swag of flour belonging to the community, black and white alike.'

'Grown on country stolen from the Nyungar.'

'So it's a Catch 22?'

'It is. Damned if you do, damned if you don't. It's still early days and you've got two opposing systems of the law. The white king has the numbers and the heavy artillery, the black king's on the defensive with his spears and country know-how.'

When the Pindjarup had taken off with the flour, he continued, Shenton had raised the alarm. Captain Ellis had rowed across to investigate, followed by the Reverend Wittenoom and Francis Armstrong, conversant in the Nyungar language.

Armstrong had rowed back to Perth and returned with two Nyungar Whadjuk trackers who had checked out the footprints, putting names to them. Then Captain Beete had arrived with a party of soldiers of the 21st regiment and he and Ellis had followed the trail until it ran cold. They'd returned empty-handed.

A few days later, Captain Ellis had taken a party of soldiers south to the Murray River estuary, where they'd staked out the store attached to the military outpost. There they'd ambushed Calyute, Marniong and Yadong when they'd turned up.

During the fight, Marniong had escaped with three bullet wounds, Calyute was bayoneted through the forearm and a stray bullet had grazed Yadong behind the ear. The soldiers had loaded the two wounded captives aboard a cart and travelled to Mandurah House on the Peel estate, where they'd arrested another two suspects, Wamba and Gummol.

Governor Stirling had been overseas at the time. On the orders of his deputy, Lieutenant Governor Richard Daniell, they'd hauled the chained prisoners in the cart to Fremantle and sent them upriver to Perth.

Wamba had been released after two settlers spoke on his behalf. The other three had been publicly flogged. Spreadeagled across the Perth gaol whipping post, Calyute had been the first to receive twenty strokes across his bare back.

'Standard punishment at the time?' Stefan suggested.

'Maybe, but he was given *sixty* lashes, bro. In a public display. At three different whipping posts, in front of the settlers on the street, men, women and children alike. I reckon he saw his humiliation as nothing short of a declaration of open war.'

'Jesus!' Stefan exclaimed, and after a pause, 'But you have to admit, by that stage the settlers must have had had a gutful.'

'No different for the Nyungar, bro. And then, when Stirling got back in August, he was out for revenge.'

LENNARD COLLECTED HIS thoughts in silence for several minutes, staring out over the sea. He visualised Calyute, dazed and lacerated, enduring the shame of an open cart ride to the Fremantle Round House prison, listening to his Pindjarup brothers' cries of anguish on his behalf as the wagon wheels turned.

What was he thinking, Lennard wondered, with his mind seared by the cruelty of the *wajbala* way? These so-called *jangga* white spirits of his ancestors had come back from the spirit lands beyond the ocean ignorant of the traditional law that all the Nyungar family groups recognised—there was a reciprocal debt to pay, a balance to be restored, moments of powerlessness to be made good. And his customary right to distribute food to his people according to family tradition to be acknowledged.

But most of all, Lennard knew, he resented their intrusion onto his Pindjarup lands to the south, over which he had absolute ancestral right of access and across which he and his extended family group travelled seasonally to feed.

Stefan broke the silence. 'You're not suggesting he should have got away scot-free?'

Lennard gazed directly at Stefan. 'You the devil's advocate now? We both know the settlers took the land because they believed it wasn't occupied. They'd even *paid* for it! In advance. Sight unseen. *In London*, of all places. Then when they discovered the Nyungar were here, they claimed it was there for the taking anyway because it wasn't being developed. Some bible quote those Wesleyans had up their sleeves. It gave them the right to take the land to turn a profit and move the savages aside, by crikey.'

Stefan coughed a suppressed laugh. 'Genesis 1:28. Be fruitful and multiply. Sorry, Ace. I know it's no laughing matter.'

'You a bible basher too?'

'Max pointed it out to me when we were talking about the law of *terra nullius*,' he replied, his smile fading.

'Max!' Lennard snorted. 'That'd be right. So the settlers had a God-given right because they had their title deeds and the Nyungar weren't farming country the European way? He knows his stuff, young Max, but don't let him get your knickers in a twist. Look, I hear it all the time from you *wajbalas*—"That's the way it was in those days. Suck it up and get over it!" Well, bro, it bloody wasn't and we bloody won't. It was up to Calyute to make sure his community was fed. To make certain they were safe.' He frowned. 'And to protect his borders.'

He went on to explain that Calyute controlled seasonal access to different areas of his country to ferment red gum honey and banksia flowers in freshwater springs for sweetened water. To collect and bury ripe zamia nuts to remove their poison before grinding them into flour. To trap wallaby and kangaroo. To dig for yams and freshwater reed rootstock. To fish for bream and mullet and migratory crabs and shoaling prawns in the shallow estuaries of Yunderup that were the arteries of his tribe's subsistence.

He downed his coffee and placed his empty mug at his feet. Stefan walked back into the glassworks to fetch the pot.

The afternoon breeze was lifting. Lennard closed his eyes as it played over him and he imagined Calyute determining that the *jangga* intrusion had to stop. They had outstayed their lack of welcome.

By tradition, his country was open only to those born to share it. The web of Nyungar blood-ties permitted other family groups during certain seasons to pass across his land to attend ceremonial gatherings when restrictions on their movement were temporarily waived.

But there was never a trespass outside that calendar that didn't incur deadly retribution—a killing spear flung from the least expected quarter at an unsuspected moment, its target the muscled flesh of thigh or buttock. There was an agreed balance to be preserved in all reciprocal relationships between the family groups. An eye for an eye.

The white *jangga* understood none of this. They'd assumed unjust rights of ownership over the land and the river and the thunder of their rifles and flash of their bayonets signalled their determination to take the land, to survey it, fence it, settle on it, farm and stock it and protect it… to survive on their stolen properties at any cost.

He opened his eyes as Stefan refilled his mug.

'Caught you dropping off there, Ace.'

'Nah. Calyute was keeping me awake.'

'So tell me more.'

FREMANTLE, 10 JUNE 1834

HE WAS IMPRISONED in the Round House until June, Lennard explained. Then he was released, but not before receiving sixty further lashes for good measure.

Several weeks later, a thoroughbred racehorse strayed from the stables on Thomas Peel's estate at the edge of the estuary in Pindjarup country. It cantered across the scrubby dunes and veered into Calyute's campsite. The warriors followed it, speared it through the chest and rump and tracked it through the heavy sand as it staggered bleeding to a leg-thrashing death, its blowing windpipe hacked through with a quartz flint. They took slabs of meat in celebration to char them on campfire embers.

Days later, Edward Barron, recently retired from army service, came down from Perth to buy the horse. Thomas Peel and his syces had searched the estate without success. As Barron mounted up to carry out another search, Private Nesbitt joined him to assist. He was stationed at the Murray barracks with a platoon of the 21st regiment, assigned to protect the local settlers.

The syce known as Soldier Man led the riders out on foot. He loped ahead of their trotting horses, through the bricked yard, past the sand wash and the first of the log-fenced paddocks where other horses grazed. He followed a grooved sand track used for the horses' exercise, occasionally detouring knee-deep through yellow Morrison flowers that left pollen powdered on his legs.

A mile beyond the paddocks, he entered an area thick with

tea tree scrub. He ran the slope of a shallow dune, cooeeing as if calling up the horse. As he did so, a party of armed Pindjarup men materialised from hiding in a sand-gully and joined him, jogging behind the trotting horses, spears held low.

Calyute led them, his back scarred with healing welts. He greeted Private Nesbitt, whom he knew. He acknowledged Edward Barron and suggested as he ran the likely places where the horse might be watering.

As their horses separated to pass each side of a thicket, the tribesmen parted with them and a number loaded their spears. Their manoeuvre alarmed Barron, who spurred his rearing horse and screamed a warning to Nesbitt. The soldier failed to respond, not sensing danger.

The loading of the spears was instantaneous, rattling as they clicked into notched woomeras. The first volley took Barron's horse in the flank and Barron in the back and kidney. He held himself low in the saddle beneath the twisted branches of the next coppice of tea trees as his terrified horse galloped along the base of the dunes and out of sight, embedded spears waving like grotesque spines.

Speared in the back and side, Nesbitt fell from his horse, his shriek silenced by a spear thrust from Merega, as Calyute, Woodan and Noonar recovered their spears from his dying body. The other fourteen members of the group then stepped in to spear him in turn, sharing in his death according to their tribal rank, twelve-year-old Berehan the last, withdrawing his spear and plunging it deep into the sand to wipe it clean, gouts of Nesbitt's blood coagulating there.

Calyute signalled for Womban, the tribal *mabarn*, the storyteller and man of magical powers, to prepare the body for its ritualised incisions. The throat and scalp were sliced through, the skull crushed to exorcise the spirit and prevent it from endangering them later, the tongue removed and replaced with the severed fingers of his right hand.

In October, Governor Stirling had returned and organised a group of fifteen horsemen in Perth, Lennard explained. They had been armed with the latest Baker muskets and bayonets, except for the chief surveyor, Septimus Roe. They had been travelling south to carry out a survey of the Pinjarra area to set up a military garrison there.

'Arresting Calyute and the tribesmen responsible for Nesbitt's murder was also on the agenda,' he said. 'They'd forced Soldier Man to give them the names of Nesbitt's killers. Fifteen were on the wanted list, including Calyute.

'They spent the night at the Peel estate where nine foot soldiers sent from the Wonup outpost joined them. They were gonna man the garrison planned for Pinjarra.' He gave Stefan a sardonic glance. 'So there they were—twenty-four *wajbalas* armed to the teeth, most of them on horses. If that's not only a survey party but a posse out to kill, bro, I don't know what is.'

'So what happened?'

'All kinds of hell broke loose.' He pursed his lips. 'And the river ran red.'

PINJARRA, 28 OCTOBER 1834

THE NEXT DAY they travelled six miles upstream following signs that a large Pindjarup group had passed through as recently as the day before. They bivouacked overnight, but it rained heavily before dawn, leaving the track sodden and washing out the footmarks they'd been following.

They reached the upper ford across the Murray River by mid-morning, the water deeper and the current stronger than expected as they crossed. They left Surveyor Roe, his assistant and four foot soldiers with the pack horses at the ford to begin mapping the area they were going to survey and made their way north along the riverbank at walking pace, zigzagging between the paperbarks and river red gums, Captain Ellis in the lead.

Six hundred metres along the embankment he stiffened, wrenched his horse to a stop and signalled for silence. Voices raised in argument drifted across the water from the opposite bank; there were tribesmen hidden from view behind the reeds and tea tree scrub.

Stirling joined him, listening keenly for several minutes. 'How many do you estimate?' he asked, his voice carrying a clipped Lanarkshire burr. 'It sounds like an altercation.'

'Hard to tell, sir. Could be three or four.'

'We should investigate who they are.' Stirling looked back at the group clustered behind him. 'Take Corporal Norcott and Heffron with two of the mounted police. Find out what you can. I'll keep going with the rest, but I'll leave Meares here. If it's Calyute or any of the other scoundrels we're after, get yourself to the riverbank and give him a signal—an open hand if you can deal with them yourself, a fist if you need support, in which case we'll come back and join you.'

'Very well, sir.'

He leaned forward in the saddle. 'I hardly need to tell you not to do anything rash. Be prudent.' He frowned. 'I'm sure you will be.'

'I will. I will, sir.'

'We're only after the men whose names we know. The rest you can leave be.' He acknowledged Ellis with a nod, then wheeled his horse to resume the walk. 'And the best of good fortune.'

When Ellis recrossed the ford with his group, Surveyor Roe followed at a distance. They advanced warily, their skittish horses tightly reined. Three hundred yards along the bank, the scrub thinned and Ellis took out his spyglass before they broke onto grassy open ground.

Behind him, Surveyor Roe did the same. He lifted the glass to his eye. 'Oh, dear God!' he exclaimed, then backed up his horse, turned and cantered back to the ford.

Ellis ran the glass across seventy or so men, women and children, young and old, spread across a broad clearing that opened onto the river, its embankment sloping into the water where several children were swimming. Fifty metres away to his left two men involved in a fiery argument faced each other across the black coals of a doused fire, several others watching on.

He recognised the rangy figure of Noonar in dusty grey military trousers, a mulga war club in his right fist, sunlight glinting from the quartz flints embedded along its shaft. His opponent, similarly armed, shorter, broad-shouldered and naked, had his back to him.

He swung the glass from left to right again, holding it steady to inspect the figures shadowed beneath each of twenty or so leafy lean-to mia mias at the far edge of the campsite. He saw a second suspect, old man Merega, in one. He was seated on a wooden stool, a thick-jowled sandy-coloured dog lying beside him with all four legs stiffly outstretched asleep. As he watched, the dog moved its head, looked directly at him, lunged to its feet and charged across the clearing, barking. Two others he hadn't noticed, both pitch black and skinny as whippets, joined it.

Before they reached him, and before he had a chance to send someone to signal Meares, Ellis swung the glass back to Noonar, then pocketed it and spurred his horse onto the grass, halting there as the first black dog snapped at his horse's rear fetlock, turning it full circle, and the other arrived to join the attack. The larger dog, its hyena-like powerful rear haunches shorter than its front legs, circled beyond range of the horse's violent double kick, snarling viciously.

Ellis dragged the horse around as Noonar stepped across the ashes to face him, his adversary beside him. Several other warriors detached themselves and snatched up spears, loping across the clearing to line up alongside Noonar. A line of twelve or so, Ellis counted... Calyute not among them.

He looked at Norcott. 'That's Noonar, I'm sure of it.'

'It certainly is,' Norcott replied, cupping a hand beside his mouth and yelling, 'Noonar! You! Noonar! Come here!'

As Noonar stepped forward, Ellis noticed in his peripheral vision a woman in a shapeless brown skirt sprint across the clearing to catch a three-year-old child by its arm and swing it through the air onto her naked back, where it clung as naturally as a dark lizard. She scooped up another two in her free hands and raced for the river, leaving a fourth screaming in the centre of the clearing, its blonde hair catching the sun, before an older woman tottered from a mia mia, snatched it up and staggered after her.

Noonar took several paces towards them, his arm carrying the war club cocked at the elbow.

'Yes!' he shouted belligerently. 'Me Noonar!'

Before Norcott could reply, one of the warriors ran three paces, leaned back and then thrust his upper body forward to hurl his spear at Heffron, who held up an arm and ducked, the musket in his other hand discharging into the air. The spear skewered his bicep and was buried partway up the shaft. He toppled slowly from his horse, his boot still in the stirrup, his horse balking. It stepped back from the clearing, dragging him with it.

Norcott shot Noonar in the chest with the first barrel of his side-by-side shotgun and wounded another with the second.

Then, as the volley of shots resounded, a barrage of spears passed between them, vibrating through the air, one striking Ellis in the forehead above his right eye and glancing off, another slicing deep into the shoulder of his horse so that it buckled to its fore-knees with a ghastly sigh, throwing Ellis across its neck.

He sat concussed with his knees up, fumbling blindly for his flintlock pistol, its barrel stuck in the ground. He was shaking the mud from it when it slid from his hand and he slumped forward, propped unconscious like a homeless beggar, blood gushing across his upturned shako hat turning its white-feathered chevron scarlet.

NORCOTT AND THE two surviving policemen dismounted, knelt and reloaded as the empty-handed warriors sprinted for the cache of spears through screaming women and children heading for the safety of the river. Four returned, each with several spears, while the others rearmed themselves and followed the women and children into the water to protect them.

Governor Stirling, alerted by the gunfire, galloped back to the opposite bank with the remaining horsemen, the foot soldiers jogging behind them. They lined the bank and he surveyed the scene, his spyglass to his eye. He saw Ellis unconscious and Norcott and the two policemen at the far side of the clearing now advancing across it. He noticed Heffron's horse head down in the scrub. He counted four warriors lying dead, another struggling to raise his head as he crawled across the clearing until a shotgun blast drove him into the grass.

Then he froze as his glass fell across what appeared to be a woman. He tore the spyglass from his eye, snapped it shut and pocketed it. *Not a woman, surely! A random unintentional errant shot. Unfortunate.* Then he noticed another woman beside her, a third lying with her leg shattered below the knee and at her feet a small naked child, limbs splayed.

Below him, frenzied women and children in the river scrambled for the reeds, while several armed warriors waded chest-deep towards him, spears raised, and others struggled downstream, assisting women and children to escape.

Two spears whistled into the trees behind him.

'Take aim and fire at your discretion,' he shouted.

To his right, he saw a group of women and children cowering in the water beneath the embankment. They had no cover. The foot soldiers had arrived and took up positions above them.

'Keep them pinned down!' he screamed. 'Let none escape! Make sure your targets are the men and only the men!'

'ONLY THE MEN,' Lennard grunted. 'Bit late for *that*!'

The firefight lasted an hour by all accounts, he went on. Those trapped mid-river, spears thrown, stood no chance in the crossfire. All but one had tried to rush the bank against the pull of water and were gunned down. The warrior who had held back ducked beneath the surface and swam unseen downstream but when he'd surfaced, a marksman's ball had struck him between the shoulders and his body had floated with the current around the bend in the river.

'Story goes, they located his rotting corpse lodged in the branches of a sunken tree beside the lower ford months later,' Lennard said. 'They added it to the number massacred.'

He said no more for several minutes, elbows on his knees and his chin in his hands, staring out towards Rottnest. Stefan broke the silence, 'What was the figure?' he asked. 'How many were killed?'

Lennard raised his eyebrows. 'It varies, bro, depending on whose report you're looking at. Anything between ten and fifty, including Calyute's wife and one of his kids.'

His voice took on a cynical edge. 'Stirling's official report to London said *fifteen* men and no women or children, which is interesting. Fifteen! An eye for an eye. Debt recovered in full. And no women or children! Pack of bloody lies!' he snarled, before taking a deep breath. 'We do know Ellis died two weeks later. He was the only *wajbala* fatality. And Stirling released the group pinned down by the foot soldiers—eight women, they reckon. They were told to spread the message among the Nyungar that they could expect more of the same if they continued playing up.'

'His report would have eased his conscience,' Stefan suggested.

'You bet, bro. If it was a massacre would he have spared them?' He stood and picked up his mug. 'Back to work. One etching down—Calyute. Let's finish off the rest.'

WHILE LENNARD SANDBLASTED the next stencil, Stefan took out his notepad and went out to the bench to jot down Calyute's story. Lennard joined him when he'd finished, wiping solvent from his hands. He rinsed them under the hose and sat beside him, drying them on a strip of cloth.

'Good to see the pen pusher hard at it,' he said and then, peering over Stefan's shoulder, 'but he's torn between the words "battle" and "massacre"! Doesn't surprise me, bro. More ink's flowed under that nit-picking bridge than you could stick a poke at.'

He slowly nodded. 'Calyute and Yagan and the others— were they freedom fighters? Were they blackfella warriors in the Nyungar 1st brigade facing *wajbala* soldiers in a war of survival? Or were they a pack of murderers, terrorists, thieves and crims facing the full force of British law? Hah! For the answer to that, don't go to the dictionary. Go to Stirling's 1829 proclamation and drill down.' He tossed the cloth into the nearby bin with a practised basketball lob. 'Want me to explain?'

'Fire away.'

'Too easy, won't take a minute. Imagine the 18th of June 1829. The wind's up, like now.'

He took five paces towards the beach, where he marked a deep cross with his heel. 'Right on this spot, let's say, Stirling sets up a flagpole and gets Captain Irwin to read the proclamation. Same one he'd declared the day before on Garden Island. A few curious Nyungar were probably watching the performance, wondering what the fuck was going on.

'So Irwin reads it out, the flag goes up and the Poms annexe the western half of the continent.' He gave a dry laugh. 'Now British sovereignty and the rule of law extends over every resident living this side of the New South Wales border! *Every resident!*'

He gave another snort, then looked at Stefan with his eyebrows raised. 'You were right at Tullamarine. According to the proclamation, the takeover *was* a settlement, but I wasn't about to let you get away with it then. But a settlement justified by what?'

After a few moments Stefan suggested, 'There was no local sovereign power to negotiate a treaty with?'

'Too right, according to them.' Lennard gestured inland. 'Never mind the Nyungar, let alone all the other groups in the state. When no one appeared waving title deeds, the takeover was done and dusted. There were a few hunter-gatherers roaming the country, bloody nuisances who could be dealt with later. Same as they were around Sydney Cove and in Tasmania. Same as they did with Calyute. See the irony?'

'I get the picture.'

'That's at the heart of it, by crikey. No treaty ceding sovereignty. No war of conquest. Just a frigging proclamation establishing a new settlement cooked up in London. In *London*, bro! Legal under European international law that's taken two hundred years of wrangling to set partly right.' He paused, and then, 'Let's face it. It was an *invasion*, pure and simple. And you wonder why it's left us with a bitter taste? But hey, you've heard all this before. You'll be thinking the needle's stuck in the groove!'

'Yeah, well,' Stefan interjected. 'It was the beginnings of Empire. Wherever you looked at the time a global land grab was going on and settling on the Swan made too much sense. If it wasn't the British, it would have been the French. Fremantle was close to India. It gave them a port in the eastern Indian Ocean. Besides, it came cheap. The settlers footed the bill.'

Lennard gave a disparaging grunt, 'It may have made sense to the *wajbala* settlers, but it made no sense to the Nyungar. Where did the proclamation leave them? They were residents in the settlement, so were they British citizens now? Were they wards of the state? Were they protected by the law, even if they didn't know it yet? Or were they relegated to the too-difficult basket?'

'They became British subjects by default?'

'You might think so, but that was never clear. They did crack one mention in the proclamation, just the one—anyone mistreating an Aborigine would be prosecuted and, in the next breath, Irwin called on every male settler between fifteen and fifty to undergo compulsory service in a local militia to take the locals on in case they turned out to be hostile!'

With an ironic, laugh he added bluntly, 'No "*in case*" about it, bro! What Irwin *didn't* read out was loud and clear—for all practical purposes, the Nyungar were pushed aside without a by your frigging leave. We both know the consequences for the Nyungar. Confusion. Dispossession. And outrage. The injustice was mind-blowing.'

'And still is?'

'Too right. Still being unravelled and set straight, right down to quibbling over the words you're struggling with in your notes there, bro. Massacre or battle?' He stretched his arms above his head, adjusted his position on the bench. 'It was *both*. You got the sequence dead right, bro! Calyute's mob took Stirling on. So battle, followed by retreat, *then* massacre, right down to the dogs.' He nodded. 'Stirling had been making noises about teaching the Nyungar a lesson they wouldn't forget. Now he'd delivered it.'

THAT EVENING AFTER dinner, Lennard brought a file from his study. He opened it at a page he'd marked with a yellow sticker and handed it to Stefan. 'You'll find photocopies of some interesting newspaper cuttings from the 1830s *Perth Gazette* in here, bro. Yagan. Calyute. Jandamarra. They all crack a mention. Alicia has been collecting them at the Beattie Library.' He rapped the page with his forefinger. 'Take a look at this one here, for starters. It refers to Yagan, but it shows the mindset of the settlers in a nutshell.'

Stefan squinted down. It was an editorial by Charles McFaull dated 1st of June 1833.

He began reading and one passage took his breath away. He gazed across at Lennard and read it aloud—

'Although we have ever been the advocates of a humane and conciliatory line of procedure, this unprovoked attack must not be allowed to pass over without the infliction of the severest chastisement: and we cordially join our brother colonists to the one universal call—for a summary and fearful example. We feel and know from experience that to punish with severity the perpetrators of these atrocities will be found in the end an act of the greatest kindness and humanity.'

He read the last sentence for the second time, before closing the file. He spread his hands across the cover. 'Kindness and humanity? What can I say?'

'Not much.' Lennard gave him a curt sideways nod. 'It's all been said.'

THE FLAME

THE EVENING THEY COMPLETED the monument, Lennard said he had a message for Stefan. He guided him out to the privacy of the veranda.

'You may wanna hear this,' he began, 'or you may not. We've had word from Richie. Alicia took the call. Tania's back. She's been back for months. She's in Sydney, working on the opening ceremony for the Games.'

Stefan took a sharp breath, staring at him in silence before asking, 'Doing what exactly?'

'She's assisting with the choreography of one of the segments. She may be appearing with the dancers, apparently. He didn't go into detail.'

'Why did he call you?'

'He knows you're working with me. He wanted to suss out how you're feeling about her these days.'

'What business is that of his?'

'Take it easy, bro. I guess he's concerned you'll find out she's back and may give her a hard time. He said he doesn't want you to contact her till after the ceremony… if you're going to.'

'Did he, now? Not much chance of that, Ace. Too much water under the bridge. I know where I stand. She's got my number and she hasn't called.' Then, after a moment's thought, 'Ah, good luck to her. Tell him I said that if he rings again.'

'No problem. So that's it?'

'That is it.'

'You sure?'

'Never been surer, Ace, even if it's taken me four years.' Then he recalled Alicia's advice and, with a shrug, conceded, 'If she *does* call, I won't slam down the phone.'

Lennard looked steadily at him with a bemused look. 'I'll pass that on when he rings back.'

BACK AT THE unit, Stefan sat on the veranda with his feet on the railing, his guitar on his lap, tuning it. His mind was racing. *Tania! Back within reach!*

He recalled the first time he'd seen her performing, after her return from Japan. She'd moved in with him and Wirruwana had called on her to replace an injured dancer in the cast of *Oceans* in Sydney. Her flawless performances that week had thrilled him, and a surge of anticipation ran through him. *They really were the very best of times... but she hasn't called me and she's been back for months. What does that signal?*

Lennard planned to unveil the cenotaph two months after the Olympics, to benefit from the euphoria and the tourists expected to visit the west coast. *How am I going to feel two months from now when I see her in the stadium?* He imagined watching her appear in the opening ceremony... and perhaps making contact. For a fleeting moment, he wondered if he should invite her over for the unveiling before a surge of bitterness drove away the thought. *Why give her the opportunity to knock me back a second time and rub more salt in the wound?*

He knew he must let the cards fall the way they would. As Alicia had suggested, the first move must come from her.

'WOULD YOU TAKE a look at that?' Lennard glanced at the others seated in an arc around the portable television set up on the back veranda. '*Now* we're getting somewhere.'

They'd tuned in to the opening of the Sydney Olympics. Alicia was gently swinging in the hammock with Skathi outstretched beneath it and Stefan and Luke were leaning against the pillars on the top step, Luke with his guitar across his lap.

Earlier that week, further news concerning Tania had filtered through to Lennard. She was assisting with a group of Arnhem Land dancers performing in a segment called *Awakenings* and she'd be participating with them.

'There's a bottle of Shiraz for the first one to spot her,' Lennard proposed. 'It shouldn't be too difficult. We've only got to watch Stefan have a coronary.'

A young Australian schoolgirl in a hot pink sundress patterned in white hibiscus flowers, her strawberry blonde hair in pink ribbons, skipped solo across the arena, its surface floodlit with sun-dappled sand. She carried a pink beach bag of woven plastic from which she withdrew a beach towel.

'Well, that's not her,' Luke muttered, 'unless she's had a serious makeover. Wonder what's coming next? Those blow-up cycling kangaroos they promised us, heading for the Tour Down Under?'

Sounds of rushing waves and the scream of gulls flooded the stadium as she laid out her towel, dug into her bag for a stick of zinc she applied to her cheeks and nose, then settled back, her head cradled in her left hand, her right arm outstretched, her eyes closed, dreaming, as the bowl of the stadium transformed into an aquarium, a 3-D underwater panorama. She was lifted high up into it, wide-eyed in her dreaming, where she began a series of floating pirouettes on cables, swimming and somersaulting her way among comic mythical sea creatures that appeared around her in a deep-sea dream sequence.

'Brilliant,' Alicia said. 'It's unexpected, offbeat, original and spectacular. But I have to say I wasn't so sure when the clichéd Man from Snowy River on his stallion opened the show full bore with his hundred and twenty stockmen.'

'And that corny "G'day"!' Lennard agreed.

'Too much like Atlanta for my taste,' Alicia admitted, 'but this, now this, I like. This is Aussie to the bone. This is quirky. This is serious fun.'

The segment ended, and they watched the girl descend into a group of white-ochre ancestral spirit beings who surrounded her. They led her to the giant spotlighted figure of

Djakapurra Munyarryun, the Wangurri songman and dancer, with his massive thighs and barrel chest streaked in ash and ochre standing high on the podium in traditional regalia, the platform smoking around him.

The effect was electric. They were transfixed as he greeted the girl climbing the stairs, the contrast between them striking as he took her hand.

'Ancient Aboriginal Australia takes young white Australia under his wing,' Alicia murmured, 'and shows her the way.'

Djakapurra descended the stairs alone, clap sticks sounding to the greeting song of the Dhalingbuy, awakening new generations of spirits as a dense circle of desert women shuffled across the arena, intoning the ancient song of the Seven Emu Sisters, calling for the family groups to join the spiritual corroboree.

The people of Arnhem Land from four different homelands appeared, singing their Macassan flag songs under triangular multi-coloured banners, followed by the islanders of the Torres Straits dancing to the syncopated muscular rhythms of the drums, all welcomed by the local Darug and Kuring-gai groups of the Eora people in a smoking ceremony designed to cleanse the stadium meeting ground.

The cleansing ceremony released the sacred Kimberley *Gjorn Gjorn* spirits, who hovered around the gathered groups on stilted legs, until the towering ancestral creation spirit of the *Wandjina* appeared, flinging an incendiary lightning bolt that ignited a bushfire, segueing brilliantly to the next display.

'How was *that* for choreography,' Lennard exclaimed. 'There must have been at least a thousand dancers in there, from who knows how many different language groups.' He turned to Stefan. 'Hey, bro, you still among the living? No sign of Tania?'

'Lost her in translation. Too many faces in the crowd.'

Lennard smiled across at Alicia. 'Saved ourselves that bottle, sister.'

Luke jumped to his feet. 'We'll drink it anyway. Whoever pulled so many different clans together deserves bottling,' he observed as he poured. 'He's done us proud. How are they gonna top that? It'll take some doing.'

They watched the fire segment unfold and then exploded with laughter when Captain Cook, wielding a telescope, rode a tandem tricycle with a rickety mainmast, a pair of square sails and trainer wheels across the arena, botanist Joseph Banks seated behind him, scribbling into a notebook with a giant quill, while naturalist Daniel Solander kept a beady eye on a caged rabbit.

'What'd'you reckon, Alicia,' Lennard called out, 'they've got the *Zuytdorp* out there, Stefan taking notes and Gerrit eyeing off frigging lunch!'

'So WHO'VE YOU got your money on to do the honours?' Luke asked when the entertainment ended at last and the flame circled the stadium, Raelene Boyle and Betty Cuthbert in her wheelchair handing the torch to Dawn Fraser.

'If it's not Dawn, it has to be Cathy,' Lennard replied, and a moment later, Cathy Freeman materialised from among the athletes to receive the flame from Debbie Flintoff-King, the spectators roaring their support.

'There you go!' he said. 'Top choice, for mine.'

Her wide-set eyes deep brown and beautiful, her black shoulder-length hair pinned behind her ears, a tic in her jaw betraying her tension, her lean, athletic body in a streamlined blue and white Lycra bodysuit with blue joggers to match, she took the flame in her right hand, held it at arm's length and gave several signature diffident smiles before turning to face the steps, five levels in all and a dozen steps in each, leading to the upper platform. All concentration, she began the climb, her run up the steps coinciding with the release of water down a floodlit chute from the summit of the stadium.

On the upper platform, she seemed to glide over water as she crossed a circular pool before turning to face the gathered athletes, a spectacular waterfall shimmering turquoise and violet in the floodlights behind her. It was an iconic moment. She bent forward to light a circle of fire, tongues of flame erupting from the water and snaking around her.

Momentarily entrapped, she smiled again as a monstrous fiery cauldron emerged from the pool, lifting slowly around her. It came to rest above her head, a gargantuan blazing crown. She stepped away with the torch still lit and turned to face the cauldron, to watch it ascend the river cascading from the summit.

And then, disaster. The cauldron jerked and shuddered to a standstill at the base of the chute.

Dramatic moments passed, then Lennard looked at his watch. 'That's one minute,' he said, as it dawned on them there was a serious hitch. 'Now they've blown it. What do they do if it's jammed there for the duration?'

'It'll be the one thing the Games will be remembered for,' Luke said. 'With the world watching, we cock up the lighting of the flame.'

Lennard looked down at his watch again. 'The fat lady hasn't sung yet.'

'She's backstage going through her breathing exercises,' Alicia murmured.

Stefan tapped the jarrah pillar. 'They'll get it going, touch wood.'

'I didn't pick you for someone superstitious, bro,' Luke said.

'I'm not, but it pays to be prudent in moments like this.'

'Three and a half minutes, and counting,' Lennard

confirmed quietly, his voice resigned, as Cathy began her descent of the stairs, her nerves evident.

Moments later, the cauldron quivered into life and a collective sigh from the spectators became deafening applause as it glided up the chute, coming to rest at the summit where a central pillar emerged, docked with it and carried it into the night sky, the Olympic flame raging, a flaring backdrop of rockets bursting in celebration.

Luke struck a resounding chord across the guitar. 'Now all Cathy has to do is win our hundredth gold medal and carry the colours round the track,' he said. 'I'm betting she'll walk it in and do us proud.'

Lennard looked around the group. 'So what's the verdict? For my money, the Corroboree and Cathy stole the show. Aboriginal Australia is alive and well!'

There was no dissent.

LATER THAT NIGHT while switching out the lights, Alicia crossed the veranda to look across the city at the ocean. She inspected the night sky as she always did, bringing closure to her day and giving her a chance to give Skathi some last-minute attention.

The Rottnest light was partly obscured; a night mist rising from the ocean, she assumed. She counted the faintly pulsing flashes—eight, as usual. But she was confused. An hour earlier when she'd glanced across the channel, the flashes had been clear and the stars, low on the horizon, pristine. This was no longer the case. If it was a mist, it had risen from nowhere and, with a blustery night breeze coming off the sea, that seemed unlikely.

As she turned to call Lennard, a flash of light close inshore caught her eye, and then another. Someone signalling a passing boat? Or a barbecue lit on Bathers Beach? And then the flash recurred, brighter now, and it persisted. She realised it was a fire.

'*Lennard!*' she shouted, startling him. 'We have a fire down near the glassworks.'

He joined her at the railing as the glow split into three distinct fiery vertical rectangles, casting a faint orange glow on the underside of a bank of rising smoke.

'That can't be the front windows of the glassworks, surely?' His voice filled with alarm. 'Was there an explosion? Call the brigade. I'll wake Luke and give Stefan a call. We'd better get down there. Right now!'

WHEN THEY REACHED the glassworks the stench of charred wood and smoke was choking, showers of sparks and ash raining down. The frames of the buckling windows were alight and through them they saw flames raging along the jarrah beams in the roof, radiating wildly across to the lacquered panels between them. Thick smoke filled the workshop, fire engulfing the benches and furnishings. The other half of the building was also ablaze, the flames not yet as fierce.

Lennard directed Luke, who'd armed himself with an axe before leaving the house, to check the pottery, its storeroom shelves stacked with enamels, acrylic paints and cans of glaze and turpentine. He shouted back that the wall between the workshops was glowing and the shelving smouldering. The blackened plate glass display window was cracked and threatening to explode.

Tenants in the flats facing the glassworks were on their patios and in their gardens in the lurid orange glow, frantically hosing down showers of embers that swirled like burning bees towards them on intermittent onshore gusts of wind.

Lennard sprinted through a cascade of flying debris to the gas mains, switching from hand to hand as he closed down the scorching tap. He knew they'd lose the furnace when the melt within it solidified and the latest exhibition piece annealing in the gas-fired mould would fracture. He had no alternative.

The monument in the converted annealing room was separated from the workshops by a passageway protected by a solid wall. Months earlier, they'd removed the polycarbonate roofing sheets so it was temporarily safe unless the fire leapt the gap or the brickwork ignited.

He cursed at the thought of three hand-held extinguishers languishing on brackets inside the building, behind locked doors. Then he recalled the oxy-acetylene tanks on the welding trolley stored beside the back door that opened to the beach.

Shocked, he screamed at Stefan, 'The oxy tanks! If they go up, they'll take out this end of the building!'

The monument would be blasted with it, along with the dividing wall to the pottery workshop and the line of windows in the flats opposite. He closed his mind to the thought of injuries among the onlookers.

He leaned across Stefan's shoulder to shout instructions over the deafening roar and they sprinted around the building through the choking pall of smoke.

Luke and Alicia followed, unaware of the reason for their alarm.

Stefan retrieved the lawn hose and struggled to disconnect the sprinkler, but it was corroded in place. He snatched Luke's axe, hacked the hose apart and soaked his T-shirt, pulling the collar over his nose as he sprayed water over Lennard, who was struggling to undo the lock, the doors ablaze on the inside, the heat unbearable.

The lock gave and Lennard hauled the left-hand door open, shielding himself behind it as a blast of flame roared out before swirling skywards in the violent updraft. A roof beam slammed to the floor, bringing down a wedge of corrugated iron, a volcanic column of fire and sparks erupting through the gap in the roof.

Lennard retreated towards the others standing on the beach.

'No choice! No time!' he shouted at Stefan. 'They're inside the door. Hose me down!'

'No you don't!' Alicia yelled out as she grasped the situation, her face ashen. 'Leave it to the fireys.' She pointed towards two firemen unrolling a length of hose from the nearest hydrant across the railway.

'Hose me down, bro,' Lennard ordered again. 'We risk losing the lot.' He turned to Luke. 'Give me your shirt, son.'

Stefan sprayed him as he bound Luke's shirt across his nose and mouth, the garish *Ingga Thaaka Rocktoberfest* poster of a Munich barmaid offering overflowing steins of beer emblazoned across it.

Alicia stepped around him. 'Over my dead body!' she screamed, placing both hands on his shoulders. 'It's not worth it!'

He waved an arm towards the annealing room. 'We've got no choice, Alicia!'

He leaned forward to embrace her, then turned away. As he did so, her fingers caught the leather thong threaded around his neck. He ducked towards the blazing door, his first step faltering as his head jerked back and the thong snapped. She looked down in horror at the pendant dangling in her hand, then turned to watch as he disappeared into the roaring inferno, bent double, a twisted black and orange shadow melting into a blast furnace.

Moments later, he staggered from the flames and smoke, racked with spasms of coughing, one hand gripping Luke's smouldering shirt across his nose and mouth, the other extended behind him hauling the oxy-acetylene trolley down the single step and out onto the grass. He flung the cylinders aside and fell prostrate.

They rushed forward to drag him away, the hair on the back of his skull singed and sparking, tongues of flame writhing down the back of his T-shirt like the mane of a chestnut horse.

HE WAS IN an induced coma for three days in the acute care burns unit in the Royal Perth Hospital, and preliminary surgery on his back, scalp and hands was undertaken as soon as feasible. Within a week, he received treatment with experimental spray-on skin cultured from his cells and the healing process began.

At first, the pain was excruciating and constant, despite the morphine, Lennard fighting to bear it, but the spasms lessened as the surgery took gradual effect.

A month later, when Stefan was at last permitted to visit him, he was returning to his irrepressible self.

'I'm gonna look like one of your mob from behind, bro, with a skullcap of new skin on the back of my head,' he said.

'Saint Francis reborn?'

'He'll do me.' Then he chuckled. 'Remember, bro, if I do look white from behind anytime soon, it's only skin deep.'

During another visit, Lennard made it plain he was determined to have the monument unveiled on time, despite his absence. 'I won't be out of here before the end of the year,' he said. 'You know the deadline we agreed. It looks like you and Alicia will have to do the honours. Any day will do, as long as it's before New Year's.'

'Trust me, Ace, we'll christen it before then, come hell or high water. And I might have the book ready for you at the same time.'

'No might about it, bro. We have a contract, you and me, signed and sealed.'

'I may have to beg for a couple of weeks' extension to prepare the final proofs.'

'On your knees then, by crikey!'

THE MONUMENT HAD survived the fire with minor staining and was quickly repaired. The Fremantle Council contractors were clearing the wreckage of the glassworks from the site. They'd removed the annealing room walls and erected a temporary fence covered in hessian to conceal the sculpture.

Stefan spent his time in the charred shell of the building retrieving whatever he could salvage as jackhammers pounded at the concrete foundations and two bobcat operators weaved among the wreckage removing slabs and bricks.

'The fireys inspected the site,' he told Lennard. 'They've confirmed it was arson. Someone sprayed the place with kerosene. He, or they, gave it a soaking, including the ceiling. They must have used a pump of some sort, before lighting it with a blowtorch, which was found in the wreckage, by the way. Whoever it was broke in through the pottery workshop.' He looked down at Lennard, frowning. 'And we've got a bone to pick with you, you old bastard.'

Reaching into the back pocket of his jeans he withdrew the coloured photocopy of a sheet of newspaper. It was a cutting from a Saturday edition of the *West Australian*, carrying in a double-column the announcement that the cenotaph was complete and would be declared open in December. A photograph of Lennard saluting the cameraman with a glass of champagne headed the article. Written in bold capitals across the page in red felt-tip marker someone had scrawled the message, '*Not on my watch, you Black Cunt!!*' A swastika in a double circle was drawn beneath it.

'Alicia found this in your writing desk.'

Lennard read the message. He grimaced an apology. 'That was the first sign of trouble we've had since you arrived, bro. I found it nailed to the glassworks door a week before the fire. I should have reported it. I didn't take it seriously enough. I stuck it in my pocket to keep you from seeing it, and I didn't want to alarm Alicia.'

'It's a bit late now.'

'And look where it's got me.'

'Alicia has given the original to the cops. God knows where that's going to lead them.'

'Straight to a pack of Neo-Nazis, bro, convinced they've got a date with destiny.' He lowered his voice and growled, 'When push comes to shove, you'll find we're a racist country under the skin. But that's not gonna stop us. No way in this world.'

Later, when Stefan was about to leave, Lennard called him back. 'Hey bro, before you go. I've got an idea I want you to give some thought to. I mentioned it to Max yesterday and he's on board.'

'I'm listening,'

'The glassworks. It's a write-off, isn't it?'

'Total, I'd say. The demolition crews are giving it a good going over.'

'Okay. So there'll be some vacant land to the right of the cenotaph?'

'Unless the council agree to put another building up.'

'That's exactly what Max is gonna convince them to do.'

'For you to lease as another glassworks?'

'No. For a meeting place.'

'For a *what*?'

'A hall. A theatre. A place where plays can be performed. And dances. Films can be shown. Stories told. Where people can debate and argue, get things off their chests.' He took a long breath. 'A *gathering* place, where we can get together to talk about the traumas in our history and iron things out.'

It took a moment for Stefan to grasp what Lennard was suggesting. 'Where people can let off steam? In a confined space? That sounds bloody risky.'

'Exactly that. We take a risk. Building the cenotaph was risky, but we've done it. Now we have to keep the spirit of the place *alive*. We both know there are two different stories—white and black. You especially; you know that.' He gave a knowing smile. 'I've watched you struggling to reconcile both versions for the last four frigging years.' His smile broadened. 'I think you still are, even though you're in denial.'

Stefan hesitated, uncomfortable with the observation. 'Knew I couldn't hide it from you.'

'No need to try.' He gazed at Stefan for several moments and then, as if to deliberately shock him, he said with quiet emphasis, 'There is no way to resolve it, bro.'

'*What?*'

'Not only with a cenotaph. It'll take a lot more than that.'

'*Now you tell me!*'

'I've been waiting for you to work it out for yourself.'

Stefan threw up his hands. 'So what are you suggesting?'

'Like I said, we build a meeting place where both stories can be told, both stories put front and centre. It'll be a game-changer. People will interact. They'll *perform*. Look at Yagan's statue! How often have vandals cut his head off with an angle grinder? Twice? Painted him white? Stolen his spear? Even tried cutting off his nuts, by crikey?'

'And you want to encourage that?'

'The Nyungar have been powerless to prevent it. So let's give the powerless a place where they'll have a voice. Give them a chance to express what they're feeling face to face, and you'll get understanding. And respect. On both sides. We'll learn to work together. We'll form relationships. Have conversations.'

'Given time?'

'Of course given time.'

'What about the damage in the meantime?'

'Think how powerful the reconciliation process will be as a result.'

Stefan looked at him for a thoughtful minute before giving a conciliatory nod. 'It's possible, I guess, but it *is* ambitious. We're up against structural racism and prejudice. We'll have to move mountains to turn *that* around.'

'That's more like it, brudda!' Lennard smiled. 'And I like that "*we*". It's a start. It'll make the cenotaph the *living* monument we want, not one that people visit less and less.' Then he gave an unexpected burst of laughter, grimacing at the pain. 'I haven't been lying here on my *manda* doing nothing. I've even thought up a Nyungar name for the building—*Babanginy Koondarnangor*. Lightning and Thunder. We've got the cenotaph—that's the lightning. Now we need the thunder.'

'*Malajarri?*'

He smiled and inclined his head. '*Malajarri*. Have a yarn with Max. See what he's got to say.'

'I'll be seeing him tonight with Alicia. It should be interesting.'

WHEN HE ACCOMPANIED Alicia on her next visit to the hospital, Stefan was carrying an old-fashioned kerosene lamp he'd found in the shed, its glass stained smoke grey. He placed it on the bedside table, a box of matches beside it.

Greetings over, he announced, 'We've come to Mt Olympus for the lighting of the flame, Ace. Can you manage that for us?'

Lennard painfully shifted his position. 'Try stopping me, brudda! Let's do the honours.'

Stefan levered open the glass, wound up the wick and

struck a match he handed to Lennard, who held the match up towards the window for several moments. Then he applied it to the lamp with great care. The wick smoked as the fuel ignited and an orange flame burned steadily behind the glass as Stefan closed it.

'Done! *Garla gambanyina*!' Lennard exclaimed, easing back into the bed with a triumphant smile that ended with a grimace. 'Whaddya say, bro, there's nothing like kerosene to start a decent fire. Now you two go and light the flame that's gonna set this continent alight!'

When Stefan reached the door Lennard called out, 'Bangarra! The dancers in the opening ceremony. You know what it means in Wiradjuri?'

'No idea.'

'Light the flame, brudda! Light that fire!'

SUNDAY 10 DECEMBER 2000. The monument towered over them, surrounded by a shallow pebbled moat in which its diffracted colours shimmered. To the left of the entrance, a single gas flame flared a brilliant orange in a bronze bowl on a pedestal of quartz excavated from Windjana Gorge. A Whadjuk Nyungar elder had lit it earlier, his *karlamarta* firestick ignited using the flame in Lennard's lamp.

A string of eucalypt saplings planted across the lawns displayed grey-green leaves above their shade-cloth windbreaks. Six senior Nyungar women dressed in ceremonial *bwoka* kangaroo skin cloaks wound their way through them, sharing a canister with the smouldering leaves of a *balga* grass tree in a smoking ceremony to prepare and cleanse the area. They were singing a Nyungar song of welcome prepared for the occasion.

'Time to go,' Stefan confirmed when the smoking ended. He stood with his camera slung around his neck.

Elegant in a simple white caftan, Alicia reached for the

albatross pendant Lennard had insisted she wear for the opening. She lifted it to her lips. 'I wish he was here.'

'He's here. He'll be thinking of us,' Luke replied, an arm around her shoulder.

She bent to hold the hand of twelve-year-old Keisha Kuranha from Waroona, winner of a poetry contest held to select the first young Aboriginal Australian to walk through the cenotaph. She was carrying a saffron yellow spray of *Mooja* tree flowers in one hand, a pair of scissors in the other.

Watched by rows of seated guests, they crossed the grass and the flagstone bridge to the entrance, accompanied by two of the senior Nyungar women, their *dwerta-dyer* headdresses resplendent with black and white *koolbardi* magpie feathers, the sound of the Wieniawski variation and didjeridoo echoing.

Keisha placed the flowers beside the flame and then, guided by Alicia, she cut the plaited red, black and gold ribbon draped across the entrance. It fell away and she followed the Nyungar women shyly into the canyon between the crystalline walls.

Alicia stepped forward to follow her and then hesitated, signalling for Stefan and Luke to precede her.

The names of the warriors glinted in the blue-grey panel to their left. Stefan acknowledged each etching, running his fingers into the recessed letters and murmuring the names. Glancing to his right, he saw them reflected in the words of the *Karni Wangkiny* song glimmering on the opposite panel.

Following Keisha, Stefan saw her reflection deep within the sculpture, its liquid mosaic gathering and gliding apart and re-forming beyond the etched names like a ghostly image.

When they were partway through, the music ended and in the sudden silence, Keisha glanced back. She caught Stefan's eye deep in the glass and it seemed to him that she was sharing for that instant the answer to a mystery familiar to her.

At the end of the passage, Stefan ran exploring fingers

into the letters of the last name—*Calyute*. When he looked back, Luke did the same, coloured light pouring across him. Then he walked out into the sun through swirling blues and aquamarine.

Shading his eyes, he peered up at the Round House prison high on Arthur Head. For an instant, he imagined the door to Calyute's cell swinging open as the prisoner emerged, blinking in the unfamiliar glare, and descending the steps to join the waiting warriors, who led him across the low dune where the cenotaph now stood, to begin his journey home.

He and Keisha watched Alicia pause at the exit, the albatross glinting at her throat. He lifted his camera as she emerged.

Then he placed a hand on Keisha's shoulder. 'This is your heritage, Keisha,' he said. 'Never forget it.'

She looked up, her smile diffident. 'Yours too,' she affirmed before averting her gaze.

And it was done.

LATER THAT EVENING, when the guests had dispersed, Stefan returned to Bathers Beach. He switched on the cenotaph floodlights and locked the gates. He sat on a bench and looked out over the darkening sea, listening to the rhythmic crunch of waves before they swished up the sand, the lingering smell of ceremonial smoke drifting.

The only other figure in the twilight was a barely discernible shadow stripped to the waist sweeping the sand with a metal detector, zigzagging up and down the slope of the beach with his dog a shadow at his heel. Stefan stifled a sardonic smile. *He must know what I know—it's a minefield and he's another searching for the Truth.*

He turned and contemplated the monument, thinking of its historical and symbolic significance when, unbidden, he was flooded by searing memories of his visit six years before to the memorial in the Lidice Garden of Remembrance outside Prague. Rows of teenage girls and children cast in bronze were clustered on a concrete foundation gazing in distress down the clover-covered hillside at the gravesite of the men and older boys, marked by a tall crucifix carrying a woven barbed-wire crown of thorns.

That memory triggered another when he was a boy, and he was distraught.

He and his father had been squeezing oranges harvested from the trees in the backyard in Geelong and his father told him that he'd helped dig the mass grave at Lidice with a team of other prisoners from Terezin Concentration Camp.

It was 11 June 1942, he'd explained, the day after the massacre. Every man and boy over sixteen from the village had been murdered in an act of revenge for the assassination of the Nazi Governor Reinhard Heydrich.

One hundred and seventy-three bodies lay strewn next to the wall of the barn beside which they'd been shot, blood-spattered mattresses propped against it. The grave was the size of half a tennis court, its perimeter marked out in lime from barrels they were instructed by the guards to use on the bodies after their disposal in the pit.

'We worked two shifts, nine of us in the grave at one time,' his father had said. 'It had to be deep enough for all the bodies. It was hard going, very rocky. On the second day, we shared some oranges from a crate one of our Czech guards found in the barn. They were dry and sour, but my quarter,' he'd looked down at the orange he was slicing, 'I will remember how it tasted to my dying day.'

He did not elaborate, despite Stefan's persistent questions, except to mention that one of the German soldiers in the firing squad salvaged a vintage portable HMV gramophone using wooden needles from one of the houses their engineers were blasting and bulldozing as they razed the village. He'd also rescued a pair of 78 records. One was a Jelly Roll Morton recording of *Wolverine Blues*, which he'd played incessantly, assigning one of the older prisoners to rewind the gramophone while the German and his fellow soldiers picked over the corpses for valuables that hadn't been handed over before the killings.

Now and then, he'd appeared at the lip of the pit, urging the prisoners to dig faster, in time with piano's rhythm.

Stefan pictured his father in the working party, armed with a shovel, sharing a slice of orange in the pit before climbing out on the shoulders of a fellow prisoner to drag the stiffening corpses to the grave's edge. They lowered them hand and foot to prisoners below, who stacked them in rows across the bottom and poured lime across them, while German engineers set fire to the dynamited village.

His father had placed a hand on his shoulder and gazed bleakly down at him. 'That memory is like a stone in my shoe,' he'd said, 'one I haven't been able to remove on my journey through life. It has been a constant reminder of my history. A reminder that you carry the past with you and learn to live with it.'

Conscious of the weight of his father's hand, Stefan had pictured his father for one excruciating moment three years later, limping on the march from Auschwitz III-Monowitz to Loslau train station in transit to Buchenwald, the worn yellow star emblazoned on his threadbare coat, a fragment of gravel in one of the shoes he'd inherited from a dead friend, unable to stop and remove it for fear of being shot and abandoned on the side of the road.

His mind had reeled, appalled by the injustice recollected in those historic moments—assassination on a street corner in

Prague and murder in the dunes on the Peel Estate, followed as night follows day, by the massacre of almost two hundred in Lidice and most of the Pindjarup family on the banks of the Murray River.

He looked up at the black ocean, fighting back tears, then held his head in his hands. Haunting questions gripped him. *Acts of revenge! Will there never be an end to the carnage? Where are the dependable landmarks with which to navigate through confusion? Where the keystones that will hold? Where the shared processes that can be relied upon?*

Once again, he looked back at the cenotaph and glimpsed beyond it the newly laid concrete pad for the meeting hall the council had approved, the gathering place Lennard had conceived. A performance theatre. A powerful place for stories to be told and heard. A place for one-on-one conversations, for conflict resolution and a place for healing.

To shake off his emotion, he tore off his shoes and walked to the sea's edge where he paced ankle-deep in the breaking waves before standing for several minutes, looking out at the light flashing on Rottnest Island. And as if hearing them spoken aloud, Lennard's words came to him, 'Listen, when I get too heavy bringing up our history and piss you off, feel free to tell me to back off and loosen up.'

'So my first lecture on Aboriginal Australian Traumascapes 101 is over?'

'Sure is, but it will never be forgotten and it won't be the last.'

And then his phone rang and he was speechless as he listened to Tania's voice, terse and matter-of-fact with nervous tension that ripped him apart. She came straight to the point. 'It's me, Stefan. I'd like to see you. Can we meet on neutral ground?'

Shock surged through him. 'How about the boathouse at Fishing Point?' he managed to ask. 'You used to like it there.'

There was silence as he fought for self-control, and then, 'I've booked it for a week over the New Year. I'm putting the finishing touches to a novel I've written.'

'The boathouse will be fine, but I'll book myself a room up in the boarding house. We can take things from there.'

'I can do the booking for you.'

'No. I'll do my own. Let me know the dates before you go.'

'I will.'

She gave him her number and rang off.

He stared down at the silent phone in disbelief. He was shaken to the core. Four years... and Alicia was right!

Surprise phone calls, he thought, as he settled back on the bench, *the story of my life*! And he recalled the first time he'd heard Lennard's voice over the telephone and hadn't recognised it, though it sounded familiar, and before he could ask who was calling, Lennard had said he had a question for him and wouldn't take no for an answer.

'Right now, I have the answer you want, bro, no questions asked.' Stefan's voice rang out across the dark water. 'The answer is *yes*, and yes again.'

Author's Postscript

B̲efore the British settlement of the Swan River Colony in 1829, the Aboriginal Nyungar people were firmly established across the southwest corner of Western Australia. They had occupied the area for over 45,000 years.

Aboriginal resistance to the European incursion in Perth and later across the state was fierce, culminating in open warfare and massacres that lasted sporadically for a century.

Two opposing historical narratives persist to this day: heroic but futile Aboriginal resistance, suppression and exclusion on the one hand; courageous European exploration, settlement and the establishment of a successful and progressive multi-cultural society on the other.

Despite considerable progress, efforts to reconcile these opposing narratives have reached a critical impasse with the call for a referendum on Truth and Reconciliation, a treaty and an Aboriginal voice to Parliament.

How does Stefan Novak, a Caucasian Australian deeply in love with an Aboriginal dancer with the Wirruwana Dance Theatre, cross that racial and cultural divide? Can he overcome the influences of his upbringing, reconcile both sides of the story and understand the need to resolve the nation's unfinished business? Or will the challenge destroy him and end the relationship?

The Glass Cenotaph is a fictional work set in Fremantle in the 1990s examining that dilemma.

2019 is the United Nations Year of Indigenous Languages. It has been a privilege to include words and phrases of the Malgana Language, spoken in the Shark Bay area, in the text. My thanks are extended to Ben Bellottie, Dr Doug Marmion and the Yamaji Language Centre in Geraldton. — **PP**

About the Author

PETER PURCHASE WAS BORN and educated in East Africa. In his novel, The Glass Cenotaph, he draws on his 30 years of experience working among Indigenous First Nations people in the Pilbara, Arnhem Land and Papua New Guinea.

Growing up in British colonial Kenya in the 1950s during the Mau Mau war of independence, he was alerted to the resentments that drive subjugated Indigenous populations to fight for their freedom.

He migrated to Australia in 1963. Working in remote locations in the mining and construction industries brought him into close contact with local Aboriginal populations.

His writing is motivated not only by an awareness of the history of the mistreatment and displacement of Australia's Aboriginal and Torres Straits Islander people but also by their fascinating culture, deep-rooted in a love of country, resilience and an unfailing sense of humour.

Peter eventually settled in Perth. He has a daughter who is a photographer and a son who works in the mining industry.